Bachelo
through, u
Jack Carsta
of the

BACHELOR
HEROES

Two brilliant page-turning
novels delivered to you by two
senstional authors

BACHELOR HEROES

A Man of Means
DIANA PALMER

Texas Hero
MERLINE LOVELACE

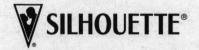

*Silhouette and Colophon are registered trademarks of
Harlequin Books S.A., used under licence.*

*This collection is first published in Great Britain 2007
Silhouette Books, Eton House, 18-24 Paradise Road,
Richmond, Surrey TW9 1SR*

BACHELOR HEROES © Harlequin Books S.A. 2007

The publisher acknowledges the copyright holders of the
individual works, which have already been published in the UK in
single, separate volumes, as follows:

A Man of Means © Diana Palmer 2002
Texas Hero © Merline Lovelace 2002

ISBN-13: 978 0 373 60500 2
ISBN-10: 0 373 60500 5

064-0107

*Printed and bound in Spain
by Litografia Rosés S.A., Barcelona*

A Man of Means

DIANA PALMER

For Cissy at Writerspace, Sara, Jill and Celeste, and all the wonderful readers, many of whom I was privileged to meet in Atlanta in 2001 at our author tea, who visit me online there at my website. Love you all. DP

One

Meredith Johns glanced around her worriedly at the out-of-control Halloween party-goers in their colorful costumes. Meredith was wearing an outfit left over from college days. She made a good salary at her job, but there was no money for little luxuries like Halloween costumes. She had to budget just to be able to pay the utility bill in the house she shared with her father.

The past few months had been traumatic, and the wear was telling on her. She needed to get out of the house, Jill, one of her colleagues, had said firmly—especially after her most agonizing experience at home. Meredith was reluctant. Her father was only just back at their house after three days. But Jill was insistent. So she'd put on the only costume she had, a bad choice in many ways, and walked the three blocks to her friend's downtown apartment. She grimaced at her surroundings. What an idiot she'd been to come to this wild party.

But it really had been a tumultuous week for Meredith

and she'd wanted to get her mind off her troubles. Her father's violent behavior at the house they shared was unnerving. They were both still grieving, but her father had taken the tragedy much harder. He felt responsible. That was why a scholarly, conservative college professor had suddenly retired from his job and turned into an alcoholic. Meredith had tried everything she could think of to get him into treatment, but he refused to go on his own accord and the treatment facilities which would have taken him wouldn't unless he went voluntarily. Only a violent episode that had landed him in jail had temporarily spared her of this saddening experience. But he was out three days later and he had a new bottle of whiskey. She still had to go home after the party. He'd warned her not to be late. Not that she ever was.

Her grey eyes were sad as she sipped her soft drink. She had no head for alcohol, and she was as out of place here as a cup of tea. Not only that, her costume was drawing unwanted attention from the men. So was her long blond hair. It had been a bad costume choice, but it was the only thing she had to wear on the spur of the moment. Going to a Halloween party in her street clothes would have made her stand out, too.

She moved away from a slightly tipsy colleague who wanted to show her around Jill's bedroom and unobtrusively put her glass on a table. She found Jill, pleaded a headache, thanked her for a "good" time and headed out the front door as fast as she could. Once on the sidewalk, she drew in a long, sweet breath of fresh air.

What a bunch of wild people! She coughed delicately, remembering the unmistakable smell of that smoke that had been thick enough to obstruct clear vision inside. She'd thought it would be fun to go to a party. She might even meet a man who would be willing to take her out and cope with her father. And cows might fly, she told herself. She hadn't been out on a date in months. She'd invited one prospective date to her home for supper. But after a good look at her father, who was mean when he drank, the prospective suitor took off. Her heart wasn't in it, anyway. Recently she'd given up trying to attract anyone. She had her hands full already. Her grief was still fresh, too.

An odd noise attracted her attention as she started back toward her own house. She felt self-conscious in her getup, and remembering the lewd remarks she'd drawn from a man who was normally very polite and gentlemanly, she was sorry she hadn't had a coat to wear. Her clothes were mostly old, because by the time she made the mortgage payment and took care of the bills, there wasn't much left over. Her father couldn't work and wouldn't get help, and she loved him too much to desert him. It was becoming a costly proposition.

She wrapped her arms around herself and hoped she was covering up enough skin to discourage stalkers. But her skirt was very short and tight, and she was wearing fishnet hose, very high heels, a low-cut blouse and a flaming pink feather boa. Her blond hair was loose around her shoulders and she was wearing enough makeup to do justice to a ballet recital. She winced, hoping she hadn't been noticed. She'd gone to the party as a burlesque dancer. Sadly she looked more like a professional hooker in her garb.

She rounded a corner and saw two shadowy figures bending over what looked like a man on the ground.

"Hey! What do you think you're doing there?!" she yelled, making as much noise as possible. Then she started running toward them and waving her arms, yelling threats as she went.

As she expected, the surprise of her aggressive presence shocked them into retreat. They jumped up and ran away, without even looking back. The best defense, she thought with faint amusement, was always a good offense. It was a calculated bluff, but she'd seen it work for women smaller in stature than she was.

She ran to the downed man and examined him the best she could in the dim glow of the streetlights.

Concussion, she thought, feeling his head and encountering a metallic smelling wetness. Blood. He'd been hit on the head by his assailants, and probably robbed as well. She felt around under the jacket he was wearing and her hand touched something small and square on his belt. She pulled it out.

"Aha," she said with a triumphant grin. A man dressed as well as he was could be expected to have a cell phone. She dialed 911 and gave the operator her location and the condition of her patient, staying on the line while the dispatcher got an ambulance en route.

While she waited for it, she sat down on the pavement beside the man and held his hand.

He groaned and tried to move.

"Don't do that," she said firmly. "You'll be okay. You mustn't move until the EMTs get here. I haven't got anything to treat you with."

"Head...hurts."

"I imagine it does. You've got a heck of a bump. Just lie still. Feel sick, sleepy...?"

"Sick," he managed weakly.

"Lie still." She lifted her head to listen for the ambulance, and sure enough, a siren sounded nearby. The hospital was less than two blocks from her home, maybe four from here. Lucky for this guy, whoever he was. Head injuries could be fatal.

"My...brothers," the man was whispering brokenly. "Hart...Ranch. Jacobsville, Texas."

"I'll make sure they're contacted," she promised.

He gripped her hand, hard, as he fought not to lose consciousness. "Don't...leave me," he ground out.

"I won't. I promise."

"Angel," he whispered. He took a long, shaky breath,

and went back into the oblivion he'd left so briefly. That wasn't a good sign.

The ambulance rounded the corner, and the headlights spilled out onto Meredith and her patient. She got to her feet as two EMTs, one male and one female, piled out the doors and rushed to the downed man.

"Head wound," she told them. "Pulse is slow, but steady. He's coherent, some nausea, his skin is cold and clammy. Blunt force trauma, probably mild concussion..."

"Don't I know you?" the female EMT asked. Her face brightened. "Got you! You're Johns!"

"That's me," Meredith said with a grin. "I must be famous!"

"Sorry, not you—your dad." She winced at the look on Meredith's face.

Meredith sighed. "Yes, he spends a lot of time on ambulances these days."

"What happened here?" the woman asked quickly, changing the subject. "Did you see anything?"

"I yelled and scared off two guys who were bending over him," she volunteered. "I don't know if they were the ones who hit him or not. What do you think?" she added as the woman gave him a professional once-over.

"Concussion, definitely," she agreed. "Nothing broken, but he's got a lump the size of the national debt here on his head. We'll transport him. Coming along?"

"I guess I should," Meredith said, waiting until they loaded him onto the gurney. He was still unconscious. "But I'm not exactly dressed for visiting a hospital."

The EMT gave her a speaking glance. "Should I ask why you're dressed like that? And does your boss know you're moonlighting?" she added wickedly.

"Jill Baxley had a Halloween party. She thought I should come."

The other woman's eyebrows levered up. "Jill's parties

are notorious for getting out of control. I've never even seen you take a drink.''

"My father drinks enough for both of us," came the reply. "I don't drink or use drugs, and I need my head examined for going to that party. I escaped early, which is how I found this guy."

"Lucky for him," the woman murmured as they loaded him into the back of the ambulance. "Judging by his condition, he could have died if he hadn't been found in time."

Meredith climbed up into the back and sat down on the bench while the driver got in under the wheel and the female EMT called the hospital emergency room for orders. It was going to be a long night, Meredith thought worriedly, and her father was going to be very upset when she got home. He and her mother had been really close, but her mother had been fond of going to parties and staying out until the early morning; sometimes with other men. Recent events had made him dwell on that behavior. Her father seemed to have transferred that old contempt to her. It made her uneasy to think of arriving home in the wee hours. Anything could happen. On the other hand, how could she leave this man? She was the only person who knew who to contact for him. She'd promised to stay with him. She couldn't let him down.

He was examined by the resident on duty in the emergency room, who diagnosed concussion. He'd been unconscious most of the way to the hospital, but he'd come out of it just once to look up at Meredith and smile, tightening his big hand around the fingers that were holding it.

His family had to be notified, and Meredith was coaxed into making the call to Jacobsville for the harassed and overworked emergency room staff.

She was given a phone and a telephone directory which also listed Jacobs County, of which Jacobsville was the county seat. She looked through it until she found a listing for Hart Ranch Properties, Inc. That had to be it.

She dialed the number and waited. A deep, drawling voice answered, "Hart Ranch."

"Uh, I'm calling for a Mr. Leo Hart," she said, having found his driver's license in the wallet his assailants hadn't had time to steal. "He's at Houston General…"

"What happened?" the voice asked impatiently. "Is he all right?"

"He was mugged. He has a concussion," she added. "He can't give the staff any medical information…"

"Who are you?"

"I'm Meredith Johns. I work…"

"Who found him?"

"I did, actually. I called the ambulance on his cell phone. He said to call his brothers and he told me where they were…"

"It's two o'clock in the morning!" the voice pointed out angrily.

"Yes, I am aware of that," she began. "It only happened a little while ago. I was walking down the street when I saw him on the sidewalk. He needs his family—"

"I'm his brother, Rey. I'll be there in thirty minutes."

"Sir, it's a long way to Houston from where you are. If you drive that fast…!" she said at once.

"We have an airplane. I'll get the pilot out of bed right now. Thanks." He added that last word as if it hurt him, and hung up.

Meredith went back to the waiting room. Ten minutes later, she was admitted to the room where the victim had been examined.

"He's conscious," the attending physician told her. "I'm going to admit him overnight, just to be sure. Any luck with his family?"

"His brother is on the way, in his own plane, apparently," she said. "I didn't get a thing out of him. Sorry."

"People get upset and they don't think," the resident said with a weary smile. "How about staying with him? We're understaffed because of that respiratory virus that's going around, and he shouldn't be alone."

"I'll stay," she said with a grin. "It's not as if I have a hectic social life."

The resident pursed his lips and smirked at her outfit.

"Halloween party," she said, grimacing. "And next time I get invited, I'll have a broken leg, I swear it!"

Forty-five minutes later, there was a problem. It was six feet tall, had black hair and dark eyes and it erupted into the hospital cubicle like an F-5 tornado, dressed in jeans and boots and a fringed rawhide jacket thrown carelessly over what looked like a beige silk shirt. The wide-brimmed hat slanted over those threatening eyes was a Stetson, one of the most expensive made, with its distinctive feathered logo pin on the hatband. He looked impressively rich, and excessively angry.

The man was livid when he saw his big brother, still drifting in and out of consciousness, on the examining table. He gave Meredith a scrutiny that could have peeled paint off old furniture, his eyes narrowing contemptuously on her costume.

"Well, that explains why you were on the street at two in the morning," he snarled angrily. "What happened? Did you feel guilty and call for help after you tried to roll him?" he added sarcastically.

"Look here," she began, rising.

"Save it." He turned to the big man on the table and laid a lean, strong hand on his brother's broad chest. "Leo. Leo, it's Rey! Can you hear me?" he asked in a tone that combined affection with concern.

The big man's eyes blinked and opened. He stared blankly up at the leaner man. "Rey?"

"What happened to you?" Rey Hart demanded gently.

Leo grinned wearily. "I was thinking about new forage grasses and wasn't paying attention to my surroundings," he murmured drowsily. "Something hit me in the head and I went down like a brick. Didn't see a thing." He winced and felt clumsily in his pockets. "Damn! My wallet's gone. So's my cell phone."

Meredith started to tell him that she had the phone and wallet in her purse for safekeeping, but before she could speak, Rey Hart gave her a furious, speaking glance and walked out of the cubicle like a man hunting a fight.

His brother drifted off again. Meredith stood beside him, wondering what to do. Five minutes later, Rey Hart walked back in accompanied by a tall man in a police uniform. He looked familiar, but Meredith couldn't quite place him. She knew she'd seen him before.

"That's her," Rey told the policeman, indicating Meredith. "I'll sign anything necessary as soon as I see that my brother's going to be okay. But get her out of here."

"Don't worry. I'll handle it," the policeman said quietly. He handcuffed Meredith with easy efficiency and pulled her out of the cubicle before she could protest.

"I'm being arrested?" she exclaimed, stunned. "But, why? I haven't done anything!"

"Yes, I know, I've heard it all before," the officer told her in a bored tone when she tried to explain what had happened. "Nobody's ever guilty. Honest to God, dressed like that, out on the streets alone after midnight, you were bound to be up to no good. What did you do with his cell phone and his wallet?"

"They're in my pocketbook," she began.

He confiscated it from her shoulder and propelled her out of the building. "You're going to be in a lot of trouble. You picked the wrong man to rob."

"See here, I didn't mug him! It was two men. I didn't see their faces, but they were bending over him as I came down the sidewalk."

"Soliciting is a felony," he pointed out.

"I wasn't soliciting anything! I'd just come from a Halloween party dressed as a burlesque dancer!" she raged, furious that she was being punished for having done someone a good turn. She read his name tag. "Officer Sanders, you have to believe me!"

He didn't say a word. He drew her with him, firmly but gently, and put her into the back seat of the police car.

"Wait," she told him before he could close the door. "You get my wallet out of my purse and look in it. Right now," she insisted.

He gave her an impatient look, but he did what she asked. He looked through the plastic inserts in her wallet and glanced at her with a changed expression. "I thought you looked familiar, Johns," he murmured, using her last name, as most people she knew at work did.

"I didn't mug Mr. Hart," she continued. "And I can prove where I was when he was being mugged." She gave him her friend Jill's address.

He gave in. He drove to Jill's apartment, went to the door, spoke to an obviously intoxicated and amused Jill, and came back to the squad car. He let Meredith out of the back of the squad car and took off the handcuffs. It was cool in the night air, and Meredith felt self-conscious and uncomfortable in her garb, even though the police officer knew the truth now.

"I'm really sorry," he told her with a grimace as he met her grey eyes. "I didn't recognize you. All I knew was what Mr. Hart told me, and he was too upset to think straight. You have to admit, you don't look very professional tonight."

"I do realize that. Mr. Hart cares about his brother, and he doesn't know what happened," she pointed out. "He walked in and saw his brother on the table and me dressed like this," she indicated her clothing, "and his brother said his wallet and cell phone were missing. He doesn't know me from a stump. You can't blame him for thinking the worst. But those two men who hit him would have gotten his wallet if I hadn't come along, and they're still on the loose.''

"Can you show me where you found him?" he asked.

"Of course. It was just down the sidewalk, that way.''

She led and he followed her, with his big wide-angle flashlight sweeping the sidewalk and the grass as they walked. She pointed to an area of flattened grass. He left her on the sidewalk and gave the area a thorough scrutiny, looking for clues. He found a candy wrapper and a cigarette butt.

"I don't guess you know if Mr. Hart smokes or likes candy?" he asked.

She shook her head. "Sorry. All he told me was his brothers' name and where they lived. I don't know anything more about him.''

He stood up. "I'll ask his brother later. Wait here while I call for one of the technicians to bag this evidence,'' he told her.

"Okay,'' she said agreeably, drawing the feather boa closer. It was getting cold standing around briefly clad, waiting for crime scene investigators. "Somebody's going to love being turned out of bed to come look at a cigarette butt and a candy wrapper,'' she stated with helpless amusement.

"You'd be surprised at what excites those guys,'' he chuckled. "Catching crooks isn't exactly a chore to them. It's high drama.''

"I hope they catch these two,'' she said firmly. "Nobody should have to be afraid to walk down the streets at night. Even after dark, dressed like this, alone,'' she added pointedly, indicating her clothes.

"Good point,'' he was fair enough to admit.

He called in his location and requested crime scene technicians. Meredith was ready to go home, but she couldn't leave until she'd given the policeman a statement for his report. She sat in his car, with the overhead lights on, writing out what she knew of the attack on Leo Hart. It didn't take long, because she didn't know much.

She handed it back to him. "Can I go home now?" she asked. "I live with my father and he's going to be upset because I'm coming home so late. I can walk. It's only about three blocks from here."

He frowned. "Your father is Alan Johns, isn't he?" he asked. His expression changed. "Do you want me to go with you?"

She didn't usually flinch at facing her irate parent. She was gutsy, and she could handle herself. But tonight, she'd been through a lot. "Would you?" she asked, uneasy because her fear was visible.

"No problem. Get in."

He drove her to her house and went to the door with her. The house was dark and there was no movement inside. She let out a sigh of relief. "It's okay. If he was awake, the lights would be on. Thanks, anyway," she said with a smile.

"If you need us, call," he said. "I'm afraid I'll be in touch again about this. Rey Hart already reminded me that his brother is our state attorney general. He's not going to let this case go until it's solved."

"I don't blame him. Those guys are a menace and they're probably still running around looking for easy targets to rob. Take care."

"You, too. And I'm sorry about the handcuffs," he added, with the first smile she'd seen on his lean face since her ordeal began.

She smiled back. "My fault, for wearing a costume like this on the streets," she admitted. "I won't do it again. Thanks for the ride."

Back at the hospital, Rey Hart sat by his brother's bedside until dawn, in the private room he'd obtained for him.

He was worried. Leo was the hardiest one of the lot, and the most cautious as a rule. He was the prankster, always playing jokes, cheering them up in bad times. Now, he lay still and quiet and Rey realized how much his sibling meant to him.

It infuriated him that that woman had thought nothing of robbing his brother while he was sick and weak and helpless. He wondered what she'd hit him with. She wasn't a big woman. Odd, that she'd been able to reach as high as Leo's head with some blunt object. He recalled with distaste the way she'd been dressed. He was no prude, but in his early twenties he'd had a fling with a woman he later found out was a private call girl. He'd been infatuated with her, and thought she loved him. When he learned her profession and that she'd recognized him at once and knew how wealthy he was, it had soured him on women. Like his married brothers had been, and Leo still was, he was wary of females. If he could find a man who could bake biscuits, he told himself, he'd never let even an old woman into the house ever again.

He recalled their latest acquisition with sorrow. He and Leo had found a retired pastry chef who'd moved in with them—the last of the Hart bachelors—to bake their beloved biscuits. She'd become ill and they'd rushed to the drugstore to get her prescriptions, along with candy and chocolates and a bundle of flowers. But her condition had worsened and she'd told them, sadly, that the job was just too much in her frail state of health. She had to quit. It was going to be hard to replace her. There weren't a lot of people who wanted to live on an isolated ranch and bake biscuits at all hours of the day and night. Even want ads with offers of a princely salary hadn't attracted anyone just yet. It was depressing; like having Leo lying there under white sheets, so still and quiet in that faded striped hospital gown.

Rey dozed for a few hours in the deep night, used to sleeping in all sorts of odd positions and places. Cattle ranchers could sleep in the saddle when they had to, he thought amusedly, especially when calving was underway or there was a storm or they were cutting out and branding calves and doing inventory of the various herds.

But he came awake quickly when Sanders, the police officer who'd arrested that woman last night, came into the room with a murmured apology.

"I'm just going off shift," Officer Sanders told Rey. "I thought I'd stop by and tell you that we've gone over the scene of the attack and we have some trace evidence. The detectives will start looking for other witnesses this morning. We'll get the people responsible for the attack on your brother."

Rey frowned. "Get 'them?'" he queried. "You've already got her. You arrested her!"

Officer Sanders averted his eyes. "Had to turn her loose," he said uneasily. "She had an alibi, which was confirmed. She gave me a statement and I took her home."

Rey stood up, unfolding his intimidating length, and glared at the officer. "You let her go," he said coldly. "Where's my brother's cell phone?" he added as an afterthought.

The policeman grimaced. "In her purse, along with his wallet," he said apologetically. "I forgot to ask her for them when I left. Tell you what, I'll swing by her house and get them on my way home…"

"I'll go with you," he said curtly. "I still think she's guilty. She's probably in cahoots with the guys who attacked Leo. And she could have paid someone to lie and give her an alibi."

"She's not that sort of woman," the policeman began.

Rey cut him off angrily. "I don't want to hear another word about her! Let's go," he said, grabbing his hat, with a last, worried glance at his sleeping brother. He wondered how the policeman could make such a statement about a woman he'd just met, but he didn't really care. He wanted her in jail.

He drove his rental car, with the off-duty policeman beside him, to Meredith's home, following the directions Officer Sanders gave him. It was in a run-down neighborhood, and the house was in poor condition. It only intensified Rey's suspicions about her. She was obviously poor. What better way to get money than to rob somebody?

He went to the door, accompanied by the policeman, and knocked. Hard.

He had to do it three times, each with more force and impatience, before someone answered the door.

Meredith Johns was disheveled and white-faced. She was clutching a bulky washcloth to her face and wearing a robe over the clothes she'd had on the night before.

"What do you want now?" she asked huskily, her voice slurred and jerky.

"Been drinking, have you?" Rey Hart asked in a blistering tone.

She flinched.

Officer Sanders knew what was going on. He read the situation immediately. He stepped past Rey, grim and silent, grimacing when he saw Meredith's face. He went by her and into the living room and began looking around.

"Hard night, I gather? It must be a continual risk, in your profession," Rey said insinuatingly, with a speaking glance at her dress in the opening of the old, worn robe. "Do your marks make a habit of beating you up?" he added with cold contempt.

She didn't answer him. It was hard to talk and her face hurt.

Officer Sanders had gone into the bedroom. He came back two minutes later with a tall, disheveled but oddly dignified-looking man in handcuffs. The man, who'd been quiet before, was now cursing furiously, accusing Meredith of everything from prostitution to murder in a voice that rose until he was yelling. Rey Hart looked at him with obvious surprise. His eyes went to Meredith Johns, who was stiff as a poker and wincing every time the man yelled at her. The policeman picked up the telephone and called for a squad car.

"Please, don't," Meredith pleaded, still clutching the ice-filled cloth to her face. "He's only just got out..."

"He isn't staying. This time, he's going to be in jail for longer than three days," the officer said firmly. "You get to the hospital and let one of the residents look at you, Miss Johns. How bad is it? Come on, show me," he demanded, moving closer.

Rey stood by, silent and confused, watching as Meredith winced and moved the bulky cloth away from her face. His breath was audible when he saw the swelling and the growing purple and violet discoloration around her eye, cheek and jaw.

"God Almighty," Rey said harshly. "What did he hit you with?"

"His fist," the policeman replied coldly. "And it isn't the first time. You have to face facts, Miss Johns," he told her. "He isn't the man he used to be. When he drinks, he doesn't know what he's doing. He'll kill you one night when he's like this, and he won't even remember doing it!"

"I won't press charges," she said miserably. "How can I? He's my father! He's the only family I have left in the world...."

The policeman looked at her with compassion. "You don't have to press charges," he told her. "I'll provide them myself. You'd better phone your boss and tell him you won't be in for a few weeks. He'll have kittens if you walk into the office looking like that."

"I suppose he would." Tears ran down her pale cheeks,

all the more eloquent for being silent. She looked at her
raging, cursing father and sadness claimed her features.
"He wasn't like this before, honest he wasn't," she told
them. "He was a kind, loving, caring man."

"Not anymore," Officer Sanders replied grimly. "Get to
the hospital and have your face seen about, Miss Johns. I'll
take your father outside until the unit comes…"

"No," she groaned. "Please, spare us that! I can't bear
to have the whole neighborhood watching, hearing
him…like that, again!"

He hesitated. "Okay. I'll watch for them out the window.
The unit can drop you by the hospital, since it's going there
first…."

"I'll take her," Rey said at once, without wondering
why he should do such an about-face. He didn't trust the
woman, or even totally believe her story. But she did look
so pitiful. He couldn't bear to leave her in that condition
to get to the hospital. Besides, whatever her motives, she
had gotten help for Leo. He could have died if he hadn't
been cared for.

"But…" she began.

"If," he added coldly, "you change clothes first. I am
not being seen in public with you in that rig!"

Two

Meredith wished she felt up to a fight. Her long blond hair was down in her face, her grey eyes were sparking fire. But she was sick to her stomach and bruised. She would rather have gone to bed if these stubborn men would just have let her alone. But her face could have broken or shattered bones. She knew that. She grimaced, hoping her insurance would cover a second "accident" in as many months.

When the unit arrived, Meredith turned away from the sight of her raging father being carried off and closed the door. Probably it wasn't surprising to the neighbors anymore, it happened so often. But she hated having everyone know.

"I'll get dressed," she said in a subdued tone.

Rey watched her go and then shoved his hands into his pockets and looked around the room. It was shabby. The only bright things in it were books—hundreds of them, in bookcases and boxes and stacked on tables and chairs. Odd, he thought. They were apparently short of cash, judging by the worn old furniture and bare floor. There was only a very small television and a portable stereo. He glanced at the CD case and was surprised to find classical music dominating the discs. What a peculiar family. Why have so many books and so little else? He wondered where the woman's mother was. Had she left the father, and was that why he drank? It would have explained a lot. He knew about missing parents, especially missing mothers—his had left the family while the five Hart boys were young, without a backward glance.

Minutes later, Meredith came back, and except for the bruised face, he might not have recognized her. She was wearing a beige sweater set, with a tweed coat over it. Her blond hair was in a neat bun and her face devoid of makeup. She wore flat-heeled shoes and carried a purse that looked new.

"Here's your brother's cell phone and his wallet," she said, handing it to him. "I forgot to give them to Officer Sanders."

He glared at them and put them in his pocket. He wondered if she'd have given them back at all if he hadn't come here. He didn't trust her, regardless of what the policeman had said. "Let's go," he said stiffly. "The car's outside."

She hesitated, but only for a minute. She wasn't going to be able to avoid a checkup. She knew the problems that negligence could cause. Even a relatively minor problem could become major.

Unexpectedly Rey opened the car door for her. She slid in, surprised to find herself in a new luxury car. She fastened her seat belt. His brother, Simon Hart, was state attorney general. Rey owned a ranch. She remembered how his injured brother, Leo, had been dressed last night, and her eyes went to Rey's expensive hat and boots and silk shirt. Of course, they were a wealthy family. Considering her state of dress—or undress—the night before, she could understand his misgivings about her character.

She sat wearily beside him, the ice-filled cloth still in her hand. She held it to the side of her face that was bruised and hoped that it would spare her some of the swelling. She didn't need a doctor to tell her that it was a bad blow. The pain was almost unbearable.

"I took a hit to the face a few years ago in a brawl," he volunteered in his deep, slow drawl. "It hurt like hell. I imagine your face does, too."

She swallowed, touched by the faint concern. Tears threatened, but she never cried now. It was a weakness she couldn't afford.

He glanced at her, puzzled. "Nothing to say?"

She managed to get her voice under control. "Thank you for taking me to the hospital," she said huskily.

"Do you usually dress like that when you go out at night?" he asked belatedly.

"I told you. There was…a Halloween party," she said. It hurt to talk. "It was the only costume I had."

"Do you like parties?" he asked sarcastically.

"My first one…in almost four years," she managed to say. "Please…hurts…to talk."

He glanced at her and then was quiet. He didn't like her. He didn't trust her. Why was he taking care of her? There was something unexpectedly vulnerable about her. But she had spirit.

He walked her into the emergency room. She filled out forms and was ushered back into a treatment cubicle while Rey sat in the waiting room between a squalling toddler and a man coughing his head off. He wasn't used to illness. He'd never seen much of it, and he didn't know how to cope with it. Accidents, sure, he was a good hand in an emergency, and there were plenty on a ranch. But he hated hospitals.

Meredith came back a good thirty minutes later with a prescription and a frown.

"What did he say?" he asked conversationally.

She shrugged. "He gave me something…for pain," she said, waving the prescription.

"They sent me to a plastic surgeon," he volunteered as they went through the automatic door.

She didn't speak.

"I had a shattered bone in my cheek that they couldn't repair," he persisted.

"I'm not…going…to any damned…plastic surgeon!"

His eyebrows arched. "Your face could be distorted."

"So what?" she muttered, wincing because it really did hurt to speak. "It's not…much of a face, anyway."

He scowled. She wasn't pretty, but her face had attractive features. Her nose was straight and elegant, she had high cheekbones. Her mouth was like a little bow, perfect. Her eyes, big and grey, fascinated him.

"You should go," he said.

She ignored him. "Can you…drive me by the pharmacy?"

"Sure."

She gave him directions and he waited while she had the prescription filled. He drove her back to her house and left her there reluctantly.

"I'll be at the hospital with Leo if you need anything," he said as if it pained him to say it.

"I don't need any help. Thanks," she added stiffly.

His eyebrows arched. "You remind me of me," he murmured, and a thin smile touched his lips—a kind one. "Proud as Lucifer."

"I get by. I really am…sorry about your brother. Will he be all right?" she asked at her door.

He nodded. "They want to keep him for two or three days. He'll want to thank you."

"No need. I would have done it for anyone."

He sighed. She was going to look bad for a long time, with her face in that condition. She'd been beaten and he felt responsible, God knew why. He took a breath. "I'm sorry I had you arrested," he said reluctantly.

She pursed her lips. "I'll bet…that hurt."

"What?"

"You don't apologize much, do you?" she asked, as if she knew.

He scowled down at her, puzzled.

She turned away. "No sweat. I'll live. So long."

She went in and closed the door. Rey, who'd done without companionship for a number of years, suddenly felt alone. He didn't like the feeling, so he shoved it out of his mind and drove back to the hospital. He wouldn't see her again, anyway.

Leo came back to himself with a vengeance late that afternoon. He had Rey lever the head of his bed up and he ate dinner with pure enjoyment.

"It's not bad," Leo murmured between mouthfuls. "But I wish I had a biscuit."

"Me, too," Rey said on a sigh. "I guess we could buy a restaurant, as a last resort," he added dejectedly. "One that serves breakfast."

"Who was that woman who came in with me?" he asked Rey.

"You remember her?" Rey was surprised.

"She looked like an angel," he mused, smiling. "Blond and big-eyed and all heart. She held my hand and sat down on the sidewalk in the cold and talked to me until the ambulance got there."

"You were unconscious."

"Not all the time. She even came in with me on the ambulance," he said. "She kept telling me I was going to be all right. I remember her voice." He smiled. "Her name was Meredith."

Rey's heart jumped. He felt uneasy. Leo usually didn't

pay much attention to strange women. "Meredith Johns," he agreed.

"Is she married?" Leo asked at once.

Rey felt threatened; it irritated him. "I don't know," he said.

"Do you think you could find somebody who knows how to get in touch with her?" his brother persisted. "I want to thank her for saving me."

Rey got up from the chair where he'd been sitting and walked to the darkened window, peering out through the blinds while he played for time. "She lives near the place where you were attacked," he said finally, unable to lie.

"What does she do for a living?"

"I don't know," Rey said, feeling uncomfortable. He couldn't get her father's accusing remarks out of his mind. She'd said she was dressed up for a party, she'd even found someone to give her an alibi, but Rey didn't completely believe her. What if that whole defense was a lie? What if she was some sort of prostitute? He didn't want his brother getting mixed up with a woman like that. He didn't trust women, especially strange women. Then he remembered her poor, bruised face and he felt bad about his suspicions.

"I'll ask one of the nurses," Leo said abruptly.

"No need," Rey told him. He turned back around with his hands in his pockets. "If you're determined, I'll go get her in the morning and bring her in to see you."

"Why not tonight?"

Rey let out an impatient breath. "Her father roughed her up because she got home late last night. I took her to the emergency room this morning before I came back here."

Leo's eyes narrowed and went cold. "Her father beat her? And you took her back home to him?" he said angrily.

"He wasn't there. They took him off to jail," he said. His face hardened even more. "She'll have a hell of a bruise. They said she couldn't go back to work for a few weeks." He moved one shoulder restlessly. "Considering the way they live, I don't know how she'll manage," he added reluctantly. "They don't seem to have much. Apparently the old man doesn't work and she's the only one bringing home any money." He didn't volunteer his opinion of how she made it.

Leo leaned back against the pillows. His big frame was without its usual vibrance. His dark eyes were dull, and his lean face was drawn. His blond-streaked brown hair was unkempt, and looked odd in the back where they'd had to shave it to put stitches in. It was a reminder of how tricky head wounds were. Leo was very lucky not to have brain damage. Rey thought about the assailants and his eyes blazed.

"I'm going to phone Simon tonight," he told Leo. "I'm sure the local police will do all they can to catch the guys who waylaid you, but they'll work even harder if they get a call from the state attorney general."

"There you go again, pulling strings," Leo mused.

"It's for a good cause."

"Did you find my wallet and my cell phone?" Leo asked.

"The woman had them. They're in my pocket."

"Good. I didn't think she had anything to do with mugging me. Don't forget your promise to bring Meredith here in the morning," he said.

Now it was "Meredith." Rey didn't like the whole idea of having Leo around the woman, but he didn't have a legitimate reason for keeping her from Leo's side. It would sound even more suspicious if Rey started throwing out sarcastic remarks about her. Leo did love to pull his chain.

"Okay," he said reluctantly.

"Good man," Leo replied with a wan grin. "Nothing like family to look after you."

"Next time, watch your back instead of daydreaming about forage grasses," Rey said firmly. Then he leaned forward in the chair. "So, tell me what sort of grasses the Cattleman's Association is advocating."

Rey got a hotel room near the hospital, so that he could have a bath and get some rest. The night staff had the phone number, so they could call him immediately if he was needed.

He phoned Simon before he went to bed.

"Leo's been mugged?" Simon exclaimed. "And you didn't call me last night?"

That tone was still intimidating, even though Rey was thirty-one. Simon was the eldest of the five brothers, and the bossiest, next to Cag.

"I was too upset to phone anybody," Rey returned, "and too busy trying to handle…another problem that cropped up. He's all right. Honest. I didn't find out until the early hours of the morning, and it's been a long day. He was already out of danger before it occurred to me that I needed to let you know."

"All right," Simon said, sounding as if he was more relaxed. "Do they have a suspect?"

"No. I thought we did, but it turned out to be a dead end," he added, without going into details about Meredith Johns. "There were two of them, and they haven't been caught. It's a miracle he wasn't killed, and that they were stopped in time before they robbed him. You might give the local police chief a call. Just to let him know we're all interested in solving the case."

"You want me to use my influence for personal gain?" Simon drawled.

"Hell, yes, I do!" Rey shot back. "This is our brother, for God's sake! If a big, strong man like Leo can get mugged in a residential neighborhood, so can anybody else! It doesn't say a lot for the security in this area."

"No, it doesn't," Simon agreed. "I'll point that out to the police commissioner, first thing tomorrow. Then I'll run down to Jacobsville and get Cag and Corrigan and we'll be right up to see about Leo.''

Rey chuckled. It was the first bit of humor he'd felt so far. The five brothers rarely went so far as to gang up on people, but considering the size and reputation of them, they got results when they did. This was an emergency, anyway. They could have lost a brother. The perpetrators had to be caught.

''They should be home by now,'' Rey replied. ''I couldn't phone them because they were showing those Japanese businessmen around the ranch and the town.''

''I'll see how much luck they had. Japan is very careful about its import beef. The fact that we run organically raised cattle will certainly go in our favor,'' Simon said.

''Yes, it will. Get some sleep. And don't worry about Leo. He's fine. I'd never have left the hospital if I'd had one doubt about that.''

''I'll stop worrying.''

''Give my love to Tira and the boys,'' Rey added.

''I'll do that. See you tomorrow.''

Rey hung up, thinking about Simon and his family. Tira was redheaded and gorgeous, and the boys favored both of them, although they had Simon's dark eyes and hair. Corrigan and Dorie had a boy and a girl. Cag and Tess had just a boy, but they were talking about how nice a daughter would be. Meanwhile, Rey and Leo enjoyed being uncles, but had no interest in joining the ranks of the married.

If it wasn't for those biscuits, Rey thought miserably. It was going to be expensive to have the local café make biscuits for them every day until they employed a new biscuit maker, but if they got desperate enough, and offered enough of an incentive, they could probably manage it.

Turning his attention elsewhere, Rey gave a thought to poor Leo with his stitches and his headache, and another to Meredith Johns's bruised face. Tomorrow, he'd have to deal with Leo's request to see her, and he wasn't looking forward to it. He wished he knew why.

Rey went to Meredith Johns's house the next morning after he'd had breakfast. It took her a minute or two to answer the door, and for an instant, he thought that perhaps she might not be in any condition to answer it. She'd been badly bruised.

But she opened the door and peered up at him bravely, even though she looked like a refugee from a bar brawl. Her left eye was swollen shut completely now.

"Leo wants to see you," he said easily, noticing how the top of her blond head only came to his shoulder. She wasn't tall. Even bruised, her face had a beautiful complexion. Her mouth was pretty. He shook himself mentally. "He wants to thank you for what you did. He remembers that you rode in on the ambulance with him. You didn't tell me that," he added with faint accusation.

"I wasn't thinking," she said. "I was worried about what would happen when I came home late."

"Have you heard any more about your father this morning?" he asked grimly.

"They're going to charge him with simple battery," she said heavily. "I can't afford a lawyer. He'll have a public defender and he'll probably have to stay in jail for a few weeks." She looked up at him. "It will be a godsend, you know, because he'll dry out completely."

He hated the compassion he felt. "Did your mother leave him?" he asked.

She averted her face. She couldn't bear to talk about it yet. "In a way," she said huskily. "Are you going to drive me?" she added, glancing at him over her shoulder. "The bus doesn't run for another thirty minutes."

"Sure," he agreed.

"Then I'll get my jacket and purse."

She went into another room and came back quickly, leading the way out the door. "Is he conscious now?"

"Very," he murmured dryly. "When I left him, he was telling a nurse what she could do with the wash basin, and how far."

She chuckled. "He didn't seem like that kind of man," she murmured. "I had him figured for a gentleman, not a renegade."

"We're all that kind of man," he replied.

"All?"

He led her to the car and put her into the passenger seat. "There are five of us. The other three are coming up this morning to have a talk with the police."

"I remember. You said that your brother was the attorney general."

"He is," he replied. "We tend to stick together."

Her eyes went to his hands on the steering wheel. He had nice hands, very lean and strong with neat, clean fingernails. He was a tough-looking man, like a cowboy.

"How's your face?" he asked unexpectedly.

She shrugged. "It still hurts. It will for a while, but I'll be fine."

"You should see that plastic surgeon."

"Why?" she asked heavily. "My insurance won't pay for cosmetic surgery, and there's not much chance that they can do any major repair on tiny shattered bones."

"You're not a doctor. Stop giving yourself medical advice."

She stared at him for a long moment and started to speak, then lost the opportunity when he pulled up in the hospital parking lot, cut off the engine, and got out.

Rey waited for her and led her up to the floor where his brother's room was located.

Leo wasn't alone. Three other men were with him, one big and dark and missing an arm, the other lean and light-eyed and handsome, and a third big one with black eyes and a threatening face towering over both the others.

"That's Cag," Rey indicated the black-eyed man. "Corrigan," he nodded toward the light-eyed man, "and that's Simon," he finished, smiling at the one-armed man. "This is Meredith Johns. She rescued Leo."

"Nice to see you and know who you are," Leo said, alert now and interested as his dark eyes swept over the neat woman just inside the door. "Miss Johns, I presume?"

She smiled self-consciously, because everybody was looking at her bruised face. "Yes," she said.

Simon Hart frowned when he got a good look at her. "What the hell happened to you?" he demanded.

"Her father," Rey said for her. "She got in late and he beat her up."

Leo looked suddenly as intimidating as the other three. "Where is he?" he asked.

"In jail," Meredith said heavily. "For several weeks, at least, and he'll have time to dry out."

"Good." Leo looked toward Simon. "Maybe you can find a way to get him into rehab before he gets out."

"I'll look into it," Simon said at once.

"And some counseling wouldn't come amiss," Rey put his two cents worth in.

"I'll see about that, too," Simon replied. "Nice to meet you, Miss Johns. We're all grateful for what you did for Leo."

"You're all very welcome," she replied. She clutched her purse, intimidated by the group of brothers.

"Come here," Leo said, holding out his hand. "They're big and they look tough, but they're really marshmallows. You don't have to feel threatened. I'll protect you."

"She doesn't need protecting from us!" Rey snapped.

The others gaped at him. It wasn't like Rey to act that way.

He cleared his throat. He didn't want them asking themselves embarrassing questions about his attitude. He shoved his hands into his pockets. "Sorry. I didn't sleep much last night," he explained.

Meredith went to stand beside Leo, who took one of her small, cold hands in his and looked up at her with interest.

"Have you seen a doctor?" he asked.

"Your brother took me to the emergency room yesterday," she said.

"Rey. His name's Reynard, but he's called Rey," Leo informed her.

She smiled. "You look much better today. Head hurt?"

"A bit, but my vision's clear and I'm not disoriented," he said, quoting the doctor. "I have a good prognosis."

"That's nice to hear. You were in pretty bad shape."

"I'd have been in a lot worse shape, but for you," Leo said. "I hear that you can't work out in public for a while, until your face heals," he added. "Can you cook?"

She blinked. "Of course," she said at once.

"Can you make bread?"

She frowned. "Bread?"

"More specifically, biscuits," he added, and had the oddest expression on his face.

She shifted her purse in the hand he wasn't holding. "Well, yes, those and rolls and loaf bread," she said, as if everybody could do it.

Leo shot a glance at Rey, who was just staring at him without daring to say a word. He knew what was coming, and he couldn't decide how he felt about it. He didn't want to think about it.

"How would you like a brief stay in Jacobsville, Texas, in a big sprawling ranch house where your only job would be to make biscuits every morning?" Leo asked with his best smile.

Rey and the other brothers were staring at her, waiting. She wondered why. And Rey was frowning, as if he didn't like the idea at all. Probably he still secretly thought she was a hooker. He couldn't seem to credit her with any sense of decency.

She thought about his attitude for a few seconds, and decided that it wouldn't be a bad idea to take the job, and show him that you really couldn't judge a book by its cover. It wouldn't hurt that arrogant cowboy to be taken down a step or two, and she was just the girl who could do it.

She smiled. It hurt her face, but what was a little pain for a good cause? She turned back to Leo. "Mr. Hart, I think I'd like that job very much!"

Three

"**G**ood for you!" Leo exclaimed, animated and smiling. "You won't be sorry, Meredith. Honest."

She smiled back at him. He was nice, like a big brother. She liked him already. "I can do housekeeping, too," she told him. "I'll earn my keep."

"You'll go on salary, of course," he insisted. "It won't be a holiday."

"Nothing is a holiday with those two," Simon murmured dryly. "They aren't kidding about biscuits. They'll run you crazy baking them."

Rey and Leo gave their brother a disgusted look.

Meredith grinned. "I don't mind," she assured Simon. "I love to cook."

"It won't be that hard," Leo promised, with another speaking glance at Simon. "We just love biscuits. But we'll make you feel right at home. Anything you need, you can have—a new stove…" he added mischievously.

She thought about her father and her job, and her smile

faltered. "I have to wrap up a few loose ends first," she began.

"No problem," Leo assured her. "I can't get out of here for another day at least, or so that doctor said," he added with impatience.

"You'll stay until he lets you out," Rey said firmly. "Concussions are tricky. You know that."

Leo grimaced. "I guess so. I hate hospitals."

"I'm not too wild about them myself," Rey had to agree.

"It would be a very sad world without them," Meredith spoke up.

She seemed irritated, Rey thought, and wondered why. "I'll run you back home when you're ready," Rey told her. "We'll be in touch before we're ready to leave."

"All right." She held Leo's hand again and squeezed it gently, to the amusement of all the Harts except Rey. "You get better. I'll see you soon."

"Thanks again," Leo told her with genuine gratitude.

"It was nothing." She gave him another smile, tugged her hand free, and let Rey herd her out the door after a quick goodbye to the other brothers.

"I thought your brother was big until I saw all of you together. Goodness, you're all huge!" she exclaimed when they were outside in the parking lot. She gave him a long scrutiny. "And there doesn't seem to be an extra ounce of fat on any of you."

"We don't sit behind desks. We're ranchers, not office workers, and we work hard, right alongside our cowboys," he said. His dark eyes cut sideways. "Leo likes you."

She smiled. "I'm glad, because I like him, too."

That set him off and he tried not to let it show. He didn't want her to like Leo. He wished he knew why. He glanced at her as he wove skillfully through traffic toward her house. "Do you have family besides your father?" he asked.

"A cousin or two near Fort Worth," she said. She

glanced out the window, absently rubbing the ring finger of her left hand, trying not to choke up over the question. "What is Jacobsville like?" she asked to divert him from any further questions.

"It's small," he said easily. "There are a lot of ranches in the area. We have good pasture and soil, and we get enough rain to manage healthy crops." He grinned. "A lot of us are heavily into organic cattle raising. And with the industry under threat right now, we'll probably keep our financial heads above water when some other ranchers are going under."

"I like organic food," she said. "It may have a few more blemishes and bug bites, but if it doesn't kill bugs, it won't kill me," she added with a grin.

He chuckled. "Good point. Do you like animals?"

"I love them. I'd like to have a cat, but it's not possible. Dad's allergic to them." She sighed wearily, leaning her head back against the headrest. Her bruises were still giving her a lot of pain. Her hand went to them and she winced.

"You should see that plastic surgeon," he reminded her.

She shook her head. "Can't afford it. Even if I could, I don't want to go through weeks of surgery."

He hesitated and then he shrugged. "Have it your way."

"I'll heal." She touched her cheek again self-consciously. "I'm not sure going to work for you is a good idea. I mean, people might think the five of you beat me up!"

He laughed wholeheartedly. "Nobody who knows us would ever think that. Especially," he added, "if you can bake. Simon was right. I'm afraid we're famous locally for our addiction to biscuits."

Actually they were famous a lot further out than Jacobsville, but he didn't want to make her think they were loopy.

She took the words at face value. "I like to cook."

He glanced at her again, taking in her very conservative

way of dressing. "You don't look like the same woman I met just after Leo was assaulted."

"I almost never dress up," she confided. "And it really was a costume," she pointed out. "I wasn't lying. I don't make my living on the streets."

"How old are you?"

Her eyebrows arched. "Old enough."

"Are you over twenty-one?" he persisted.

"I'm twenty-three, almost twenty-four," she replied.

"And not married?"

"I've had responsibilities for the past few years," she said distantly, staring out the windshield. "My father has become the largest of them. I've been afraid to leave him alone."

"He's obviously dangerous when he drinks."

She hesitated, fingering her purse. "He seemed to lose himself in the bottle overnight. I thought I could handle him, control him, break the cycle. I couldn't even get help for him. My father doesn't think he has a drinking problem, so nobody would take him." She looked over at him. "I'm very grateful to your brother for his help. As I mentioned the night he was arrested, my father has only been like this for the past few months. It's not a long-standing problem. But I couldn't solve it alone."

"You're going to work for us," Rey said. "And it's not that much of a problem for Simon. He's good at his job."

"Is it a big ranch?" she asked unexpectedly.

"Enormous," he replied, "and one of five ranches we own as a family. Things get hectic during roundup, as you'll find out if you're still there next Spring."

"I won't be," she said with some certainty. "When I heal, I have to get back to my job."

"What do you do?" he asked curiously. "Is it house-cleaning or working as a cook in a restaurant?"

She almost bit her tongue at the demeaning comment. "You don't think I'm qualified to do anything else?"

He averted his eyes to the road. "I don't know you, Miss Johns," he commented carelessly. "But you seem pretty domestic to me."

She didn't feel well enough to retaliate. But one day, she promised herself, she was going to make him eat those condescending words.

"I've made beds and done light cleaning," she said, talking around her actual profession.

"Aren't you ambitious?" he persisted, with a faint frown. "Most women are, these days."

"That sounded bitter," she commented. "Did you get thrown over by an ambitious woman?"

"By a couple of them," he said curtly, and his expression became hard.

She hadn't thought of him that way. They'd been adversaries from the first contact. But it occurred to her as she gave him a quick, covert scrutiny, that he was a sensuous man. He wasn't handsome—except for Corrigan Hart, the rest of the brothers seemed cursed by a lack of conventional good looks.

But Rey had a lithe, graceful stride, and a strong face. He had good hands, clean and long-fingered. She liked the blackness of his straight hair, the high cheekbones, the long, thin, chiseled mouth. He was the sort of man who could have attracted women, except for his personality. The Harts didn't strike her as particularly gregarious or good mixers from her brief acquaintance with them. Leo was the one with the warmest personality. He made her feel at ease. The man beside her made her uncomfortable, insecure, nervous. She wasn't usually so strung-out by a man's proximity. Not that she'd had a lot to do with men in very recent years. Her father's overprotective, possessive nature had seen to that. He'd been so certain that she was going to end up like her mother.

She closed her eyes briefly, hating the memories.

"If you want to go and see your father before we leave for Jacobsville, I'll ask Simon to arrange it."

She stiffened. "I don't want to see him again until he's sober," she replied. "We both need time to get over what happened."

"Is your face the only place he hit you?" he asked unexpectedly.

"He got me in the back and the side, too, but those were only bruises. The doctor checked me over thoroughly." She sighed wearily. "I'm so tired," she murmured absently.

"I'm not surprised. You can get some rest. I'll phone you tomorrow, when we'll know more about Leo's condition and when he'll be released."

"Okay."

He stopped in front of her house and parked the car, walking to the door with her. He looked down at her while she fumbled the key into the lock. She was, in some ways, the most vulnerable woman he'd ever met. But there was steel in her makeup. He sensed that she wasn't like this usually, that she was fiery and independent and determined.

"This isn't the first time your father's laid into you, is it?" he asked suddenly.

She glanced at him, surprised. "No. But until this happened, it was more humiliating than painful." She frowned. "How did you know?"

He seemed concerned. "When I was in school, I had a couple of friends whose fathers got violent during binges. There's an...attitude, a posture, that people get when they've been beaten. I can't explain it, but I recognize it when I see it."

"Do you want to know what it is?" she asked with a world-weary smile. "It's a feeling of futility, of knowing that no matter what you do, you can't hold out physically against a man who's enraged and bent on hurting you. Because you know if you fight back, it will be even worse, maybe fatally worse. I don't like it," she added, her pale eyes beginning to glow, "and he's never getting the chance to do this again. He's my father. I love him, and I feel sorry for him. But I'm nobody's victim. Not even his."

He pushed his hands into his slacks' pockets and smiled at her. Her face was bright with color, and her eyes were alive, like peridots in sunlit water. He remembered her long blond hair around her shoulders and he wondered what she'd look like in pink silk. The thought shocked him and he scowled.

"Did I glue my nose on upside down?" she asked, raising her eyebrows.

He let out a short laugh. "No. I had a wild thought. Do you need an advance on your salary? I mean, is there anything you have to get for the trip that you can't afford?"

"I don't have a car," she began, and hated remembering why.

He glared. "I didn't say you were going to have to get to Jacobsville on your own. You'll go with Leo and me. Simon drove my car up from Jacobsville."

"Do I get to ride in the car, or have you got me earmarked for the trunk?" she returned.

He pursed his lips. Odd feelings were kindling inside him. "Keep that up and you'll be riding on the back bumper."

She wrinkled her nose. "Nice. Real nice. I can see you're going to be a great boss."

"If you don't burn the biscuits, I will be," he said.

"I'll stick close to your brother," she promised. "He'll protect me."

He didn't like that, but he wasn't going to let it show. "Leo's a tease," he said flatly. "Don't get your hopes up. He's not a marrying man. Neither am I," he added deliberately.

Her eyes widened. "Well, gee whiz, that's a major disappointment! And to think, I was only willing to take the job because of the marriage prospects!"

His face shuttered. "Sarcasm doesn't get you any points with me. I'm just making the position clear. We need a cook, not a prospective soul mate."

"Speak for yourself," she told him, turning back to her door. "I think Leo likes me already."

"I just told you…!"

She opened the door and looked back at him with pure irreverence. "Your brother can speak for himself. You don't own him, and you don't own me. I'll do what I please."

"Damn it…!"

"With charm like that, it's no surprise to me that you're still single," she said as she walked into the house.

"I can be charming when I've got a reason to be," he said icily. "But that's something you'll never know!"

"Lucky me!"

He started to speak, closed his lips tight, and walked back to his car.

She closed the door quickly and leaned back against it, almost shivering with anger. Of all the conceited, infuriating men she'd ever met, that one took the cake!

The next day, Rey phoned her midmorning to tell her that he and Leo would pick her up at one for the drive down to Jacobsville.

She had her suitcase packed and the house closed up when the big luxury car pulled into the driveway. It was a late-model car, and it looked odd, sitting in front of the shabby little house.

As she walked to the car, Meredith saw curtains fluttering and knew that the neighbors were getting an eyeful. They probably thought she was being carried off by the mob. That amused her and she smiled, glad that something diverted her mind from her father and her pain, and the misery of the past few months.

"We hadn't planned to ask you to help us move cattle,"

Rey drawled when he saw how she was dressed, in jeans and a striped shirt and boots.

"I haven't volunteered, either," she assured him. "But I didn't think you'd want me to do housework in a dress." She gave him a wry glance. "Those old black-and-white sitcoms weren't historically accurate, you know. I never saw a woman vacuum the carpet wearing a dress and high heels and pearls!"

"You can do housework in a suit for all I care, as long as you can bake me a pan of biscuits every morning," Rey said, taking the suitcase and putting it in the trunk.

"Good morning," Leo called from the open window of the front seat, grinning as Rey opened the back door and helped her inside.

"Good morning," she said brightly. "You look much better."

"I feel better, except for the headache." He gave her a long look. "You aren't in very good shape yourself. Face hurt?"

"Yes. I guess we're both like walking wounded, huh?" she asked with a grin as she leaned back into the warm leather seat.

"Maybe we should take a nurse with us," Rey muttered as he got in and started the car.

Meredith cleared her throat, but before she could speak, Leo turned to his brother. "I don't need nursing, thank you very much!" Leo said curtly.

"Neither do I!" Meredith agreed.

Rey glanced at them as he pulled out into the street. "I've seen accident victims who looked better than the two of you."

"Don't let him insult you, Meredith," Leo told her. "I'll tell you all about his weak spots so that you can deal with him."

She wouldn't have expected Rey to have any of those, but she was keeping her mouth shut and her options open for the time being. Her new boss looked formidable, and even Leo seemed curious about his lack of warmth.

"Are you all from Jacobsville originally?" Meredith changed the subject.

"No, we're from San Antonio," Leo said. "We inherited the Jacobsville property and it needed a lot of work, so we made it our headquarters. It's convenient to Houston and San Antonio, and frankly, it's isolated and gives us some privacy. We don't like cities as a rule."

"Neither do I," she said, recalling her grandmother's beautiful flower garden at the old place near Fort Worth. She smiled. "I wish Dad hadn't taken the job in Houston in the first place."

"What does he do?" Leo asked.

"He's retired," she said, not wanting to go into specifics. It hurt to talk about her family. Her father was a sore spot just now, anyway.

"Simon talked to the authorities," Rey interrupted. "They're going to make sure he gets counseling and he won't be released until he's kicked the alcohol habit." He glanced over the seat at her, his dark eyes intent. "They think it will be better if you don't have any contact with him for a few weeks, until he's through the worst of the withdrawal symptoms."

"I know about withdrawal," she replied, absently smoothing her hand over her jeans. "Bad habits are hard to break, even new ones."

"You two must read a lot," Rey replied. "I never saw so many books in one place as I did at your house. Even our library isn't that stuffed, and we all read."

"I love reading," she agreed. "We have a television, but neither of us had much time to watch it. Until recently," she added reluctantly, and winced at the thoughts that went through her mind. "I hope they get those men who mugged you, Mr. Hart," she told Leo fervently.

"Leo," he corrected. "It's really Leopold, but nobody

calls me that," he added with a grin. "We're pretty informal with our employees."

"Do you have a lot?" she asked curiously.

"A good many in Jacobsville," he replied. "Although we don't have a full-time vet, we do have several accountants, livestock managers, computer programmers, salesmen…you name it, we've got one. It's big business these days to run cattle. We even have a man who does nothing but keep up with legislation that may impact us."

"Do you have dogs and cats?" she asked.

"Always," Rey replied. "We have border collies that help us herd cattle, and we keep cats in the barn to help handle the rats."

"We had a cat in the house," Leo added, "but it was Cag and Tess's, and they took it with them when they moved into their new house. At least she won't have to cope with Herman," he told his brother, and laughed.

Rey smiled involuntarily. "You might not have wanted to work for us if we still had Herman."

"Who's Herman?" she wanted to know.

"He was Cag's albino python," he told her. "He weighed a hundred and ten pounds and lived in a cage in Cag's bedroom. He gave Herman up when he married Tess. He said it would be crazy to keep an animal that big and dangerous around their son. They're still over the moon about that little boy."

"Yes, but there are people who don't even consider things like that," Meredith murmured absently. "I remember a little girl who had to have plastic surgery because she was bitten in the face by her father's pet boa constrictor."

"Herman didn't bite, but Tess almost had a heart attack when she first came to work for us and found him in the washing machine."

"I can sympathize with her," Meredith said. "I haven't come across many snakes. I'm not sure I want to."

"We have rattlers and water moccasins around the

place," Rey told her. "You have to watch where you walk, but we've only had one person bitten in recent years. Snakes are always going to be a hazard in open country. You can't be careless."

"I'll remember."

"We've got a big garage apartment," Leo told her. "It's got picture windows and a whirlpool bath. Tess lived there until she and Cag married. I think you'll like it."

"I don't mind where I stay," she said easily. "I'm grateful to have a job at all. I really couldn't go to work in Houston looking like this. It would have been embarrassing for my boss."

"You won't have people staring at you on the ranch," Leo assured her. "And it won't take too long for those bruises to heal."

"I'll be fine, but you'll have to take it easy for a few days still, I'm sure they told you that," she returned at once. "No violent exertion. Concussion is tricky."

"I know that," Leo told her. "We had a man who was kicked in the head by a horse. He dropped dead three days later while he was walking into the corral. It was a hard lesson about head injuries. None of us ever forgot it."

She averted her eyes. She didn't like thinking about head injuries just now.

"I've got to stop for gas," Rey said as they reached the outskirts of the city and he pulled into a self-service gas station. "Anybody want something to drink?"

"Coffee for me," Leo said. "Meredith?"

"I'd like a small coffee, black, please."

"I'll go get it after I fill the tank," Rey said. He got out and started pumping gas.

Leo leaned his arm over the back seat and looked at Meredith openly, his dark eyes quiet and gently affectionate.

"You're still having a hard time with Rey, aren't you?" he asked her.

"He doesn't really like me," she confessed with a wry smile. "And I have to admit, he puts my back up, too. He seems to want to think the worst of me. He was convinced that I mugged you."

He chuckled. "You aren't tall enough to have knocked me out," he said. "But Rey doesn't like women much. He had a bad time of it with a young woman who turned out to be a call girl," he added, noticing absently how stunned Meredith seemed to be at that remark. "He had the ring bought, the honeymoon spot picked out, and then he found out the truth about her. It took him years to get over it. He was crushed."

"I guess so," she said heavily. "Good Lord, no wonder he thought the worst when he saw how I was dressed."

Leo frowned. "I just barely remember the rig you had on. What was it, some sort of costume?"

"I'd been to a wild Halloween party and had just escaped when I saw those men bending over you," she told him. "I ran at them waving my arms and yelling, and frightened them off."

"That was taking a hell of a chance!" he exploded.

She shrugged. "I've done it before," she said. "I learned it from my…from my brother's best friend," she amended, forcing the words out. It was much too soon to try to talk about her tragedy. "He taught karate in the military. He said that sometimes all it needed was a yell and the element of surprise to spook an attacker and make him run. It works."

"Not all the time," Leo said darkly, "and not for women. I'm all for equality, but most men are bigger and stronger than most women, and in hand-to-hand, you'd lose. You can't count on a man running, loud noise or not."

"Well, it worked for you," she amended, and smiled at him. "I'm glad, because I couldn't have wrestled those guys down."

He nodded. "See that you remember it," he told her. "Don't take chances. Get help."

"Some help those partygoers would have been," she scoffed. "Half of them were drunk, and the other half probably wouldn't have walked across the street to save a grandmother from a mugging!"

"Then why were you at a party with them?" he asked reasonably.

She picked at a fingernail. "A girl I know from work said I needed a night off and insisted that I come. I wore an old costume, the only one I had, and thought I'd enjoy myself. I don't do drugs or drink, and one of the men made a blatant pass at me." She wrapped her arms around her body in a defensive posture that betrayed her fear. "I was anxious to get away from the whole mess, luckily for you," she added with a grin.

"I don't like parties much, either," he said. "Getting drunk isn't my idea of a good time."

She glanced out the window. Rey had finished pumping gas and was inside the convenience store now. "Does he drink?" she asked.

"Very rarely. I've been known to, under provocation, but Rey's levelheaded and sober. He can be mean, and he's got the blackest temper of all of us, but he's a good man to have on your side when the chips are down."

"He doesn't like me," she repeated.

"He'll come around, give him time," Leo told her. "Meanwhile, you've got a job and a place to stay while your face heals. We all have hard times," he added gently. "But we get through them, even when we don't expect to. Give yourself time."

She smiled. "Thanks," she said huskily. "You really are a nice man."

"Nice, clean, sober, modest and incredibly handsome," he added with a wicked grin. "And I haven't even gotten to my best points yet!"

"Compared to your brothers," she began, "you—"

The door opened before she could hang herself, and Rey shoved a cup of coffee at her before he handed the second one to Leo.

"It's hot," he told them as he slid in and took the soft drink out of his jacket pocket and put it in the cup holder.

"Cold caffeine," Leo said, shuddering. "Why can't you drink coffee like a normal man?"

"I drink coffee at breakfast," Rey told him haughtily.

"So do I, but you don't have to have rules on when to drink it!"

Rey started the engine with a speaking glance.

"See that look?" Leo indicated it to Meredith. "When he looks like that, you've already lost whatever argument you're in the middle of. We call it 'the look.' I once saw him break up a fistfight with it."

"I don't plan to argue," Meredith promised.

Rey gave her "the look," and it lingered before his attention turned back to the windshield.

Meredith sat back against the leather seat and wondered suddenly if she wasn't making the biggest mistake of her life.

Four

The Hart Ranch was almost as Meredith had pictured it, with neat wooden fences concealing electrified fencing, improved pasture land and cattle everywhere. There were also pastures with horses, and there was a barn big enough to store a commercial jet. But she loved the house itself, with its graceful arches reminiscent of Spanish architecture, and the incredible number of small trees and shrubs around it. In the spring, it must be glorious. There were two ponds, a decorative one in the front of the house and a larger one behind the house in which a handful of ducks shivered in the November sun.

"Do you have goldfish in the pond?" she asked excitedly as Rey stopped the car in front of the house on an inlaid stone driveway.

"Goldfish and Koi," he answered, smiling reluctantly at her excitement. "We have a heater in the pond to keep them comfortable during the winter. There are water lilies in there, too, and a lotus plant."

"Does the other pond have goldfish, too, where the ducks are?" she wondered.

Leo chuckled. "The other one is because of the ducks. We had to net this pond to keep them out of it so we'd *have* some goldfish. The ducks were eating them."

"Oh, I see." She sighed. "It must be beautiful here in the spring," she said dreamily, noting the gazebo and the rose garden and stone seats and shrubs around the goldfish pond.

"It's beautiful to us year-round," Leo told her with lazy affection. "We all love flowers. We've got some more roses in a big flower garden around the back of the house, near a stand of pecan trees. Tess is taking courses in horticulture and she works with hybrids."

"I love roses," Meredith said softly. "If I had time, I'd live in a flower garden."

"I suppose cleaning rooms is time-consuming," Rey murmured sarcastically as he got out of the car and went in the front door of the house.

Leo glanced at her curiously while Rey was out of earshot. "You clean rooms?"

"I don't," she told him with a sharp grin. "But I'm living down to your brother's image of my assets."

Leo pursed his lips. "Now, that's interesting. You sound like a woman with secrets."

"More than you'd guess," she told him heavily. "But none that I'm ashamed of," she added quickly, just in case he got the wrong idea.

"Rey doesn't like you, does he?" he murmured, almost to himself. "I wonder why? It's not like him to pick on sick people."

"I'm not sick," she assured him. "I'm just battered, but I'll heal."

"Sure you will," Leo promised, smiling. "You'll be safe here. The only real chore you'll have is baking. By the time you're completely back on your feet, your father will be sober and in counseling, and your home life will have changed drastically.''

''I hope so,'' she said huskily.

He watched her eyes grow tragic and haunted. He frowned. ''Meredith,'' he said slowly. ''If you need to talk, ever, I can listen without making judgments.''

She met his clear dark eyes. ''Thanks, Leo,'' she said with genuine gratitude. ''But talking won't change a thing. It's a matter of learning to live with…things.''

''Now I'm intrigued.''

''Don't push,'' she said gently. ''I'm not able to talk about my problems yet. They're too fresh. Too painful.''

''And more than just your father, or I'm a dirt farmer,'' he drawled.

She shrugged. ''Perhaps.''

''Anyway, just take your time and let the world pass you by. You're going to love it here. I promise.''

''Am I?'' She watched Rey come back out of the house with an elderly lady in tow, wringing her hands on her apron.

''That's Mrs. Lewis,'' Leo told her. ''We talked her into coming back to bake biscuits for us, even though she'd retired, but now we're losing her to arthritis. She's going to show you the ropes. But not right now,'' he added quickly.

''No time like the present,'' Meredith disagreed with a smile. ''Busy hands make busy minds.''

''I know how that works,'' Leo murmured drolly.

Rey opened the back door and helped Meredith out. ''Mrs. Lewis, this is Meredith Johns, our new cook. Meredith, Annie Lewis. She's retiring. Again.'' He made it sound like a shooting offense.

''Oh, my, yes, I'm losing the use of my hands, I'm afraid,'' Mrs. Lewis said. ''Glad to meet you, Miss Johns.''

''Glad to meet you, too, Mrs. Lewis,'' Meredith replied.

"I'll take your bag to your room, while Mrs. Lewis shows you around the house," Rey added.

"She just got here," Leo protested.

"And there's no time like the present to show her the house," Rey replied.

"That's just what she said," Leo sighed.

Rey glanced at Meredith, who gave him a wicked grin and followed along behind Annie Lewis, who was making a valiant effort not to ask about the terrible bruises on Meredith's face.

"It's a big, sprawling house, and it takes a lot of cleaning," Mrs. Lewis said as she led Meredith down the long hall and opened doors to the very masculine bedrooms both with dark, heavy Mediterranean furniture and earth tones in the drapes and carpets. "The men aren't messy, thank God, but they track in all that mud and dust and animal fur! They had beige carpeting when I came here." She glanced at Meredith with a shake of her head. "Red mud just won't come *out* of beige carpet!"

"Or anything else," Meredith added on a soft laugh.

"They work hard, and they're away a lot. But the foreman lives in the bunkhouse with a couple of bachelor cowboys, and they'll look out for you."

"I don't know that I'll be here very long," Meredith replied quietly. "They offered me the job so that I can have time for these to heal." She touched her face, and looked straight at the older woman, who was struggling not to ask the question in her eyes.

"Nobody will hurt you here," Mrs. Lewis said firmly.

Meredith smiled gently. "My father got drunk and beat me up, Mrs. Lewis," she explained matter-of-factly. "He's a good and kind man, but we've had a terrible tragedy to work through. He hasn't been able to cope with it except by losing himself in a bottle, and now he's gone too far and he's in jail." She sighed. "I tried so hard to help him. But I couldn't."

Mrs. Lewis didn't say a word. She put her arms around Meredith and rocked her in them. The shock of it brought the tears that she'd held back for so long. She wept until her body shook with sobs.

Rey, looking for her, stopped dead in the doorway of his bedroom and met Mrs. Lewis's misty eyes over Meredith's bowed shoulders. It shocked him to see that feisty, strong woman collapsed in tears. It hurt him.

Mrs. Lewis made a gesture with her eyebrows and a severe look. Rey acknowledged it with a nod and a last glance at the younger woman as he walked back down the hall.

Supper was riotous. Meredith had made a huge pan of homemade biscuits and ferreted out all sorts of preserves to go with them. For an entrée, she made fajitas with lean beef and sliced vegetables, served with wild rice and a salad. Dessert was fresh fruit and fresh whipped cream, the only concession besides the biscuits that she made to fat calories. She'd also found some light margarine to set out.

"This is good," Rey commented as he glanced at her. "We usually have broiled or fried steak with lots of potatoes."

"Not bad once a week or so, but terrible for your cholesterol," she pointed out with a smile as she finished her salad. "Lean beef is okay for you, but not in massive doses."

"You sound like a dietician," Leo chuckled.

"Modern women have to keep up with health issues," she said evasively. "I'm responsible for your health while I'm working for you. I have to be food-conscious."

"That's fine," Rey told her flatly, "but don't put tofu and bean sprouts in front of me if you want to stay here."

Her eyebrows arched. "I hate tofu."

"Thank God," Leo sighed as he buttered another biscuit. "I got fed tofu salad the last time I went to Brewster's for supper,'' he added with absolute disgust. "I ate the olives and the cheese and left the rest."

"I can't say that I blame you," Meredith said, laughing because he looked so forlorn.

"Janie Brewster thinks tofu is good for him," Rey commented. "But she thinks he needs therapy more. He doesn't like fish. She says that has some sort of connection to his fear of deep water." He glanced at his brother with wicked affection. "She's a psychology major. She already has an associate degree from our local junior college."

"She's twenty," Leo said with a twist of his lower lip. "She knows everything."

"She just got her associate degree this spring," Rey added.

"Good. Maybe she'll get a job in New York," Leo said darkly.

"Why New York?" Meredith asked curiously.

"Well, it's about as far east as she can go and find her sort of work," Leo muttered. "And she'd be out of my hair!"

Rey gave him a covert glance and finished his fajitas.

Meredith finished her own meal and got up to refill coffee cups. She had a feeling that Leo was more interested in the nebulous Brewster girl than he wanted to admit.

"We need groceries," she told them when she'd served dessert and they were eating it. "Mrs. Lewis made me a list."

"You can use one of the ranch trucks to drive to town," Leo suggested carelessly.

Her fingers toyed with her fork. "I haven't driven in several months."

"You don't drive?" Rey exclaimed, shocked.

She couldn't meet his eyes. "I take buses." Cars made her feel guilty.

"Why?"

She remembered a day she should have driven. The memories were horrible...

"Meredith, it's all right," Leo said gently, sensing something traumatic about her behavior. "I'll drive you. Okay?"

"You won't," Rey replied. "You're in worse shape than she is. Which brings up another point. You don't need to be walking around town like that," he told her.

She wasn't offended; it was a relief. She even smiled. "No, I don't guess I do. Will you do the shopping?" she asked him, her wide, soft eyes steady on his.

He felt wild little thrills shooting through his body at the impact. It had been years since he'd been so shaken by eye contact alone. He didn't move. He just stared at her, his dark eyes unblinking, curious. His body rippled with vague hunger.

Leo, watching the eye contact, tried not to grin. He cleared his throat, and Rey seemed to remember that he had a forkful of fruit halfway to his mouth. He took it the rest of the way and chewed it carefully before he spoke.

"I'll get the groceries," Rey volunteered. He glared at both of them, noting the shaved place where Leo had stitches near the back of his head. "Obviously I'm the only one here who can walk around without drawing curious stares from bystanders!"

Leo buttered another biscuit. "That sounds like sour grapes to me. If you want attention, try walking around without your pants."

"I didn't say I wanted attention," Rey returned hotly.

"Good thing." He glanced at Meredith with a mischievous smile. "He looks like hell without his pants," he said conversationally. "Hairiest legs of the bunch."

"That's debatable," Rey shot back. "Yours aren't much better."

"What a good thing you two aren't Scottish," Meredith said demurely.

It took a minute for them to get it, then Leo burst out

laughing, trying to picture his younger brother in a kilt. Rey lifted a corner of his thin mouth, but he wasn't in a smiling mood. It bothered him, that Meredith had been crying in Mrs. Lewis's arms, that she didn't drive, that she was so mysterious about her life. She was twenty-three, almost twenty-four. Most women by that age had been involved in a serious relationship, some more than one. Many had been married.

His heart skipped. Was that her secret? He remembered watching her rub her ring finger in the car. He glanced at it curiously. She didn't wear a ring, and there was no sign that she'd been wearing one there. She didn't act married. She hadn't talked about having a husband. She was single, apparently by choice. But had there been men in her past? He was still carrying scars from his one great love affair, from the deception he'd endured. Meredith had gone out walking to a party in a rig that made her look like a prostitute, and she'd been comfortable doing that. It wasn't something an innocent girl would have considered.

Knowing that, he looked at her in a different way, speculatively. She had a nice figure and she wasn't all flushing smiles like Janie Brewster when Leo was around. Meredith was oddly mature for her age, almost matronly. She seemed to be used to giving instructions, too. She was a puzzle that disturbed him. What if she was hiding something sordid in her past? He and Leo had taken her in on faith and pity, but now he wondered if they'd made a terrible mistake. If she were in league with the men who'd robbed Leo, they might have a dangerous situation developing. What if she'd planned the whole thing as a means to an end?

Basically Rey didn't trust her. He wasn't going to let down his guard, either, no matter if looking at her did raise his blood pressure. She wasn't going to know that she did. And he'd keep his eyes open, all the time, just in case.

The days turned to a week. Meredith's painful bruises faded slowly. She lost some of the brooding sadness that seemed to cling to her like the jeans she wore around the house when she was working. She found the slower, easier pace strange, and she missed the urgency of her daily routine. But as the days went by lazily, she realized that she hadn't really given herself time to think. She'd avoided it, ignored it, hoping that the past would vanish. Now she was face to face with it, forced to reflect on what had happened.

She sat beside the fishpond one sunny afternoon, between chores, and watched the goldfish under the surface of the dark water as they moved sluggishly. The water wasn't frozen, but it was cold. The pond heater only kept a small area heated, so the fish were limited in movement. She could imagine how it would be to sit here in the summer and watch them move around in their watery world, with flowers blooming all around.

She'd loved planting flowers. She missed her home, her bulbs and shrubs, the familiar things that she'd accumulated around her. Now it was all gone, sold without a second thought to make the memories bearable. It was too late, and she wished she'd been more sensible. There were things she should have kept. Mike's stupid baseball cap, the one he always wore on the rare occasions when he wasn't working, and when he went fishing. She missed her mother's collection of small silk Chinese boxes and her pretty evening gowns. She'd thrown all those things away. At the time, it had seemed reasonable to cut all the ties with the past. It didn't, now.

The sound of a truck pulling up to the front door caught her attention. Rey and Leo had been out of town for two days, attending another cattle convention, this time in Denver.

They climbed out of the cab of the big six-wheeled pickup truck and retrieved their suitcases from the back, waving as the ranch truck pulled right out again and took off down the road.

Meredith got up and went to join them.

"Want some coffee and pie?" she asked with a smile.

"That would really hit the spot," Leo said, returning the smile. "I hate commercial flights."

"You're the smart guy who said our jet needed to be overhauled," Rey reminded him.

"It did," Leo replied.

Rey was looking at Meredith openly. "The bruises are fading," he remarked. "You have more color, too."

"I've been getting out in the sunlight," she replied easily. "I like to watch the fish, even though they don't move much."

"We might put a big aquarium inside," Rey remarked, unaware of his brother's quick, curious glance. "I like fish myself."

"They've done studies," Meredith volunteered as they stood aside to let her enter the house first. "They say watching fish swim is calming. It helps relieve stress."

"God knows, we could use some of that," Leo chuckled. "Especially when cattle prices fall and feed prices go through the roof."

"Cattle raising must be a complex process," she remarked.

"Very complex," Rey said. He frowned as he watched her walk. "Hip sore?" he asked.

She laughed self-consciously. "Well, yes, it is. How did you know?"

"You've got a light limp on the right side. Barely noticeable."

She rubbed her hip self-consciously. "I fell on that side, the night Dad hit me," she told him. "The floor's pretty hard."

"There's a whirlpool bath in your bedroom," Rey reminded her. "It'll help the soreness."

"I discovered that," she said, grinning. "What a luxury! We only have a shower at home, and it's temperamental."

Rey gave her a long look. "When we've had time to

catch our breath, I'll see what I can find out about your father, if you'd like.''

Her face brightened. ''That would be nice.''

He smiled slowly, liking the way her pale eyes seemed to glow when she was pleased. She wasn't bad-looking at all, and her figure was just about perfect. He wondered how she could have remained single for so long, with her home-making skills, not to mention her sweet personality and that knockout body.

She was watching him with equal appreciation, and totally unaware of it. He had a lithe, powerful physique that made her think of rodeo. He walked with a unique sort of grace, and he didn't stoop or slouch, ever. She liked his eyes best of all. They were almost a liquid-brown, and they had black rims around the pupils. He was rugged and sensuous, and she looked at his wide thin mouth and wondered for the first time how it would feel to kiss it.

Her thoughts horrified her. She dragged her eyes away and excused herself in an absolute fluster to go make coffee.

Leo lifted both eyebrows and stared at his brother after she was out of earshot. ''Well, well,'' he murmured. ''You do seem to be making an impression on her.''

''Cut it out,'' Rey said testily.

''And vice versa,'' came the irritating reply.

Rey made a rough sound in his throat and stomped off down the hall to his room. He put down his suitcase, took off his suit and dress shirt and got into jeans and a checked long-sleeved work shirt. He glanced at himself in the mirror as he buttoned it, his eyes blank as he recalled the wild flush on Meredith's cheeks. It shouldn't please him. He didn't trust her. She could be trying to play them all for suckers. But he smiled, just the same.

Meredith had coffee and cherry pie in saucers on the table by the time the brothers were changed and walking into the kitchen.

"Coffee's fresh," she said.

"Aren't you having any?" Rey asked.

"I have to get the clothes into the dryer," she excused herself with a quick smile. "Yell if you need anything."

She was gone in a flash.

Rey stared broodingly at his pie and frowned. She didn't want to have coffee with them. Why?

"You make her nervous," Leo said, answering the unspoken question. "She knows you don't trust her."

Rey frowned as he nibbled at his pie and sipped coffee. "I don't know her," he replied. He gave his brother a speaking glance. "We've always done background checks on employees," he added firmly. "I don't think we should make an exception of her, even though she's temporary."

"Translated, that means you want to know more about her than you do," Leo drawled, grinning.

"Maybe I do," Rey confessed. "But she's in a position to do a lot of damage if she isn't what she seems. You could have been killed, or suffered brain damage," he added quietly. "If she's in cahoots with the guys who mugged you…" He let the sentence trail off meaningfully.

Leo grimaced. "I don't like poking into peoples' private business," he replied. "But you're right. It's risky not to check her out."

"I'll get the agency on it first thing tomorrow," Rey said. He took another bite of the pie. "She's a hell of a good cook," he murmured.

"Makes good coffee, too," Leo commented.

They looked at each other and grimaced. It was going to upset Meredith if she found out what they were up to. But it was too much of a gamble not to find out what they could about her background and character. On the other hand, Leo promised himself, he was going to intercept that background check before Rey had a chance to see it. If Meredith

had secrets she was hiding for a good reason, he wasn't
going to give her away to Rey.

It took several days for the private detective to get to the
case and send a report to the Harts.

Rey was out of town at a one-day seminar on a new
spreadsheet computer program the brothers were using for
herd records when the report arrived. Leo carried the report
into his office and closed the door while he read it.

When he finished, he let out a harsh breath. So that was
Meredith's secret. No wonder her father drank. No wonder
she was so reticent and quiet about her past. He smiled as
he considered her true profession, and he was determined
that Rey wasn't going to know about it until disclosure was
inevitable. Rey was too prone to conclusion-jumping and
rushing to judgment. It was about time he had a set down,
and Meredith was just the woman to give it to him. Meanwhile, he'd let Rey work on hanging himself. Obviously
Meredith was enjoying her anonymity, and considering the
high-powered pressures of her daily job, it wasn't surprising that she found mundane housekeeping a nice change.
It wouldn't hurt to let her enjoy the vacation from stress,
without probing into her feelings. No doubt she still felt
the grief, even after several months.

He touched the report with idle fingers, frowning as he
recognized one of the names on it. Mike had been a Houston policeman. He was also a friend of Colter Banks, a
Texas Ranger and cousin of the Harts, who worked out of
the Houston ranger office. It really was a small world. He
wanted to tell Meredith that he remembered Mike, but he
didn't want to blow her cover. He also didn't want her to
know that they'd been checking up on her.

He put the file into the filing cabinet, deliberately putting
it under the wrong letter of the alphabet. If Rey asked, he'd
just tell him that the agency was working on it but had
other, more urgent cases to assign agents to first.

* * *

Meredith was alone in the house when Rey came in, late that night, from his business trip. Leo had gone to dinner at the Brewsters' house again, presumably at the invitation of Janie's father, to talk about a new breeding bull the Brewsters were trying to sell him.

She'd just started the dishwasher and was ready to turn the lights off in the kitchen when she heard Rey come in.

He paused in the kitchen doorway, a black Stetson slanted over one dark eye, wearing a grey vested suit that clung lovingly to the hard, muscular lines of his tall body. Meredith felt ragged by comparison in her jeans and red T-shirt, and barefoot. Her hair was disheveled because she'd been scrubbing the floor with a brush, and she wasn't wearing makeup. She hadn't expected to see either of the brothers before she went to bed.

Rey's dark eyes went to her pretty feet and he smiled. "You don't like shoes, do you?"

She grimaced. "No, and it's not good to go without them. No arch support." She studied his lean face. He had dark circles under his eyes. "Would you like some coffee and something to eat?"

"I would," he said heavily. "They gave me peanuts on the plane," he added with absolute disgust.

She chuckled. The sound was pleasant, and Rey was surprised at how it touched him to hear her laugh.

"I'll make you a nice thick low-fat ham sandwich with sauce."

"Thanks," he said, sliding a chair out so that he could straddle it. He tossed his hat into the chair beside him and ran a hand through his thick dark hair. "Make the coffee first, Meredith. I've got paperwork that has to be done tonight before the accountant comes to do the books in the morning."

"Can't it wait?" she asked gently. "You look worn to a frazzle. You need an early night."

His eyes searched hers intently. "I don't need mothering," he said, angered out of all proportion.

She flushed and turned away. She didn't apologize or say another word, but her hands shook as she filled the coffeepot and started it brewing.

Rey cursed himself silently for snapping at her. It was unkind, especially after she'd volunteered to feed him. She'd been working hard, too, he could see the spotless floor and the brush and bucket she'd been using on it. She must have done it on her hands and knees. It was a big kitchen, too. He wasn't the only one who was tired.

He got up from the chair and moved to stand just behind her. His lean hands caught her small waist and pulled her back against him. "I'm sorry," he said, his voice deep and husky with sudden emotion.

Her cold fingers came to rest on his and her whole body went rigid as a flash of white-hot pleasure shot through it. She caught her breath. He heard it. His own body tautened and the hands around her waist suddenly grew possessive, rough, insistent, as they pulled her tight against him.

He could hear her breathing change. He could feel the faint tremor of her hands over his. Impulsively he bent his head and his mouth touched the side of her neck.

Five

Meredith knew her knees were shaking. She hoped she wasn't going to fall on the floor at his feet with sheer excitement. It had been years since a man had made her feel such a rush of pleasure, and even then, it had been one-sided. She'd been crazy about a man who only saw her as a sort of unrelated sister. But even that wasn't as powerful as what she was feeling with Rey Hart.

His mouth became insistent as it moved slowly up her neck. He began to turn her, in the silence that was suddenly alive with passion. His hard lips traveled to the hollow of her throat, where a tiny pulse hammered, and then up to her chin. His teeth nibbled her chin, moving on to her lower lip. He tugged it away from the top one and tasted it with his tongue. All the while, his lean, strong hands were sliding up and down at her waist, smoothing her body completely against him.

His teeth nipped at her top lip with a sensual approach that made her breath shiver in her throat. He was experienced, far more so than she was. For all her professional capability, in this way she was a novice, and it showed.

He noticed her lack of sensual response with absent curiosity. She was attracted to him, that was obvious, but it was as if she didn't know what to do.

He guided her hands to his vest and flicked open buttons while his lips teased around hers. She fumbled and he laughed softly, his nose rubbing against hers as he moved her hands and unfastened the buttons on his vest and shirt with deft efficiency. He coaxed her hands inside, against thick hair and hard, warm muscle, while his mouth began to bite at hers, tempting her lips to part. She was stiff, trying not to respond, but her body was hungry.

"Like this," he whispered gently, teaching her mouth the lazy, sensual rhythm he wanted from it. "Taste my mouth, the way I'm tasting yours. Don't fight what you're feeling."

She heard the words as if through a fog. She didn't understand what he was saying, but her body obeyed him. She was in a sensual limbo, her hands flat against his chest, her head lifted, her eyes slitted and looking up into his as he began to increase the teasing pressure of his mouth. She followed his lips. She relaxed into the curve of his powerful body with a little shiver.

He devoured her mouth roughly, again and then again, tempting her until her mouth followed his, returning the arousing pressure. She could see the glitter grow in his narrow eyes, feel the grip of his lean hands as he pushed her hips against the sudden hardness of him. She gasped with embarrassment and then lost all sense of it as his mouth opened and pushed down hard against her parted lips, drowning her in passion.

It was like flying, she thought dazedly. He hesitated for an instant and her eyes opened, drowsy and curious. Her mouth was swollen, soft, tremulous. She looked at him with fascination, utterly helpless in his embrace. He felt an unfamiliar protectiveness toward her. It had been years since he'd kissed an innocent. Meredith's lack of experience was obvious. He was enjoying it.

"Yes," he murmured gruffly, and he bent again. His arms enfolded her, tender arms that no longer forced her into intimacy. His mouth was tender, too, exploring hers with slow mastery, careful not to overwhelm her.

She sighed into his hard mouth, relaxing against him. Her hands moved restlessly on his broad, bare chest, and contracted in the thick mat of hair that covered him.

He lifted his head, staring down into her wide eyes with somber delight. His hands smoothed hers deeper into his thick hair and hard muscle. He traced the edges of her short nails with his thumbs. His breath was jerky. He didn't like having her see that he was vulnerable. There were too many things he still didn't know about her, and he didn't trust her. She seemed innocent, but he couldn't forget the dress she'd been wearing and the accusations her father had made about her. He didn't dare trust her on such short acquaintance. On the other hand, his body was singing with pleasure from the long, hot contact with hers. He couldn't force himself to let her go. Not just yet.

"Why did you do that?" she asked huskily.

One dark eyebrow lifted. He didn't smile. "Why did you let me?" he shot back.

She felt uncomfortable. Despite the effort it took, she moved away from him. He let her go with no show of reluctance. He watched her struggle for composure while he refastened buttons with easy confidence, concealing the effect she had on him. He didn't even look ruffled.

"The coffee must be done by now," he pointed out when she seemed unable to move.

She turned stiffly and went to fill cups and put them, along with cream and sugar, on the table.

While he fixed his coffee, she made him two thick ham sandwiches with hands that slowly lost their tremor. She was devastated by a kiss that didn't seem to have disturbed him at all. She remembered the sudden hardness of his body, but she knew all about anatomy. A man couldn't help that reaction to anything feminine, it was part of his makeup. It wasn't even personal.

Somehow, it made things worse to know that. She felt his eyes on her back, and she knew he was measuring her up. She had no idea why he'd kissed her, but she didn't trust his motives. He didn't like her. She couldn't afford to let her guard down. Rey Hart would be hell on a woman who loved him. She knew that instinctively.

By the time she had the sandwiches made, her hands were steady again and she was able to put them on the table with a cool smile.

"I have to tidy up the living room…" she began.

He caught her hand as she started past him. "Sit down, Meredith," he said quietly.

She sat. He sipped coffee and studied her for a long moment. "I talked to Simon while I was away," he said. "Your father has been released from jail and placed in an alcohol treatment center. It's early days yet, but the prognosis is good. It helps that he hasn't been drinking that heavily for a long time."

She looked relieved and anxiously waited to hear what else Rey had to say about her father.

He continued. "The therapist wouldn't reveal any intimate details to Simon, you understand, but he was able to say that your father had been unable to deal with a family tragedy. Now that he's sober, he's extremely upset about what he did to you." He looked grim. "He doesn't remember doing it, Meredith."

She averted her eyes to her coffee cup. For something to do, she lifted it and took a sip of blistering black coffee, almost burning her lip. "That's common in cases of alcohol or drug abuse," she murmured absently.

He studied her over the rim of his coffee cup. "You

won't be allowed to communicate with him until he's through the treatment program, but he wanted you to know that he's desperately sorry for what he did.''

She ground her teeth together. She knew that. Her father wasn't a bad man. Until he'd started abusing alcohol, he'd been one of the gentlest men alive. But, like all human beings, he had a breaking point which he reached when tragedy erupted into his life.

"He isn't a bad man,'' she said quietly. "Although I know it must have seemed like it.''

"I've seen drunks before,'' Rey replied. "My brothers have gone on benders a time or two.'' He smiled faintly. "In fact, Leo holds the current record for damage at Shea's Bar, out on the Victoria road. He doesn't cut loose often, but when he does, people notice.''

"He doesn't seem the sort of man who would do that,'' she remarked, surprised.

"We're all the sort of men who would do that, given the right provocation,'' he told her.

She smiled. "Do you get drunk and wreck bars?'' she couldn't resist asking.

"I don't drink as a rule,'' he said simply. "A glass of wine rarely, nothing stronger. I don't like alcohol.''

She smiled. "Neither do I.''

He leaned back in his chair and studied her quietly. His hair was still faintly disheveled where her hands had caught in it when he was kissing her, and his lower lip was swollen from the pressure of her mouth. She knew she must look almost as bad. Her hand went unconsciously to her unruly hair.

"Take it down,'' he said abruptly.

"Wh…what?''

"Take your hair down,'' he said huskily. "I want to see it.''

She'd just gotten her wild heart under control, and now

it was galloping all over again from that sultry tone, from the dark, intent caress of his eyes on her face.

"Listen, I work for you," she began with a tremor in her voice.

He got up from the chair and moved toward her with a lazy, almost arrogant stride. He drew her up in front of him and started pulling out hairpins. Her hair, unbound, fell in soft waves down her back, almost concealing one eye.

"It's hard to manage when it's down," she said self-consciously.

"I love long hair." He tangled his lean hands in it and coaxed her face up to his. He searched her eyes at point-blank range. "I've kissed girls years younger than you who knew even more than I do. Why are you still a novice?"

She swallowed hard. He was making her knees weak again. She couldn't quite get a whole breath of air into her lungs. Her hands rested on his chest lightly and she felt her heart choking her with its rapid beat as she stared into his narrowed, dark eyes.

"What?" she asked, barely having heard much less understood the question.

His hands were exploring the cool length of her hair with fascination. "You're not bad-looking, Meredith. Surely you've dated."

"Yes," she said, disconcerted. "But I'm old-fashioned."

Both eyebrows went up over a cynical smile. "That's a pitiful excuse in this day and age."

"Why?" she asked, her clear grey eyes staring up into his with no thought of subterfuge. "The whole reason for the women's movement is so that women can have the freedom to do as they please. I'm not promiscuous. Why should I need an excuse?"

He blinked. She made his question sound unreasonable. "I thought sexual liberation was the soul of the movement," he drawled.

"Being chaste is sexual liberation, in my book," she

replied. "You'd be amazed how many women in my graduating class practiced abstinence."

"In high school, I gather," he said absently, tracing the length of her hair with his hands.

She almost corrected him, but then, she really mustn't destroy the illusions he had about her as a domestic. "Yes. In high school."

He moved closer to her, his lean body a sensual provocation that made her breath catch. He laughed softly. "Care to test the hypothesis?" he murmured softly.

"I work for you," she repeated, playing for time.

"So?"

"So it's not wise to mix business..."

"...with pleasure?" He caught her waist and drew her close. "It's been a while since I found a woman so desirable," he whispered, bending to her mouth. "Experience bores me. You," he bit off against her soft lips, "are a challenge."

"Thank you, but I don't want to be," she whispered, trying to pull away.

He lifted his head and searched her eyes. "No curiosity about the great unknown?" he taunted.

"No desire to treat it as a sophisticated game," she corrected abruptly.

He hesitated, but only for an instant. His lean hands contracted and then released her. He went back to his chair and sat down. "Touché," he said with a curious glance. "All right, Meredith, I'll sit here and eat my sandwiches and we'll pretend that we're still strangers physically."

"Good idea," she approved. She reached down for her half-empty coffee cup and put it in the sink.

He was halfway through a sandwich when she excused herself and went to fluff up the pillows in the living room and put magazines and books back in their places. Leo had left things strewn about before he'd gone to the Brewsters'.

She was glad, because it gave her a valid reason not to sit next to Rey with her emotions in turmoil.

By the time she'd gone back to the kitchen, Rey had finished his sandwiches and coffee and was coming out the door.

"You're safe," he drawled. "I'm going to change and get to work in the study. Where's Leo?"

"Having supper at the Brewsters' house," she told him. "He said he'd be early."

"That means he'll be late," he mused. "Janie Brewster will have found twenty excuses to keep him talking to her father. She's one determined young lady, but Leo's equally determined. He doesn't want ties."

"Doesn't that sound familiar?" she murmured wickedly.

His eyes slid up and down her body in a silence that teemed with tension. "I never said I didn't want ties," he corrected. "I said I didn't want marriage. There's a difference."

"Don't look at me," she said carelessly. "I don't have time for relationships."

"Of course. All that cleaning must demand a lot of you," he said deliberately.

She flushed. He had no idea what her life was like on a daily basis, and she wanted very badly to tell him. But he was so almighty arrogant and condescending that he put her back up. She wasn't going to tell him a thing. He'd find out soon enough.

She put her hands on her hips and stared at him. "And what's wrong with being a housekeeper?" she demanded, going on the offensive. "Where would you and your brother be right now if there weren't women you could hire to bake and clean for you? I guess you'd have to get married then, or learn to cook, wouldn't you?"

He glared at her. "I could cook if I wanted to."

"You're the sort of man who makes a woman wish she

didn't have a culinary skill to her name," she said icily. "You are so 'lord of the manor-ish', Mr. Hart!"

"It isn't a manor," he pointed out. "They have those in England. We call this a ranch."

She glared at him.

He grinned. "You really do rise to the bait beautifully," he murmured, and something flashed in his dark eyes. "The sandwiches were good," he added.

She looked surprised. "Nothing but ham and a home-made sauce," she faltered.

"You do that a lot with food," he remarked gently. "I like the way you experiment with dishes. I even like the way you garnish the plates. You make things look appetizing."

She didn't realize that he'd even noticed. "I learned that from a dietician," she said without thinking. "If food is decorative, sometimes it makes up for bulk."

He smiled quizzically. "You can't decorate biscuits," he teased. "But you make really good ones."

"Thanks." She smiled back. "I'll tidy up the kitchen if you're through."

"I am. Don't stay up too late," he added and his eyes were suddenly bright with mischief. "You need plenty of rest so that you can make biscuits for breakfast!"

"Okay. I'll get an early night." She laughed and went on past him to the kitchen.

He stared after her for several long seconds with an expression that he was glad she didn't see. He liked the taste of her. That hadn't been wise, kissing her that way. He was going to have to make sure it didn't happen again. He didn't need complications.

Nothing was the same between Meredith and Rey after that day. They were aware of each other. It wasn't blatant, but she could feel tingling in her spine when Rey was in a room. It was instinctive. Her eyes followed him like puppies, and she flushed wildly when he caught her at it and gave her that amused, wordily glance.

Leo noticed, too, and it worried him that Rey was encouraging Meredith. He knew Rey too well to think he'd had a change of heart toward his bachelor status.

"You're leading her on," Leo accused his brother one evening when they were alone in the study with the door closed. "Why?"

Rey gave him a surprised glance. "You make it sound like a crime to flirt with her."

"In your case, it is," his brother said flatly. "You're a rounder. She isn't."

Rey shrugged. "She's not exactly off limits," he told his brother. "Not at her age."

"And what do you have in mind? Seduction?" Leo persisted irritably. "She's already been damaged enough by what happened with her father. The bruises are barely healed, and the mental scars are still there. Don't play games with her."

"Aren't you self-righteous all of a sudden?" Rey shot back angrily. "You've been stringing Janie Brewster along for weeks, and we both know you don't have any intention in hell of getting serious about her. All you want is first chance at that damned seed bull they're thinking of selling! Does she know?" he added maliciously.

Leo's eyes began to glitter. "Janie is a child," he said furiously. "I pick at her, and not because of any damned bull. I'm certainly not hell-bent on seduction!"

"She's not a child," Rey countered. "You're leading her down a blind alley, when you know full well she's in love with you."

Leo looked shocked. "She's not in love with me! Maybe she's got a crush. That's all!"

"You don't see the way she looks at you, do you?" Rey replied solemnly.

Leo cleared his throat. "We're talking about Meredith," he said firmly.

Rey's eyes narrowed. "Meredith is an adult."

"And she works for us," Leo went on relentlessly. "I'm not going to stand by and let you make an amusement of her."

"Jealous?" his brother taunted.

Leo was very still. "Is that the draw?" he asked softly. "Are we competing for a woman again?"

Rey's eyes flashed. "I would never have known about Carlie if you hadn't started propositioning her in front of me. Do you think I can forget that?"

"I keep hoping you will someday. She would have taken you for the ride of your life," Leo said quietly. "You're my brother. I couldn't stand by and do nothing."

Rey turned away with a muttered curse. Leo was right; he had saved him from even worse heartache, but the memory was still raw enough to hurt.

"Don't try to take it out on Meredith," Leo told him firmly. "She's had enough tragedy. Let her do her job."

Rey glanced at him over his shoulder. "I would, if she'd remember why she's here," he said venomously. "It's not my fault that every time I turn around, she's drooling over me! A saint could be tempted by a woman whose eyes worship him like that. I'm only human!"

"Don't raise your voice," Leo cautioned.

"Why? Do you think she's standing outside the door eavesdropping?" Rey drawled sarcastically. "What if she did hear me? It's the truth. She wants me. A blind man could see it."

"That's no reason to take advantage of her. She's not like your usual women."

"No, she's not. She has no ambition, no intellect. Besides that, she's so inexperienced, it's unreal. I never thought kissing a woman could be boring, until she came along," Rey added coldly, trying not to let Leo see how attracted he was to their housekeeper. "She's so naive, it's nauseating."

Outside the door, Meredith stood poised like a statue with a cup of coffee in a saucer shaking in her hands. She'd come to offer it to Rey, and overheard words that had never been meant for her ears. She fought tears as she turned around and went quickly and silently back down the hall to the kitchen.

Hearts couldn't really break, she told herself firmly, as she dabbed at the tears with a paper towel. She was just feeling the aftereffects of her devastating experience at home. It wasn't as if she was really drooling over Rey Hart.

She felt like sinking through the floor when she realized that she did spend an inordinate amount of time staring at him. He was handsome, sensuous, attractive. She liked looking at him. And maybe she was infatuated, a little. That didn't give him the right to say such horrible things about her.

If she hadn't been listening, she'd never have known about them in the first place. She'd have gone right ahead, mooning over him and having him know it and be amused by it. Her pride felt tattered. She'd never been one to wear her heart on her sleeve, but Rey had kissed her as if he enjoyed it, and she'd built dreams on those kisses. She realized now how truly naive it had been. The first man who paid her any attention in years, and she fell head over heels for him. Seen in that context, perhaps it wasn't surprising after all. She'd heard Leo accuse him of being a rounder, and she had to admit that his experience ran rings around hers. Apparently he was accustomed to playing sensual games with women. That was all those devastating kisses that had brought her to her knees had meant to him—just a game. And she'd taken it seriously!

Well, she told herself firmly, he needn't worry that she'd throw herself at his feet again. From now on, she was going to be the perfect employee, polite and courteous and eager to please—but she'd never stare at him longingly again. Thank God she'd overheard what he said to Leo. It had spared her a terrible humiliation. A little hurt now was far better than being wrung out emotionally down the road because she'd been ignorant of the facts. Wasn't she herself always telling people that the truth, however brutal, was always best in the long run? It was time to take her own advice.

When Rey and Leo came in to breakfast the next morning, she put bacon and eggs and biscuits on the table with a cool, professional smile.

Rey was oddly subdued. He didn't give her the arrogant scrutiny that had become force of habit in recent days. In fact, he didn't look at her at all. Leo kept up a pleasant conversation about the day's chores. They were moving some sick cattle into a pasture near the house so the vet could examine them, and stock was being shifted into closer quarters as well, within easier reach of the hay barn.

"I thought you had those big round bales of hay?" Meredith asked curiously.

"We do," Leo agreed. "But we still bale it the old-fashioned way and stack it in the barn. You lose some of the round bales through weathering by sun and rain. The hay that's kept dry in the barn has less deterioration and better nutrition."

"But you feed more than hay?"

Leo chuckled. He buttered a second biscuit. "You are sharp. Yes, we have a man who mixes feeds for better nutrition. No animal proteins, either," he added. "We're reactionaries when it comes to ranching. No artificial hormones, no pesticides, nothing except natural methods of pest control and growth. We're marketing our beef under the Hart Ranch label, as well, certifying it organic. We've already got several chain supermarkets carrying our product, and we've just moved onto the Internet to extend our distribution.''

"That's amazing," Meredith said with genuine interest. "It's like having custom beef," she added, nodding.

"It is custom beef," Leo told her. "We're capitalizing on the move toward healthier beef. Quick profit methods are going to fail producers in the long run, especially with the current attitude toward hormones and antibiotics and animal-product proteins for feed. We think that once organic beef catches on, the market will justify the added expense.''

"Word of mouth will take you far, too," Meredith said. "Hospitals teach nutrition these days, not only to patients but to the community. Tailored beef will find a market among consumers with heart problems, who'll pay the extra cost for healthier cuts of meat grown organically.''

Rey was listening. He finished his biscuit and poured himself another cup of coffee from the carafe on the table. "J.D. Langley pioneered that organic approach locally," he remarked. "He and the Tremayne boys got into terrific fights with other producers at seminars for a while. Then we saw the disasters overseas and suddenly everybody else was jumping on the bandwagon.''

"They'll be glad they did, I think," Meredith said.

"Which reminds me," Leo said, eyeing her. "Mrs. Lewis said her larder hadn't been opened since you came here. So…what are you making these biscuits with?''

She gave them a wary glance. "Light olive oil," she said slowly.

Rey gaped at his biscuit as if it had suddenly sprouted hair. "Olive oil?!" he gasped.

"Listen," she said quickly, aware of horrified stares, "olive oil is so healthy that people who live on a Mediterranean diet have only a fraction of the vascular problems we have in abundance in this country. The fat content is still there, but it's a vegetable fat, and it's actually good for you. Until I told you, you didn't even know you'd given up great gobs of animal fat in those biscuits!''

The brothers looked at each other. "Well," Leo had to admit, "they taste just as good as the others did."

"That's true," Rey agreed reluctantly.

"And we're getting older," Leo continued. "We don't want clogged arteries giving us heart attacks and strokes."

"Or bypass surgery," Rey sighed.

"So I guess olive oil isn't so bad, after all," Leo concluded, with a grin at Meredith.

She grinned back. "Thank goodness. I had visions of being tarred and feathered," she confessed.

"I'm not giving up butter, though," Rey told her firmly, dipping his knife into the tub next to the biscuit basket. "Nothing tastes like real butter on a biscuit."

Meredith didn't look at him. She couldn't confess that what he was eating was not butter, but rather a light margarine that actually lowered cholesterol levels. She only smiled and poured herself another cup of coffee.

Leo and Rey had started moving bulls into the lower pasture, where new forage grasses were thriving even in autumn, when a mangy old longhorn bull suddenly jerked his head and hooked Leo in the shoulder.

Leo yelled and threw a kick at him, but the aggravating animal was already trotting nonchalantly into the new pasture without a backward glance.

"How bad is it?" Rey asked, leaving the cowboys to work the cattle alone while he looked at his brother's shoulder.

"Probably needs stitches," Leo said through his teeth. "Drive me to the house and let me change shirts, then you can take me to Lou Coltrain."

"Damned bull," Rey muttered as he put his brother into the ranch truck and took off home.

Meredith was sweeping off the back steps when they drove up. She gave Leo's bloodstained shirt a quick glance.

"Come on in here, let me have a look," she said gently.

Disconcerted, Leo let her remove the shirt from his shoulder and bathe the blood away with a clean cloth.

She probed around the edges of the cut and nodded. "You'll need stitches. Here. Hold this tight against the cut until you get to town."

"I need to change shirts," he began.

"You need to get to the doctor. Which one do you use?" she persisted, picking up the mobile phone she kept on the table.

"Dr. Lou Coltrain," he said.

"I'll phone and tell them you're on the way," she said firmly.

Rey gave her a curious glance, but he hustled Leo out the door and into the truck again.

When they got to the office, Dr. Lou Coltrain's nurse, Betty, came right out to meet them and guide them back into a cubicle.

Lou walked in, took a professional look at the cut, and grinned. "Stitches," she said. "How about a tetanus jab?"

Leo grimaced. "Well…"

She patted him on the shoulder that wasn't injured. "We'll have you fixed up and out of here in no time."

He sighed, glancing at his brother. "I hate shots."

Rey shrugged. "You'd hate tetanus more," he told Leo. "Besides," he added, "I hear she gives sugarless gum to the good patients."

Leo made a face at him.

When Leo was stitched up and given his tetanus shot, Rey drove him back to the house, where Meredith made him a cup of coffee and cut him a slice of cherry pie, making sure he had a cushion for his back in the straight chair at the table.

Rey glared at the special treatment his brother was getting. "Maybe I should get gored," he commented drolly.

Meredith stared at him, and she didn't smile. "You'd get a vinegar dressing and a cup of cold coffee," she said.

He glared at her, too. He felt as if he'd been put in the corner without supper. It wasn't a feeling he liked. He gave them both a hard look and went back out the door, smoldering with bad temper.

Six

"I shouldn't have said that," Meredith said wryly when Rey was gone. "I set him off again."

"It won't hurt him to have one woman who doesn't fall all over herself when he's around," Leo told her flatly. "Sometimes too much success can ruin a good man."

She toyed with her coffee cup. "Women like him, I guess," she said.

He gave her a quick glance that she didn't see before he started on his pie. "He's had girlfriends since he was in grammar school. But there was only one serious one. She turned out to be a real loser," he added quietly. "She soured him on women."

She sipped coffee. "You can't judge an entire sex by one woman," she pointed out.

"Well, we had our mother as an example, too," he continued. "She left Dad with five young boys and never looked back. We haven't been overawed with sterling examples of womanhood, although Simon and Corrigan and Cag have made good marriages in spite of that.''

She smiled absently as she looked at him. ''I had a brother of my own,'' she said without thinking.

''Yes, I know,'' Leo replied, surprising her into silence. ''His name was Michael Johns. He worked for Houston PD.''

Her gasp was audible. ''How…do you know about him?''

''Remember Colter Banks?''

''Yes. Colter was Mike's best friend.''

''Well, Colter's our second cousin,'' he told her. ''I knew Mike, too. I'm sorry.''

She clenched one fist in her lap and tried not to give way to tears. ''Do the others…know?''

''No, they don't,'' he replied. ''They weren't that close to Colter, and they never met Mike. I haven't told them, and I'm not planning to.''

She searched his dark eyes. ''What else do you know about me, Leo?'' she asked, because of the way he was watching her.

He shrugged. ''Everything.''

She let out a long breath. ''And you haven't shared it with Rey.''

''You wouldn't want me to,'' he murmured dryly. ''He's having too much fun being condescending. When the time comes, he's got a few shocks coming, hasn't he?''

She laughed softly. ''I hadn't meant to be cloak-and-daggerish. It's just that it still hurts too much to talk about,'' she said honestly.

''Colter told me the circumstances. It wasn't your fault,'' he replied. ''Or your father's. I gather that he drinks because he feels responsible?''

She nodded. ''We both dined out on 'what-if' just after it happened,'' she confessed. ''I know that it probably wouldn't have made any difference, but you can't help wondering.''

"It doesn't do any good to torment yourself over things that are history,'' Leo said gently.

"I don't do it intentionally,'' she murmured.

"The first step was getting your father into treatment,'' he said. "Getting you out of your rut was the second. You don't have any memories to contend with here. I've noticed the difference in you just in the past week.'' He smiled. "You're changing already.''

"I suppose so.'' She smiled back. "I've never even been on a ranch before. I could love it here. It's such a change of pace.''

"When you're back to normal, we've got plenty of opportunity around here for your sort of job,'' he pointed out.

She chuckled. "Don't rush me. It's far too soon to think about leaving Houston.'' She didn't add that she didn't want to be that close to Rey, considering his opinion of her at the moment. "I've only been down here a week.''

"Okay. I'll let it drop, for now.'' He leaned back in his chair and winced, favoring the arm he'd had stitched. "Damned bull,'' he muttered.

"Did they give you something for the pain?''

"No, and I didn't ask for anything. I have over-the-counter painkillers if it gets really bad. So far, it hasn't.''

"You know, of course, that statistically farm and ranch work have the highest ratio of accidents,'' she said.

"Any job can be dangerous,'' he said easily.

She pursed her lips and lifted her coffee cup to them. "Your brother's a walking job hazard,'' she said thoughtfully.

"Oh? In what way, exactly?'' he asked.

She wouldn't have touched that line with a pole. She laughed. "He's abrasive. I don't think he wants me here.''

"I've noticed his attitude. I hope you haven't let it get to you?''

"I haven't. Anyway, he'll mellow one of these days," she said.

"He could use some mellowing. He's a disillusioned man."

She smoothed the lip of the cup. "Did he love her very much?"

He knew she was talking about Carlie. He sighed. "He thought he did. His pride suffered more than his heart." He hesitated. "I didn't help matters. I made a play for her deliberately, to show him what she was. That was a miscalculation. A bad one. He's never forgiven me for it. Now, if I pay any attention to a woman, he tries to compete with me…"

She noticed the way his voice trailed off, and she averted her eyes. "I get the picture," she said.

"It's not like that, not with you," he began.

She forced a smile. "He's not interested in me," she said bluntly. "And just in case you're worried that I might be falling all over him, there's no danger of that, either. I was outside the door when he was talking to you. I wasn't eavesdropping, but he was speaking rather loudly. I heard what he said. I'd have to be certifiable to lose my heart over a man like that."

He grimaced as he read the faint pain that lingered in her eyes. "I wouldn't have had you hear what he said for the world," he said deeply.

She managed a smile. "It's just as well. It will keep me from taking him seriously. Besides, I'm not really down here looking for a soul mate."

"Just as well, because Rey isn't any woman's idea of the perfect partner, not the way he is right now. I love him dearly, but I can afford to. It's another story for any woman who loses her heart to him." He studied her warily. "Just don't let him play you for a fool."

"I wouldn't dream of it," she said. "Even if I got the chance."

He nodded. He finished his pie and coffee and got to his feet. "I'd better change and get back to work. Thanks for running interference, by the way. You're a cool head in an emergency," he remarked with a smile.

"I've had lots of practice," she said modestly and grinned. "But try to stay away from horned things for a while."

"Especially my brother, the minor devil," he said, tongue-in-cheek, and grinned back when she got the reference and started laughing.

After Leo went back to work, Meredith went out to gather eggs. It seemed very straightforward. You walked into the henhouse, reached in the nest, and pulled out a dozen or so big brown eggs, some still warm from the chicken's feathered body.

But that wasn't what happened. She paused just inside the henhouse to let her eyes adjust to the reduced light, and when she moved toward the row of straw-laced nests, she saw something wrapped around one nest that wasn't feathered. It had scales and a flickering long tongue. It peered at her through the darkness and tightened its coils around its prey, three big brown eggs.

Meredith, a city girl with very little experience of scaly things, did something predictable. She screamed, threw the basket in the general direction of the snake, and left skid marks getting out of the fenced lot.

Annie Lewis, who was doing the laundry, came to the back door as fast as her arthritis would allow, to see what all the commotion was about.

"There's a...big black and white *snnnnnakkkkkke*...in there!" Meredith screamed, shaking all over from the close encounter.

"After the eggs, I reckon," Annie said with a sigh. She wiped her hands on her apron. "Let me get a stick and I'll deal with it."

"You can't go in there alone with the horrible thing and try to kill it! It must be five feet long!"

"It's a king snake, not a rattler," Annie said gently, recognizing the description. "And I'm not planning to kill it. I'm going to get it on a stick and put in the barn. It can eat its fill of rats and poisonous snakes and do some good out there."

"You aren't going to kill it?" Meredith exclaimed, horrified.

"It's a king snake, dear," came the gentle reply. "We don't like to kill them. They're very useful. They eat rattlesnakes, you know."

"I didn't know." Meredith shivered again. "I've never seen a snake except in a zoo, and it was a python."

"You'll see lots of them out here in the country. Just remember that if one rattles at you, it means business and it will strike. Rattlesnakes are venomous."

Meredith looked around as if she expected to be mobbed just at the mention of them.

"You can finish the washing," Annie said, trying not to grin. "I'll take care of the snake."

"Please be careful!"

"I will. After all, you get used to things like…"

Rey drove up and stopped the truck just short of the two women, exiting it with his usual graceful speed.

"What's going on?" he asked as he pulled a box of assorted bovine medicines out of the boot of the truck.

"There's a snake in the henhouse!" Meredith exclaimed.

He stopped with the supplies in his arms and stared at her curiously. "So?" he asked.

"I'm just going to move it for her, Rey," Mrs. Lewis said with a grin. "It sounds like a king snake. I thought I'd put him in the barn."

"I'll get him for you." He put the box on the hood of the truck. "Scared of snakes, are you?" he scoffed.

"I'd never seen one until a few minutes ago," she said

huffily, and flushed. He was looking at her as if she were a child.

"There's a first time for everything," he said, and his eyes made a very explicit remark as they lingered on her breasts.

She gave him a glare hot enough to fry bacon, which he ignored. He walked right into the chicken lot and, then, into the henhouse.

Barely a minute later, he came back out with the snake coiled around one arm, its neck gently held in his other hand.

"Would you look at this, it's Bandit!" he exclaimed, showing it to a fascinated Mrs. Lewis. "See the scar on his back where he got caught in the corn sheller that time?"

"So it is!" she said. "Hello, old fella!" She actually petted the vile thing under the chin.

"How can you touch that thing?!" Meredith groaned. "It's a snake!"

Mrs. Lewis glanced at Rey. "Reckon we should tell her that he used to live in the house?"

"Probably not," Rey suggested, aware of her white face. "I'll just stick him up in the loft. Come on, Bandit, I'll put you in a safe place."

Meredith was holding both chill-bump laden arms with her hands and shivering.

"There, there," Annie said gently. "He wouldn't bite you unless you provoked him. He's very gentle."

"If you say so."

"I do. Now you go back in there and get the eggs. Don't let Rey see how frightened you are. Trust me, he'll take advantage of it. You'll find rubber snakes in the refrigerator, the blender, the washer…"

"No!" Meredith exclaimed, horrified.

"Just grit your teeth and go back in the henhouse," Annie suggested. "Quick, before he comes back out."

Meredith took a quick breath and gave Annie a miserable glance, but she did as she was told.

Her skin crawled when she had to pick up the basket and gather the eggs, especially the ones the snake had been curled around. Now, every time she went to the henhouse, she'd be shivering with apprehension.

You've looked at gunshot wounds, accident victims, every sort of horror known to human eyes, she told herself firmly. The snake wasn't even lacerated! So get it done and move on.

She did, walking back out into the sunlight with a full basket of eggs and a forced look of composure on her soft face.

Rey was waiting for her, leaning against the bumper of the truck with his arms crossed and his hat pulled low over his eyes.

She didn't dare look at him for long. In that indolent pose, his lean, muscular body was shown to its very best advantage. It made her tingle to think how it had felt to be held against every inch of that formidable frame, to be kissed by that long, hard mouth.

"You get thrown, you get right back on the horse," he said with approval. "I'm proud of you, Meredith. It would be hard for even a ranch-born girl to go back into a henhouse where a snake had been lurking."

She took a slow breath. "We don't face things by running away from them, I guess," she agreed.

His eyes narrowed under the wide brim of the hat. "What are you running away from, Meredith? What is your father running away from?"

She clutched the basket to her chest. "That's nothing that you need to concern yourself with," she said with quiet dignity.

"You work for me," he replied.

"Not for long," she pointed out. "In another week or so, I'll be a memory."

"Will you?" He lurched away from the bumper and went to stand just in front of her, a tall and sensual threat. His fingers touched her soft mouth lightly. "Those bruises still look pretty fresh," he pointed out. "And you did ask for a month's leave, or so you said. Did you?"

She grimaced. "Well, yes, but I don't have to stay here all that time."

"I think you do," he returned. He bent and drew his mouth slowly over hers, a whisper of a contact that made her breath catch. He smiled with faint arrogance as he stood up again. "Anything could happen," he drawled. "You might like ranch life."

"I don't like snakes already."

"That was a fluke. They're generally hibernating by November, but it's been unseasonably warm. Spring is generally when you have to watch where you put your hands. But you don't need to worry. I'll protect you from snakes. And other perils."

"Who'll protect me from you?" she asked huskily.

He raised any eyebrow. "Why would you need protection?" he asked. "You're well over the age of consent."

"I've lived a very sheltered life," she said flatly.

He pursed his lips as he studied her, examining the statement. "Maybe it's time you walked out of the cocoon."

"I'm not in the market for an affair."

"Neither am I." He smiled slowly. "But if you worked at it, you might change my mind."

"I don't think so," she said. Her eyes were cool as they met his. "I wouldn't want you to think I was 'drooling' over you," she added deliberately.

His face changed. He knew immediately that she'd overheard what he'd said to Leo. He was sorry, because it wasn't true. He'd been desperate to throw Leo off the track. He didn't want his brother to know how attracted he was to her.

"Eavesdroppers never hear anything good about themselves, don't they say?" he asked quietly.

"Never," she agreed. "Now, if you'll excuse me, I'll go wash the eggs."

"I said something else that you'll remember with sordid ease," he murmured as she started past him. He caught her by the shoulder and tugged her close, bending to drag his mouth roughly across hers. "But I didn't mean that, either," he whispered against her parted lips. "Your innocence makes my head spin. I lay awake at night thinking of all sorts of delicious ways to relieve you of it."

"You'd be lucky!" she exclaimed, shocked.

He laughed softly as he let her go. "So would you," he drawled. "I've been called 'sensual hell' in bed, and I can assure you it wasn't meant to be a derogatory remark."

"Rey Hart!" she burst out.

"But why take anyone else's word for it?" he teased. "I'll be glad to let you see for yourself, anytime you like."

"If you think…I have never…of all the…!"

"Yes, it does tend to make women flustered when I mention what a great lover I am," he said with a wicked grin.

She couldn't get one coherent sentence out. She stomped her foot hard, turned around, and stormed into the kitchen, almost knocking herself down with the door in the process. It didn't help that Rey stood out there laughing like a predator.

If she expected Rey to be apologetic about what he'd said, she was doomed to disappointment. He watched her with narrow, assessing eyes as she went about her household duties. He didn't harass her, or monopolize her. He just watched. The scrutiny made her so nervous that she fumbled constantly. Her heart ran wild at the attention from those dark, steady eyes.

"Why don't you want to do something else besides keep house?" Rey asked her one evening when she was putting supper on the table. Leo, as usual, was late getting in. Rey had volunteered to set the table while she fixed Mexican corn bread and chili.

"Keeping house has less stress than most outside jobs," she said, not looking at him.

"It pays lousy wages," he continued, "and you could get into a lot of trouble in some households, with men who'd see you as fair game."

"Do you see me that way?" she asked, wide-eyed.

He glowered at her. "No, I don't. The point is, some other man might. It isn't a safe career. In a profession, there are more laws to protect you."

"Most professional people have degrees and such. Besides, I'm too old."

"You're never too old to go back to school," he replied.

She shrugged. "Besides, I like cooking and cleaning."

He eyed her curiously. "You're very good at handling injured people," he said suddenly. "And you're remarkably calm in an emergency."

"It's good practice for when I have kids," she said.

He drew in a short breath. "You like being mysterious, don't you?"

"While it lasts, it's fun," she agreed.

His eyes narrowed. "What dark secrets are you keeping, Meredith?" he asked quietly.

"None that should bother you, even if you found them out," she assured him. She smiled at him from the stove. "Meanwhile, you're getting fresh biscuits every day."

"Yes, we are," he had to agree. "And you're a good cook. But I don't like mysteries."

She pursed her lips and gave him a teasing glance over her shoulder. "Too bad."

He put the last place setting on the table and sat down at his place, just staring at her, without speaking. "You know," he said after a minute, frowning, "there's something familiar about your last name. I can't quite place it, but I know I've heard it somewhere.''

That wasn't good, she thought. He might remember Leo talking about her brother. She didn't want to have to face the past, not just yet, when she was still broken and bruised and uncomfortable. When she was back on her feet and well again, there would be time to come to grips with it once and for all—as her poor father was already doing.

''Think so?'' she asked with forced nonchalance.

He shrugged. ''Well, it may come back to me one day.''

Fortunately Leo came in and stopped his train of thought. Meredith put supper on the table and sat down to eat it with the brothers.

The next morning, Rey came out to the kitchen with a bright silver metal gun case. He set it down beside the counter, out of the way, before he started eating his breakfast.

''Going hunting?'' Meredith asked impishly.

He gave her a wary glance. ''Skeet shooting,'' he corrected. ''The season's over, but I practice year-round.''

''He won two medals at the World championships in San Antonio, this year,'' Leo told her with a grin. ''He's an 'A' class shooter.''

''Which gauge?'' she asked without thinking.

Rey's face became suspicious. ''All of them. What do you know about shotguns?''

''I used to skeet-shoot,'' she volunteered. ''My brother taught me how to handle a shotgun, and then he got me into competition shooting. I wasn't able to keep it up after I grad...after high school,'' she improvised quickly. She didn't dare tell him she gave it up after she finished college. That would be giving away far too much.

He watched her sip coffee. ''You can shoot, can you?'' he asked, looking as if he were humoring her. He didn't seem to believe what she claimed.

"Yes, I can," she said deliberately.

He smiled. "Like to come down to the range with me?" he asked. "I've got a nice little .28 gauge I can bring along for you."

By offering her his lowest caliber shotgun, he was assuming that she couldn't handle anything heavier.

"What's in the case?" she asked.

"My twelve gauge," he said.

She gave him a speaking glance. "I'll just shoot that, if you don't mind sharing it. Uh, it doesn't have a kick or anything…?" she added, and had to bite her tongue to keep from grinning at her innocent pose.

He cleared his throat. He didn't dare look at Leo. "No," he said carelessly. "Of course it doesn't have a kick."

In truth, it would kick worse than any other of the four gauges, but Rey was planning to call her bluff. She was putting on an act for his benefit. He was going to make her sorry she tried it.

"Then I'll be just fine with that gun," she said. "More apple butter?" She offered him an open jar and spoon.

"Thanks," he replied smugly, accepting the jar. He put it down and buttered another biscuit before he spooned the apple butter into it. "Don't mind if I do. Leo, want to come along?" he asked his brother.

Leo was also trying not to grin. "I think I will, this time," he told his brother. This was one shooting contest he wasn't about to miss. He knew that Mike Johns was a champion shooter. If he'd been the one who taught his sister, Meredith would shock Rey speechless when she got that shotgun in her arms. He was going along. He didn't want to miss the fun.

"The more the merrier, I always say," Rey chuckled.

"Funny thing, that's just what I was thinking," Leo replied, tongue-in-cheek.

Meredith didn't say another word. She finished her breakfast, waited until they finished theirs, and put the dishes in the dishwasher. Then she dressed in jeans, boots, and a long-sleeved flannel shirt with a down-filled vest and a bib cap, and went off to let Rey show her how to shoot a shotgun.

The target range was unusually busy for a lazy Friday afternoon in November. It was a cool day, with a nice nip in the air. Meredith felt good in the down vest. It was one she'd often worn when she went to the firing range with Mike in cold weather. Coats were cumbersome and often got in the way of a good, quick aim.

Rey and Leo stopped to pass the time of day with two elderly shooters, both of whom gave Meredith a warm welcome.

"This is Jack, and that's Billy Joe," Rey introduced the white-haired men, one of whom was tall and spare, the other overweight and short. The short one had walked briskly the short distance from the red pickup truck parked at the clubhouse, and he was out of breath already. "We all go to district, state and national shoots as a team from our club."

"But we get honorable mention, and Rey wins the medals," Billy Joe, the shorter man, chuckled, still trying to catch his breath. "We don't mind. We're just happy that somebody from our club breaks records!"

"Amen to that," Jack agreed, smiling.

"All right, let's get to shooting," Billy Joe said, turning back to his truck. "Stay where you are, Jack. I'll bring your gun, too!"

He turned back toward the truck, rushing and still breathless. Meredith frowned. His cheeks were unnaturally pink, and it wasn't that cold. His complexion was almost white. He was sweating. She knew the symptoms. She'd seen them all too often.

"You might go with him," Meredith said abruptly, interrupting Jack's banter with Rey.

"Excuse me?" Jack asked.

Just at that moment, Billy Joe stopped, stood very still for a minute, and then buckled and fell forward into a crumpled heap at the door of his truck.

Meredith took off at a dead run. "Somebody get me a cell phone!" she called as she ran.

Leo fumbled his out of the holder on his belt and passed it to her as she knelt beside Billy Joe.

"Get his feet elevated. Find something to cover him with," she shot at the other men. She was dialing while she spoke. She loosened the man's shirt, propping the phone against her ear—the worst way to hold it, but there was no other way at the moment—and felt down Billy Joe's chest for his diaphragm. "Get his wallet and read me his weight and age from his driver's license," she added with a sharp glance in Leo's direction.

Leo dug out the wallet and started calling out information, while Rey and Jack stood beside the fallen man and watched with silent concern.

"I want the resident on duty in the emergency room, stat," she said. "This is Meredith Johns. I have a patient, sixty years of age, one hundred and eighty pounds, who collapsed without warning. Early signs indicate a possible myocardial infarction. Pulse is thready," she murmured, checking the second hand of her watch as she took his pulse with her fingertips, "forty beats a minute, breathing shallow and labored, grey complexion, profuse sweating. I need EMTs en route, I am initiating cardiopulmonary resuscitation now."

There was a long pause, and a male voice came over the line. With her voice calm and steady, Meredith gave the information again, and then handed the phone to Leo as she bent over the elderly man and did the spaced compressions over his breastbone, followed by mouth-to-mouth breathing.

Rey was watching, spellbound at her proficiency, at the

easy and quite professional manner in which she'd taken charge of a life-or-death emergency. Within five minutes, the ambulance was screaming up the graveled road that led to the Jacobsville Gun Club, and Billy Joe was holding his own.

The EMTs listened to Meredith's terse summary of events as they called the same resident Meredith had been talking to.

"Doc says to give you a pat on the back," the female EMT grinned at Meredith as they loaded Billy Joe onto the ambulance. "You sure knew what to do."

"Yes," Rey agreed, finding his tongue at last. "You've obviously had first-aid training."

He probably meant it as praise, but it hit Meredith in the gut. She glared at him. "What I've had," she emphasized, "is five years of college. I have a master's degree in nursing science, and I'm a card-carrying nurse practitioner!"

Seven

Rey stared at his new cook as if she'd suddenly sprouted feathers on her head. His summation of her abilities was suddenly smoke. She was someone he didn't even know. She was a health care professional, not a flighty cook, and certainly not the sort of woman to streetwalk as a sideline.

She nodded solemnly. "I figured it would come as a shock," she told him. She turned her attention back to the EMTs. "Thanks for being so prompt. Think he'll be okay?"

The female EMT smiled. "I think so. His heartbeat's stronger, his breathing is regular, and he's regaining consciousness. Good job!"

She grinned. "You, too."

They waved and took off, lights flashing, but without turning on the sirens.

"Why aren't the sirens going?" Rey wanted to know. "He's not out of danger yet, surely?"

"They don't like to run the sirens unless they have to,"

Meredith told him. "Some people actually run off the road and wreck their cars because the sirens rattle them. They use the lights, but they only turn on the sirens if they hit heavy traffic and have to force their way through it. Those EMTs," she added with a smile, "they're the real heroes and heroines. They do the hardest job of all."

"You saved Billy Joe's life," Jack said huskily, shaking her hand hard. "He's the best friend I got. Thank you."

She smiled gently and returned the handshake. "It goes with the job description. Don't try to keep up with the ambulance," she cautioned when he went toward Billy Joe's truck, which still had the key in the ignition. The two men had come together.

"I'll be careful," the older man promised.

"Whew!" Leo let out the breath he'd almost been holding, and put up his cell phone. "You're one cool lady under fire, Meredith."

She smiled sadly. "I've had to be," she replied. She glanced at Rey, who looked cold and angry as it occurred to him, belatedly, that she'd played him for a fool. "I can see what you're thinking, but I didn't actually lie to you. You never asked me exactly what I did for a living. Of course, you thought you already knew," she added with faint sarcasm.

He didn't reply. He gave her a long, contemptuous look and turned away. "I've lost my taste for practice," he said quietly. "I want to go on to the hospital and see about Billy Joe."

"Me, too," Leo added. "Meredith…?"

"I'll go along," she said. "I'd like to meet that resident I spoke with. He's very good."

Rey glanced toward her. "You'll get along. He keeps secrets, too," he said bitterly, and got behind the wheel.

Leo made a face at Meredith, opening the third door of the big double cabbed truck so that she could sit in back.

He put the gun cases in the boot, in a locked area, and climbed in beside Rey.

The resident turned out to be a former mercenary named Micah Steele. He was married to a local girl, and he'd gone back to school to finish his course of study for his medical license.

"I couldn't very well carry a wife and child around the jungles with me," Micah told her with a grin. He was tall and big, and not at all bad-looking. She could picture him with a rifle in one arm. But now, in a white lab coat with a stethoscope thrown carelessly around his neck, he seemed equally at home.

"When's Callie due?" Leo asked.

"Any minute," he said, tongue-in-cheek. "Can't you see me shaking? I'm the soul of self-confidence around here, but one little pregnant woman makes me a basket case!"

"Callie's quite a girl," Rey agreed, smiling at the big man.

Micah gave him a look. "Yes, and isn't it lucky for me that you hardly ever went into her boss Kemp's office for legal advice, while she was still single?"

Rey pursed his lips. "Kemp eats scorpions for breakfast, I hear. I like my lawyers less caustic."

"Last I heard, the local bar association had you down as a contagious plague and was warning its members to avoid you at all costs," Micah replied wickedly.

"I never hit any local lawyers." Rey looked uncomfortable. "It was that Victoria lawyer, Matherson," he muttered. "And I didn't even hit him that hard. Hell, he's lucky I wasn't sober at the time! Otherwise, he'd have had twice the number of stitches!"

Meredith listened to the repartee with wide, fascinated eyes, but Rey wouldn't meet her eyes and Micah, too, cleared his throat and didn't pursue the subject.

"Matherson took a client who accused us of assault,"

Leo volunteered. "Cag had hit him, several times, after he got drunk and assaulted Tess, who's now Cag's wife. But the bounder swore that he was the injured party, that we falsely accused him and all took turns pounding him. He convinced a jury to award him damages. Not a lot of money," Leo added solemnly, "but the principle was what set Rey off. He was in a bad mood already and he had a few too many drinks at Shea's Bar, out on the Victoria road. To make a long story short," he added with a chuckle, "Matherson was having a quiet beer when Rey accused him of handling the ex-employee's case for spite because he lost an argument with us over Tess when he was handling her inheritance. Matherson took exception to Rey's remarks, and the two of them set about wrecking the pretty stained-glass window that used to overlook the parking lot."

"Used to?" Meredith fished, sensing something ominous.

"Yes, well, Matherson made a rather large hole in it when Rey helped him into the parking lot the hard way," Leo concluded.

Micah Steele looked as if it was killing him not to burst out laughing.

"He," Leo jerked his thumb toward Steele, "had to remove quite a number of glass particles from Matherson's rear end. *And* we got sued again, for that!"

"But the jury, after hearing Kemp's masterful summation of our grievances," Rey interrupted, "decided that Matherson was only entitled to the cost of the repair job on his butt. Shea had insurance that replaced the stained-glass window with one of comparable age and exclusivity." Rey smiled smugly. "And the judge said that if she'd been sitting on the first case, the rat Matherson was representing would have gotten a jail sentence."

Leo chuckled. "Only because Kemp put Tess on the stand and had her testify about what really happened the night Matherson's client took her on a date. The jury felt that Rey was justifiably incensed by the former verdict." He glanced at Meredith wryly.

"Yes, but I understand that Shea's two bouncers meet Rey at the door these days and won't let him in if he's not smiling," Micah contributed.

Rey shrugged. "I never get drunk anymore. I've learned to handle aggression in a nonphysical manner."

The other two men actually walked down the hall. Meredith noticed their shoulders vibrating.

Rey took a step toward Meredith, half irritated by the character assassination job his brother and Micah Steele had just done on him, and even more put out by Meredith's unmasking.

"You knew I had no idea about your education," Rey accused Meredith. "Why didn't you say something at the outset, when Leo first went to the hospital?" he demanded in a low, deep tone. "I may have jumped to conclusions, but you provided the springs, didn't you?"

She grimaced. "I guess so. But it was only a little jump from telling you about my job to talking about the reason Daddy started drinking. It's…still very fresh in my mind," she added huskily. "It's only been six months. The memories are—" she swallowed and looked away "—bad."

Unexpectedly he reached out and caught her fingers in his, tugging her closer. The hall was deserted. In the background there were muted bell-tones and announcements and the sound of lunch trays being distributed. "Tell me," he said gently.

She bit her lower lip hard and lifted her tormented eyes to his curious ones. "Not…yet," she whispered tightly. "One day, but…not yet. I can't."

"Okay," he said after a minute. "But I'd like to know how you learned to shoot."

"My brother, Mike, taught me," she said reluctantly, staring at his broad chest. She wanted to lay her head on

it and cry out her pain. There hadn't been anyone to hold
her, not when it happened, not afterward. Her father withdrew into his own mind and started drinking to excess at
once. Her job was all that had kept Meredith sane. She
hadn't been able to let out her grief in any normal way.

Rey's mind was working overtime. He stared down at
her, still holding her fingers entwined tightly with his own,
and he frowned as bits and pieces of memory began fitting
themselves together.

"Mike. Mike Johns." His eyes narrowed. "Our cousin
Colter's best friend, and one of Leo's acquaintances. He
was killed…!"

She tried to tug her fingers away. He wouldn't let her.
He pulled her into his arms, holding her there even when
she struggled. But a few seconds of resistance were all she
had. She laid her flushed cheek against his broad chest and
let the tears flow.

Rey's arms contracted roughly. He smoothed his hand
over her nape, caressing, soothing. "There was a bank rob-
bery in Houston," he recalled quietly. "Mike was a cop.
He was at the bank with your mother. It was Saturday. He
was off duty, but he had his service revolver under his
jacket." His arms tightened as her sobs grew painful to
hear. "He drew and fired automatically, and one of the
robbers sprayed fire from one of those damned little automatic rifles in his general direction. He and your mother
died instantly…"

Meredith's fingers dug into his wide back. He rocked her,
barely aware of curious glances from passersby.

"Both men were caught. You don't kill a cop and get
away with it in Texas," he added softly. "They were ar-
raigned and treated to a speedy trial just a month ago. You
and your father testified. That was when your father really
went off the deep end, wasn't it, when he had to see the
autopsy photos…"

Micah and Leo came back down the hall, frowning when

they saw the condition Meredith was in. Even as they watched, her eyes rolled back and she would have fallen to the floor except for Rey's strong arms lifting her.

Later, she wouldn't recall much except that she was hustled into a cubicle and revived. But when she started sobbing hysterically, they'd given her a shot of something that put her out like a light. She came to back at the ranch, in her own little garage apartment.

She opened her eyes, and there was Rey, sitting by the bed, still wearing the same jeans and shirt and boots he'd worn to the shooting range. Meredith was aware of the bedspread covering her up to her waist. Her boots were off, but she was also wearing the same clothes she'd started out in that morning.

"What time is it?" she asked in a husky, slightly disoriented tone.

"Five hours past the time you flaked out on me," he said, smiling gently. "Micah knocked you out. He thought some sleep might help." The smile faded into quiet concern. "You don't sleep much, do you, Meredith?" he asked surprisingly.

She sighed, brushed back her disheveled blond hair, and shook her head. "When I go to sleep, I have nightmares. I wake up in a cold sweat, and I see them, lying there on the floor, just the way they looked in those vivid crime scene photos." She closed her eyes and shivered. "People look so fragile like that, they look like big dolls, sprawled in pitiful disarray on the floor. Everybody stares at them..."

He brushed back her hair with a lean, gentle hand. "They got the guys who did it," he reminded her. "Including the trigger man. He'll serve life without any hope of parole. He'll pay for it."

Her pale eyes were tormented as they met his. "Yes, but it won't bring them back, will it?" she asked. "And do you know why they said they did it? For a bet. For a stupid bet, they killed two innocent people!"

"They also ruined their own lives," he reminded her, "and the lives of their own families."

She looked at him blankly, scowling.

"Don't you ever think about that?" he asked softly. "Criminals have families, too. Most of them have loving, decent parents who took care of them and disciplined them and blame themselves for what their children do. It must be pure hell, to have your child kill someone, and feel responsible for it."

"I haven't considered that," she admitted.

He continued. "When I was in high school, one of my best friends was arrested for murder. He killed the old man next door in the process of stealing his wallet. He wanted to buy his girl a diamond necklace she liked, and he didn't have any money. He figured the man was old and didn't need money anyway, so he might as well take it. He was sorry about it, but he never figured on killing the man or getting caught."

"Was he a good friend?" she asked.

He looked at their linked fingers. He nodded. "We were pals since grammar school. He wasn't quite as bright as some of the other boys, but he had a gentle nature. Or so we thought." He met her eyes. "His mom and dad always had a houseful of other peoples' kids. They were everybody's mom and dad. It shattered them when Joey went to prison. Even the children of the old man felt sorry for them."

"Funny," she mused. "I never even thought of how it would feel to have a child or a parent or a sibling who broke the law in some terrible way." She met his eyes. "I guess I'd feel guilty, too."

"Most kids are raised right. But some of them have a wild streak that nobody can tame, others have poor impulse control. Many are handicapped. Nobody goes to jail because he wants to."

"I never thought of you as a sensitive man," she blurted out, and then flushed at the insult.

His eyebrows lifted. "Who, me? I stop to pick worms out of the highway so my tires won't bruise their little bodies, and you think I'm insensitive?"

It took a minute for the words to make sense, and then she burst out laughing.

"That's better," he said. He smiled and squeezed her fingers. "You're going to be okay. You've had a lot of traumatic experiences just lately. No wonder you caved in."

"Lucky for you," she shot back.

"Me? Why?"

"Because if we'd unpacked those shotguns, I'd have destroyed your ego," she said with a smug smile. "At Mike's gun club, they used to call me 'dead-eye.'"

"Oh, they did, did they?" he challenged. "Well, we'll see about that when you step up to my gun range."

She studied his lean face. He wasn't handsome, but he had strong, stubborn features. He was familiar to her now, almost necessary. She thought about going back to Houston with real panic.

He touched her cheek where the bruises were a mixture of purple and yellow, much less vivid now. "He really knocked you around," he said, and his face hardened visibly. "I don't care if a man is drunk, there's no excuse for hitting a woman."

"Shades of primitive man," she chided with a smile.

"Women are the cradles of life," he said simply. "What sort of man tries to break a cradle?"

"You have a unique way of putting things."

"We had Spanish ancestors," he told her. "They were old-world men, conquerors, adventurers. One of them made his way to Texas and was given a huge tract of land under a Spanish land grant, for services to the crown of Spain."

He noticed a start of surprise on her face. "Do you know the legend of the Cid?"

"Yes!" she exclaimed. "He was a great Spanish hero. Cid is for the Arabic 'Sidi' which means Lord."

"Well, our ancestor wasn't El Cid," he said on a chuckle. "But he fought his way through hostile neighbors to claim his land, and he held it as long as he lived. Our family still holds it, through our late uncle, who left us this ranch."

"This is the original grant?" she exclaimed.

He nodded. "It isn't nearly as big as it was a couple of hundred years ago, but it's no weekend farm, either. Didn't you notice the antique silver service in the dining room?"

"Yes, I've been afraid to touch it. It looks very old."

He smiled. "It came from Madrid. It's over two hundred years old."

"An heirloom!" she breathed.

"Yes. Like the ranch itself." He tilted his head and studied her for a long time. "Now I understand. Your father wasn't violent until the killer's trial, was he?"

"No, he wasn't." She looked down at Rey's big, warm hand wrapped around her own. It made her feel safe. "He told Mike to drive Mama to the bank," she added reluctantly. "He had papers to grade. He couldn't spare the time, he said, and he snapped at her when she protested that Mike was spending his day off, carting her all over Houston." She glanced at him. "I was called in to work at a clinic my boss holds in the Hispanic community every Saturday. There's a regular nurse, but she was at home with a sick child. I went to stand in for her." Her eyes fell to his broad chest. "I could have asked someone to go in my place. I didn't. So he and I both have our guilt."

"Because you lived and they didn't," Rey said bluntly.

She gasped. "No, that's not true!"

"It is true." His black eyes held hers relentlessly. "The same thing happens to people who survive airplane crashes, automobile wrecks, sinking ships. It's a normal, human re-action to surviving when other people don't. It's worse when the victims include close relatives or friends.''

"Where did you learn that?" she asked.

"From Janie Brewster," he said.

She frowned. "That name sounds familiar."

"We've mentioned her to you. She's the daughter of a neighboring cattleman," he related. "She got her associate degree in psychology from our community college, and now she's studying it in Houston," he added with a grin. "She's almost twenty. They let her take college courses while she was still in high school, so she's ahead."

"Oh."

"She's not hard on the eyes, either," he murmured, avoiding her eyes. "She and her father live alone. Leo and I have a standing dinner invitation, any time we care to show up."

She started to say "oh" again, and realized how juvenile she was behaving. She straightened her shoulders against the pillow that was propping her up, and tugged at the hand Rey still held. "Then if she can bake biscuits, you're saved when I leave, aren't you?" she asked coolly.

"Well, she can't exactly bake stuff," Rey had to admit.

"Why?"

"She has no sense of time. She sets the timer and it goes off, and she never hears it. So the chicken bounces, the heat-and-serve rolls usually come out black, and I won't even mention what happens to vegetables she tries to cook on *top* of the stove." He gave her a sad look. "She did try to make us a pan of biscuits once." He actually shuddered.

"Not a successful try?" she fished.

"We had to take the damned things home, or her father would never have let us near the Salers heifers he was offering for sale." He glanced at her. "Leo just bought us a big Salers bull, and we needed purebred heifers to breed to him. Purebred breeding stock brings a big price, especially if you show cattle and win ribbons.'' He shrugged. ''So we took the biscuits home.''

''Did you eat them?'' she persisted.

He shook his head and he shuddered again.

''Then what did you do with them?'' she asked, thinking he probably fed them to the cattle dogs or some livestock.

''Well, actually, we took them out to the skeet field and used them for clay pigeons,'' he confessed with a grin. ''They were the best damned targets we ever had, but we didn't dare say where we got them!''

She put her face in her hands and burst out laughing. ''Oh, the poor girl!'' she chuckled.

''Don't worry, we'd never tell her,'' he promised. ''But we did ask her for another pan of biscuits, without telling her why.'' He sighed. ''That woman has a ready-made profession as a target maker, and we haven't got the guts to tell her so. Hell of a shame!''

She brushed at her eyes with the hem of her blouse. Poor Janie. And she'd been jealous.

''What does she look like?'' she asked, curious.

''She comes up to my shoulder. She's got light brown hair, longer than yours, and her eyes are green. If she didn't know everything, and tell you so every time you saw her, she might get married one day.''

''You don't want to marry her?'' she teased. ''Not even for an inexhaustible supply of skeet targets?''

''I don't want to marry anybody,'' he said bluntly, and he looked her straight in the eye when he said it. ''I love my freedom.''

She sighed and smiled. ''So do I,'' she confessed. ''I don't think I could ever settle for diapers and dishes. Not with my background.''

''You were a science major, weren't you?'' he asked abruptly.

''Yes. Chemistry and biology, genetics—stuff like that. I made good grades, but it was hard work. Then I went right to work for my boss, straight out of college. I need to be two people, just to catch up. I run my legs off. The stress is pretty bad sometimes.''

"No wonder keeping house and baking biscuits seemed like a holiday to you," he said to himself.

"It's been fun," she agreed. "I love to cook. I do it a lot, at home. I used to when Mama was alive," she recalled. "She hated housework and cooking. I came home from work and did it all."

"I've read about the sort of work you do," he commented, recalling articles he'd seen in the daily newspaper. "You're second only to a physician in authority. The only thing you can't do is write a prescription without his supervision."

"That's true." She smiled.

He studied her slender body, her exquisite figure nicely outlined by the garments she was wearing. "All those years, nothing but textbooks and exams and, then, a hectic career. No men?" he added, with a calculating stare.

"I dated," she replied. "I just couldn't afford to get serious about anybody. My father scraped and begged and borrowed to get the money to finance my nursing education," she told him. "Even Mike...contributed to it." She drew in a steadying breath and locked her fingers together on her lap. "It would have been so petty of me to throw all that up, just so I could go to parties and get drunk with the other students."

"Surely there wasn't much of that, at a community college?"

She laughed. "You'd be surprised. There was all too much, for my taste. But I didn't live on campus. I lived at home and commuted." She met his searching gaze. "That party I was at, when Leo was attacked—the woman who gave it was a college classmate who works for a doctor in our practice. I knew she sort of had a reputation. I guess I should have realized how wild things would get, but I was so depressed that I let her pressure me into going to the party. It was a mistake.''

"A lucky mistake, for my brother,'' Rey said gently. "He might have been killed, if you hadn't come along when you did.'' He scowled. ''You said, you ran at the attackers, waving your arms.''

She nodded. ''Mike taught me about shock tactics,'' she said sadly. ''I was afraid it wouldn't work, but I had no weapon, no other way of stopping them. So I took the risk.''

"I'm grateful that you did.'' He shook his head slowly. "But it was an act of lunacy, Meredith. You could have been lying on the grass next to Leo.''

"But I wasn't.'' She hunched her shoulders as if she felt a chill. ''I think there might be a force behind every single chain of events,'' she said thoughtfully. ''I don't believe in chaos,'' she elaborated. ''The body is such a messy, beautiful miracle. A single cell has chemical processes that are so complex, so meticulously crafted, that I can't believe life is an accident. If it isn't accidental, it has to be planned.'' She shrugged. ''That's simple logic. That's why I don't think God is a myth.''

They were silent for a moment. ''You're the most intriguing woman I've ever met,'' he murmured, and his dark eyes fell to her soft, full mouth.

"Surely not?'' she asked demurely. ''I don't have any secrets left.''

"That's what you think,'' he said in a soft, low tone.

She looked up and he moved toward her, one hand catching the wooden headboard as he levered his hard mouth down against her soft one.

Her hands instinctively went to his chest, but its muscular warmth was fascinating. She'd never done anything really intimate with her infrequent dates, having been completely turned off by men with fast reputations. She preferred gentlemen to rounders. She knew that Rey had been a rounder. She wanted to draw away. She really did.

But Rey Hart was completely out of her experience. He wasn't aggressive and insistent, as one of Meredith's rare dates had been. He didn't rush at her. He didn't insist. He wasn't insulting with the speed of his advances. He simply bent and kissed her, slowly and gently, with nothing more intimate than his hard, tender lips touching hers. He nibbled her upper lip and lifted his mouth slowly.

"You're doing a surfboard imitation," he murmured. "There's no need. I'm too good a cattleman to rush my fences."

She was trying to understand the slow, sensuous speech when his lips came down on hers again and caressed her upper lip. Her hands pressed flat against his muscular chest. She liked the way he felt. She could feel the quick, strong pulse of his heart under her palms. She could feel the growing rise and fall of his breathing.

His teeth nibbled her lips again, tenderly, and she found her hands moving under his arms and around him. She wanted to be held close, tight. She wanted him to envelop her against him. She wanted something more than this torturous teasing of his mouth on hers.

She made a husky, high-pitched little cry into his mouth and her nails bit into the solid muscles of his back.

"What do you want?" he whispered just above her lips.

"Kiss me," she moaned huskily.

"Kisses are dangerous, didn't you know?" he murmured, smiling against her responsive mouth. "They can be very addictive."

She was following his lips mindlessly. Her body was on fire. She'd never felt such headlong desire. Belatedly she realized that his hands were at her rib cage. Whether by accident or design, they were moving slowly up and down, up and down, so that his long fingers just lightly brushed the underswell of her breasts. It was extremely provocative. It was arousing.

She caught her breath as they moved ever closer to entrapment, and her eyes locked into his.

"Don't you like it this way?" he asked at her lips, brushing his mouth against them.

"Like…it?" she murmured mindlessly. Her body was reaching up toward those tormenting hands. She was shivering with every pulsating motion of her body, trembling with new and exciting surges of pleasure.

He laughed softly, sensuously. "Never mind." He lifted a hand to her hair and tugged out the hairpins, so that her beautiful long hair fell down around her shoulders. He tugged aside the top she was wearing, so that her shoulder was bare. Then he bent to it with his mouth, and she felt the warm, moist press of his lips right in the hollow of her shoulder.

Her nails dug into him. She lifted toward his mouth with a hoarse moan as she felt the slow tracing of his tongue against skin that had never known a man's touch. She was on fire. She was going to go up in flames right here. She didn't want to think, see, hear anything. She only wanted Rey to keep on touching her, to keep on holding her, to never, never stop…!

Eight

Just when the world was spinning away in a warm, pleasurable oblivion, the sound of loud, urgent footsteps echoed down the hall and brought Rey upright.

He looked at her with narrow, blank eyes as the sound grew louder. He cursed under his breath and got to his feet, keeping his back to her as he moved to the window, gripped the curtains and stared out at the pasture beyond.

Meredith dragged the bedspread up under her arms, over her clothes, and tried to steady her breathing. When she remembered what she and Rey had been doing, she blushed.

The door, ajar, was pushed completely open, and Leo came in with a tray. On it were a china cup and saucer, with a silver coffeepot, a silver cream and sugar service and a napkin and spoon. On a china plate were some dainty little chicken salad sandwiches.

"I thought you might be hungry," Leo said with a gentle smile as he put the tray on her lap. It had legs, so it would stand alone over her lap. "Mrs. Lewis came over to fix supper, and I had her make you these."

"Thank you!" she exclaimed. "And thank Mrs. Lewis, too. I was just starting to feel empty!"

Rey made an odd sound and she reached for a tiny sandwich very quickly, not daring to glance at him after the enthusiastic and unwise remark she'd just made.

Leo turned his eyes toward his brother. "Something wrong with you?" he asked curiously.

"Stomach cramp," Rey said without turning. "I had chili and salsa for lunch. Heartburn's killing me!"

"You should go and take an antacid tablet," Leo advised. "And drink some milk."

"I guess I'd better." Rey took a long breath and turned around, feeling more normal, finally. He glanced at Meredith. "I'm glad you're okay."

"I'll be fine. Thanks for the conversation," she said, and wouldn't meet his eyes. But she smiled shyly.

He just looked at her. Suddenly his dark eyes began to burn. He studied her intently, as if something had just happened that shocked him.

"Are you all right?" she asked impulsively.

He took a slow breath. He was still staring at her, to his brother's covert amusement. With her hair around her shoulders like that, sitting up in bed, smiling at him, he felt as if his whole life had just shifted five degrees. She was uncommonly pretty with her hair down. She had a warm, kind heart. She'd put her life on the line for a total stranger. Why hadn't that occurred to him in Houston, when they first told him that she'd saved his brother from attackers?

"Leo probably owes you his life," Rey said carefully. "But it bothers me that you risked your own to save him."

"Wouldn't you have done that same thing, even for a total stranger?" she mused.

He hesitated. "Yes," he said after deliberating for a few seconds. "I suppose I would have."

"See? You have all sorts of potential as a prospective husband," she added with a wicked smile, which got wider when he reacted. "You're sexy, you're rich, you drive a nice car, and besides all that, you like animals." She began nodding her head. "Definite potential."

His high cheekbones flushed and he glared at her. "I don't want to get married."

"Don't worry about it," she said soothingly. "It's perfectly natural for a bachelor to resist matrimony. But you'll come around." She wiggled both eyebrows. "If you get me a ring, I'll let you see my collection of used chewing gum wrappers and bottle caps."

He was still glaring.

Leo chuckled. "I'd love to see your used chewing gum wrappers, Meredith," he said enthusiastically. "In fact, I may start collecting right now!"

Rey stared a hole through his brother while, inside him, something froze.

"I'll even consider marrying you," Leo added wickedly.

She laughed, not taking him seriously. "Sorry. It's Rey or nobody. My heart's set on him." She frowned. "Pity I couldn't trade you something for him," she murmured to Leo.

Rey was getting angrier by the second, and uncomfortable at the idea that Leo was trying to cut him out.

"Make me an offer," Leo told her. "But he can't cook, and he has a temper worse than a sunburned rattler. Besides that, you can't domesticate him. He wears his spurs to the dinner table."

"So do you!" Rey accused.

"I sit more daintily than you do," Leo said imperturbably.

Rey rammed his hands into the pockets of his jeans and glared at Meredith again. "You can't give people away."

"I'm not trying to give you away," Leo said calmly. "I

want to make a profit.'' He scowled suddenly and his eyes widened as he looked at his brother's boots.

Meredith was staring at them, too. She pursed her lips and exchanged a look with Leo.

Rey glared back at them belligerently. ''What?'' he demanded hotly.

Both Leo's eyebrows went up, along with both hands, palms out. ''I didn't say a word!''

''Neither did I,'' Meredith assured him.

Rey looked from one to the other and finally looked down. There, on one of his feet, was a dainty little foot sock with a tassel on it, covering the steel toe of his brown cowboy boot. He'd unknowingly picked it up under Meredith's bed while he was kissing her.

Rey jerked it off, cursed royally, shot a furious glance at Meredith and his brother, who were trying valiantly not to look at him, and stomped out.

Helpless laughter erupted from the two people left in Meredith's room, and the sound of it infuriated Rey.

Leo was obviously ready to set up shop with their recently disclosed nurse, and Rey didn't like it. Leo was the plague of housekeepers everywhere, but he was also easier on the eyes than the other brothers, and he was charming. Rey had never learned how to use charm. He always looked uncomfortable when he smiled. Especially with women like Meredith, who was painfully shy and naive. He wasn't used to such women. But what made it so much worse was the dropping sensation in his stomach that he'd experienced when he'd stared at Meredith. He hadn't had anything like that since Carlie, who made his pulse race almost as fast as Meredith did when he kissed her.

He could still taste Meredith on his mouth. She didn't know much, but she made up for her lack of knowledge with enthusiasm and curiosity. He thought about carrying the lessons much farther, about baring her to the waist. His heart began to slam into his throat as he tried to imagine what she looked like under her blouse. He already knew that the skin of her shoulder was warm and soft, like silk. He remembered her husky moan when he'd kissed her there, the way her fingers had bitten into his back like little sharp pegs.

He'd been away from women for a long time, but he still knew what to do with one, and his imagination was working overtime just now. Meredith had attracted him when she was just his cook. Now that he knew about the intelligent, capable woman underneath the flighty camouflage, he was fascinated with her. She was everything a man could wish for.

Not that she wanted him, oh, no. She'd made it plain. But that teasing speech about marriage had unnerved him. His freedom was like a religion. He didn't want to get married. Of course he didn't!

But it was natural to think of Meredith with children. He could picture her baking biscuits for him every morning and holding a child in her arms at night while they watched television. He could picture her playing catch with a little boy out in back, or picking wildflowers with a little girl at her skirts. She was kind and sweet. She'd make a wonderful mother.

There was her job, of course. He knew something about her profession, that it was supposed to be high pressure. She'd be called upon to make life and death decisions, to comfort the sick and grieving, to make herself involved in the daily lives of her patients so that she should counsel them on how to maintain good health. Besides all that, she had a college degree.

Rey was college educated, too, with a degree in management and a minor in marketing. He was the mind behind the business decisions, the coordinator of the labor pool, and the director of marketing for the brothers' cattle co-operative. He was good at what he did. He enjoyed conversations with other educated people, and he'd convinced himself that Meredith wouldn't know Degas from Dali, Domingo from Dwight Yoakum, Hemingway from Dr. Seuss. Now he knew better, and his respect for her increased.

She'd saved Billy Joe's life at the gun club. He recalled that she must have known what to do for Leo as well, when she'd found him after he was mugged. Leo really did owe her his life. She was competent, confident, and she wasn't hard on the eyes, either. She had wonderful qualities.

But he didn't want to marry her. He wasn't sure about Leo. His eyes narrowed as he recalled the way Leo conspired with her. Leo had known all about her already. Obviously they'd been talking together since her arrival at the ranch, because Leo hadn't been a bit surprised when she rushed over to manage Billy Joe's heart attack.

Why hadn't he noticed that? Leo had called for Meredith when he was in the hospital. He was obviously fond of her. Maybe he was interested in her romantically, too. He'd been interested in Tess, before Cag had walked off with her, but Tess hadn't realized it. Or if she had, she'd ignored it. Leo wasn't hard on the eyes, either, and when it came to charm, he had his share and Rey's as well.

As he walked down to the barn to talk to one of his men, Rey had a terrible premonition that Leo had been serious when he joked about being willing to marry Meredith. Would she be desperate enough, lonely enough, frightened enough, to marry Leo and give up her job and living with her father? Her father had beaten her badly. She might be looking for a way out of the torment, and there was Leo, successful and handsome and charming, just ready to take her in and protect her.

Rey felt himself choke on dread. He couldn't imagine living in a house with Meredith if she was married to his brother. He'd rather throw himself headfirst into a cement mixer!

But, then, Leo had been teasing. Leo was always teasing. Rey forced himself to breathe normally and at least give the appearance of someone who was relaxed. Sure, it was just a joke. He didn't have to worry about the competition. There wasn't any. He pulled his hat lower over his eyes and walked on down the aisle to the man who was doctoring a heifer.

Several days later, Meredith received a huge bouquet of assorted roses from Billy Joe, now out of the hospital and back on the shooting range. She put them in water in the kitchen, along with the card, which the brothers blatantly read.

"He'd marry you," Rey drawled with pure acid in his tone as he dragged out a chair and sat down to lunch. "He's been widowed twenty years."

Meredith gave Leo a mischievous glance and fiddled with putting biscuits in a linen-lined basket. "He's not bad-looking for a man his age, and it wouldn't hurt him to have a nurse under his roof." She glanced at Rey's eloquent back. "But can he cook?"

Rey sipped coffee noisily.

"And does he slurp his coffee?" she added without missing a beat.

"That was done deliberately, to show you that I don't give a damn about manners!" Rey growled.

"All right, just don't expect me to take you to any nice restaurants while we're courting," she said easily, setting the basket of biscuits on the table.

"Lady, you aren't taking me as far as the mailbox," he said curtly.

He looked ferocious. That black temper was already kindling. Meredith studied his bent head curiously. You never knew about men. She'd seen some very mild-mannered ones come to the emergency room with wives who'd been beaten within an inch of their lives. It didn't hurt to see how far a man would go when he got mad. Especially after her experience with her father.

"You'll have to learn to scrape the mud off those enormous boots, too," she went on in a conversational tone. "And not slurp your soup. Your hair could use a good trim…"

"Damn it!"

He shot to his feet, eyes blazing in a rigid face, with a dusky flush creeping along his high cheekbones with all the warning color of a poisonous reptile.

Meredith stood her ground, watching him clench those big fists at his side.

"Rey," Leo cautioned abruptly, and started to get to his feet.

Meredith went right up to Rey, looking him in the eyes, quiet, still—waiting.

Rey was breathing through his nostrils. His jaw was clenched with fury. But intelligence won easily over bad temper. His chin raised slowly. "You're testing me," he said out of the blue. "You want to know if I'll hit you."

"It's something a woman needs to know about a man," she said very quietly. "And she needs to find it out where she can get help if she needs it." She didn't look at Leo, but Rey knew that was what she meant. She smiled gently. "No, you don't hit," she said in a soft, quizzical tone. "You do have a temper, but it's not a physical one."

He was still breathing through his nose. "If you were a man, it might be," he told her bluntly.

"But I'm not a man," she replied.

Her eyes were almost glowing with feeling. He got lost in those soft, warm, grey eyes. He hated the way he felt when he was near her. He'd been fighting it ever since he carried her up to her garage apartment after she'd fainted at the hospital. He liked the feel of her in his arms. He liked kissing her. He liked the way she picked at him and teased him. No woman had ever done that before. As his older brothers had been before they married, he was taciturn and uncommunicative most of the time. His very attitude put most women off.

It didn't put Meredith off. She wasn't afraid of his temper, either. She made him into a different person. It wasn't something he could easily explain. He felt comfortable with her, even while she was stirring him to passion. He could imagine just sitting in front of the television with her and holding hands, late at night.

The image intimidated him. He sat back down, ignoring Meredith, and started putting butter and strawberry preserves on four biscuits.

Leo gave him a measuring look. "Don't eat all the biscuits."

"I'm only getting my share. She," he jerked his thumb towards Meredith, "didn't make but eight this morning. That's one for her, four for me, and three for you."

"And why do you get four?" Leo asked belligerently.

"Because she proposed to me," he said with pure smug arrogance, and a look that made Leo's teeth snap together.

"I did not," Meredith said haughtily, sitting down across from him. "I said I was thinking of you as a marriage prospect, not that I actually wanted to go through with a ceremony." She cleared her throat. "I'll have to see how you work out."

Rey smiled faintly. "That sounds interesting."

He didn't necessarily mean what it sounded like he meant. She mustn't jump to any conclusions here. But her cheeks were getting very rosy.

He noticed that. It was a devilish game they were playing, and he could do it better. He stared pointedly at her soft mouth as he put a cube of fresh pear into his mouth, slowly and deliberately.

She felt very uncomfortable in odd places when he did that. She ate her beef and gravy and tried to ignore him.

"I like having fresh fruit," Rey said with a slow smile.

He speared a grape with his fork and eased it slowly between his lips.

She moved restlessly in her chair. "It's healthy stuff."

"No wonder you were trying to get us to eat right," Leo said, trying to break the growing spell Rey was casting on her. "You teach nutrition, I suppose."

"In a way. I'm supposed to counsel patients on changing bad habits and making lifestyle changes when they're warranted," she explained. If only her hand didn't shake while she was holding the stupid fork. Rey saw it and knew why, and she hated that damned smug smile on his lean face!

He picked up a piece of perfectly cooked asparagus spear and slowly sucked it into his mouth, using his tongue meaningfully.

"I have to fix dessert," Meredith choked, jumping to her feet so quickly that she knocked her chair winding and had to right it.

"I saw that chair jump right out and trip you, Meredith," Rey commented dryly. "You ought to hit it with a stick."

"I ought to hit *you* with a stick instead!" she raged at him, flushed and flustered and out of patience.

"Me?" Both eyebrows arched. "What did I do?"

She pictured hitting him across the jaw with the biggest frying pan she had. It was very satisfying. Pity she couldn't do it for real.

She went to the cupboard and drew out the ingredients for an instant reduced fat pudding. She had some low-fat whipped cream in the freezer that she could top it with. Meanwhile, Rey would finish his meal and stop using fruits and vegetables to torment her with. She could have kicked him.

Behind her, Rey was talking comfortably to Leo about some new equipment they were ordering, and about routine chores that had to be completed before Thanksgiving this month and the Christmas holidays next month. Most of the ranch hands would have Thanksgiving, the day after, and that weekend free. Next month, they'd have Christmas Eve and Christmas Day free, along with four days before or after, depending on the schedule. Some of the men had families in far-flung locations and they had to travel a distance for the holidays. The Harts made a practice of giving the men time off to go home during the holiday season by staggering work schedules, so that there was an adequate crew here to work when days off were assigned.

Then they moved on, naturally, to a discussion about Thanksgiving dinner.

"You're going to stay until after Thanksgiving, aren't you?" Rey asked Meredith.

She had her back to them. "Yes, I'd like to," she said, because she'd already been planning special menus and light, noncaloric desserts for it. "Unless you're planning to go away for it," she added quickly.

"The family has a Christmas party, when we all get together. We sort of save Thanksgiving for just us, so the others can have the day with their wives and kids," Leo told her. "It's been sort of hit and miss since Mrs. Lewis has been plagued with arthritis. As you know, we got her to come back to work just briefly, but her hands won't hold out to make bread and do any scrubbing with them, despite medicine. She has her children up from Corpus Christi for the holidays and cooks for them. We sort of got leftovers."

She grimaced. "Well, I'll make sure you have a big Thanksgiving dinner this year," she said gently. "With all the trimmings. Including biscuits," she added when they both looked her way.

She finished whipping the pudding, and put it in bowls in the refrigerator to chill before she sat back down. "That will make us a nice dessert tonight," she commented. "I don't suppose you want it any sooner?"

They shook their heads. "I've got a meeting with our marketing staff in half an hour," Rey said, checking his multifunction watch.

"And I've got to go over the new equipment list with our mechanic and see if we've got everything ready to order," Leo added.

"How about a nice Greek salad for supper?" Meredith asked. "I make it with Feta cheese and black olives and eggs. I bought the ingredients yesterday at the store. Except for the eggs, of course. I'll get those out of the henhouse."

"Sounds nice," Leo said with a grin.

"Watch where you put your hands," Rey murmured without looking right at her. "I haven't seen my pet snake in the barn lately."

She gave him a cold look. "If I see him, I'll get him on a stick and put him right back in the barn," she said with pure bravado.

Rey glanced at her with dancing dark eyes. "I'd pay real money to see you do that," he chided.

So would I, she thought, but she didn't say it. She just smiled smugly.

The brothers finished their last swallows of coffee and went out the door still talking business.

Later, Meredith went out to the henhouse to gather the eggs, with her straw basket on her arm. Rey had unnerved her with his comment about the damned snake. Now she was sure it was in there, waiting for a gullible victim to frighten.

She took a deep breath and walked carefully into the dim confines of the henhouse. She bit her lower lip and approached the nest slowly. She stopped dead. There was actually a snake in there. He was wrapped around the eggs. He was licking his snaky lips.

She shivered with fear, but she wasn't going to let the stupid thing make her a laughingstock twice.

She saw a long, thick stick on the straw-covered floor. She put her basket down, still watching the snake, and picked up the stick.

"It's okay, old fellow," she said to the snake. "It's okay.

I'm just going to ease you out of the nest. Don't get mad, now. I won't hurt you. It's okay.''

While she was talking, softly, she eased the stick under its coils and very carefully lifted it. It was very still, not moving its head except to hiss. So far, so good. She had it up on the stick. It was heavy.

As she pulled it out of the nest, she noticed that it was really quite long. It really didn't look much like that black and white one Rey had put in the barn. This one had a pretty brown pattern on its back and had a white underbelly. But, then, it wasn't striking at her or anything, so she wasn't worried.

She held it far out in front of her and stepped carefully out of the henhouse into the bright light. As she did, the snake hung from the stick, looking rather bored by the whole thing.

She carried it through the yard and out toward the barn. One of the men was standing by a truck, watching her progress. His jaw fell. She wondered what was wrong with him. Maybe he'd never seen a woman carry a snake around before.

"Nice day," she called to him.

He didn't answer. She shrugged and kept walking.

The barn was empty, except for the bales of hay that were stacked neatly on the bottom and the loft of the huge structure. Over against one wall there was a corn crib with stacks and stacks of dried corn, and a machine that shelled them.

"Here we go, old fellow," she told the snake. She eased him over the wooden box and slid him down into the piles of unshelled corn.

He drew back in a threatening pose and hissed at her again.

Odd, the shape of his head, she thought, frowning as she studied him. It looked like an arrowhead. That other snake's head had been rounded.

Well, it might be some other species of king snake, she supposed. Weren't there several?

She walked back out of the barn into the daylight, whistling softly to herself as she started back to the henhouse. She was so proud of herself. She'd gotten the snake on the stick all by herself, without screaming once, and she'd carried him all the way to the barn and put him in the corn crib. She wasn't afraid of the snake anymore. As Rey had said, they were beneficial. It wasn't right to kill something just because you were afraid of it, she told herself.

The man who'd been standing by the truck was nowhere in sight, but the truck was still running and the driver's door was standing wide-open. She wondered where the driver had gone. He must have been in a hurry for some reason.

Meredith went back to the henhouse, put the stick down, picked up her basket and went to gather eggs. There were no more snakes, but there were plenty of eggs. She could boil several to go in her nice Greek salad. The spinach she'd bought to make it with was crisp and cold and almost blemishless. The brothers would love a salad if it had enough eggs and cheese and dressing.

She got the last egg into the basket and walked back out again, pausing to reach down and pet one of the big red hens who came right up to her and cocked its head curiously toward her face.

"Aren't you a pretty girl?" she said, smiling. She liked the way the chicken felt. Its feathers were very smooth and silky, and the chicken made the sweetest little noises when she petted it. She'd never been around farm creatures. She found that she enjoyed the chickens and the cattle dogs and the endless cats that hung around outside begging for handouts.

Two other hens came up to her, curious about the tall creature in jeans and tank top. She petted them, too, laughing as they crowded close. But then one started to peck the eggs, and she stood up again.

She turned back toward the house, her mind on the snake and her bravery. She'd have to remember to tell Rey and Leo about it…

"Meredith!"

The loud, urgent deep voice sent her spinning around. Rey was running toward her, bare-headed, with the cowhand who'd been next to the running pickup truck at his heels.

"Hi, Rey," she said hesitantly. "What's wrong?"

He stopped just in front of her. He caught her a little roughly by the arms and took the basket away from her, setting it aside, while he looked at every inch of her bare arms and hands. He was breathing rapidly. He seemed unnaturally pale and tight-lipped.

"It didn't bite you?" he demanded.

"What?"

"The snake! It didn't bite you?" he snapped.

"No, of course not," she stammered. "I just got it on a stick, like you did, and put it in the corn crib."

"Get my Winchester," Rey told the other man in a harsh tone. "Load it and bring it back here. Hurry!"

"I don't understand," Meredith said with noticeable confusion. "What's wrong with you? Why do you need a gun?"

"Oh, baby," he whispered hoarsely. He pulled her against him and bent to kiss her in view of the whole outfit, his mouth hard and rough against hers. "Baby!"

She had no idea what was wrong, but she loved the faint tremor in his hard arms as they crushed her against his body. And she loved the way he was kissing her, as if he couldn't get enough of her mouth. He'd called her "baby…"

She held on and moaned under the crush of his lips.

He drew back. "I'm sorry. It was such a shock. I was

scared out of my wits, I didn't even stop to grab my hat when Whit came into the office…!''

Her mouth was pleasantly swollen. She looked up at him dreamily and smiled.

"You don't have a clue, do you?'' he asked huskily, searching her soft grey eyes.

"Mmm. About what?'' she murmured, only half hearing him.

The other man came out with a rifle. He handed it to Rey. "Safety's on,'' the man advised.

"Thanks, Whit.''

He moved back from Meredith. "I'll go kill it.''

"Kill it?'' Meredith exclaimed. "You can't! It will eat the rats, it's harmless…!''

"Sweetheart,'' he said very gently, "you were carrying a copperhead moccasin.''

"Yes?'' She stared at him blankly.

"It's one of the most poisonous snakes in Texas!''

She stood looking after him with her mouth open and her heartbeat choking her. She'd been carrying the damned thing on a stick, with it hissing at her. She felt the blood leave her head. Seconds later, she was lying on the hard ground. Fortunately she missed the basket of eggs on the way down.

Nine

"**Y**ou're making a habit of this lately," Rey murmured as he carried Meredith up the stairs to the garage apartment. "I never figured you for a fainter, Meredith," he added dryly.

He was still bare-headed, but he wasn't grim now. He was smiling.

"Of course I fainted! I picked up a poisonous snake!" she gasped, still in shock.

"Well, you've got guts, woman, I'll give you that," he said with a slow smile, shifting her a little closer. "Picked up a poisonous snake with a stick and carried it all the way to the barn, and it didn't bite you. Now I've heard everything."

"It did hiss a little," she recalled, shivering.

"It had eaten three eggs," he murmured. "Probably it was too busy digesting to care where it went at the time. Lucky for you."

She laid her cheek against his broad, strong shoulder and

held on tight. She had a sudden thought. "It didn't bite you?" she asked worriedly.

"It didn't get the chance. Didn't you hear the shot? I got it as it was crawling down from the corn bin onto the floor." He chuckled. "If I hadn't gotten it, though, Bandit would have. King snakes are natural enemies of any poisonous snake. They eat them. I hate to kill even a copperhead, but we can't have poisonous snakes around the livestock, or the men. Or, especially," he added with a warm glance at her, "in the henhouse. At the very least, a bite from one can put a man in the hospital."

She shivered, and her arms tightened around Rey's neck. "I was so proud of myself," she murmured. "I had no idea I was taking my life in my hands. It didn't look exactly like the other snake, but the patterns were sort of similar. I know about snake bites because I've helped treat them, but I don't know one snake from another unless I see pictures of them!" she added defensively.

"You'll learn." He kissed her forehead with breathless tenderness. "My brave girl," he whispered. "You'll never know how scared I was when Whit came running to tell me what you were doing."

It made soft little ripples of pleasure run through her body when he said that. He was being protective about her. She closed her eyes and drank in the warm nearness of him, the easy strength of his arms as he carried her. She felt safe as she'd never felt in her whole life. It was nice to lean on somebody strong, just for a little while.

He felt the vulnerability. He told himself that he wouldn't take advantage of it, but who was he kidding? She was soft and cuddly like this, and it was almost an involuntary action when his mouth slowly moved over hers as he reached her door.

The pressure was light, comforting. She sighed under the warmth and delight of it, and her lips parted, just the least little bit.

His whole body contracted with desire at that faint response. He looked down into her half-closed, misty eyes with growing hunger.

The look was as new as the tenderness. She couldn't tear her eyes away from that dark hunger in his. She forgot the snake, the scare, the people outside in the yard, everything. He bent back to her, and she met his mouth hungrily with her own, her arms clinging fiercely to his shoulders.

He groaned aloud. It was too soon, but he didn't care. He managed to open the door and close it behind them, making a beeline for the neatly made-up bed. He barely took time to put her down on the coverlet before his body slid against and over her own, his arms under her, taking his weight while his mouth made new, insistent demands on her innocence.

He lifted his head a torturous few seconds later, and his eyes blazed into her own. One lean hand slid deliberately under the hem of her tank top. At the same time, one long, powerful leg eased between both of hers and his hard mouth began to tease around the corners of hers.

"Danger will do it every time," he murmured deeply.

"Will...do what?" she asked, burning with new longings as his hand began to move up her rib cage toward the lacy little bra she was wearing under the top.

"This." His mouth opened on hers and became quickly insistent. While he kissed her, his fingers found the catch on her bra and flicked it open. She jumped when she felt his hand on flesh that had never known a man's touch before. He lifted his head and looked into her eyes. "I know. It's new territory," he said gently. His fingers stroked the delicate, warm flesh as lightly as a breeze. "Try to think of it as a rite of passage."

She felt strange new sensations. There was a tightening, a swelling, in her breasts as he touched them. She lifted involuntarily, and her eyes mirrored her surprise.

"Innocence is a rare, rare thing these days," he said at

her lips. "I respect it. And you'd better thank your lucky stars that I do," he added as his mouth bit hungrily at hers. "Because with an experienced woman, I'd lock the door and I wouldn't hesitate a minute."

She felt the words like the caress of his hands on her body. She moaned huskily under the demanding crush of his mouth. She felt his tongue tracing her lips, teasing under them, darting and touching and withdrawing. She felt his teeth, too, in a sensual caress that only intensified the new sensations he was teaching her to feel.

She felt her back arch again as he traced around the curves of her breast without ever touching the hard, taut nipple. She wanted him to touch it. Her body ached to have him touch it. She didn't understand why it should be such a violent, aching need…!

He laughed in a soft, sexy way against her lips. "Is this what you want?"

He caught the nipple between his thumb and forefinger and she lifted off the bed with a sharp cry. Heat spread over her, through her. Her short nails dug into his back fiercely and she gasped with pleasure.

"Baby," he groaned roughly, aroused by her unexpectedly ardent response. "Baby, you turn me on so hard…!"

The top was suddenly around her collarbone and his mouth—his mouth!—was right on her nipple, suckling her while his tongue tasted the hardness with a subtle caress that made her shiver. Her hands caught in the thick strands of his dark hair and held him to her body while he explored it with his mouth. She'd never imagined that she was capable of so much passion, and so unexpectedly swift. He could do anything to her, and she didn't have the willpower to stop him. Even a simple "no" was beyond her now. She wanted more. She wanted his eyes on her, his hands on her. She wanted his body closer.

As if he knew that, both lean hands smoothed up from her waist and onto her soft breasts. His fingers were rough from hard work, but their touch was pure heaven. She caressed his nape, moving rhythmically with each slow brush of his fingers, lost in pleasure.

He lifted his head to look at what he'd uncovered. She was beautiful, not too big or too small. She was just right. He loved the way her body moved when he touched it. He loved knowing how innocent she was. He'd never been with an innocent. Making love to one was a whole new experience, with levels of pleasure he'd never tasted. Her soft little moans excited him as much as those enthusiastic fingers caressing his back.

She felt his eyes and she opened hers, looking up at him. "Am I doing it right?" she whispered breathlessly.

His body tautened even more. "Yes," he whispered. "Just right."

He bent and drew his mouth gently over hers with a soft, cherishing pressure. He felt it open under his, felt her arms pulling at him. It wasn't a good idea to let this go any farther than it already had. While he was thinking it, he was moving slowly between her long legs until his body rested in the fork of hers. He eased down against her, letting her feel the slow burgeoning of his body against her belly.

She caught her breath.

He heard it, and lifted his head. His eyes were smoldering with desire, his body was rigid with it. He was getting little surges of insistent pleasure that ran the length of his spine. Her hips moved as if they were responding helplessly to the touch of him. She was making him ache like hell.

His hand moved to her hip and bit into the soft flesh, stilling the faint motion of her hips instantly while he rested on the elbow of his other arm. "Meredith," he said softly. "That will get you seduced. Right now."

She felt hot all over. Her mind seemed barely under her control. She searched his dark eyes with wonder. Her hands were against his shirt, right on the buttons. She felt him against the lower part of her body, and it felt right. It felt wonderful. She wanted to writhe under him and tempt him into intimacy.

His hand contracted and he gave her a wise, challenging stare as he read the look on her face. "Don't do it," he said huskily. "I'm years ahead of you in experience, but I can still lose my head. You don't want me to do that. Not really."

She pulled at a stabilizing breath. Her heart was still whacking around at the walls of her chest, as if she'd been running a race. "Are you sure I don't want you to do that? I mean, if you get pregnant, I'll marry you," she said breathlessly, and with deathbed humor. "Honest!"

He looked at her as if he couldn't believe his ears. The passion drained out of him, replaced by howling amusement. He started laughing. "Damn you, that wasn't fair!" he accused.

"Well, I like that! You're laughing, and here I've made you a solemn promise," she persisted, eyes twinkling.

"Hell!" He rolled away from her and sat up on the edge of the bed to run a lean hand through his disheveled hair. He glared down at her. "Now you've got fingerprints and lipstick and perfume all over me. The men will laugh themselves sick if I go to work smelling like a flower garden."

She tugged down her top and gave him an impish grin. "We could rush into my bathroom and shower it off, together," she offered wickedly.

He laughed again. He'd never laughed as much in his life as he did with her. Was this the way she'd been, before the tragedies of the past year that had marred her life? She'd said she didn't date much, but how in the world could men ignore a sweet, pretty little woman like that?

"I can't believe you spend your weekends watching television with your father," he murmured.

"I don't. I work."

He frowned. "On the weekends?"

She sat up, reaching under her blouse to refasten the bra

he'd unsnapped. She wondered why she didn't feel embarrassed. "Seven days a week, for the past six months," she said honestly. "Before that, six days a week, and I had to rest on Sunday. I usually work ten-hour days, sometimes longer if we have an emergency."

He didn't like that. "You don't have any free time, do you?"

She shook her head. "I've been dedicated to the job since I got out of college."

"And no men," he murmured with a speculative glance.

She grimaced. "Well, there was one I liked very much. We went out together for four months, and I was very nearly in love with him. But he never touched me. I thought he was building up to it, or something." She sighed. "Then I saw him, with another man." She shrugged. "He thought of me as a friend. I thought of him as a boyfriend. I sort of lost confidence in myself after that."

"It happens, in the modern world," he replied quietly.

"Before that, I had crushes on boys who never noticed me, except to ask me to help them with math or chemistry." She searched his eyes. "Of course, I didn't exactly look like this until last year."

"How did you look?" he asked curiously.

She got off the bed, went to get her purse, and took out a plastic insert. She pulled a photo from behind a credit card and handed it to him.

His eyes widened. "Good heavens!"

She winced. "I was sixty pounds overweight, and I couldn't lose it at all. I guess I tried every diet known to man. Then I took nutrition classes and learned how to get it off the sensible way. That's why I know so much about low-fat cooking."

He looked from the photo to her face and smiled. "You were pretty before, too," he said slowly. "You know, Meredith, it's not the outside that attracts people. It's what you are, how you treat other people, that makes friends of them.

You risked your life to save my brother, then you stayed with him until his family came. I wasn't very flattering to you when we first met, but I've had a lot of time to think about what you did. You're good people. Really good people.''

She flushed and cleared her throat. ''Thanks.'' She gave him a mischievous look. ''So, would you like to get married Friday, or is Monday better for you?'' she added with a grin.

He chuckled. ''Sorry, I have to wash my dogs.''

She sighed. ''Rejected again.''

He pursed his lips and let his eyes run over her slowly. ''You could lie back down and we could discuss it again.''

''Absolutely not. I only have so much willpower. You shouldn't throw yourself at women that way unless you're asking to be seduced. It's unfair.''

''You're not bad yourself, kid,'' he murmured with a warm smile. He got up. ''I've got to go back to work. Come here.''

She went to him. ''Changed your mind?'' she asked. ''I can get a ring today…''

He put a finger over her mouth. ''How do I smell?''

''Is that all you want?!'' she exclaimed. ''Good Lord, you got me all the way over here to *smell* you?''

He bent and kissed her hungrily, pulling her so close that she could feel him against every cell of her body. But before she could cling, he put her away. ''How do I smell?'' he persisted.

She sniffed him. ''You smell like aftershave.''

He bent and sniffed her, and frowned. ''You're not wearing perfume, are you?''

She shook her head. ''I'm allergic to most strong fragrances.''

''You smell like flowers.''

She smiled. ''Herbal shampoo. Flowers don't bother me. Well, real ones do sometimes, but not flowery scent. I can use scented shampoos and wear one or two colognes, but no perfumes. They're too strong."

"At least I don't smell womanly," he said with mocking relief. "I'd never live that down."

She cocked her head and stared up at him. "There goes the shower," she sighed.

He tapped her nose. "Now, cut that out." His fingers traced the fading bruises on her cheek and jaw and his eyes narrowed. "He'll never touch you again, I swear he won't," he said in a low, dangerous tone.

Her heart lifted at the look on his face. "Oh, my, aren't we getting possessive?" she teased.

He didn't smile. "Careful," he told her quietly. "I'm not teasing."

Her eyes widened with something like wonder.

"Hasn't anyone ever stood up for you?" he asked curiously.

"Just my brother. But he never had to protect me from Daddy. I know it looks really bad, but my father was the most gentle man on earth until we lost Mama and Mike. He goes crazy when he drinks, and he never remembers what he did." Her eyes fell to his chest. She toyed with his shirt buttons, wondering absently how it would feel to smooth her fingers over his bare chest. "I miss my brother terribly," she added simply.

"I'm sure you do. And your mother."

She grimaced. "She and I weren't really very close," she confessed. She searched his eyes. "You see, what Daddy yelled about her that night you were at the house was pretty much true. She was a very attractive woman, and she had lovers." She winced. "I hated knowing that. You can't imagine what it did to Daddy. She even bragged about them."

"She doesn't sound like much of a wife," he murmured.

"She didn't act like one, either. She did love to spend money, though. That's why she picked rich lovers." Her face clouded. "I was so ashamed of her. I guess she saw herself as a modern woman. I'm not. There's a big difference between sleeping with someone you truly love, and jumping into bed with anyone who has some money."

He nodded and touched her soft, swollen mouth. "She's soured you on men, hasn't she?"

"Sort of. Until you came along, at least," she admitted, without looking at him. She stared at his shirt button. "Bad temper and all, you've got some wonderful qualities."

He gave her a wry look. "I'll have to tell my brothers. They didn't know."

She chuckled. "Thanks for letting me come here to heal, anyway."

He felt uneasy. "That sounds like goodbye, Meredith."

She sighed. Her fingers stilled on his buttons. "I can't stay much longer," she said sadly. "Even though I'd like to. My boss is shorthanded as it is, and the woman filling in for me doesn't like leaving her kids in day care. She retired when she had the second one."

"Retired?"

"Yes. She said keeping two kids in day care ate up her whole paycheck." She lifted her eyes to his. "Since her husband got a raise, it was actually cheaper for her to stay home with the kids than it was to work. She loves it."

There was a strange look on his face. He rubbed his fingertips over her short fingernails absently. "Would you want to stay home with your kids?"

She stared up at him, transfixed. "Yes, I would. Those first few years are so important. If I could find any way to do it, I would, even if I had to sacrifice some little luxuries."

"That would be tricky. You're a highly trained professional."

"One of my friends was a highly trained doctor," she replied. "She gave up her job and stayed home with her little boy until he was in kindergarten. Even then, she arranged her schedule so that she'd be there when he got home in the afternoons.''

He was frowning, and his fingers were still smoothing over hers. He wanted to ask if she thought she could get used to ranch life and snakes. He was afraid to say it. The act of commitment was still very new to him. He couldn't rush her.

He sighed, troubled. ''What does your father do, by the way?'' he asked suddenly.

''Oh, he teaches in the veterinary department of his college in Houston.''

His hand stilled on hers. ''He's a veterinarian?''

''He has a doctorate in veterinary medicine, yes. Why?''

Wheels were turning in his head. He stared at her thoughtfully. ''Will he have a job to go back to, after all the trouble he's had with the law?''

''You're very perceptive,'' she said after a minute. ''Actually, no, he won't. The college phoned before his last bender and told him not to come back. You can't blame them, either,'' she added sadly. ''What would it do to the college's image, to have an alcoholic on staff with a dangerous temper?''

''Not much,'' he had to admit. ''Did he drink before the shooting?''

''Never. Not even a beer,'' she replied. ''But he's set records in the past six months. I couldn't get him near a treatment center. At least he's in one, now.''

''Not only in it, but improving by the day,'' Rey said unexpectedly. ''He'd like you to come see him. I can run you up there Sunday, if you'd like to go.''

That was surprising. ''You've spoken to him?'' she asked.

He nodded. ''I had Leo phone Colter. He has contacts who helped arrange it.'' He drew in a deep breath. ''Your father seems pretty rational right now. Of course, he isn't drinking, either.'' His eyes darkened. "I meant exactly what I said. He'll never touch you again in anger.''

"When he's sober, he never would. I can't believe...he really wants to see me?'' she asked haltingly.

He brushed his hand against her cheek. "He loves you. I'm sure you love him, too. You don't throw people away because they make a mistake—even a bad one. You get help for them.''

"I tried.''

"Sure you did. But it's better this way. When he comes home, we'll decide where to go from there. For now, I'll drive you to Houston on Sunday to see him. Want to go?''

"Oh, yes,'' she said. Her expression was soft, wondering. "You'd do that, for me?''

He smiled. "Anything you want, kiddo,'' he murmured. "It's the least I can do for the only woman who's ever proposed to me.''

She pursed her lips and gave him an impish look. "We could lie down and talk about it.''

"No, we couldn't,'' he told her firmly, and chuckled as he removed her hands from his shirt. "I have to get back to work. I was in the middle of a meeting when you did your snake charmer routine. I left twelve employees sitting in the boardroom with glasses of water and no ashtrays. At least six of them smoke, despite all the regulations. I expect they've attacked the other six with chairs by now, or vice versa. I've got to get back. Quick.''

"I'd love to go Sunday,'' she said.

"Fine. I'll run you up there Sunday afternoon. We can go to church first.''

Her eyebrows lifted. "I'm Methodist.''

He grinned. "So are we. It's a date.'' He opened the door. Before he went out it, he glanced back over his shoulder. "And stay out of the henhouse for the rest of the day, will you?''

"Anything for my prospective fiancé," she said with a theatrical gesture of her arm.

He shook his head and walked out, still chuckling.

Later, she wondered what he'd meant, about making decisions when her father got out of rehab. She didn't dare think too hard about it. But it sounded very much as if he wanted to go on looking out for her.

She was a modern woman. She could look out for herself. But it was kind of nice to have a man act protective and possessive, especially one like Rey, who didn't seem the sort to do it habitually. She remembered the hunger in his lean body when he held her, when he kissed her. She remembered the strange tenderness he reserved for her. It was an adventure, just being around him. They'd known each other such a short time, really, but she felt as if she'd known him all her life. The thought of going back to Houston without him was suddenly frightening.

She did the routine things until Sunday, except that when she gathered eggs, she was overly cautious about going into the henhouse. She'd learned from Rey that snakes often traveled in pairs, so she was careful to look before she stepped anywhere that the ground was covered.

She'd become something of a legend among the Hart ranch hands already. They removed their hats when she walked by, and they spoke to her in respectful tones.

"It's really strange," she remarked at the dinner table on Saturday evening, glancing from Leo to Rey. "The men seem sort of in awe of me."

Rey chuckled and exchanged an amused look with his brother. "They are. None of them has ever picked up a copperhead on a stick."

"It let me," she reminded him.

"That's the awesome thing," Leo remarked. "You see, Meredith, copperheads have a nasty reputation for attacking without provocation. It's kind of mystic, what you did."

He pursed his lips and gave her a teasing glance over his buttered biscuit. "Any snake charmers in your family?"

"No, but Mike had a pet boa for a while, until it ate one of the neighbor's rabbits," she sighed.

"Yuccch!" Rey said, and shivered.

"It was an accident," Meredith insisted. "It escaped out the window and was gone for three weeks. We figured it was starving, because it hadn't been fed in so long. Besides that," she added, "the rabbit was vicious. It attacked everybody who opened the cage."

"Why did the neighbor keep rabbits?"

"He sold them for meat to a specialty grocery store."

Rey chuckled. "Maybe the boa was a reincarnated taste-tester," he mused.

Leo made a face. "I wouldn't eat a rabbit if I was starving. On the other hand, snake's not so bad. Remember when we were in Arizona on that hunting trip, camping out, and our guide caught that big, juicy rattler?"

"Sure do," Rey agreed, nodding. "Tasted just like chicken!"

Obviously that was a private joke, because the brothers looked at each other and burst out laughing.

"What became of the boa?" Leo asked, interested.

"Mike had just sold it to a breeder," she recalled sadly. "He was engaged to the sweetest, kindest girl I ever knew. It devastated her when he was killed. They had to sedate her for two days, and she couldn't even go to the funeral." She shook her head. "I felt as sorry for her as I did for Dad and me."

"What happened to her?" Leo asked.

She finished her coffee. "She became a missionary and went to South America with a group of them." She winced. "She had the worst luck…it was that plane that was mistaken for drug smugglers and shot down. I think she was one of the survivors, but she didn't come back to America with the others."

"Poor kid," Rey said.

"Colter was upset over the shooting for a long time, too," Leo recalled. "Just between you and me, he was sweet on Mike's girl, but too much a gentleman to do anything about it. He thought the sun rose and set on Mike."

"I never knew," Meredith said softly.

"Neither did Mike. Or the girl," Leo added with a smile. "Colter's a clam. He never talks."

"Is he still with the Texas Rangers?" Meredith asked.

Leo nodded. "Got promoted to lieutenant just recently. He's good at his job."

She pushed back from the table. "If you two are through, I'll just wash up. Rey's going to drive me up to see my dad tomorrow."

"What a sweet guy!" Leo exclaimed with a wide-eyed look at his brother.

"He's being nice to me, because I'm the only woman who ever proposed to him," Meredith volunteered with a wicked grin. "He feels guilty because he turned me down."

"Good. I'll marry you, Meredith," Leo volunteered at once. "You just name the time and place, and I'll buy a new suit…!"

"Shut the hell up!" Rey said curtly, and hit his brother with his Stetson.

Leo protected his shoulder. "Meredith, he's picking on me!" he wailed.

"Do you want biscuits for breakfast?" she asked Rey.

He stopped flogging his brother. "All right. But only for biscuits," Rey said. He got up and deliberately bent and kissed Meredith, right in front of Leo. "Don't stay up too late. Leo and I have to check the livestock in the barn."

"Okay. Wear a jacket," she said, smiling up at him.

He bent and brushed his mouth against hers one more time. "It's not cold."

"It is. Wear a jacket," she insisted.

He sighed and made a face, but he picked up his lightweight denim jacket from the hat stand by the back door as he went out.

Leo followed him, but with a new expression on his face. He'd seen something he hadn't expected during that teasing exchange. He wondered if Rey realized that he was in love with that sweet little biscuit-making woman. And unless he missed his guess, it was mutual.

Ten

The next morning, Meredith sat next to Rey in church and felt his hand holding hers almost all the way through the service. She felt different with him than she'd ever felt with anyone else. Rey made her feel as if she could do anything. He made her feel strong and confident and safe.

She glanced up at him while they shared a hymnal and he forgot what he was singing. They searched each other's eyes slowly, until they realized that everybody else had stopped singing and were sitting down. Smiling sheepishly, Rey sat down and tugged her down beside him.

After the service, they got amused, affectionate looks from bystanders who knew Rey and had heard about his new cook.

But he didn't seem to be the least bit embarrassed by the attention. In fact, he made a point of introducing Meredith to several people, adding the little known information that she was a licensed nurse practitioner as well as a great biscuit chef.

Meredith flushed, because it sounded as if he were very proud of her, especially when he related how her quick thinking had probably saved Billy Joe's life at the target range. Billy Joe was well-known and liked locally, so that brought even more smiles. She clung to his hand with unashamed delight when they left.

"See, you're already a local celebrity," he teased. "And I didn't even get around to mentioning the snake."

"We should forget the snake," she said quickly.

He chuckled. "No, we shouldn't. It wins me points if I have a…cook who isn't even afraid of poisonous snakes."

She heard that hesitation before "cook," as if he wanted to say something else instead. It made her tingle all over. She couldn't stop smiling, all the way to the Jaguar convertible he drove when he wasn't working.

"This is a very flashy car," she commented as he put her in on the passenger side.

"I like sports cars," he said with a grin.

"So do I," she confessed. She didn't even put on a scarf. In fact, she pulled the pins out of her hair and let it fall around her shoulders.

"Won't it tangle in the wind?" he asked when they were seat-belted in place.

"I don't care." She looked at him and smiled warmly. "I like to feel the wind."

"Me, too."

He started the car, put it in gear, and pulled out onto the highway. When they were on the interstate, heading toward Houston, he let the powerful car do its best.

"Now this is a HORSE!" he called over the roar of the wind.

She laughed with pure delight. It was the most wonderful day of her life. She even forgot where they were going in the excitement of being with him in the elegant vehicle.

But all too soon, they were pulling up at an impressive brick building with its function discreetly labeled on a

metal plate near the door. It was a substance abuse reha-
bilitation center, three stories tall, and staffed impressively
with psychologists, psychiatrists, and health professionals,
including physicians.

Rey held her hand to the information desk and then up
to the second floor waiting room, where her father would
be brought to visit with them.

"They don't like visitors the first week," Rey explained
to her. "You probably knew that," he added, remembering
her profession.

"I've never had anybody in here," she said quietly. She
was nervous and she looked it.

He caught her fingers in his again and held them tight.
"It's going to be all right," he said firmly.

She met his eyes and took a deep breath. "Okay," she
said after a minute, and her body lost some of its rigidity.

There were footsteps and muffled voices. A minute later,
her father came in the door, wearing slacks and a knit shirt,
and behind him was a uniformed woman with a clipboard.

"Miss Johns? I'm Gladys Bartlett," the woman introduced herself with a firm handshake. "I'm the staff psychologist on your father's case."

"Hello, Merry," her father said hesitantly. He winced
when he noticed the faded bruises on her face. "I'm sorry,
my dear," he choked.

Meredith let go of Rey's hand and went forward to hug
her father warmly. Mr. Johns closed his eyes and hugged
her back, hard. His lips trembled as he forced them together, but tears ran down his lean, pale cheeks. "I'm so
sorry," he sobbed.

She patted him on the back and tears fell hotly from her
own eyes. "It's okay, Daddy," she whispered brokenly,
comforting him the way he'd once comforted her and Mike
when they were little, and something had hurt them. He'd

been a wonderful father. "It's okay," she said again. "You're going to be fine. We both are."

"My son. My boy!" He shook all over. "I said I was too busy to take her to the bank. I asked him...I *asked* Mike...to go instead. He'd be alive, but for me!"

"Now, Mr. Johns," the counselor said gently, "we've been over this several times already. You can't assume blame for the lawless acts of other people. Ninety-nine times out of a hundred, nothing would have happened if you'd asked your son to go to the bank on your behalf."

"But this was the one out of a hundred," he husked. "And I can't live with the guilt!"

"I've had my own problems with it," Meredith confessed. "I could have refused to go in to work that day and taken her instead."

"And you'd be lying dead instead of Mike," her father replied curtly. "And I'd be just as eaten up with guilt!"

"You're both missing the point," Rey said, standing up. "You can't control life. Nobody can."

They all looked at him. He stood quietly, his hands deep in his slacks pockets, and stared back. "Einstein said that God didn't play dice with the universe, and he was right. Even in seeming chaos, there's an order to things, a chain of events that leads inevitably to conclusions. People are links in the chain, but people don't control the events. Life has a pattern, even if we don't see it."

"You've studied philosophy," Mr. Johns said quietly.

Rey nodded. "Yes, I have."

The older man, with thinning hair and glasses and a faintly stooped posture, moved away from Meredith and smiled. "I took several courses in it, myself. You have a degree, haven't you?"

"I do, in business. A master's, from Harvard," Rey volunteered, something that Meredith hadn't even known.

"Mine is in medicine. Veterinary medicine. I'm..."

"I know. You're Dr. Alan Johns," Rey said, shaking

hands. "Your daughter is staying with us on the ranch in Jacobsville, baking biscuits, while she recovers."

Dr. Johns winced and flushed. "They told me what I did to you," he said, glancing shamefaced at his daughter. "I swear before God, I'll never take another drink as long as I live!"

"You won't get the chance," Rey said. "I intend to watch you like a red-tailed hawk."

"Excuse me?" Dr. Johns stammered.

Rey studied his boots. "We don't have a vet on staff. We have to call one down from Victoria, because our vets are overworked to death. It would be nice to have our own vet. We pay competitive salaries and you'd have your own house."

Dr. Johns sat down quickly. "Young man, I…!"

Rey lifted his head and stared him in the eyes. "You made a mistake. People do. That's why they put erasers on pencils. You can work for us. We'll keep you straight, and you won't have to take some sort of menial job in Houston just to make ends meet. You'll like the ranch," he added. "We have a good crew."

"Someone might know what I did," Dr. Johns stammered.

"Everybody knows already," Rey said, and shrugged. "It's no big deal to us. We've got one man who came back from cocaine addiction—let me tell you, that was a story and a half—and another one who was a habitual DWI for six years until we hired him and helped him get straight." He smiled. "We don't hold a man's past against him, as long as he's willing to stay straight and work hard."

Dr. Johns was having a hard time keeping control of himself, and it was obvious. "Young man, I'll work without a salary, if that's what it takes. And I promise, you'll never have cause to regret giving me a job."

"Not unless you keep calling me 'young man,'" Rey

said with a grin. "I'm Reynard Hart, but everybody calls me Rey."

"Glad to meet you," the older man said. "Rey."

Rey nodded. "How much longer will they keep you?" he asked, and glanced at the woman with the clipboard.

"Another week should do it," she said with a big smile. "And how nice, to see him with a settled environment to look forward to the day he leaves! I believe in minor miracles, but I don't see many. This is certainly one."

Rey gave her a complacent smile. "Miracles only happen for people who believe in them," he said, chuckling.

"Thanks, Rey," Meredith said huskily.

He only shrugged. "How could I ignore the father of the only woman who ever proposed to me?" he said, matter-of-factly, and with a smile that made her blush.

"You proposed to him?" her father asked with raised eyebrows.

"Several times," she said with mock disgust. "But he has to wash his dogs, so he can't marry me."

Dr. Johns laughed heartily.

The counselor relaxed. This was going to work out. Dr. Johns was never going to end up in rehab again, she was certain of it. She only wished she could say the same for more of her poor patients.

On the drive back to Jacobsville, Meredith was on top of the world. "Not only does he get a new job, but one doing what he always loved best, working around large animals."

"He likes cattle, does he?" Rey asked absently, enjoying Meredith's animated company.

"He grew up on a cattle ranch in Montana," she explained. "He was even in rodeo for six or seven years before he went to college."

Rey expelled a breath. This was going to work out even better than he'd dreamed. Amazing, he thought, how a single act of kindness could expand like ripples around a rock dropped into a pond.

"He's not much good on a horse anymore," she continued chattily, "but he really knows veterinary medicine."

"He might go back to teaching one day. Not in Houston," he added gently. "But Texas is a big state, and when he's been away from alcohol a couple of years, who knows?"

"The ranch will be good for him. You did mean it, didn't you?" she added quickly. "It wasn't something you said to help him want to get better?"

"I very rarely say things I don't mean, Meredith," he replied. "Well," he added with a frown, "I wasn't exactly telling the truth about washing the dogs."

"Excuses, excuses." She toyed with her purse. "Rey, thank you for giving him a second chance."

He laughed gently. "I've got an ulterior motive," he murmured dryly. "When you come to the ranch to visit him, you can make me a pan of biscuits."

"Just you? Not one to share with Leo?"

He shifted behind the wheel. "He can go find someone to make him biscuits," he said. "Surely, somewhere in Texas, there's a woman who'd do it just for him."

"Your other brothers, do their wives bake?"

"Dorie and Tess do," he said. "But Tira hasn't got a clue how to," he added on a sigh. "Simon doesn't mind. They have a cook who can. Although he's really not much on biscuits, so it doesn't matter." He grinned. "You should see him with his sons. Two of them now. They're still toddlers, and he's a whiz at fatherhood. Dorie and Corrigan have a boy and a girl and Cag and Tess have a son. That makes me an uncle five times over! Christmas is going to be a real treat this year."

She thought about Christmas. It was going to be a lonely one for her, with her father down here on the ranch.

He saw the look on her face and reached out to catch

her hand in his. "Hey," he said softly, "you're invited for Christmas, you know. We'll pack up the kids and go over to the annual Christmas party at the Doctors Coltrain. They have huge layouts of Lionel trains that they run every year, especially with a little boy of their own who'll be big enough to play with them in a couple of years. Draws a big crowd. Do you like train sets?"

She smiled. "I do." It lifted her heart to know that she was going to be included in the family get-together. She loved children. It would make the season less traumatic for her and her father, because they were missing two members of their immediate family.

"We'll make it a happy Christmas," he said softly.

She tangled her fingers into his. "I'll have that to look forward to, when I go back."

"It's premature right now, but if you decide to move down here, too, I'd bet good money that Micah Steele would offer you work."

She looked at his big, warm hand holding hers. "I like Jacobsville."

His fingers grew possessive. "I like *you*."

"Thanks. I like you, too, and if you'll loan me your cell phone, I'll call the minister right now and we can set a date," she added with wicked haste.

He chuckled. "Hold on, tiger, I may have been lying about washing the dogs, but marriage is a big step. You have to look out for me. I know you can tame snakes and handle heart attacks, and you bake good biscuits. But how do you look in a suit, and can you dance?"

"I look great in a suit," she said firmly, "and I can do Latin dances."

He grimaced. "I can't. How about a nice, slow two-step?"

"I can do that, too!"

He glanced at her. "What do you like to read?" he asked.

The next few minutes were spent in gleeful harmony, going over things they had in common. They liked the same basic forms of relaxation, and they even thought alike on politics and child-raising. It was a very good start. Meredith had seen far too many relationships start out with nothing more than sex for a foundation, and they didn't last. It took common interests, common beliefs, friendship, to make a lasting marriage.

Marriage. That word, once so warily approached, now seemed as natural as letting Rey hold her hand all the way back to Jacobsville. She wondered where they were going together in the future, and hoped it was someplace nice.

She had to go back to work the following week. Friday morning she had her suitcase packed. She was wearing her tailored beige suit with her blond hair in a neat ponytail when she followed Rey out the front door. He carried her suitcase to his car and put it in the trunk.

"I'll be back late this afternoon," he told Leo. "If you need me, I'll be on my cell phone." He patted the cell phone carrier on his belt.

"Oh, I think I can cope," Leo drawled with a wink at Meredith. "Don't be a stranger, Meredith," he added. "We'll miss you. But thanks for making us all those pans of frozen biscuits!"

"It's a good thing you have a walk-in freezer, is all I can say," she mused, chuckling. "But don't forget the directions on how to cook them," she added. "They're only dough until then."

"I'll have it all down pat in no time," Leo promised. "Meanwhile," he added, rubbing his big hands together with visible delight, "there are still six biscuits left over from breakfast!"

"No use asking you to save me a couple, is there?" Rey asked on a sigh.

"Blood is thicker than water, except where biscuits are involved," Leo shot back. "Sorry."

Rey got in the car and started the engine without another word.

Meredith was quiet most of the way to Houston. She was oddly reluctant to go back to work, although she loved her job. She was going to miss Rey and Leo and Mrs. Lewis. She was even going to miss the chickens.

"You can come down anytime you want to," Rey reminded her, when he noticed that she was brooding. It had been hard, but he'd kept his hands to himself for the duration of her stay at the ranch. He was planning a frontal assault in the near future. This wasn't the time, though.

"I know." She stared out the window at the bare trees and chilly flat landscape. "Thanksgiving comes along pretty soon."

"Your father will be working for us by then. You can come and spend a few days while you're off."

"I might still be on call," she worried.

He was grim and silent himself, after she said that. The rest of the way to Houston, he had the radio on, letting it fill the cool silence.

He dropped her off at her father's house. It looked cold and unwelcoming as she unlocked the front door so that he could sit her suitcase inside.

She turned back to him, her grey eyes wide and sad as they met his dark ones. He hadn't removed his hat, and it was hard to see his face in the shadow of it.

"Well, thanks for everything," she began.

He stared down at her with a sense of loss. After their ride up to Houston to visit her father, there seemed to be a curtain between them. They'd been very close that Sunday. But he'd gotten cold feet, he admitted to himself, and he'd drawn back. He felt the threat of her in his heart and he was trying to run from it. Suddenly it was like trying to run from himself.

"You'll be here alone," he said quietly. "Make sure you keep your door locked. We haven't had any reports that they caught the guys who rolled Leo. Just in case, don't let your guard down."

"I'll be fine," she promised him.

She looked so small and vulnerable standing there. He hated leaving her.

"You wear your jacket when it's cold like this," she told him firmly, noticing that he was standing in the cold wind in just the shirtsleeves of his chambray shirt.

"And my raincoat when it's raining," he said with a mocking smile. "You wear yours, too."

She hesitated. "Well, goodbye," she said after a minute.

"You and I won't ever say goodbye, Meredith," he replied. "It's 'so long.'"

She forced a smile to her lips. "So long, then."

He was still hesitating. His face was absolutely grim.

"I know where a jeweler's is open this early," she said suddenly, with mischievous enthusiasm.

It warmed him to hear her tease, to see that wonderful smile. "Do you, really?"

She nodded. "You can even have a diamond. But it would have to be a small one."

His dark eyes twinkled. "You just hold that thought," he said gently. "One of these days we might talk about this marriage hang-up of yours. Meanwhile, I've got to…"

"If you say 'wash the dogs,'" she interrupted, "I'll slug you!"

He chuckled. "I wasn't going to say that. I've got to get back and finish my marketing strategy for the next year before we have our year-end board meeting."

"I guess that's pretty complicated."

"No more than treating diseases and plotting nutrition,"

he replied. He studied her quietly. "I'll miss you. Don't stay away too long."

"Why?" she prodded.

"You have to save me from attacks on my virtue from hordes of amorous, sex-crazed women," he said without cracking a smile. "Who knows when I might weaken and give in to one of them, and then where would we be?"

"I've got my heart set on a virgin," she informed him.

He laughed helplessly. "Sorry, honey, you missed the boat by a decade or so."

She snapped her fingers. "Damn!"

"On the other hand, I didn't," he said in a deep, soft voice, and moved closer. He framed her face in his lean hands and studied it hungrily for several seconds. "You make me ache every time I touch you," he whispered, bending. "I'll starve to death before you get back."

"Starve...?" She wasn't thinking. She was watching his long, hard mouth come closer. She held her breath until it settled, ever so softly, on her parted lips. And then she didn't think at all for several long, tempestuous seconds.

Too soon, he caught her by the arms and pushed her away. "You stop that," he muttered breathlessly. "I refuse to be seduced on the front lawn."

She was trying to catch her own breath. "No problem. There's a nice soft carpet just five steps this way," she indicated the hall.

"I'm not that kind of man," he said haughtily.

She made a face at him.

He chuckled and kissed her one last time, teasingly, before he pulled back and started toward his car. "I'll call you."

"That's what they all say!" she cried after him.

"Then you call me, honey," he said in that deep, sexy voice that made her melt. "You've got my number, even if you don't know it yet." He winked and went on to the car. He didn't look back, even as he drove away. Meredith's eyes followed the car until it was out of sight. She didn't cry until she was inside, behind the closed door.

She was back at work and going crazy in no time, overrun by people with everything from stomach viruses to the flu. She had a good immune system, and she didn't catch any of the ailments, but she missed Rey terribly.

Three days before Thanksgiving, her father telephoned her from the ranch, full of excitement about his new job. He seemed like a different person. He told her he was still going to therapy sessions, but in Jacobsville with a psychologist. He was doing much better, and he was going to make everything up to his daughter, he swore it. And wasn't she coming for Thanksgiving?

It took real nerve to tell him the truth, that she hadn't been able to get off because of the time she'd already missed. There was simply nobody available to replace her. She'd have Thanksgiving Day, but nothing more.

She'd tried to beg the time off to have a long weekend, but her boss hadn't been pleased and he refused. He wanted her on call that weekend, and she couldn't be and go to Jacobsville. The office held a huge clinic for the local immigrant population on Saturdays, as well as Sunday afternoons, and Meredith was competently bilingual in medical terms. It made her indispensable. Not that she minded. These people were desperately in need of even the most basic health care, and Meredith was a whiz at preventive medicine. She counseled them, advised them on nutrition and wellness, and tried not to let her heart break at the sight of little children with rotting teeth and poor vision and a dozen other ailments that money could have corrected easily. The disparity between the rich and the poor was never more evident than in minority communities.

But the fact was, she had one day off for Thanksgiving and no real time for herself. It was a reminder of just how pressured her job really was, and how demanding. She loved what she did, but she hated being made to feel guilty when she asked for time off—something she hadn't done since her brother's and mother's untimely deaths. Actually it had been a battle royal to get time off for bereavement leave, and the funerals, and she'd had to go right back to work the day after the burials. It had been too soon, but she'd thought work would be good medicine.

Perhaps it had been, but she was living on nerves. The weeks at the Hart ranch had given her a taste of a whole other life. It was one she recalled with joy and missed every day. Most of all, she missed Rey. Now she wouldn't even see him. Her father said that he'd ask someone to loan him a vehicle, and he'd come to have Thanksgiving with her. That cheered her up a little, but it would mean she wouldn't see Rey. It was a bad blow. She told her father that she'd make dinner, which cheered him up as well.

Thanksgiving Day came, and Meredith got up before daylight to start cooking. She was determined that she and her father were going to have the best Thanksgiving dinner she could manage. She'd bought a turkey and a small ham, and raw ingredients to make dressing and sweet potato soufflé, green beans, ambrosia, homemade rolls and cherry and pumpkin pies.

She'd just taken the last pie out of the oven when she heard a car pull up in front of the house. She didn't stop to take off her apron or run a brush through her disheveled hair. She ran to the front door and opened it, just in time to see her father and Rey come up on the porch.

"Happy Thanksgiving, Merry," her father said, and hugged her warmly.

Rey grinned. "We thought you might like company to help you eat all that food," he told her.

"I didn't make any biscuits," she said worriedly. "Just homemade rolls."

"I love rolls." He held out his arms. "Well, come on,"

he chided when she hesitated. "You can't treat a red-hot matrimonial prospect like me to the cold shoulder! You'll never get me to say 'yes' from arm's length!"

Her father coughed. "I'll just, uh, check on the turkey," he said with an impish smile and went into the kitchen.

Rey nudged Meredith back inside the house, closed the door, and kissed her to within an inch of her life. He barely stopped to breathe before he was kissing her again, enfolding her in a bearish embrace while he made up for what seemed like years of abstinence.

"You'll smother me," she complained weakly.

"Stop complaining and kiss me," he murmured against her swollen lips. He kissed her ever harder.

"I'm not...complaining!" she gasped when he finally stopped.

He bit her lower lip ardently. "I am," he groaned. "Come on, woman, ravish me!"

"Here?" she exclaimed, wide-eyed.

"Well, give your father a quarter and send him to the store for cigarettes!" he asked with comical desperation between kisses.

"Nobody here smokes," she pointed out.

"Excuses, excuses," he murmured against her lips, using her own favorite complaint. His arms tightened and he only stopped when he had to breathe. "What a long, dry spell it's been, Merry," he whispered huskily. "Come back here..."

She kissed him and kissed him with no thought of the future. It was wonderful to be held and cuddled and wanted. She thought she'd never felt so much joy in her whole life as she did here, in Rey's hard arms.

"There's that carpet you mentioned when I left here last time," he said breathlessly, indicating the floor. He wiggled both eyebrows. "We can lock your father in the kitchen and you can ravish me, right here!"

"Not on your life." She linked her arms around his neck.

"I won't ravish you until you agree to marry me," she managed unsteadily.

"Is that a proposal?" he murmured huskily.

"Sure. You can have a ring. I think there's a ten-year-old cigar around here somewhere with a band on it…"

He was still kissing her between words. "I'll phone the minister first thing tomorrow. You can have a blood test at work. I already had Micah Steele do one on me. He said he'd love to have a nurse practitioner of his very own, by the way, if you're interested. We can have a Christmas wedding in Jacobsville."

Her mind was spinning. She couldn't quite understand what he was saying. Of course, he was kissing her and she could hardly think at all. "Blood test…work for Micah…Christmas wedding?" she murmured.

"Mmm-hmm," he whispered, kissing her again. "You can get me a ring whenever you like, but I got you one already." He fumbled in his jacket pocket and pulled out a velvet-covered jeweler's box. He opened it and showed it to her. Inside was a glorious emerald solitaire, and a diamond and emerald wedding band. "If you don't like it, we can throw it in the fishpond and go buy you something else…"

"I love it!" she exclaimed, flustered by the sudden turn of events.

"Good. Here." He took out the engagement ring, pocketed the box and slid it gently onto her ring finger. "Now it's official. We're engaged. Remember what you just promised," he added with a wicked grin. "The minute your father leaves, I'll let you ravish me on the carpet!"

Eleven

"But, Rey, Daddy won't leave," she whispered. "There's a turkey in the kitchen!"

"He can take it with him," he said generously.

She laughed and hugged him very hard. "I can't believe this."

"Neither can I," he said, nuzzling his cheek against hers. His arms tightened. "Even when I was suspicious of you, I couldn't bear you out of my sight. I still can't. This past week has been endless. I thought we could cool it for a few weeks, while I got things into perspective. But the only thing I got into perspective was how lonely I was without you." He lifted his head and looked down into her wide, rapt eyes. "I love my freedom. But not as much as I love you."

"And I love you, Rey," she said huskily. "I was lonely, too. I feel as if I've known you for centuries."

"Same here," he replied. "We're going to make a good marriage."

"A very good marriage," she agreed, and lifted her face so that he could kiss her again. He did, at length and very nicely, until her father came out of the kitchen with a turkey leg in one hand and asked if there were plans to take the dressing out of the oven before it got any blacker. Rey told him their news while Meredith took off at a dead run to rescue dinner.

Meredith worked out a two-week notice and gave up her job, to the dismay and regret of her boss, who hadn't wanted to lose her. He did see that she couldn't have a husband in Jacobsville and a job in Houston, however, and he made them a wedding present of a beautiful faceted crystal bowl.

Micah Steele offered her a job at his office, which she accepted with pleasure, on the understanding that she could work three days a week instead of six. Micah understood being a newlywed, since he and his Callie were still newlyweds as well, even with a baby on the way.

The only hitch was that all Rey's brothers got together and took over the wedding plans, to his dismay and Meredith's horror.

"It's going to be a humdinger of a wedding," Leo promised with relish, rubbing his hands together. "Cag had this great idea for entertainment."

"I don't want to hear it," Rey said firmly.

"You'll love this," Leo continued, unabashed. "He's got this great hard-rock band from Montana coming down to play their new hit record. They just had a hit single about getting married," he added with a rakish grin. "And they're having a caterer from San Antonio bring down the buffet lunch. The wedding gown is coming from one of the couture houses in Paris…"

"But you don't even know my size!" Meredith protested breathlessly.

"We looked in your dresses," he said imperturbably.

"Got your shoe size, too, and we also looked in your drawers and got the, ahem, other sizes." He grinned sheepishly. "Everything is couture, and silk. Only the best for our new sister-in-law," he added sweepingly.

Meredith didn't know whether to laugh or scream.

"We booked you a room at a five-star hotel for your honeymoon," he continued, glancing at Rey. "You still speak French, don't you?"

"French?" Meredith gasped.

"Well, your rooms are in Nice," he said. "The French Riviera. You've got a suite, overlooking the beach. Monaco is just on down the beach from there."

Rey whistled. "Not bad, for a rush job."

"We try to be efficient," Leo said, and his eyes twinkled. "We even ordered her a trousseau with formal gowns and casual clothes. Lots of pinks and blues and soft beige colors. We thought pastels would suit her."

Her mouth was open. She was trying to take it all in without fainting. She was only beginning to realize that the horror stories she'd heard from Tess about weddings and the brothers were true.

"You did kidnap Dorie and tie her in a sack with ribbon and carry her home to Corrigan!" she gasped.

"He didn't have a Christmas present," Leo explained patiently. "We gave him one. Look how well it worked out!"

"You hooligans!"

"Our hearts are all in the right place," Leo protested. "Besides, Dorie could bake. Which brings us to Tess, who could also bake…"

"You blackmailed Callaghan into marrying her, I heard!" Meredith was getting her second wind now.

"He's very happy. So is Tess."

"And poor Tira," she continued, unabashed. "You arranged her wedding and she didn't even get to choose her own gown, either!"

"She was pregnant. We had to hurry, there was no time," Leo explained matter-of-factly.

"I am not pregnant!" she exclaimed, red-faced.

Leo gave Rey a quick, speculative glance. "Yet," he replied. He grinned.

"If you would just give me a little time to organize my own wedding," she began, exasperated, and thought, I'm being nibbled to death by ducks...!

Leo checked his watch. "Sorry, I'm running late. The printer is waiting for me to check the proofs."

"Of what?" she burst out.

"Oh, just the wedding invitations. We're overnighting them to the people we invited. The governor's coming, so is the lieutenant governor. The vice president wanted to come, but he has to be in Singapore..." He frowned and checked his back pocket. "There they are! I almost forgot the interview questions. Here." He handed Rey two folded sheets of paper. "You'll have time to look them over before the camera crews move in."

Meredith and Rey exchanged wide glances. "What camera crews?" she asked.

"Just a few reporters," Leo waved them away with a lean hand. "You know, CNN, Fox, the international press...got to run!"

"International press!" Meredith choked.

"We've just signed an important export deal with Japan, didn't I mention it?" Leo called back. "They love organic beef, and we've got some. I mentioned it to our public relations people and they called the news people for us. Your father's writing the statement we're giving them. He's sure got a way with words, hasn't he?"

He waved again, climbed into his truck, and sped off.

"Invitations," Meredith said haltingly. "Clothes. Honeymoons. Reporters."

"Now, now," he said, pulling her into his arms. "Just think of all the work they've saved you. You'll have nothing to do but dress and say yes, and fly off to the Riviera with your brand-new husband!''

"But, but," she blurted.

"I want to marry you right away," he added. "You're a qualified health professional, and I have a terrible pain that you can cure in only one night."

She got the idea, belatedly, and hit him.

He chuckled, bending to kiss her gently. "It's no use trying to stop them," he said. "Besides, they're very good at it. I used to be, too." He scowled. "Somehow, it's not as much fun being on the receiving end, though."

She just shook her head.

The wedding was beautiful, despite her misgivings. Meredith wore the most gorgeous gown she'd ever seen, with yards and yards of exquisite lace over satin, with a long veil made of the same lace and a bouquet of pure white roses. Her father gave her away, and all four of Rey's brothers were best men. Tess, Cag's wife, stood with Meredith as her matron of honor. In a very short time, the two women had become close friends.

Most of Jacobsville turned out for the affair, but Meredith had eyes only for her handsome husband, who was dressed to the hilt as well. They exchanged rings and Rey lifted the veil very slowly. He'd been romantic and gentle and teasing over the days before the wedding. But when he looked at her now, his eyes were quiet and loving and very solemn. He bent and kissed her with such tenderness that she knew she'd remember the moment for the rest of her life.

They clasped hands and ran down the aisle and out of the church together, laughing gaily as they were pelted with rice and rose petals. At the waiting limousine, Meredith turned and tossed her bouquet. Surprisingly it was caught by Janie Brewster, notorious locally for her rubber chicken dinners and trying to catch Leo Hart's eye. She blushed vividly and clutched the bouquet, her eyes on it and not on anyone nearby. Which was as well, because Leo looked suddenly homicidal as the ranch foreman elbowed him and grinned.

The newlyweds waved and dived into the limousine, already packed and ready to take them to the airport. They'd already announced that the reception would have to go on without them, to the brothers' shock and dismay.

"I hated for us to miss it," Rey told her on the way to the airport, "but I know my brothers. They'd have found some way to embarrass us."

She chuckled, snuggling close to him. "Well, we're safe now."

The flight to France was long and boring. They held hands and couldn't sleep as the little computers above the seats marked the long trail on a map, showing the progress of the flight. When the jumbo jet finally landed, they walked like zombies into the airport to go through passport control and then on to wait for their luggage so that they could get through customs and to the waiting car that would take them to their hotel. The driver, holding a sign that read Hart Newlyweds had met them at the gate and arranged to meet them at customs. Meredith was yawning visibly when they found the driver and followed him and the wheeled luggage out the door. He and Rey exchanged comments that went right over Meredith's head.

"I don't speak French," she said worriedly when they were in the car. "I took a double minor in German and Spanish."

"No Latin?" he teased.

"There's a special course of it for nursing students," she replied with a smile. "Fortunately you don't have to learn the whole language anymore, although I wouldn't have minded. I'm so tired!"

"We'll have a nice long rest when we get to the hotel."
He pulled her close. "I could use a little sleep myself!"

The car pulled up under the covered entrance and a bell-
boy came out to get the luggage. Rey paid the driver and
made arrangements to contact him when they were ready
to go sightseeing in a day or two.

Meredith followed Rey and the luggage to the desk clerk
and waited while he got the key to their suite.

It didn't take long. Rey unlocked the door and opened
it. And the bellhop burst into helpless laughter.

There, on the bed, very obviously courtesy of the Hart
boys, were two life-size blow-up dolls, a blond female and
a dark-haired male, in the midst of a garden of thornless
roses of every color known to man. They were obviously
engaged in a notorious newlywed ritual.

Rey tipped the bellhop and opened the door himself,
waving the man out while he tried not to bend over double
laughing.

When he closed the door again, Meredith was removing
the dolls and roses with tears of mirth running down her
cheeks.

"Just wait until they break something, anything," she
threatened. "We can have them put in body casts for a
sprained ankle…!"

He came up behind her and caught her around the waist.
"And I'll help you. But, later, sweetheart," he added in a
soft, hungry tone as he turned her into his arms. "Much,
much…later!"

She was a professional health care worker. She knew all
the mechanics of marriage. In fact, she counseled young
wives in them. This was totally out of her experience.

Rey undressed her with slow precision, while he kissed
every soft inch of skin as he uncovered it. He never rushed.
He seemed to have committed the whole night to her

arousal, and he went about it like a soldier with a battle plan.

She was teased, caressed, kissed until she felt as if there wasn't a bed under her at all. The roses were scattered over the carpet by now, along with half the bed linen. She was under him and then over him as he increased the insistence of his hands and mouth on her body. She heard high-pitched little cries of pleasure and barely realized that they were coming from her own throat.

One particularly enthusiastic embrace landed them on the carpet, cushioned by the sheet and blanket and, under them, the thick comforter.

"The bed," she whispered, trembling with unsatisfied hunger.

"It will still be there when we're finished," he replied breathlessly as his mouth bent again to her taut, arching breasts. "Yes, do that again, sweetheart!" he added when she pulled his head down to her.

He guided her hands along his lean, fit body to his hips and pressed them there as he suddenly shifted between her soft legs and his mouth ground into hers with intent.

The abrupt shift in intensity took her by surprise and lessened the sharp pain of his possession of her. His hard mouth absorbed the tiny cry that pulsed out of her tight throat, and his hands moved under her hips to caress her.

After a few seconds, she began to relax. He shifted again and found the place, and the pressure, that made her lift toward him instead of trying to escape the downward rhythm of his hips.

She clung to his damp shoulders as the little bites of pleasure became great, shivering waves. She could feel him in every cell of her body, and she wanted to look at him, to see his face, but she was intent on some distant goal of pleasure that grew by the second. Her mouth opened against the hollow of his shoulder and she moaned, her eyes closed, her body following the lead of his own as the heated minutes lengthened.

Her nails suddenly stabbed into his back and she gasped.

"Yes," he groaned at her ear. "Now, baby, now, now...!"

As if her body had given him some secret signal, his hips became insistent and the rhythm increased to madness. She reached, reached...reached...until the pleasure exploded inside her and began to spread in racking hot waves from her head to her toes. She rippled with him, sobbed against his skin, as the ecstasy she'd never known flamed through her with hurricane force.

"Rey!" She cried out pitifully as the wave peaked, and she felt her body go incandescent with joy.

His hands gripped her hips as he riveted her to his insistent hips. She heard his breathing become raspy and hoarse and then stop as he groaned endlessly against her throat and his entire body convulsed over her.

She felt him shake as the madness began to drift away.

"Are you all right?" she whispered urgently.

"I'm...dying," he choked.

"Rey!"

She held him close until the harsh contractions of his body slowed and then stopped. He collapsed on her with his whole weight, his breathing as labored as his heartbeat. His mouth burrowed into her throat hungrily.

"Never like that, Mrs. Hart," he whispered huskily. "You just made me a whole man!"

"Did I, really?" she whispered with a silly giggle.

He laughed, too. "That's what it felt like." He sighed heavily and lifted his head to look at her. His hair was as damp as hers, and he looked exhausted. He brushed loose blond strands away from her cheeks. "I'm glad we waited. I hope you are."

"Yes." Filled with wonder, she touched his hard mouth, which was swollen from its long contact with hers. "I think

I swallowed the sun,'' she whispered. ''It was…glorious!''
She hid her face in his throat, still shy of him, especially
now.

He laughed again, lazily brushing his mouth over her
closed eyes. ''Glorious,'' he agreed with a long sigh. He
rolled away from her gently, onto his back, and pulled her
against him. ''We fell off the bed,'' he remarked after a
minute.

''I thought we were thrown off it,'' she murmured sleepily. ''You know, by the hurricane.''

''Hurricane.'' He kissed her forehead gently. ''That's
what it felt like.''

''I'm sleepy. Is it normal?''

''Yes, it is, and it does worlds for my masculinity,'' he
drawled. ''Feel free to tell anyone you like that you rav-
ished me to such an extent that I fell out of bed in my
excitement, and you went to sleep from the tidal wave of
pleasure!''

She managed one tired little chuckle. ''I'll take out an
ad in a magazine,'' she promised. She wrapped her arms
and one leg around him, completely uninhibited now. ''I
love you, but I have to go to sleep now.''

''Suit yourself, but I hope you're not throwing in the
towel. I'm a brand-new bridegroom, remember, you can't
just roll over and go to sleep once you've had your way
with me…Meredith? Meredith!''

It was no use. She was sound asleep, worn-out by the
pace of the wedding and her first passion. He lay watching
her sleep, his eyes quiet and tender and loving. It had already been, he mused, one hell of a wedding night, even
if they hadn't waited for it to get dark.

When she woke up, she was wearing a nightgown and
lying on the bed, under the covers. Rey was sipping coffee
and sniffing freshly cooked food under silver lids. He

glanced up as Meredith sat up in bed and blinked her eyes sleepily.

"Supper?" she asked.

He grinned. "Supper. Come and eat something."

She pulled herself out of bed, feeling a little uncomfortable and grinning as she realized why. She sat down beside Rey, who was wearing a pair of blue silk pajama bottoms and nothing else, and looked under lids.

"Seafood," she sighed, smiling. "My favorite."

"Mine, too. Dig in, honey." He reached over and kissed her softly and gave her a wicked grin. "It's going to be a long, lovely night!"

And it was.

They came back to the ranch after several magical, wonderful days together to find the house deserted. There was a note propped up on the kitchen table, obviously left by Leo, because his name was signed to it.

"Goodbye, cruel world," it read. "Have run out of biscuits. No relief in sight. Can't go on. Have gone into Jacobsville to kidnap a cook or beg door-to-door for biscuits. If I fail, drag the river. P.S. Congratulations Meredith and Rey. Hope you liked the wedding present. Love, Leo."

"He wouldn't really kidnap a cook," Meredith said.

"Of course not," Rey agreed. But he had a very odd look on his face.

"Or beg door-to-door for a biscuit."

"Of course not," Rey repeated.

Meredith went to the telephone. "I'll call Dad."

He waited while she dialed the cottage her father occupied and tapped his foot while it rang and rang.

"Dad?" she asked suddenly. "Have you seen Leo?"

There was a pause, while Rey gestured with his hands for her to tell him something. She flapped a hand at him while she listened and nodded.

"Okay, Dad, thanks! Yes, we had a lovely honeymoon! We'll have you up for supper tomorrow. Love you, too!"

She hung up and sighed. "Well, Leo's gone to San Antonio."

"What the hell for?" he exclaimed.

"Apparently he walked out of Barbara's café with a cook in his arms and put him in the ranch truck..."

"*Him?*" Rey exclaimed.

"Him." She sighed. "The cook escaped out the other door and ran to get Chet Blake."

"The chief of police?" Rey looked horrified.

"Chet was laughing so hard that he didn't get to the café before Leo took off in a cloud of dust, barely escaping public disgrace. He tried to hire the little man to bake him some biscuits, but the cook refused, so Leo took harsh measures." She chuckled. "Dad said he phoned halfway to San Antonio and said he'd be back in a few days. He thinks he'll go to that genetics workshop until the heat dies down here."

"We'll never live that story down," Rey sighed, shaking his head.

"There is a solution," she remarked. "We can find him a nice wife."

He laughed even harder. "Leo's the one of us who'll have to be dragged to the altar behind a big horse," he told her. "For all that Janie Brewster is desperate to marry him, he's as elusive as smoke."

"Janie's pretty," she recalled, because the girl caught her bridal bouquet at the wedding.

"She's a doll, but she can't boil water," Rey told her. "He'd never get a biscuit if he married Janie. Besides, she's not mature enough for him."

"She could change."

"So could he, sweetheart," he drawled, pulling her close to kiss her. "But I wouldn't hold my breath in either case. Now here we are, at home, and all alone, and I'll give you one guess what I'd like you to do next," he whispered suggestively.

She smiled under his lips. "Would it have something to do with flour and olive oil and skim milk and a hot oven?" she whispered back.

He actually gasped. "Darling!" he exclaimed, and kissed her even harder.

She linked her arms around his neck. "So," she whispered, moving closer, "Just how badly do you want that pan of biscuits, sweetheart?" she teased.

Chuckling, he bent and lifted her clear of the floor and turned down the hall. "Let me show you!"

Eventually he got a pan of fresh biscuits and a whole jar of fresh apple butter to go on them—along with a nice pat of low-fat margarine. And he didn't even complain!

*   *   *   *   *

Texas Hero

MERLINE LOVELACE

MERLINE LOVELACE

spent twenty-three years as an air force officer, serving tours at the Pentagon and at bases all over the world, before she began a new career as a novelist. When she's not tied to her keyboard, this RITA® Award-winning author and her husband of thirty years, Al, enjoy travelling, golf and long lively dinners with friends and family.

This book is dedicated to my own handsome
hero, who I first met in the shadow of the
Alamo. Many thanks for all those wonderful
San Antonio memories, my darling.

Prologue

"Thank God for air-conditioning!"

Swiping a forearm across his dirt-streaked forehead, the tall, flame-haired grad student followed his team leader into the welcoming coolness of San Antonio's Menger Hotel.

"If I'd had any idea how muggy it gets down here in July," he grumbled, "I wouldn't have let you talk me into assisting you on this project."

"Funny," the woman beside him responded with a smile, "I seem to recall a certain Ph.D. candidate *begging* me to let him in on the dig."

"Yeah, well, that was before I realized I'd be branded as a defiler of history and practically run out of Texas on a rail."

Elena Maria Alazar's smile faded. Frowning, she shifted the strap of her heavy field case from one aching shoulder to the other and stabbed at the elevator buttons. Eric's complaints weren't all that exaggerated. He and everyone else working the project had come under increasingly vitriolic fire in recent days.

Dammit, she shouldn't have allowed the media to poke around the archeological site, much less elicit a hypothesis as to the identity of the remains found in the creek bed. She was an expert in her field, a respected member of the American Society of Forensic Historians, for pity's sake! She headed a highly skilled team of anthropologists and archeologists. She knew better than to let her people discuss their initial findings with reporters. Particularly when those findings held such potentially explosive local significance.

She couldn't blame anyone but herself for the howls of outrage that rose when the *San Antonio Express-News* reported that Dr. Elena Alazar, niece of Mexico's President Alazar and professor of history at the University of Mexico, was rewriting Texas history. According to the story, Ellie had found proof that legendary William Barrett Travis, commander of the Texans at the Alamo, hadn't died heroically with his men as always believed. Instead, he'd run away from the battle, was hunted down by Santa Anna's troops and was shot in back like a yellow, craven coward.

Ellie and her team were a long way yet from *proving* anything, but try telling that to the media! The *Express-News* wasn't any more interested in running a disclaimer than a correction to identify her as a professor of history at the University of *New* Mexico. Never mind that Ellie had been born and raised in the States. To the reporter's mind—and to the minds of his readers—she was an outsider attempting to mess with Texas history.

Thoroughly disgruntled, she made another stab at the brass-caged elevator. It was an antique, like everything else in the hundred-year-old hotel located just steps from the Alamo. Until the story broke, Ellie had thoroughly enjoyed her stay at the luxuriously appointed establishment. Now, she felt the weight of disapproval from every employee at the hotel, from desk clerks to the maid who cleaned her room.

She didn't realize just how much she'd earned the locals' displeasure, however, until she unlocked the door to her suite. Startled, she stopped dead. Behind her, Eric let out a long, low whistle.

''Folks around here sure let you know when they're not happy. I haven't seen a room trashed this bad since pledge week at the frat house. Come to think of it, I've *never* seen a room trashed this bad.''

The two-room suite hadn't been just trashed, Ellie soon discovered. It had been ransacked. Her laptop computer was gone, as was the external drive that stored the data and thousands of digital images her team had collected to date.

The loss of her equipment was bad enough, but the message scrawled across the mirror above the dresser made her skin crawl.

Mexican bitch.
I've got you in my crosshairs.
Get the hell out of Texas!

Chapter 1

Washington, D.C., steamed in the late afternoon
July heat. On a quiet side street just off Massachusetts Avenue, in the heart of the embassy district, the
chestnut trees drooped like tired old women and tar
bubbled in the cracks of the sidewalk. The broad-
shouldered man who emerged from a Yellow Cab
took care not to step in the sticky blackness as he
crossed the sidewalk and mounted the front steps of
an elegant, Federal-style town house located midway
down the block.

He paused for a moment, his gaze thoughtful as
he studied the discreet bronze plaque beside the front
door. The inscription on the plaque identified the
three-story town house as home to the offices of the

President's special envoy. Most Washingtonians considered the special envoy's position a meaningless one, created years ago for a billionaire campaign contributor with a yen for a fancy title and an office in the nation's capital. Only a handful of insiders knew the special envoy also served as the head of a covert agency whose initials comprised the last letter of the Greek alphabet, OMEGA. An agency that, as its name implied, was activated only as a last resort in instances when other, more established organizations like the CIA or the Department of Defense couldn't respond for legal or practical reasons.

This was one of those instances.

Squaring his shoulders, the visitor entered the foyer and approached the receptionist seated behind a graceful Queen Ann desk.

"I am Colonel Luis Esteban. I'm here to see the special envoy."

"Oh, my! So you are."

Elizabeth Wells might have qualified for Medicare a number of years ago, but her hormones still sat up and took notice of a handsome man. And Colonel Luis Esteban, as OMEGA agent Maggie Sinclair had reported after a mission deep in the jungles of Central America, was gorgeous—drop-your-jaw, boggle-your-eyes gorgeous.

Elizabeth managed to keep her jaw from sagging, but the colonel's dark, melting eyes, pencil-thin black mustache and old-world charm did a serious number on her heart rate.

"I believe the special envoy is expecting me."

"What? Oh! Yes, of course. Mr. Jensen's in his office. With Chameleon, as you requested."

"Ah, yes." A small, private smile played about the colonel's mouth. "Chameleon."

Elizabeth's pulse tripped again, but not with pleasure this time. Having served as personal assistant to both Maggie *and* her husband, Adam Ridgeway, during their separate tenures as director of OMEGA, Elizabeth wouldn't hesitate to empty the Sig Sauer 9 mm tucked in her desk drawer into anyone who tried to come between them. With something very close to a sniff, she lifted the phone on her desk and buzzed her boss. Her gaze had cooled several degrees when she relayed his reply.

"Go right in, Colonel."

"Thank you."

Luis walked down a short hall, opened a door shielded from attack by a lining of Kevlar, took one step inside and plunged into chaos. There was an ear-shattering woof. A flash of blue and orange. A chorus of shouts.

"Dammit, he's doing it again."

"Radizwell! No!"

"Shut the door, man!"

A hissing, bug-eyed lizard the size of a small hound darted between Luis's legs. A second later, a

huge sheepdog tried to follow. Knocked sideways,
Luis grabbed the door handle while the furiously
barking hound raced after the iguana. Doubling back,
the lizard leaped for the safety of a polished mahog-
any conference table. Once there, it whipped out a
foot-long tongue and spit at the jumping, madly woof-
ing hound.

"Nick!" Half-laughing and wholly exasperated,
Maggie Sinclair shouted an appeal to OMEGA's current director. "Get Radizwell out of here."

The man who answered her plea sported a lean,
well-muscled body under his elegantly tailored suit,
but it took all his strength to drag the vociferously
protesting hound out of the office. Deep, mournful
howls followed him when he returned. Closing the
door to muffle the yowls, he smoothed his blond hair
with a manicured hand and shot Luis a wry smile.

"Nick Jensen, Colonel. I'd apologize for the noisy
reception, but…" He glanced at the still hissing giant
iguana. "I understand you were the diabolical fiend
who gave Maggie her pet in the first place."

"Yes, he was." A smile lighting her eyes, Maggie
Sinclair came across the spacious office and held out
both hands. "Hello, Luis. How are you?"

Esteban's gaze took in her glowing face, dropped
to her gently rounded stomach. Regret punched
through him. He'd had his chance with this woman
a number of years ago. She slipped away from him

then, as changeable and lightning quick as her code name implied.

Luis had come to Washington on urgent business at the request of the president of Mexico. Only he knew that he also brought with him the half-formed idea of reigniting the sparks that had once flared between Maggie and him. He'd heard she'd left OMEGA to finish writing a book and raise her two small daughters. He'd thought perhaps she might be bored and ready for a touch of excitement. He could see at a glance that wasn't the case, however. Maggie Sinclair wore the look of a woman well and truly loved.

Swallowing a small sigh, he lifted her hands and dropped a light kiss on the back of each. "I'm well, Chameleon. And you... You are as lively and beautiful as ever."

"I don't know about the beautiful part, but my family certainly keeps things lively." Rueful laughter filled her honey brown eyes. "I thought you might want to see how your gift has grown over the years. Unfortunately, Terence won't go anywhere these days without his buddy, the sheepdog you just met. They're best of pals until Radizwell, er, well..."

"Gets the hots for the damned thing," the third person in the room said. He strolled forward, his blue eyes keen in his aristocratic face. "Adam Ridgeway, colonel."

"Ah, yes," Luis drawled, returning both the

strong grip and rapierlike scrutiny. "Maggie's husband."

"Maggie's husband," he affirmed with a smile that sent an instant and unmistakable message. "Hope you don't mind if I sit in on your meeting. I'm told it involves one of the agents I recruited for OMEGA."

Instantly all business, Luis Esteban nodded. "Yes, it does. Jack Carstairs. I understand he's on his way to San Antonio."

"He left a few hours ago," Nick Jensen replied, gesturing the other three to seats well away from the conference table occupied by the wary, unblinking iguana. "What *we* don't understand, however, is how Renegade's mission concerns you."

"Allow me to explain. When I first met Chameleon, I was chief of security for my country. I've since retired and established my own firm. I do very private, very discreet work for a number of international clients. The President of Mexico is one of them. He asked me to run a background check on Jack Carstairs."

Nick's brows lifted. "Did he?"

"Yes. You know, of course, that Carstairs once had an affair with President Alazar's niece."

"We know. Which made us wonder why he requested Carstairs for this mission in the first place."

"He didn't, actually. The request came from his niece."

Flicking his shirt cuff over his gold Rolex, Luis picked his way through a potentially explosive international minefield.

"As you're aware, Elena's father—President Alazar's youngest brother—emigrated to the States as a young man. He and Ellie's mother met in Santa Fe and married after a whirlwind courtship. Unfortunately, Carlos Alazar died before his daughter was born, but his wife made sure Ellie spent summers with her father's family in Mexico. During one of those visits, Ellie met a Marine pulling guard duty at the U.S. Embassy. Their affair was brief and, I'm told, rather indiscreet."

"Indiscreet enough to get Gunnery Sergeant Carstairs sent home in disgrace and subsequently booted out of the Marines," Nick acknowledged.

"Evidently Ellie feels a lingering responsibility for ruining the man's military career. When her uncle decided she needed a bodyguard, she insisted it be Carstairs. Which is why President Alazar hired me to check him out."

"How did you get past Renegade's cover and make the link to OMEGA?" Nick asked, not liking the idea that one of his agents had been compromised.

Luis merely smiled. "I think Chameleon will attest that I, too, possess certain skills. Suffice to say I uncovered his connection to OMEGA and advised President Alazar, who subsequently made the call to your President, requesting Carstairs's services.''

''And now President Alazar's having second thoughts about the request?''

''Let's just say he's worried that Carstairs's past involvement with his niece might get in the way of his ability to maintain the detachment required for this job.''

Nick Jensen, code name Lightning, didn't for a second doubt Jack Carstairs's ability to do his job. During Nick's days as an operative, he'd gone into the field with Renegade more than once and had gained a profound respect for his skills. Nick also, however, possessed a Gallic understanding of the power of passion.

Once a skinny, perpetually hungry pickpocket who called the back streets of Cannes home, Henri Nicolas Everard had been adopted by Paige and Doc Jensen, moved to the States and had grown to manhood in a house filled with love. He'd parlayed the near starvation of his childhood into a string of high-priced restaurants scattered around the globe.

Nick was now a millionaire many times over. His cover as a jet-setter gave him access to the world of movie princes and oil sheikhs. It had also led to a number of discreet affairs with some of the world's most beautiful women. A true connoisseur, he could understand why Jack Carstairs had sacrificed his military career for a fling with Elena Maria Alazar. The background dossier compiled by OMEGA's chief of communications had painted a portrait of an astonishingly vibrant, incredibly intelligent woman.

Not unlike OMEGA's chief of communications herself, Nick thought. A mental image of Mackenzie Blair replaced that of Ellie Alazar and produced a sudden tightening just below his Italian leather belt. Both amused and perturbed by the sensation, Nick offered his assurances to Colonel Esteban.

"OMEGA wouldn't have sent Renegade into the field if we weren't absolutely confident in his ability to protect Dr. Alazar. If it will ease President Alazar's mind, however, I'll pass on his concerns."

"Perhaps you might also keep me apprised of the situation in San Antonio," Esteban suggested politely.

Everyone in the room recognized that they were treading tricky diplomatic ground here. Relations between the United States and Mexico had reached new, if somewhat shaky, levels with the recent North American Free Trade Association Treaty. The last thing either president wanted right now was an ugly international incident souring an economic agreement that had taken decades to hammer out.

"Not a problem," Nick said smoothly. "Once we ascertain that's what President Alazar wishes, of course."

"Of course." Rising, the colonel dug into his suit

pocket and produced a business card. "You can contact me day or night at this number."

His gaze drifted to Maggie, who rose and gave him a warm smile.

"Don't worry, Luis. Renegade's one of the best field operatives in the business. He wouldn't be working for OMEGA otherwise."

With that blithe assurance, she strolled across the office and clipped a leash on the unblinking iguana. Identical expressions of repulsion crossed the faces of Nick and the colonel as the creature's long tongue flicked her cheek in a quick, adoring kiss. Adam merely looked resigned.

"We'll walk you out," he said to Esteban. "Lightning has some calls to make."

OMEGA's acting director made the calls from the control center located on the third floor.

Mackenzie Blair ruled OMEGA's CC, just as she used to rule the command, control and communication centers aboard the Navy ships she'd served on. She loved this world of high-tech electronics, felt right at home in the soft green glow from the wall-size computer screens—far more at home than she'd ever felt in the two-bedroom condo she and her ex had once shared.

One of the problems was that she and David had never stayed in port together long enough to establish joint residency. He'd adjusted to the separations better than Mackenzie had, though. She discovered that when she returned two days early from a Caribbean cruise and found the jerk in bed with a neighbor's wife.

She'd sworn off men on the spot. Correction, she'd planted a very hard, very satisfying knee in David's groin when he'd grabbed her arm and tried to explain, *then* sworn off men.

Lately, though, she'd been reconsidering forever. Her itchy restlessness had nothing to do with her boss. Nothing at all. Just a woman's natural needs and the grudging realization that even the most sophisticated high-tech gadgets couldn't *quite* substitute for a man.

Which was why goose bumps raised all over her skin when Lightning strolled over to her command console with the casual grace that characterized him.

''Patch me through to the White House.''

She cocked a brow. She wasn't in the Navy now.

''Please,'' Lightning added with an amused smile.

All too conscious of his proximity, Mackenzie transmitted the necessary code words and verifications, then listened with unabashed interest to the brief conversation between Lightning and the Prez. When it was over, she leaned back in her chair and angled OMEGA's director a curious look.

''Sounds like Renegade's got the weight of the free world riding on his shoulders on this one.''

''The weight of North America, anyway.''

His gaze lingered on her upturned face. Mackenzie had almost forgotten how to breathe by the time he murmured a request that she get Renegade on the line.

His eyes, narrowed and rattlesnake-mean behind his mirrored sunglasses, Jack Carstairs snapped shut the phone Mackenzie Blair had issued him mere hours ago. The damned thing was half the size of a cigarette pack and bounced signals off a secure telecommunications satellite some thirty-six thousand kilometers above the earth. Lightning's message had come through loud and clear.

Renegade was to keep his hands off Elena Maria Alazar.

As if he needed the warning! He'd learned his lesson the first time. No way was he going to get shot down in flames again.

Hefting his beat-up leather carryall, he walked out of the airport into a flood of heat and honeysuckle-scented air. A short tram ride took him to the rental agency, where he checked out a sturdy Jeep Cherokee.

The drive from the airport to downtown San Antonio took only about fifteen minutes, long enough for Jack to work through his irritation at the call. Not long enough, however, to completely suppress the prickly sensation that crawled along his nerves at the thought of seeing Ellie Alazar again.

His jaw set, he negotiated the traffic in the city's center and pulled up at the Menger. Constructed in 1859, the hotel was situated on Alamo Plaza, right next to the famous mission. The little blurb Jack had read in one of the airline's magazines during the flight down indicated the Menger had played host to a roster of distinguished notables. Reportedly, Robert E. Lee rode his horse, Traveller, right into the lobby. Teddy Roosevelt tipped a few in the bar while organizing and training his Rough Riders. Sarah Bernhardt, Lillie Langtry and Mae West had all brought their own brand of luster to the hotel.

Now Elena Maria Alazar was adding another touch of notoriety to the venerable institution. One Jack suspected wasn't particularly appreciated by the management.

He killed the engine, then climbed out of the Cherokee. A valet took the car keys. Another offered to take his bag.

"I've got it."

Anyone else entering the hotel's three-story lobby for the first time might have let their gaze roam the cream marble columns, magnificent wrought-iron balcony railings and priceless antiques and paintings. Six years of embassy guard duty and another eight working for OMEGA had conditioned Jack to automatically note the lobby's physical layout, security camera placement and emergency egress routes. His boot heels echoing on the marble floors, he crossed to the desk. There he was handed a message. Ellie was waiting for him in the taproom.

After the blazing sun outside and dazzling white marble of the lobby, the bar wrapped Jack in the welcoming gloom of an English pub. A dark cherry-wood ceiling loomed above glass-fronted cabinets, beveled mirrors and high-backed booths. A stuffed moose head with a huge rack of antlers surveyed the scene with majestic indifference, wreathed in the mingled scents of wood polish and aged Scotch.

Instinctively, Jack peeled off his sunglasses and recorded the bar's layout, but the details sifted right through his conscious mind to be stored away for future reference. His main focus, his only focus, was the woman who swiveled at the sound of his foot-steps.

His first thought was that she hadn't changed. Her mink brown hair still tumbled in a loose ponytail down her back. Her cinnamon eyes still looked out at the world through a screen of thick, black lashes. In her short-sleeved red top and trim-fitting tan shorts, she looked more like a teenager on vacation than a respected historian with a long string of ini-tials after her name.

Not until he stepped closer did he notice the dif-ferences. The Ellie he'd known nine years ago had glowed with youth and laughter and a vibrant joy of life. This woman showed fine lines of stress at the corners of her mouth. Shadows darkened her eyes, and he saw in their brown depths a wariness that echoed his.

She didn't smile. Didn't ease her stiff-backed pose. Silence stretched between them. She broke it, finally, with a cool greeting.

"Hello, Jack."

He'd expected to feel remnants of the old anger, the resentment, the fierce hurt. He hadn't expected the punch to his gut that came with the sound of her voice. His head dipped in a curt nod. It was the best he could manage at the moment.

"Thanks for coming," she said cooly.

He moved closer, wanting her to see his face when he delivered the speech he'd been preparing since Lightning informed him of the nature of his mission.

"Let's get one thing straight, right here and right now. My job is to protect you. That's the reason I'm here. That's the *only* reason I'm here."

Her chin snapped up. The fire he remembered all too well flared hot and dark in her eyes.

"I didn't imagine you'd make the trip down to San Antonio for any other reason. We had our fun, Jack. We both enjoyed our little fling. But that's all it was. You made that quite clear when you walked away from me nine years ago."

His jaw tightened. He had no answer for that. There *was* no answer. Eyes hard, he watched her slide off the bar stool. Her scent came with her as she approached, a combination of sun and the deli-

cate cactus pear perfume she'd always worn. It was
her mother's concoction, he remembered her telling
him. He also remembered that he'd been nuzzling her
neck at the time. Deliberately, Jack slammed the door
on the thought.

When she raised a hand to shove back a loose
tendril of hair, however, the gleam of silver circling
her wrist brought another, sharper memory. The two-
inch-wide beaten silver bracelet had cost him a half-
month's pay. He'd slipped it onto her wrist mere moments before her uncle's police had arrived to arrest
him.

"Let's go upstairs," he instructed tersely. "I want
to see the message your friend left you."

Chapter 2

Wrapping her arms around her middle, Ellie stood just inside the door of the trashed suite.

"I moved to another room. The hotel wanted to clean up the mess, but I asked them to leave it until you got here."

His face impassive, Jack surveyed the mess. "Did the police find anything?"

"They dusted for prints, interviewed the hotel staff and asked for a complete inventory of the missing items, but as far as I know, they haven't come up with any concrete leads. In fact…"

"In fact?"

Her shoulders lifted under the chili red top. "The detective in charge was somewhat less than sympathetic. Evidently he read the story about me in the *Light* and doesn't take kindly to Mexicans determined to rewrite Texas history. It doesn't seem to make a whole lot of difference to some folks that I'm as American as they are.''

''No, it wouldn't.''

Jack had seen more than his share of bigotry during his overseas tours, both in the Marines and as an OMEGA agent. It didn't matter what a person's race, creed or financial circumstances might be. There was always someone who hated him or her because of them. With a mental note to establish liaison with the detective handling Ellie's case as soon as he conducted his preliminary assessment of the situation, he eyed the message on the mirror.

The wording suggested a man, someone familiar with weapons and not afraid to let Ellie know it. The obvious inference was that the threat stemmed from her work. Jack never trusted the obvious.

''I want a complete background brief on the members on your team,'' he told her, making a final sweep of the premises. ''Particularly anyone who might or might not have a grudge against the team's leader.''

Startled, she dropped her arms. ''You think one of my own people is responsible for this?''

''I don't think anything at this point. I'm just assessing the situation.''

Her eyes huge, she stared at him. Jack could see

the doubt creep into their cinnamon brown depths, followed swiftly by dismay. Only now, he guessed, was it occurring to her that the leak to the press might have been more deliberate than accidental. That one of her team members might, in fact, be working behind the scenes on some hidden agenda of his or her own.

The years fell away. For a moment, he caught a glimpse in her stricken face of the trusting, passionate girl she'd once been.

He'd come so close to loving that girl. Closer than he'd ever come to loving anyone who didn't wear khaki. Until Ellie, the Marines had been his life. Until Ellie, the Corps had constituted the only family he'd ever wanted or needed. He'd never known his father's name. He'd long ago buried the memory of the mother who left her four-year-old son in the roach-infested hotel room and drove off with some poor slob she'd picked up in a bar. After years of being passed from one foster home to another, Jack had walked into a recruiting office on his eighteenth birthday, signed up and found a home.

He shot up through the ranks, from private to corporal to gunnery sergeant in minimal time. He learned to follow and to lead. Because of his outstanding record, he was selected for the elite Marine Security Guard Battalion. His first tour was at the U.S. Embassy in Gabon, Africa, his second at the plush post in Mexico City.

The debacle in Mexico City had ended his career and destroyed all sense of family with the Corps. Thankfully, he'd found another home in OMEGA. This one, he vowed savagely, he wouldn't jeopardize by tumbling Ellie into the nearest bed.

"I also want a copy of your list of missing items."

The dismay left Ellie's face. Stiffening at his curt tone, she gave him an equally succinct response. "I'll print you out a copy. It runs to more than fifty pages."

"Fifty pages!"

The exclamation earned him a condescending smile. "My team's been on-site for almost a week now. We've recorded hundreds of digital images, cross-indexed them and made copious notes concerning each. The data was all stored in the external FireWire drive that was stolen. Thank God I backed the files up via the university's remote access mainframe!"

With that heartfelt mutter, she led the way down the hall to the new set of rooms the hotel had assigned her. Jack followed, forcing himself to keep his gaze on her back, her hair, the stiff set to her shoulders under her top. On anything, dammit, but the seductive sway of her hips.

A swift prowl around the spacious corner suite she showed him to had him shaking his head. "Pack your things."

"I beg your pardon?"

"I'll call the front desk and get them to move us."

"Why?"

He dragged back the gauzy curtains covering the corner windows. One set of wavy glass panes fronted the street. The other set faced the brick wall of the River Center complex next door.

"See the roof of that building?"

"Yes."

"It's on a direct line with these windows. Anyone with a mind to it could get a clear bead on a target in this room. Or climb up on the roof of that IMAX theater across the street and stake you out."

The color leached from her cheeks. "If you're trying to scare me, you're doing one heck of a good job."

"You should be scared. That wasn't a valentine your visitor left on that mirror, you know."

"Of course I know! To paraphrase your earlier remark, the viciousness of that threat is the reason, the *only* reason, I agreed to the nuisance of a bodyguard."

Hooking his thumbs in his jeans pockets, Jack tried to get a handle on the woman who'd emerged from the girl he'd once known.

"So why are you hanging around San Antonio, Ellie? Why offer yourself as a target to the kook or malcontent who issued that warning?"

"Because I refuse to let said kook or malcontent interfere with my work. In all modesty, I'm good at what I do. Damned good.'' She speared him with a hard look. ''You predicted I would be. Remember, Jack? Right about the time you and Uncle Eduardo jointly decided finishing college was more important to me than my... Let's see, how did he phrase it? My passing infatuation with a hardheaded Marine.''

They'd have to scratch at the old scars sometime. Better to do it now and give the scabs time to heal again. If Jack was to protect her, he needed her trust. Or at least her cooperation. He wouldn't gain either until he'd acknowledged his culpability for the hurt she'd suffered all those years ago.

''You were only nineteen, Ellie. I thought... Your uncle thought...''

''That I didn't know my own mind.'' Her chin came up. ''You were wrong. I knew it then. I know it now.''

She couldn't have made her meaning plainer. Jack Carstairs wouldn't get the chance to wound her again. He accepted that stark truth with a nod.

''Why don't we get settled in different rooms, and you can tell me exactly what it is you're so good at. I need to understand what you're doing here,'' he said to forestall the stiff response he saw coming, ''and why it's roused such controversy.''

The hotel staff moved them to adjoining suites two floors down. The rooms looked out over the inner courtyard of the hotel instead of the street. Like the rest of the historic hotel, they were furnished with a combination of period antiques and modern comfort. A burned-wood armoire held a twenty-seven-inch TV and a well-stocked bar. The wrought-iron bedstead boasted a queen-size mattress and thick, puffy goose-down comforter.

While Jack checked phones, door locks and ceiling vents, three valets transferred boxes of files and equipment on rolling dollies. Ruthlessly rearranging the furniture to meet her work-space needs, Ellie promptly turned her sitting room into a functional office. She'd already replaced the stolen computer and hard drive, which she now hooked up to an oversize flat LCD screen.

A smaller unit sat beside the computer. Jack studied it with a faint smile. Mackenzie Blair, OMEGA's chief of communications, would light up like a Christmas tree if she caught sight of all those buttons and dials and displays. The palm-size unit was probably crammed with more circuitry than the Space Shuttle.

Evidently Ellie Alazar shared Mackenzie's fascination with electronic gadgetry. She gave the small metal box the kind of pat a fond mother might give a child.

"This holds the guts of a technology I developed the summer after we…" Her brown brows slashed down. Obviously impatient with her hesitation, she plowed ahead. "The summer after I met you. I didn't make the trip to Mexico City that year. I didn't go down for several years, as a matter of fact.''

Jack wasn't surprised. Elena's emotions ran close to the surface. In the short months he'd known her, she'd never once reined them in. Looking back, he could see that was what had drawn him to her in the first place. Everything she thought or felt was all there, in her eyes, her face. Impatience, passion, anger—whatever emotion gripped her, she shared. Honestly. Openly.

She'd certainly shared her feelings the day her uncle sent his police to arrest Jack. She'd been furious with Eduardo Alazar. But not half as angry as she'd became with the Marine who refused to stand and fight for her.

''You didn't go to Mexico that summer,'' Jack acknowledged, steering the conversation to less volatile subjects. ''What did you do?''

''I worked for the National Park Service on a dig in the Pecos National Park. We were excavating the site of the battle of Glorietta Pass. The battle took place in 1862 and was one of the pivotal engagements in the Civil War.''

''The Gettysburg of the West. I've heard of it.''

She gave him a look of approval. ''Then you know the battle turned the tide against Confederates and sent Silbey's Brigade scuttling back to Texas in total disarray.''

Another Texas defeat. Evidently Ellie had started

her career at the site of one disastrous conflict for the Lone Star state. Now she was up to her trim, tight buns in controversy over another. No wonder some loyal local citizens wanted to roll up the welcome mat and send her on her way.

"We used metal detectors to locate shell casings at the battle site," she explained, warming to her subject. "We marked their location on a computerized grid, then categorized the casings by make and caliber. We also analyzed the rifling marks on the brass to determine the type of weapon that fired them."

"Sounds like a lot of work."

"It was. Three summers' worth of digging and mapping. Plus hundreds of hours of detailed research into the weaponry of the time. The Confederates tended to carry a wide variety of personally owned rifles and side arms. Union weapons were somewhat more standardized. By matching spent shell casings to the type of weapon that fired them, we were able to map the precise movement of both armies on the battlefield. We also built a massive database. For my Ph.D. dissertation, I expanded and translated the raw data into a program that allows forensic historians to reliably identify shell casings from any era post-1820."

"Why 1820?"

"The copper percussion cap was invented in the 1820s. Within a decade, two at most, almost every army in the world had converted its muzzle-loading flintlocks to percussion. More to the point where my research was concerned, the copper casing retained more defined rifling marks, which aided in identification of the type of weapon that fired it.''

Jack was impressed. He could fieldstrip an M-15, clean the components and put it back together blindfolded. He'd qualified at the expert level on every weapon in the Marine Corps inventory, as well as on the ones OMEGA outfitted him with. Yet his knowledge of the science of ballistics didn't begin to compare with Ellie's.

''So how do we get from the invention of the percussion cap to your finding that the hero of the Alamo deserted his troops and ran away?''

''It's not a finding.'' She shot the answer back. ''It's only one of several hypotheses I surfaced for discussion with my team. Honestly, you'd think simple intellectual curiosity would make folks wait to see whether the theory is substantiated by fact before they get all in a twit.''

''You'd think,'' Jack echoed solemnly.

Flushing a bit, she backpedaled. ''Sorry. I didn't mean to snap. I'm just getting tired of having to deal with outraged letters to the editor, picketers at the site, skittish team members and a nervous National Park Service director who's close to pulling the plug on our funding.''

There they were again. The fire, the impatience.

She hadn't learned to bank, either. Jack found himself hoping she never did.

"And this hypothesis is based on what?" he asked, the evenness of his tone a contrast to hers. "Start at the beginning. Talk me through the sequence of events."

"It would be better if I showed you." She speared a glance at her watch. "It's only a little past two. If you want, we can start here at the Alamo, then drive out to the site."

"Good enough. Give me ten minutes."

With the controlled, smooth grace that had always characterized him, he executed what Ellie could only describe as an about-face and passed through the connecting door. It closed behind him, leaving her staring at the panels.

The old cliché was true, she thought with a little ache. You can take a man out of the Marines, but you never quite took the Marine out of the man.

Like dust blown by the hot Texas wind, memories skittered through her mind. She could see Jack the night they'd met. She'd accompanied her aunt and uncle to a formal function at the American embassy. As head of the security detail, Gunnery Sergeant Carstairs had stood just behind the ambassador, square-shouldered, proud, confident. And so damned handsome in his dress blues that Elena hadn't been able to take her eyes off him all evening.

She'd been the one to ask him to dance. *She'd*

called him a few days later, inviting him to join her for a Sunday afternoon stroll through Chapultapec Park. *She'd* let him know in every way a woman could that she was attracted to him.

And that's all it was. A sizzling, searing attraction. At first.

How could she know she'd fall desperately in love with the man? That she'd find a passion in Jack's arms she'd never come close to tasting before? That she'd swear to give up everything for him—her scholarship, her family, her pride—only to have him throw them all back in her face.

If she closed her eyes, she could replay their final scene in painful, brilliant color. Jack was already under house arrest. Her uncle's overly protective, knee-jerk reaction to his niece's affair had forced the U.S. ambassador to demand Sergeant Carstairs's immediate reassignment and possible disciplinary action.

Steaming, Ellie had ignored her uncle's stern orders to the contrary, marched to the marine barracks and demanded to see Jack. He'd come to the foyer, stiff and remote in his khaki shirt and blue trousers with the crimson stripe down each leg. With brutal honesty, he'd laid his feelings on the line.

Ellie still had a year of college and at least three years of grad school ahead of her. He was going home to face a possible court-martial and an uncertain future. He refused to make promises he might not be able to keep. Nor would he allow her put her future on hold for his.

He was so noble, Ellie had railed. So damned, stupidly obstinate. Traits he continued to demonstrate even after they both returned to the States.

Cringing inside, Ellie recalled the repeated attempts she'd made to contact Jack. He wouldn't return her calls. Never answered her letters. Finally, her pride kicked in and she left a scathing message saying that he could damned well make the next move. He never did.

Now here they were, she thought, blowing out a long breath. Two completely different people. She'd fulfilled the early promise of a brilliant career in history. Jack, apparently, had bottomed out. Despite his extensive training and experience in personal security, he'd evidently drifted from one firm to another until going to work for some small-time operation in Virginia. Ellie wouldn't have known he was in the bodyguard business if one of her colleagues hadn't stumbled across his company on the Internet while preparing for a trip to Bogotá, Colombia, the kidnap capital of the universe.

It was guilt, only guilt, that had made her insist on Jack when her uncle urged her to accept the services of a bodyguard. She'd caused the ruin of his chosen career. Her own had exceeded all expectations. The least she could do was throw a little business his way.

From the looks of him, he could use it. She didn't know what was considered the appropriate uniform for bodyguards, but her uncle's security detail had always worn suits and ties and walked around talking into their wristwatches. She couldn't remember seeing any of them in thigh-hugging jeans or wrinkled, blue-cotton shirts with the sleeves rolled up. Or, she thought with a small ache just under her ribs, black leather boots showing faint scuff marks.

More than anything else, those scratches brought home the vast difference between the spit-and-polish sergeant she'd once loved and the man in the other room. Her throat tight, Ellie turned to gather her purse and keys.

Jack flipped open the palm-size phone and punched a single key. One short beep indicated instant connection to OMEGA's control center.

"Control, this is Renegade."

OMEGA's chief of communications responded with a cheerful, "Go ahead, Renegade."

As little as a year ago, operatives at the headquarters stood by twenty-four hours a day to act as controllers for agents in the field. Mackenzie Blair's improvements in field communications allowed for instant contact with headquarters and eliminated the need for controllers. Instead, Mackenzie and her communications techs monitored operations around the clock.

Mostly Mackenzie, Jack amended. The woman spent almost all her waking hours at OMEGA. She needed a life. Like Jack himself, he thought wryly.

"I've made contact with the subject."

The terse report no doubt raised Mackenzie's brows. After all, the background dossier she'd compiled had included a summation of Elena Maria Alazar's affair with Sergeant Jack Carstairs.

"Tell Lightning I'm working the preliminary threat assessment. I'll report back when I have a better feel for the situation."

"Roger that, Renegade."

After signing off, Jack slid the small, flat phone into his shirt pocket and hiked his foot up on a handy footstool. His movements were sure and smooth as he drew a blue steel short-barreled automatic from its ankle holster. He made sure the safety was on, released the magazine, checked the load and pushed the magazine back in place. A tug on the slide chambered a round. With the 9 mm tucked in its leather nest, he shook his pant leg over his boot and rapped on the door to Ellie's room.

"Ready?"

Pulling on a ball cap in the same chili-pepper red as her top, she hooked a bag over her shoulder.

"Yes."

Chapter 3

Outside, the July sun blazed down with cheerful brutality. Exiting the hotel, Ellie turned right toward Alamo Plaza. Jack walked beside her, his eyes narrowed against the glare as he scanned the crowd.

It included the usual assortment of vendors and tourists, with a heavy sprinkling of men and women in Air Force blue. They were basic trainees, released for a few precious hours from the nearby Lackland Air Force Base. With their buzz-cut hair and slick sleeves, they looked so young, so proud of their uniform. So unprepared for the crises that world events could plunge them into at any moment.

What they didn't look like were riled-up patriots seeking vengeance on a historian who dared to question the courage of a local legend. Nonetheless, Jack didn't relax his vigilance.

"What do you know about the Alamo?" Ellie asked as they approached the mission.

"Not much more than what I absorbed from the John Wayne movie of the same name."

And in the data Mackenzie had pulled off the computers. Jack kept silent about the background file. Right now, he was more interested in Ellie's version of the Alamo's history.

"It's one of a string of five missions located along the San Antonio River, founded in the early 1700s," she informed him. "Originally designated Mission Antonio de Valero, it didn't become known as the Alamo until much later."

With a sweep of her arm, she gestured to the adobe structure dominating the wide plaza ahead.

"There it is. The shrine of Texas liberty."

The distinctive building stirred an unexpected dart of pride in Jack. As a symbol of independence, its image had been seared into his consciousness. Of course, all those John Wayne movies might have had something to do with the sensation.

"Originally the mission compound sat by itself, well across the river from the settlement of San Antonio de Bexar," Ellie related. "Now, of course, the city's grown up all around it."

They wove a path through sightseers snapping photo after photo. A red-faced, grossly overweight candidate for a stroke backed up to frame a shot, banging into several fellow tourists in the process. Swiftly, Jack took Ellie's elbow to steer her around the obstacle.

Just as swiftly, he released her.

Well, hell! Here it was, going on nine years since he'd last touched this woman. Yet one glide of his fingers along her smooth, warm skin set off a chain reaction that started in his arm and ended about six inches below his belt.

For the first time since Lightning's call some hours ago, Jack conceded maybe Eduardo Alazar had reason to be concerned. The fires weren't out. Not entirely.

Jack had been so certain the embarrassment he'd caused Ellie and himself had doused any residual sparks. The sudden flare of heat in his gut screamed otherwise. Clenching his jaw against the unwelcome sensation, he tried to concentrate on Ellie's recitation.

"A series of droughts and epidemics decimated the mission's religious population," she related. "In 1793 the structure was turned over to civil authorities. At that point, Spanish cavalry from Alamo de Parras in Mexico took occupancy, and the fort became known at the Pueblo del Alamo. When the Spanish were driven out of Mexico, Mexican troops moved in. About the same time, the Mexican government opened the province of Texas to foreign settlers.''

''Foreign meaning Americans?''

''Americans and anyone else who would put down roots and, hopefully, help stem attacks on settlements by the Commanches and Apaches. Given the proximity to the States, though, it's only natural that most immigrants were Americans. Led by Stephen Austin, they flooded in and soon outnumbered the Mexican population five to one. It was only a matter of time until they decided they wanted out from under Mexican rule.''

''Those pesky Texans,'' Jack drawled.

''Actually,'' she replied with a smile, ''they called themselves Texians then. Or Tejanos. But they *were* pretty pesky. Tensions escalated, particularly after General Antonio Lopez de Santa Anna seized control of the Mexican government and abrogated the constitution. In the process, he also abrogated most of the rights of the troublesome immigrants. There were uprisings all over Mexico—and outright rebellion here in Texas.

''After several small skirmishes, the Americans declared their independence and sent a small force to seize the Alamo. When Santa Anna vowed to march his entire army north and crush the rebellion, the tiny garrison sent out a plea for reinforcements. William Travis, Jim Bowie and Davy Crockett, among others, answered the call.''

The names sounded like a roll call of America's heroes. Jim Bowie, the reckless adventurer as quick with his wit as with his knife. Davy Crockett, legendary marksman and two-term member of Congress from Tennessee. William Barrett Travis, commander of the Texas militia who drew a line in the sand with his saber and asked every Alamo defender willing to stand to the end to cross it. Supposedly, all but one did so.

Those who did met the fate Ellie related in a historian's dispassionate voice.

"When Santa Anna retook the Alamo in March, 1836, he executed every defender still alive and burned their bodies in mass funeral pyres. Or so the few non-combatants who survived reported."

"But you think those reports are wrong."

"I think there's a possibility they *may* be."

With that cautious reply, she led the way through the small door set in the massive wooden gates fronting the mission. Inside, thick adobe walls provided welcome relief from the heat. A smiling docent stepped forward to greet them.

"Welcome to the Alamo. This brochure will give you… Oh!" The smile fell right off her face. "It's you, Dr. Alazar."

"Yes, I'm back again."

"Our museum director said you'd finished your research here."

"I have. I'm playing tourist this afternoon and showing my, er, friend around."

The docent's glance darted from Ellie to Jack and back again. Suspicion carved a deep line between her brows. "Are you planning to take more digital photos?"

"No. I've taken all I need."

"We heard those were stolen."

"They were," Ellie replied coolly. "Fortunately, I make it a practice to back up my work."

The volunteer fanned her brochures with a snap. "Yes, well, I'll let Dr. Smith know you're here."

"You've certainly made yourself popular around here," Jack commented dryly.

"Tell me about it! The exhibits are this way."

Exiting the church, they entered a long low building that had once served as the barracks and now housed a museum of Texas history. Ellie let Jack set the pace and read those exhibits that caught his interest.

They painted a chillingly realistic picture of the thirteen-day siege. There was Santa Anna's army of more than twelve hundred. The pitiful inadequacy of the defending force, numbering just over a hundred. Travis's repeated requests for reinforcements. The arrival of the Tennesseeans. The wild, last-minute dash by thirty-two volunteers from Goliad, Texas, through enemy lines. The final assault some hours before dawn on March sixth. The massacre of all defenders.

The mass funeral pyres that consumed both Texan and Mexican dead. The pitiful handful of non-combatants who survived.

The original of Travis's most famous appeal for assistance was preserved behind glass. Written the day after the Mexican army arrived in San Antonio, the letter still had the power to stir emotions.

Commander of the Alamo
Bexar, Fby 24th, 1836
To the People of Texas and All Americans in the World
Fellow Citizens & Compatriots

I am besieged by a thousand or more of the Mexicans under Santa Anna. I have sustained a continual bombardment & have not lost a man. The enemy has demanded a surrender at discretion, otherwise the garrison are to be put to the sword if the fort is taken. I have answered the demand with a cannon shot, and our flag still waves proudly on the walls. I shall never surrender nor retreat.

Then, I call on you in the name of Liberty, of patriotism, & of everything dear to the American character, to come to our aid with all dispatch. The enemy is receiving reinforcements daily & will no doubt increase to three or four thousand in four or five days. If this call is neglected, I am determined to sustain myself as long as possible and die like a soldier who never forgets what is due to his own honor & that of his country.

Victory or death

William Barrett Travis

Lt. Col. Comdt

P.S. The Lord is on our side. When the enemy appeared in sight, we had not three bushels of corn. We have since found in deserted houses 80 or 90 bushels & got into the walls 20 or 30 head of Beeves.

Travis.

"Whew!" Jack blew out a long breath. "No wonder the mere suggestion that this man didn't die at the Alamo has riled so many folks. He certainly made his intentions plain enough."

Nodding, Ellie trailed after him as he examined the exhibits and artifacts reported to belong to the defenders, among them sewing kits, tobacco pouches and handwoven horsehair bridles and lariats. A small, tattered Bible tugged at her heart. It was inscribed to one Josiah Kennett, whose miniature showed an unsmiling young man in the wide-brimmed sombrero favored by cowboys and vaqueros of the time. Silver conchos decorated the hatband, underscoring how closely Mexican and Tejano cultures had blended in the days before war wrenched them apart.

When Jack and Ellie emerged into a tree-shaded courtyard, the serene quiet gave no echo of the cannons that had once thundered from the surrounding walls. Tourists wandered past quietly, almost reverently.

"Okay," Jack said, summarizing what he'd read inside. "Susanna Dickinson, wife of the fort's artillery officer, said that Travis died on the north battery. Travis's slave Joe said he saw the colonel go down after grappling with troops coming over the wall. They make a pretty convincing argument that William B. stuck to his word and died right here at the Alamo."

"An argument I might buy," Ellie agreed, "except that Susanna Dickinson hid in the chapel during the assault. After the battle, she reportedly saw the bodies of Crockett and Bowie, but never specifically indicated she saw Travis's. She probably heard that he died on the ramparts from other sources."

"What about Joe's report?"

"Joe saw his master go down during the assault, then he, too, hid. Travis could have been wounded yet somehow survived. The only document that indicates his body was recovered and burned with the others is a translation of a report by Francisco Ruiz, San Antonio's mayor at the time. Unfortunately, the translation appeared in 1860, years after the battle. The original has never been found, so there's no way to verify its authenticity."

She knew her stuff. There was no arguing that.

"On the other hand," she continued, "rumors that some of the defenders escaped the massacre ran rampant for years. One held that Mexican forces captured Crockett some miles away and hauled him before Santa Anna, who had him summarily shot. There's also a diary kept by a corporal in the Mexican army who claims he led a patrol sent out to hunt down fleeing Tejanos."

Her eyes locked with Jack's.

"Supposedly, his patrol fired at an escapee approximately five miles south of here, not far from Mission San Jose. The corporal was sure they hit the man, but they lost him in the dense underbrush along the river."

"Let me guess. That's the site you're now excavating."

"Right."

It could have happened, Jack mused. He'd experienced the confusion and chaos of battle. He knew how garbled reports could become, how often even the most reliable intelligence proved wrong.

Still, as they moved toward the building that housed a special exhibit of weaponry used at the Alamo, he found himself hoping the theory didn't hold water. A part of him wanted to believe the legend— that William Barrett Travis *had* drawn that line in the sand, then heroically fought to the death alongside Davy Crockett, Jim Bowie and the others. Texas deserved its heroes.

The museum director evidently agreed. Short, rotund, his wire-rimmed glasses fogging in the steamy heat, he stood in front of the door to the exhibit with legs spread and arms folded and greeted Ellie with a curt nod. "Dr. Alazar."

"Dr. Smith."

"Were you wishing access to those artifacts not on public display?"

"Yes, there's one rifle in particular I want to show my, er, associate."

Jack flicked her an amused glance. Obviously, Ellie wasn't ready to admit she'd been intimidated into acquiescing to a bodyguard.

"I'm sorry," the director replied with patent insincerity. "I must insist that you put all such requests in writing from now on."

Ellie's eyes flashed. Evidently Smith had just drawn his own line in the sand.

"I'll do that," she snapped. "I'll also apprise my colleagues in this and future endeavors of your generous spirit of cooperation."

She left him standing guard at his post. Jack followed, shaking his head. Elena Maria Alazar might be one of the foremost experts in her field, but she wouldn't win a whole lot of prizes for tact or diplomacy.

"Damn Smith, anyway," she muttered, still fuming. "I suspect he's the one who raised such a stink with the media. He seems to think I'm attacking him personally by questioning his research."

It sounded to Jack as though the man might have a point there. Wisely, he kept silent and made a mental note to have Mackenzie run a background check on the museum director.

"I'll show you the images of that shotgun later," Ellie said as they retraced their steps.

"Why is that particular weapon so significant?"

"It's a double-barreled shotgun, reportedly recovered after the battle. Records indicate William Travis owned just such a weapon, or one similar to it. It's almost identical to the one we recovered at the dig."

Tugging her ball cap lower on her brow to shield her eyes against the blazing sun, she wove a path through the milling crowd outside the Alamo and made for the elaborate, wrought-iron façade of the Menger.

"I wish I could convince Smith that I'm still wide open to all possible theories. And that I have no intention of caving in to threats, obscene phone calls or petty nuisances like putting my requests for access to historical artifacts in writing."

Her mouth set, she rummaged around in her shoulder bag, dug out a parking receipt and approached the parking valet.

"Why don't I drive?" Jack said easily, passing the

attendant his receipt instead. ''I want to get the lay of the land.''

He also wanted to make sure someone skilled in defensive driving techniques was at the wheel whenever Ellie traveled.

She didn't argue. When the Cherokee came down the ramp, its tires screeching at the tight turns, she tossed her bag into the back and slid into passenger seat. The ball cap came off. With a grateful sigh for the chilled air blasting out of the vents, she swiped the damp tendrils off her forehead.

''Which way?'' Jack asked.

''Take a left, go past the Alamo Dome, then follow the signs for Mission Trail.''

Propping her neck against the headrest, Ellie stared straight ahead. For the second time in as many hours, Jack sensed the accumulated stress that kept the woman beside him coiled as tight as a cobra.

''Tell me about these obscene phone calls. How many have you received?''

''Five or six.'' Her nose wrinkled. ''They were short and crude. Mostly suggestions on where I could stick my theories. One of the callers was female, by the way, which surprised the heck out of me.''

Nothing surprised Jack any more. ''Did the police run traces?''

''They tried. But the calls came through the hotel switchboard, and there's something about the routing system that precluded a trace.''

Jack would fix that as soon as they returned. The electronic bag of tricks Mackenzie had assembled for this mission included a highly sophisticated and not exactly legal device that glommed onto a digital signal and wouldn't let go.

"See that sign?" Ellie pointed to a historical marker in the shape of a Spanish mission. "This is where we pick up Mission Trail. You need to hang a left here."

"Got it."

Flicking on his directional signal, Jack turned left. A half mile later, he made a right. That was when he noticed the dusty black SUV. The Ford Expedition remained three cars back, never more, never less, making every turn Jack did. Frowning, he navigated the busy city streets for another few blocks before spinning the steering wheel. The Cherokee's tires squealed as he cut a sharp left across two lanes of oncoming traffic.

"Hey!" Ellie made a grab for the handle just above her window. "Did I miss a sign?"

"No."

He flicked a glance in the rearview mirror. The SUV waited until one oncoming vehicle whizzed passed, dodged a second and followed.

Ellie had figured out something was wrong. Craning her neck, she peered at the traffic behind them while Jack whipped around another corner. When the

SUV followed some moments later, he dug his cell phone out of his pocket and punched a single button.

"Control, this is Renegade."

"Renegade?"

Ignoring Ellie's startled echo, Jack waited for a response. Mackenzie came on a moment later.

"Control here. Go ahead."

"I'm traveling west on…" He squinted at the street sign that whizzed by. "On Alameda Street in south San Antonio. There's a black Expedition following approximately fifty meters behind. I need you to put a satellite on him before I shake him."

"Roger, Renegade. I'll vector off your signal."

"Let me know when you've got the lock."

"Give me ten seconds."

Jack did a mental count and got down to three before Mackenzie came on the radio.

"Okay, I see you. I'm panning back… There he is. Black Expedition. Now I just have to sharpen the image a little…" A moment later, she gave a hum of satisfaction. "He's tagged. I'm feeding the license plate number into the computer as we speak. How long do you want me to maintain the satellite lock?"

"Follow him all the way home. And let me know as soon as you get an ID."

"Will do."

"Thanks, Mac."

"Anytime," OMEGA's communications chief answered breezily.

Jack snapped the transceiver shut and slipped it into his shirt pocket. A quick glance at Ellie showed her staring at him in astonishment.

"Your company has a satellite at their disposal?"

"Several. Hang tight, I'm going to lose this joker."

Jack could see the questions in her eyes but didn't have time for answers right now. The first rule in personal protective services was to remove the protectee from any potentially dangerous situation. He didn't know who was behind the wheel of the SUV or what his intentions were. He sure as hell wasn't about to find out with Ellie in the car.

Stomping down on the accelerator, he took the next intersection on two wheels. Ellie gulped and scrunched down in her seat. Jack shot a look in the rearview mirror and watched the larger, heavier Expedition lurch around the corner.

Two turns later, they'd left the main downtown area and had entered an industrial area crisscrossed by railroad tracks. Brick warehouses crowded either side of the street, their windows staring down like unseeing eyes. Once again, Jack put his boot to the floor. The Cherokee rocketed forward, flew over a set of tracks and sailed into an intersection just as a semi bearing the logo of Alamo City Fruits and Vegetables swung wide across the same crossing.

"Look out!"

Shrieking, Ellie braced both hands on the dash. Her boots slammed against the floorboards.

Jack spun the wheel right, then left and finessed the Cherokee past the truck with less than an inch or two to spare. Smiling in grim satisfaction, he hit the accelerator again.

The bulkier Expedition couldn't squeeze through. Behind him, they heard the squeal of brakes followed by the screech of metal scraping metal. Still smiling grimly, Jack made another turn. A few minutes later, he picked up Mission Trail again, but this time he headed into the city instead of out.

"We'd better put off our visit to the site until tomorrow," he told Ellie. "By then I should have a better idea of who or what we're dealing with."

"Fine by me," she replied, wiggling upright in her seat.

Actually, it was more than fine. After that wild ride, her nerves jumped like grasshoppers on hot asphalt, and her kidneys were signaling a pressing need to find the closest bathroom.

Jack, on the other hand, didn't look the least flustered. He gripped the steering wheel loosely, resting one arm on the console between the bucket seats, and divided his attention between the road ahead and the traffic behind. She couldn't see his eyes behind the mirrored sunglasses, but not so much as a bead of nervous sweat had popped out on his forehead.

"Do you do these kinds of high-speed races often in your line of work?" she asked.

"Often enough."

"And you've been in the same business since you left the Corps?"

"More or less."

"How do you handle the stress?"

He flashed her a grin that reminded her so much of the man she'd once known that Ellie gulped.

"I'll show you when we get back to the hotel."

Chapter 4

"Yoga?"

Ellie's disbelieving laughter rippled through the sun-washed hotel room.

"You do yoga?"

"According to my instructor," Jack intoned solemnly, "one doesn't 'do' yoga. One ascends to it."

"Uh-huh. And who is this instructor?" she asked, forming a mental image of a tanned, New Age Californian in flowing orange robes.

"One of the grunts in the first platoon I commanded."

"You're kidding!"

"Nope. Dirwood had progressed to the master level before joining the Corps."

She shook her head. "You know, of course, you're blowing my image of United States Marines all to hell."

"Funny," Jack murmured, "I thought I'd pretty much already done that."

He peeled off his sunglasses, tucked them in his shirt pocket and propped his hips against the sofa back. His blue eyes spent several moments studying Ellie's face before moving south.

She withstood his scrutiny calmly enough but knew she looked a mess. Sweat had painted damp patches on her scoop-necked top, and her khaki shorts boasted more wrinkles than Rip Van Winkle. She was also, as Jack proceeded to point out, a bundle of nerves.

"You're wound tighter than baling wire. You have been since I arrived."

No way was she going to admit that a good chunk of the tension wrapping her in steel cables stemmed as much from seeing him again after all these years as from the problems on the project.

"I've had a lot on my mind," she replied with magnificent understatement.

"It takes years to really master yoga techniques, but I could teach you a few of the basic chants and positions to help you relax."

Somehow Ellie suspected that getting down on the floor and sitting knee-to-knee with Jack would prove anything but relaxing. Part of her wanted to do it, if for no other reason than to test her ability to withstand the intimacy. Another part, more mature, more experienced—and more concerned with self-preservation—knew it was wiser to avoid temptation altogether.

"Maybe later," she said with a polite smile.

"It's your call."

"So what do we do now?"

"We wait until I get a report on the SUV."

Sitting twiddling her thumbs with Jack only a few feet away didn't do any more to soothe Ellie's jangled nerves than getting down on the floor with him would have.

"Since we've got the time now," she suggested, "why don't I show you some of the digital images I took at the Alamo and at the excavation site?"

"Good enough."

"I'll boot up the computer. Drag over another chair."

More than agreeable to the diversion, Jack hooked a chair and hauled it across the room. It was obvious why she'd shied away from his offer to teach her some basic relaxation techniques. She was jumpy as a cat around him. Not a good situation. For either of them.

A tense, nerve-racked client could prove too demanding and distracting to the agent charged with his or her protection. Jack's job would be a whole lot easier if he could get her to relax a little. Not enough to let down her guard. Not so much she grew careless. Just enough that the tension didn't leave her drained of energy or alertness.

Still, he had to admit to a certain degree of relief that she'd turned down his offer. The mere thought of folding Ellie's knees and elbows and tucking her into the first position was enough to put a kink in Jack's gut. Breathing in her potent combination of sun-warmed female and cactus pear perfume didn't exactly unkink it, either. Scowling, he focused his attention on the long list of files that appeared on the computer screen.

"We'll start at the Alamo," Ellie said, dragging the cursor down the list. "I want to show you the shotgun I was talking about."

"The one the museum director refused to let us see this afternoon?"

"Yes. I think the armament images pick up right about..." The cursor zipped down the indexed files. "Here."

Brilliant color flooded the seventeen-inch active matrix screen. There was Ellie in the Alamo's courtyard, smiling at the short, rotund director who gestured with almost obsequious delight to the entrance of the building housing his prized arms exhibit. Tourists crowded the courtyard around and behind them.

One mugged at an unseen camera. Another waited with an expression of impatience for Ellie and Smith to move out of the way. But the shot of Smith's face was clear and unobstructed.

"I'd like to send a copy of this image to a security analyst," Jack said. "Can you flag it for later reference?"

"Yes, of course. But..." Looking uncomfortable, Ellie turned to face him. "Smith is just trying to protect his turf. I don't like the idea of invading his privacy or compiling a secret file on him. Or on any of my colleagues, for that matter."

"We won't be compiling secret files," he answered mildly. "Merely exploiting those that already exist. You'd be amazed at how much data is floating around out there about John Q. Public."

"Yes, but..."

"Flag the image, Ellie."

With obvious reluctance, she went to the menu at the top of the screen and bookmarked the file.

Jack leaned forward, peering intently at the images that flashed by after that. More shots in the courtyard. The interior of the museum, with room after room of weaponry of the type used during the siege of the Alamo. The special exhibits, not open to the public.

"For the most part," Ellie explained, "these are pieces that have yet to be authenticated. They were either excavated in or around the Alamo or donated by descendants of the combatants.''

A click of the mouse brought up a vividly detailed image of a long-barreled rifle.

''This is a Brown Bess, so known because the troopers allowed the steel barrel to burnish and thus prevent glare that could distort their aim. This smooth-bore musket served as the standard infantry rifle carried by the British during the Napoleonic Wars. After the war, the Brits sold their excess inventories to armies all over the world.''

''Including the Mexican army?''

''Yes, well, Mexico was still ruled by Spain then. When it won its independence, its army pretty well retained the standard-issue armaments. Historical documents indicate Santa Anna's infantry was armed with the Brown Bess. Most had been converted from muzzle-loading flintlock to percussion by then.''

She flashed up another image of the musket and highlighted the differences in the firing mechanism.

''By contrast,'' she continued, ''the Tejanos who fought at the Alamo carried weapons as diverse as the defenders themselves. They weren't members of a regular army, remember. They were settlers—farmers, ranchers, doctors, lawyers, ministers and slaves—all rebelling against Santa Anna's edicts dispossessing them of their rights under the former Constitution. They were also adventurers like Jim Bowie.

Patriots like Davy Crockett and his Tennesseeans. Slaves, like Bowie's man Joe. They came armed with everything from Spanish blunderbusses to French muskets to long-barreled Kentucky hunting rifles, fowlers and shotguns.''

She ran through a series of images, identifying each weapon as it came up. When the image of a particular shotgun filled the screen, her voice took on an unmistakable hint of excitement.

''We know from various accounts that Travis arrived at the Alamo armed with a double-barrel shotgun like this one. He'd written several letters to Stephen Austin, advocating the gun as the standard weapon for the newly organized Texas cavalry. It didn't have the range of long rifle, of course, but it provided lethal firepower at closer range.''

With a click of the mouse, she rotated the three-dimensional image.

''Note the stock. It's made of curly maple, sometimes called tiger tail or fiddleback.''

Another click zoomed in on the silver inlays on the side of the stock.

''See the gunsmith's mark on the butt plate? It traces to a gunsmith in Sparta, South Carolina.''

Close at her shoulder, Jack could feel her controlled excitement straining to break loose as she returned to the index, scrolled down several pages and clicked on another file.

An outdoor scene was painted across the screen. A narrow creek twisted through the background, its banks almost lost amid a dense tangle of cotton-woods. A small group stood at the edge of one bank. Ellie and her team, Jack guessed, scrutinizing each of their faces in turn.

"Flag this photo, too," he instructed.

Her lips thinned, but she bookmarked the file. That done, she zoomed in on one of the objects lying on a piece of canvas at the team's feet. It was a shotgun, similar to the one she'd brought up on the screen moments ago. But this barrel sported a thick coat of rust. The silver mountings had tarnished to black, and wood rot riddled the stock.

Ellie enlarged the image again. "Look at the butt plate on this one. The gunsmith's mark is hard to read, but it's there."

Jack leaned closer, squinting at the screen. "Looks like the same mark."

"It is. Did I mention the gunsmith lived in Sparta, South Carolina?"

"You did."

"And that William Barrett Travis grew up, went to school and opened his first law practice in Sparta?"

"No, You saved that bit for last." Grinning at her air of triumph, he played devil's advocate. "Okay. I'm a betting man. I'd say you could lay odds Travis carried a gun made for him by a smith in his home-town *into* the Alamo. But someone could have picked up the gun when Travis went down and carried it *out,* including any one of a thousand Mexican soldiers.''

''As a matter of fact, Deaf Smith, a scout for Houston, captured a Mexican courier a month later using saddlebags monogrammed W.B. Travis.''

She swiveled her chair sideways, her eyes alive with the enjoyment of an intellectual debate.

''Who's to say those saddlebags weren't taken off a horse found wandering beside a creek five miles south of the Alamo? We're, uh, hoping DNA testing will help…you know…confirm…''

She stuttered to a halt. They were close. Too close. Almost nose to nose. Jack could see the gold flecks in her eyes. Feel the warm wash of her breath on his skin. If he leaned forward an inch, just another inch…

Abruptly, he jerked back in his seat.

Ellie made the same move at precisely the same moment. Chagrin, dismay and a touch of irritation chased across her face. She opened her mouth, only to snap it shut again when the small device in Jack's shirt pocket gave off a high-pitched beep. He pulled out the phone, glanced at the digital display and swung to his feet.

''Renegade here. Go ahead, control.''

Mackenzie Blair came on the line. "I ran the Expedition's tag. It's registered to a Mr. Harold Berger, 2224 River Drive, Austin, Texas."

"What have you got on the man?"

"Nothing much, seeing as Mr. Berger died two years ago. His wife reports that he never owned an Expedition, black or otherwise."

Jack's glance went to Ellie, still seated in front of her computer. The tension that had jolted through him seconds ago returned, doubled in intensity.

"Interesting," he muttered.

"Isn't it?" Mackenzie replied. "I did a screen of credit cards issued to Mr. H. Berger at his Austin address. I found an American Express and a Visa card, issued six months after he died."

Jack paced the sitting room, the phone tight against his ear. "What about the Expedition's driver? Did you get a picture of whoever emerged from the vehicle after it hit the truck?"

"Negative. He didn't get out of the vehicle. Not at the scene, anyway. He backed up, peeled off and squealed into a five-story parking garage about a mile away. Unfortunately, our spy satellites can't look through five layers of concrete, so I didn't get a shot of him exiting the vehicle. I contacted the San Antonio police and asked them to check it out. They found it abandoned and wiped clean of prints."

"Figures."

"I thought you should know one of their gun-sniffing dogs alerted on it. They found traces of gunpowder residue in the front seat."

Jack wasn't liking the sound of this. A stolen identity. Gunpowder residue. No prints. His gut told him they weren't talking a short, balding museum director here. Or a highly credentialed member of a scientific team. They were talking a pro.

"I'm going to send you a batch of digital images," he told Mackenzie. "We'll put names to the folks we know. I want you to run complete background checks on them and screen the rest for anyone or anything that looks suspicious."

"No problem."

"When can I expect results?"

"I don't know. How many images are we talking about?"

"Hang on." He cut to Ellie. "How many digital files have you got stored on the computer?"

"About six hundred."

"How many of those do you estimate include images of people?"

Her forehead wrinkled in concentration. "Live persons, I'd guess about two hundred. If you include the skeletal remains, another hundred or so."

"We'll start with those folks who are still breathing," Jack drawled. "Get ready to send copies."

Her brows soared. "Of all two hundred?"

"All two hundred."

"Two hundred!" OMEGA's chief of communications gave a groan. "And here I actually planned to beat the traffic home tonight, order a pizza and sneak in a little tube time."

"Sorry, Mac. Have your pizza delivered to the Control center and charge it to me."

"Don't think I won't," she grumbled. "Okay, I'll stand by to receive. Tell Dr. Alazar to fire off those files when ready."

They started popping up on the Control Center's screens fifteen minutes later. Dr. Alazar had converted the images contained in each file to JPEG format, thank goodness. JPEG files took a little longer to load but produced clear, sharp pictures.

Mackenzie worked the easy ones first, those with flags indicating Dr. Alazar had identified the individuals in the photos. One by one, she fed the names into a program linked to financial, government, merchandising and criminal databases worldwide. Within moments, she'd know whether any of these scholarly looking individuals had ever been cited for jaywalking, rented porn movies or fudged on his income taxes.

"Anything I can help you with, chief?"

Dragging her eyes from the screen, Mackenzie

glanced at her subordinate. John Alexander had put
in at least five more years at OMEGA than she had
but cheerfully cited his wife and four kids as reason
for remaining as a mid-level tech with semiregular
hours instead of moving up to the chief's job when
it had come open. With all his experience, John was
a good man to have at headquarters and a wizard in
the field when it came to planting bugs that absolutely defied detection.

"As a matter of fact," Mackenzie said with a grin,
"I was just going to send the cavalry to search for
you. Renegade sent us a tasking."

She got him started on the unflagged files. Since
they didn't have IDs on the folks in those photos,
John would have to scan the images one by one and
run them through a program that captured each subject's skin, hair and eye color, estimated weight and
height and any discernible scars, tattoos or disfigure-
ments. The physical characteristics would then be fed
into FBI, CIA and national crime information center
computers for potential matches. Information extracted by this method wasn't as accurate as fingerprints, DNA sampling or retinal scans, but the
matches ran something close to seventy percent. If
nothing else, they provided a starting point.

"Geez," John muttered as he opened the first file.
"There must be ten or twelve people in this shot.

They look like a bunch of tourists. Do you want me to scan all of them?''

"Let me see.''

Mackenzie rose out of her seat and bent over the console to view his screen. That was how Lightning found her when he strolled into the control center a moment later, a pizza carton held shoulder-high and balanced on his fingertips.

He paused for a moment, unabashedly enjoying the view. Most days, Nick looked, acted and thought like an American, but he'd been born in Cannes and possessed a Frenchman's esteem for the finer points of the female form. And Mackenzie's round, trim rear certainly qualified as fine.

Unfortunately, the same rules that prohibited an agent from becoming involved with a subject during operations applied in triplicate to OMEGA's director and his chief of communications. As long as one of his agents was in the field, Lightning couldn't allow himself or anyone on his staff to become distracted. Still, his eyes glinted with masculine appreciation as he made his way across the control center.

"This was just delivered downstairs," he said casually. "I assume you ordered it."

Mackenzie scrambled off the console. "If it's a sausage, double pepperoni and jalapeño special, I did."

Nick's eyes closed in something close to real pain. Dear Lord. Sausage, double pepperoni and jalapeño.

"Have you ever tasted pizza the way they make it along the Riviera?"

"My last cruise in the Navy was to the Med," Mackenzie informed him, lifting the lid to sniff appreciatively. "We dropped anchor just off San Remo. As I recall, the northern Italians doused everything, including their pizzas, in white cream sauce. Yuck!"

"A good cream sauce can be one of life's most decadent pleasures," Nick replied with a lift of one brow. "You'll have to let me take you to one of my restaurants sometime so you can sample it done right."

And that would be, Mackenzie thought, right about the time she developed a severe death wish.

She didn't play in Nick Jensen's league and knew it. If her short, disastrous marriage had taught her nothing else, it was to avoid smooth, handsome charmers like this one at all costs. Now if only she could keep her nerves from crawling around under her skin when he came to stand beside her.

"What are you working?"

"A request from Renegade. He's forwarded a series of images and asked for IDs and background checks."

Nick's blond brows drew together. In the blink of

an eye, he transitioned from every woman's ultimate sex fantasy into OMEGA's cool, take-charge director.

"I don't like that business with the Expedition this afternoon. Give Renegade whatever he asked for and then some."

Whipping to attention, Mackenzie snapped him a salute. "Aye, aye, *sir!*"

He eyed her for a moment, his expression inscrutable. She held the exaggerated pose until he left the control center, then turned to her assistant with a wry grin.

"Guess that answers your question, John. Scan every warm body in those photos."

Chapter 5

Ellie's team returned to the hotel from the excavation site a little past six that evening. The first team member to rap on her door was a tall, rangy, twenty-something male with a shock of dark red hair. He looked surprised when Jack answered his knock. Even more surprised when Ellie introduced the newcomer as an old friend.

"Jack's in the security business," she explained. "He flew in this morning to help us deal with some of the nastiness we've been subject to recently. Jack, this is Eric Chapman. He's one of my graduate students at the University of New Mexico."

Chapman's handshake was casual enough, but Jack picked up on the subtle signals that only the male of the species would recognize. Unless he missed his guess, the kid had a bad case of the hots for his professor and didn't particularly like the idea of another man poaching on his territory.

"So are we having a team meeting tonight, Ellie?"

"Yes. Eight o'clock, here in my room. Pass the word along to the others, would you?"

"Sure. How about dinner? Want to go down on the river and grab a quick bite?" His glance drifted to Jack. "If you two don't have plans, that is."

"We do," Jack answered, preempting Ellie's response.

She threw him a cool look but didn't contradict him. "I'll see you at the meeting, Eric. Tell the team I'd like a complete report of the afternoon's activities."

"Right."

When the door closed behind him, Ellie returned to the sitting room and regarded Jack with a slight frown. "I think we better establish some ground rules here, the first being that you consult with me before making arbitrary decisions."

"Like where you'll have dinner and who you'll have it with?"

"Exactly."

"Were you really that eager to go back out in the heat and chow down with the kid?" he asked, suddenly, acutely curious.

The intensity of his need to know whether she reciprocated Chapman's interest both surprised and irritated Jack. Somehow, he'd just skidded right past professional into personal. Very personal. Why the hell should he care if Ellie was providing the kid with private instruction after hours? Unless their relationship impacted Jack's ability to protect her, it wasn't any of his business. Technically.

Ellie evidently shared that opinion. Her voice chilly, she set him straight.

"No, I'm not all that eager to go back out in the heat. I simply prefer that you not make decisions for me. Or undermine my authority with my team," she added pointedly.

"Then you'd better make up your mind how you want me to interact with them. As your bodyguard or as old friend."

The chill didn't leave her eyes. If anything, it deepened. Toying with the silver bracelet banding her wrist, she debated her response.

Jack understood her hesitation. He'd piled up enough experience as an embassy guard and as a freelancer after leaving the Corps to appreciate how much take-charge executives hated to admit their fear. Hated, too, the helplessness that came with becoming a walking target. People in Ellie's position were used to calling the shots, not dodging them.

"Why don't we just stick with the explanation I gave Eric?" she suggested after a moment. "You *are* an old friend. You're also an expert in the security business. You flew in to assess the seriousness of the threats against me and my team.''

''Fine. We'll go with that. Now, about dinner. Mind if we order room service? I want you to give me a complete rundown on your team members before they assemble.''

Mackenzie would provide in-depth background dossiers once she'd screened the files they'd sent earlier, but Jack wanted Ellie's take. She'd worked with these people. She knew their strengths and weaknesses.

Now that she'd had time to think about it, she might also have some insight into whether one of them had deliberately leaked her controversial preliminary hypothesis to the media.

She didn't.

Flatly rejecting the idea that that a member of her group might be trying to sabotage the project, she spent the next two hours alternately detailing their impressive credentials and passionately defending them.

She hadn't changed much in that regard, Jack thought when he left her to prepare for the meeting and went next door to grab a quick shower. She'd defended a certain hardheaded Marine just as fiercely to her uncle...until Jack killed her arguments and her passion by rejecting both.

He'd taken the right stand, he told himself as he leaned against the shower tiles and lifted his face to the stinging needles. The *only* stand he could have taken, given the circumstances. Ellie had been so young then, with her whole future ahead of her. Jack couldn't see any future beyond being sent home in disgrace to face a possible court-martial, with all its potential for publicity.

The paparazzi would have eaten it up. The niece of the president of Mexico. An American Marine with a father whose name was a question mark and a mother who could be turning tricks in Detroit for all Jack knew. He'd never cared enough to track her down.

Then there were those searing, stolen hours in Mexico City. If the sensation-hungry media had gotten wind of those, the shinola would have hit the fan for sure. Jack had been insane to give in to Ellie's urgings, crazy to think he could give her release while holding back his own. On fire with impatience and need, she'd taken matters into her own hand. Literally. Even now, Jack could remember how her hot, eager fingers had brushed his aside and tugged at his zipper.

The memory slammed into him, hitting like a fist to the gut. He stiffened, felt himself get hard. Painfully hard. Cursing, he reached out and gave the shower knob a savage twist. Ice cold pellets shot into his skin from his neck to his knees. Gritting his teeth, Jack ducked his head under the stream.

His skin still prickled when he rapped on the connecting door fifteen minutes later. So did his temper, but he disguised his edginess behind a bland expression as Ellie's team began to congregate.

There were three besides Chapman. Orin Weaver, a noted forensic anthropologist who, Ellie explained, frequently acted as consultant for local, state and national law enforcement agencies. Janet Dawes-Hamilton, an archeologist from Baylor University. Sam Pierce, a field archeologist on the staff of the National Park Service, which owned the land on which the remains were discovered.

All except Chapman possessed Ph.D.s and an impressive string of published credits. All, including Chapman, eyed Jack with varying degrees of wariness. Like Ellie, they seemed to think the addition of a security specialist to their little group added a disturbing note of authenticity to the ugliness swirling around them.

"Sorry I didn't make it back to the site this afternoon," she said once the team had made themselves comfortable. "We were on our way but got involved in a high-speed chase through the streets of San Antonio."

The dry announcement produced the expected reactions. Gray-whiskered Orin Weaver blinked. The red-haired Chapman demanded to know if she was serious.

"Who was chasing whom?" Dr. Dawes-Hamilton asked in a cool, clipped voice.

"Person or persons unknown were after us," Jack answered. "We don't know who or why. Yet."

Pierce frowned and leaned forward, his callused hands clasped loosely between his knees. The National Park Service staffer didn't come across as a man out to harass his colleague into abandoning a dig or a particular theory, but Jack wasn't going to cut him any more slack than the others.

"I'll have to notify my headquarters about this latest incident," he said to Ellie. "They're already concerned over the adverse publicity our project has generated. One more mishap or media frenzy and...well..."

"The director may decide to shut down the dig," she finished for him. "With funding for future projects up before Congress," she explained to Jack, "he's nervous about offending the powerful Texas Congressional delegation."

"Not to mention the equally powerful President, who just happens to hail from the Lone Star state," Pierce put in dryly.

Jack kept to himself the fact that it was the President who'd requested OMEGA send an agent to San Antonio with instructions to protect Dr. Alazar and defuse the situation, if at all possible. From what he'd observed in the past eight hours or so, it might not be de-fusable.

Which is what he reported to Lightning later that night.

It was late, well past midnight. The meeting had broken up a little past ten. Jack waited until he was sure Ellie had settled into bed before slipping out to make his rounds. By the time he'd tested the hotel's security systems and satisfied himself as to the night staff's alertness, he was ready to drop into the rack himself. First, though, he gave Lightning his initial take on the situation.

"It's not smelling right. I'll make contact with the San Antonio police tomorrow to see what they've turned up, but that business about the Expedition being wiped clean bothers me."

"Me, too."

"How's Mac coming on those IDs and background checks?"

"Last time I checked, her pizza had gone stone cold and she had some rather uncomplimentary things to say about you."

"I'll bet."

"Hopefully, she and her folks will complete the runs within twenty-four hours. I'll stay on her."

Jack cocked a brow at the odd note in Lightning's voice. He'd dodged bullets and side-stepped pit vipers with the man during one memorable mission but

still couldn't quite read him. None of the OMEGA
agents could. Jensen came across as smooth and sophisticated, yet no one who'd ever witnessed his skill
with a knife would willingly go blade-to-blade with
him.

After signing off, Jack set the phone on the night-
stand beside his bed and unbuttoned his shirt. His
thoughts drifted to the time Lightning had lived up
to his name and saved Jack's life with one lethal
throw. Jack had returned the favor some months later
while helping take down a band of gunrunners.
Grunting with satisfaction at the memory, he shucked
his shirt and had just reached to unbuckle his ankle
holster when he heard the crash of metal and shat-
tering glass next door.

Ellie's cry came through the wall, sharp with dis-
tress. Jack hit the connecting door a half second later,
swearing viciously when he found it locked on the
other side. One brutal kick with his heel splintered
the wood and sprang the lock, slamming the door
against the wall.

He dived through. Hit the floor in a roll. Came up
in a crouch, the blue steel automatic aimed squarely
at the woman who shrieked and stumbled back a few
steps.

"Jack! Good God!"

Her obvious astonishment eased his blood-
pumping tension a fraction. Only a fraction. Heart
hammering, Jack swung in a full circle. There was

no one else in the room. Only then did he straighten and record two separate impressions.

The first was an overturned room service tray, spilling the dinner Ellie had hardly touched across the carpet.

The second was her sleep shirt.

At least, that's what Jack assumed it was. It looked like a man's white cotton T-shirt, cut off a good six inches above the skimpiest damned pair of bikini briefs he'd ever laid eyes on. If that bite-size bit of nylon and lace wasn't a thong, it was close enough to raise an instant sweat on his palms.

Which, he realized belatedly, still gripped the automatic.

Swinging the barrel away from Ellie's midsection, he thumbed the safety. His breath came fast and hard through his nostrils, and his voice was distinctly unfriendly when he demanded to know what the hell she was doing.

"I was hungry," she fired back, shaken but recovering fast. "I intended to finish the salad I didn't eat earlier and tipped over the tray. I'm sorry I woke you."

Her stiff apology didn't cut it.

"I'm not talking about the damned tray! Why did you lock the door?"

His snarl snapped her chin up. Lips thinning, she speared a glance at the shattered wood.

"I wasn't afraid you were going to pay me a late-night visit and jump my bones, if that's what you're thinking.''

He wasn't. Now that she'd planted the idea, though, he knew he'd have to pry it out of his head with a crowbar. Along with the all-too-vivid image of her bare belly and long, slender flanks.

''Evidently an unlocked door is one of those ground rules we didn't cover,'' she said stiffly. ''Maybe we'd better sit down and spell them all out.''

Yeah. Right. With Jack stripped down to the waist and her in a scrap of nylon and last.

Not hardly!

''We'll spell them out tomorrow. For tonight, leave the door propped shut. And for God's sake, don't trip over any more trays.''

''I'll do my best.''

The sarcasm didn't win her any points. Shooting an evil look across the room, Jack made sure the dead bolt on the door to her suite was set, checked the window locks once more and retreated. His side of the connecting door closed with a small thud. A few seconds later, the shattered door on her side hit with a bang.

He was up before dawn the next morning. Showered and shaved, he took perverse pleasure in rapping on the door just past seven.

Some moments later, Ellie yanked it open. She'd

pulled a short silk robe over her T-shirt, thank God. Her hair spilled over her shoulders in a rumpled free fall. Sleep added a hoarse note to her voice when she croaked at him.

"What?"

"I'm going to make a quick visit to the San Antonio police department. Don't leave the hotel until I get back."

Still groggy, Ellie grunted an assent.

Never a morning person, she felt about as fresh and perky as last week's leftovers. Her eyelids scraped like sandpaper. Her mouth had that cottony fuzz that cried for Scope. The fact that Jack was wide awake, showered and looking lean and tough in snug jeans and a black knit shirt that stretched taut across his shoulders only added to her disgruntlement.

As she closed the door behind Jack, though, she would have traded mouthwash and toothpaste *and* half her next month's salary for a cup of black coffee. She considered calling room service to order a pot, but the prospect of explaining the broken dishes and shattered connecting door nixed that notion. Any more damage to their historic hotel and the Mengers' management would probably call in the sheriff to escort her out of town.

Shaking her head, Ellie padded into the bathroom and turned the shower to full blast. Steam soon wreathed the room. After shedding her robe and undies, Ellie stepped into the stall and waited for the hot jets to work their restorative magic.

By the time Jack returned, she was dressed in a fresh pair of khaki shorts, a tan tank and a sleeveless khaki vest that came equipped with a half dozen handy pockets. With her hair tucked under a ball cap and a thick slathering of insect repellent coating all exposed areas of skin, she once again felt ready to take on all comers.

Jack included.

Chapter 6

"The police don't have anything on the Expedition yet."

Ellie accepted Jack's terse report with a nod. After her less than positive experience with the detective investigating her ransacked hotel room and the threats scrawled across her mirror, she hadn't really expected much.

"Have you had breakfast?" she asked, trying to tamp down her impatience to get out to the site. She'd already lost almost a whole day of work. With the National Park Service director waffling over the funding for the project, she didn't want to lose any more.

"I downed a cup of coffee and a breakfast burrito

while I was waiting for Detective Harris to put in an appearance at the precinct,'' Jack replied. ''How about you?''

''I'll grab some coffee on our way through the lobby.''

''You need more than that.''

''That's all I ever have in the mornings.''

Draping her heavy canvas bag over her shoulder, Ellie waited for him to join her at the door. Jack went out first, armed the anti-intrusion devices he'd installed and followed her down the hall.

Thankfully, the hotel provided complimentary coffee for its guests. Downing the hazelnut blend in quick, grateful gulps from a cardboard cup, Ellie settled into the passenger seat of Jack's rented Cherokee. This time, the drive down Mission Trail proved uneventful. No dusty SUVs with darkened windows chasing after them. No high-speed twists and turns. Only Ellie and Jack, thigh-to-thigh in the close confines of the rental vehicle.

By the time they pulled into the parking lot of Mission San Jose, she felt the need to put some immediate distance between her and the hard, muscled contours of his body.

''We could drive around to the dig,'' she informed him, shouldering open her door, ''but I thought you might want to see the mission compound first. It'll give you a better sense of what the Alamo was like back at the time of the siege.''

Slinging her canvas field bag over one shoulder, Ellie led the way down a gravel path. As always, Mission San Jose's tranquil setting and superb restoration thrilled both the historian and the aesthete in her. San Jose had been the largest and most active of the Texas religious settlements and, in her considered opinion, richly deserved its title as the Queen of the Missions.

The church boasted a large cupola dome, an exquisitely ornamented façade and the beautiful but curiously misnamed Rose Window, with elaborate carvings not of flowers but pomegranates. A rectangular granary with an arched roof dominated the opposite side of the compound from the church. The walls surrounding both were twelve feet thick, a potent reminder that these missions served secular as well as religious purposes.

"San Jose was founded in seventeen twenty," Ellie told Jack, their boots crunching the gravel path in a synchronized beat. "Just a few years after the Alamo. Like the other Texas missions, its purpose was to convert the local population to Catholicism, extend Spanish civilization in the New World and buttress the northern frontiers. At one time, the mission housed a population of more than three hundred priests, soldiers and Coahuiltecan Indians."

Signs spaced at intervals on the path pointed to various points of interest, including the park headquarters and gift shop. Ellie steered Jack past the main structures toward a gate in the far wall.

"The Indians farmed the surrounding countryside, producing corn, beans, potatoes, sugar cane and cotton, among other crops. They also maintained large herds of cattle, sheep and goats. Naturally, a rich settlement like this made for an irresistible target for hostile raids. When the Apache or Comanche threatened, the residents would drive their livestock inside the compound and hunker down behind San Jose's massive walls. Reportedly, they were never breached."

"Unlike those at the Alamo," Jack commented.

"Also unlike the Alamo, San Jose is still an active Catholic parish. Masses are said in the church, and I'm told it's a popular spot for weddings. The diocese maintains the church, and the National Park Service is responsible for the other structures and the outlying grounds."

Once through the small gate, they faced a wide, grassy field banded on three sides by a split rail fence. A twisting line of cottonwoods defined the fourth. As Jack and Ellie crossed the field toward the tree-lined creek, grasshoppers buzzed in the early morning heat and leaped out of their way. About halfway across the grassy field Ellie pointed out a series of small squares dug in the earth. Staked strands of wire surrounded each square. Red tags dangled from the wire.

''We've been using metal detectors to scan this field. Each of those tags marks a spot where we found spent cartridge shells. Most of the shells have rifling marks which suggest they were fired from Brown Besses similar to those used by the Mexican army. We also found several we think were fired by the shotgun we excavated down by the creek. We won't know for sure until we run a full ballistics analysis.''

She tried to keep her voice properly dispassionate, but the thrill of discovery added a vibrancy she couldn't quite disguise. ''Notice how those digs run in almost a straight line from north to south?''

Jack took a quick fix on the sun and nodded. Carefully, Ellie emphasized her point.

''The trail of expended bullets extends from the far corner of the Mission San Jose Park almost to the creek.''

''By extrapolation,'' he said slowly, picking up on her lead, ''from the Alamo to this spot five miles south, where a desperate defender might have raced for the tangle of trees to escape his pursuers, firing as he rode.''

She beamed at him. ''Exactly!''

His instant grasp of the significance of those small digs didn't surprise her. Jack Carstairs was no dummy. Except, she amended, when it came to his long-ago relationship with a passionate nineteen-year-old.

"The bullets track right to the spot where the skeletal remains were found," she related.

"Who found them?"

"The bullets or the bones?"

"The bones."

"A couple of boys. They snuck out of Sunday Mass and slipped away to play by the creek. When they spotted the bones, they ran yelling for their mom."

"Probably had nightmares for a month after that."

"I don't think so," Ellie replied, laughing. "I saw the news cam videotapes taken right after the find. The boys mugged like mad for the cameras. They seemed to think they'd landed right in the middle of a grand adventure. Even more so after the police and ME determined from the artifacts found with the bones that the find had historical significance."

"Is that when you were called in?"

"Yep. Because I'd done so much work for and with the National Park Service, the director contacted me and asked me to head up the team. He hasn't said so," she added with a wry grin, "but I'm pretty sure he's regretting his choice."

They were almost to the creek when Eric Chapman stepped out of the shadows and into the blazing sunlight. A metal detector extended from his left arm like a long, mechanical claw. When he spotted Ellie, a look of profound relief crossed his face.

"Hey, boss lady. You got here just in time."

"Uh-oh. What's up?"

"Another TV reporter, with cameraman in tow. Sam's trying his best to fob her off with the press release we hammered out last night, but she wants down and dirty details."

Ellie threw a glance at the trees. Just what she needed to start her day. A camera crew and more adverse publicity. Swallowing a sigh, she eyed the detector strapped to Eric's arm.

"We've pretty well covered this open field. Work the grids closer in to the mission today."

"Will do."

Jack's knowledge of metal detectors was thin, at best, but even with his limited frame of reference, he could tell the piece of equipment cuffed to Chapman's arm was no ordinary treasure hunter's toy.

"It's my own design," Ellie told him, noting the direction of his gaze. "Remember that little black box that contained the database I developed after those summers at Glorietta Pass?"

"Yes."

"It's a duplicate of the one that fits right here, on the neck of the metal dectector."

She signaled Chapman to raise the instrument for Jack's inspection. Grunting, the grad student lifted the heavy wand to waist level.

"I call this baby Discoverer Two," she said with a touch of proprietary pride. "Discoverer One was the prototype."

Like most metal sweepers, Discoverer came with a large, flat disk at the bottom end of its arm. At the top, where the wearer could comfortably read it, sat the computerized brain box Ellie referred to.

"One ping gives you a good idea of what you've found," Chapman added. "A low tone indicates iron, gold and nickel. A medium tone, lighter metals like aluminum pull tabs and zinc. Brass, copper and silver return a high pitch."

"In addition to the type of metal found," Ellie elaborated, "Discoverer will tell you how deep it's buried. The built-in computer also uses the signal return to paint a picture of the object here on this little screen. When we lock on something that looks, sounds and smells like a shell casing, the pre-programmed data from my prior research gives us a pretty good indication what type."

His arm sagging with the weight of the wand, Chapman waited patiently for her to finish describing some of the more technical aspects of the equipment. Once the grad student had trotted off to begin his sweeps, Ellie drew in a deep breath, braced herself and plunged into the shade of the cottonwoods.

The rest of her crew was there, doing their best to dodge the questions of a news reporter with a waist-length curtain of black hair and an air of dogged inquisitiveness. Sam Pierce stood solidly in front of the camera and greeted Ellie's arrival with barely dis-guised relief.

"Here's Dr. Alazar now. She can give you a better estimate of when we'll release our findings."

Jack stepped to the side and out of the picture as the camera locked onto Ellie.

"Dr. Alazar. Deborah Li, Channel Six news. We understand you've sent bit of bone from the remains you recovered to the police lab for DNA sampling."

"That's correct."

"When will you have the results?"

"Hopefully, by the end of the week."

"Then you're going to run a match against a sample from one of William Travis's descendents?"

"A great-great-grandniece has volunteered a sample," she confirmed. "So have descendents of several other Alamo defenders."

After all the bad press, Ellie only hoped the donors would still provide the samples as promised. Several had already voiced doubts. She didn't share that bit of information with the reporter, however.

"What if there's no match?" Li asked. "Pardon the pun, but won't that shoot your theory that the remains might belong to William Barrett Travis all to heck?"

"At this point, it's only a theory," she reminded the reporter with unruffled calm. "One of several we're working. If you like, I'll show you around the site. There's not much to see at this point, though," she warned. "We're almost finished here. By next week, we hope to switch from field to full laboratory mode.''

As curious as the reporter, Jack trailed along. It was quite an operation, he discovered. Two vans held racks for the team's equipment, which included an impressive array of computers, field microscopes, digital imaging cameras and chemicals for sampling soil, wood and metal fragments. The excavation site was cut into the bank of the creek. It formed a flat, level bed where what looked like a hundred or so cubic yards of mud and debris had been removed bit by careful bit.

''As I said, there not much to see at this point. The major artifacts we recovered have been photographed, catalogued and shipped to Baylor University, where Dr. Dawes-Hamilton and her assistants will complete the authentication process. The skeletal remains were transported to the San Antonio morgue pending DNA identification and possible burial by family. If we make no ID, the bishop of the diocese has agreed they should be buried here, in San Jose's old mission cemetery.''

At this point, Ellie explained, the team was working the final phase of on-site activity. Reconfirming exact coordinates of the finds. Digging additional exploratory sites up and downstream to make sure they hadn't missed any artifacts. Making last, expanded sweeps with the metal detector.

Jack found the excavations fascinating, the decisive authority Ellie projected even more so. She was at once coolly professional and vibrantly passionate about her work. She never allowed the reporter to throw her off stride or pull information she preferred not to give.

When the news crew departed a half hour later, her skin wore a pearly sheen of perspiration and her boots were caked with mud, but no one viewing her on the news tonight could doubt her credentials or the intellectual honesty she brought to the project.

Not that either would protect her from a nut bent on safeguarding his preferred version of history. Or a professional hired for the same purpose.

His senses on full alert, Jack turned his attention to the group who remained after the TV crew departed. In addition to the professional members of the team, a number of amateur archeologists, high school students and interested volunteers had turned out to help.

"We don't have as many volunteers as we did at the start of the project," Ellie explained. "As a result of the adverse publicity, a number have defected."

Those who hadn't were already hard at work. As Jack soon discovered, even the last stages of field-work involved labor-intensive effort. He wasn't quite sure how Ellie roped him into it, but by mid-morning he was up to his knees in creek mud, digging an exploratory site alongside Sam Pierce and a fresh-faced sophomore.

Later that afternoon, he tried a turn with the metal detector. It took a few swipes to get into a smooth rhythm, keeping the bottom flat to the ground and the swing in a controlled arc. It also took muscle power. The contraption weighed only about eight or ten pounds, but felt more like twenty or thirty after Jack had covered the length of the compound's south wall a half dozen times.

True to Eric Chapman's predictions, the digital displays lit up like fireworks at any hint of metal. The number and variety of objects buried beneath the earth astounded Jack. Discoverer Two hit on bridle bits, nails and barrel hoops from the nineteenth century, beer cans, bobby pins and dimes from the twentieth, and just about everything in between. His prize find was a blackened, dented silver disk.

"It's a concho," Ellie informed him after scrutinizing the object. "From the size of it, I'd say it's most likely off a bridle or sombrero. The concho was the decoration of choice on hats favored by both Mexicans and Tejanos. At least until a New Jersey hatter by the name of Stetson traveled west for his health and produced his version of the ten-gallon hat."

"I always wondered if those things really held ten gallons," Jack mused, recalling once again the Westerns he'd seen, where scouts and cowboys poured precious canteen water into their hats for their panting ponies.

Smiling, Ellie shook her head. "Only about three, actually, although that had nothing to do with the name. Gallon is a derivation of the Spanish word *galon,* which means braid. A ten-gallon hat simply refers to the amount of braiding around the brim."

"Another Hollywood myth shot down in flames," Jack muttered, shaking his head as she added the metal disk to the inventory of historical artifacts to be turned over to the National Park Service.

All too aware that they were working on borrowed time, the team remained at the dig until seven that evening. Once back at the hotel, Ellie conducted a quick wrap-up before sending her crew off to hit the showers and find dinner.

Jack was ready for both. When he knocked on the connecting door a half hour later, his stomach rumbled like a '56 Chevy with bad pipes. His hunger took on a whole different edge, however, when Ellie answered his knock. She'd changed into a long, gauzy flowered skirt in shades of green and lavender, topped by a lilac scoop-necked top. A silver crucifix on a thin chain circled her neck. Silver hoops dangled from her ears. As always, Jack noted with a kick to his gut, the bracelet he'd given her so many years ago banded her wrist.

But it was her hair that drew his gaze. She'd caught it back with combs at either temple and left the still damp, shining mass to tumble down her back, the way she used to when they'd first met.

Like hard right jabs, the memories hit him. Of tugging those combs free. Burying his face in that fragrant mass. Tunneling his fingers through the silky curtain to bring her mouth down to his.

Christ!

Clenching his fists, Jack managed to ask in a relatively normal voice where she wanted to have dinner.

"After last night's fiasco with room service, I suggest we go downstairs. Or better yet, out on the Riverwalk. I'll take you to my favorite Mexican restaurant. It's only a block away."

"Lead the way."

As Ellie had indicated, Casa del Rio was only a short walk from the hotel. They could have covered the distance in five minutes if not for the crowds jamming the popular Riverwalk.

"I've never seen it this packed," she told Jack as they took the stairs down to the river and plunged into the ebb and flow.

Crowded was an understatement. Tourists strolled shoulder-to-shoulder along the stone walks lining both sides of the placid green waterway. Many toted plastic drink cups and called to friends on the opposite side of river, pitching their voices to be heard over the music that spilled from the hotels and outdoor restaurants crowding the flagstone walk. A good number of the revelers wore wide-brimmed sombreros. Unlike the hats Jack and Ellie had discussed only this afternoon, these were cheap straw imitations decorated with red and green pom-poms instead of leather braid or silver conchos.

"There must be a convention in town," Ellie murmured, surveying the sea of straw.

"There is."

The comment came from a tourist decked out in an ankle-length red sundress and one of the distinctive sombreros. Dipping her head, she pointed to the lettering on the high-peaked crown.

"The American Travel Agents Association annual convention. Tonight's our big opening gala. You'll see the fireworks shooting up from the convention center later on."

Smiling her thanks, Ellie wedged sideways to make way for the woman and her companions. The movement brought her close to the river. Too close. Her heel caught on the edge.

"Careful!"

Jack's hand whipped out and caught her arm. He spun her away from the murky water. She landed awkwardly against his chest. Fingers splayed against his shirtfront, she blinked at him.

Ellie had never believed the silly cliché about time standing still, but for some reason the moment seemed to stretch forever. She could feel Jack's heat and the strong, steady beat of his heart under her fingertips. Her pulse skipped a beat, two, then drummed like thunder in her ears.

She didn't expect the hunger that leaped up and grabbed her by the throat. Wasn't prepared for it. Yet everything in her burst into a fever of need.

"Jack…"

He must have felt it, too. His muscles tensed. The arm he'd slipped around her waist to steady her tightened to a steel band. Ellie strained against him, aching, wanting, only to crash back to reality at the sound of a chuckle.

"Excuse us, folks. Hate to intrude on your little tête-à-tête, but we need to get by. Don't want to be late for the opening gala."

A glance over her shoulder showed a circle of grinning travel agents. Her cheeks warming, Ellie pulled out of Jack's arms. "Sorry."

"No apologies necessary, sweetie!" The woman in the red knit sundress laughed and let her gaze drift over Jack with unabashed feminine appreciation. "If a world-class hottie looked as hungry for me as this one just did for you, I sure as heck wouldn't be sorry."

Her glance dropped to Ellie's left hand. Grinning, she dug into her straw tote.

"Here's my card. Give me a call when you two are ready to make it legal, and I'll get you a heck of a deal on a honeymoon package."

Ellie's cheeks went from warm to downright hot

as she accepted the card the woman pressed on her and slipped it into her skirt pocket. Mute, she steered through the crowds toward the restaurant.

Jack kept his jaw clamped shut and his hand on Ellie's arm. *Not* because he couldn't bring himself to let her go. And certainly not because the press of her body against his for those brief moments had set spark to a fire in his belly he was doing his damnedest to douse.

The fact was he didn't like these crowds. Liked even less the advantage the restaurants and hotels on either side of the walkway gave a shooter. Anyone could check into the Hyatt or Hilton. Take a room on one of the upper floors. Line up a clear shot at the merrymakers flowing by below. His nerves crawling, Jack tucked Ellie closer to his side. She frowned when their hips bumped a time or two, but said nothing.

The restaurant she'd selected didn't provide any better cover. Case del Rio sat right on a bend of the river, its open-air patio a kaleidoscope of umbrellas and colored lights strung from tree to tree.

"Let's eat inside," Jack muttered, guiding Ellie away from the exposed patio and into the air-conditioned interior. Only after the waiter had showed them to a booth set well away from the windows and he'd scoped out the clientele did he allow his shoulders to slump against the back of the booth.

Ellie's brown eyes met his. He knew she'd felt it,

too. The way his muscles leaped under her touch. The instant heat every time they came in contact. He read the question in her eyes but didn't have an answer that would satisfy either one of them. He thought he caught a flash of disappointment, maybe even regret, before she picked up the menu and used it as a shield between them.

"I'll have combination number three," she told the waiter who plopped down a basket of chips and cups of salsa. "And a margarita."

"Same here," Jack said, tossing aside his menu. "No margarita, though. Just water."

"Just water?" Ellie echoed when the waiter departed. "As I recall, your drink of choice used to be an icy cold Corona."

"It still is, but not while I'm on duty."

"That's right." Frowning, she stabbed a chip into the salsa. "How could I forget? You're on duty."

The word hung between them, as solid as a brick wall and twice as impenetrable. In her last, furious tirade all those years ago, Ellie had accused him of caring more about the Corps than he did about her. Of letting his sense of duty take precedence over what they had together. What they could have together.

Like an uninvited guest who wouldn't take the hint and leave, the echoes of that ugly argument stayed at the table all through the meal. As a result, conversation was stilted, at best. Ellie shook her head when the waiter asked if she wanted another margarita, then abruptly changed her mind.

By the time she slurped up the last of her drink and they left the restaurant, dusk had softened to night, and colored lights twinkled all along the river. The late hour hadn't diminished the foot traffic. If anything, the crowds had increased. Barges filled with sightseers jammed hip-to-hip floated over the dark water. From another barge, a mariachi band poured a soaring rendition of "Una Paloma Blanca" into the night. The music drew cheers and applause from the appreciative crowd, most of whom, Jack noted, sported straw sombreros. The travel agents had descended on the Riverwalk en masse.

His muscles tensed in instinctive response to the crowd. Throngs like this could provide an excellent protective shield. Conversely, they could also mask the approach of unfriendlies.

Jack kept Ellie on the inside, away from the river, and forged a path toward the stairs leading up to street level. They were just a few feet from the steps when he heard a muted pop and the crack of rock splintering.

He took Ellie down in one swift lunge, covering her body with his on the way down. Before they hit the ground, the night exploded around them.

Chapter 7

Pinning Ellie to the stone, Jack yanked out his automatic and twisted around. In the heart-pounding seconds that followed, he registered the startled faces of tourists. The lights strung through the trees. The deafening booms that exploded into starbursts of glittering red and green.

"Hey!" one of the bystanders exclaimed over the flashes of color. "What the heck do you think you're doing?"

With a snarl, Jack whipped his weapon toward the source of the shout. The man's face went chalk white beneath his sombrero. Stumbling against his companions, he jerked up both palms.

"Take it easy, pal! Take it easy!"

There was another earsplitting series of pops. Red and green balloons pinwheeled through the sky. As the sound faded, Ellie gasped and wiggled under the dead weight pinning her to the flagstones.

"What's going on?"

Jack didn't take his eyes from the crowd. "I heard a gunshot."

"That—that was the fireworks," the white-faced travel agent stuttered, his hands still high. "Really, pal, all you heard was the fireworks."

As if to add emphasis to his nervous explanation, another series of booms exploded right overhead. Rockets of brilliant red and green shot into the night sky, trailing long, sparkling tails. A chorus of oohs and ahs rose from the spectators not engaged in the small drama occurring at the foot of the stairs.

"Jack." Ellie panted, wiggling frantically. "Please! I can't breathe."

He had to get her out of here. The single thought hammered in Jack's head. He rolled to his feet, the automatic tight against his thigh. Wrapping his free hand around Ellie's arm, he hauled her up.

The travel agent and his friends gaped as Jack hustled Ellie up the stone stairs. She was panting when they gained street level and decidedly unhappy when they arrived at the Menger. While the elevator whizzed them upward, she collapsed against the brass cage.

"That's twice now you've pulled that gun and

scared the dickens out of me. Tell me you haven't gone all Rambo since leaving the Marines.''

"I haven't gone all Rambo.''

"Then what's with the rather dramatic reaction to a few fireworks?''

"I recognize the sound of a gunshot fired from a silenced weapon when I hear it.''

Ellie opened her mouth, snapped it shut again. She didn't say a word during the walk down the hall to her room or while Jack checked the intrusion detection devices he'd set when they left the hotel. Satisfied no one had been in the rooms, he turned to face her.

She stood in the middle of the room, hugging her crossed arms. Her face and throat showed a decided pallor against the soft lilac of her top.

"If you did hear a gunshot,'' she said slowly, "it was timed perfectly to go off with the fireworks.''

"That's what I'm thinking.''

"So if there *was* a shooter, he's not some nutcase trying to scare me away.'' A shudder rippled down her body. Her fingers dug into her arms, making white marks in the tanned skin. "He's planning each move.''

As much as Jack wanted to shield her from the ugly suspicions he'd been harboring for the past twenty-four hours, he knew he had to level with her. She wasn't the young girl he'd once dreamed of keeping safe and warm in his arms. She was Dr.

Elena Maria Alazar, the woman he'd been sent to protect. As such, she had to understand the nature of the threat as he perceived it.

"I think we're dealing with a pro, Ellie. Someone who knows exactly what he's doing."

Briefly, he related the information he'd received from Mackenzie yesterday. Ellie's eyes narrowed as he detailed the assumed identity, the gunpowder residue, the Expedition carefully wiped clean of all prints.

"Why didn't you tell me all this before now?"

"I should have," he admitted.

She was furious, as she had every right to be. Eyes spitting fire, she marched up to him and jabbed a blunt-tipped finger into his chest.

"I'd suggest you remember who hired you, Carstairs."

"Your uncle, I was told."

"Wrong!" Her finger struck again. "Uncle Eduardo insisted I have a bodyguard. I insisted it be you."

"You were behind this job?" His hand closed over hers, stilling it before she could take another jab. "Why?"

"I felt guilty."

"Guilty?" That threw him. "For what?"

"For causing you to be sent home in disgrace," she snapped. "For ruining your military career. For making you start over as a hired hand with some obscure company no one's ever heard of.''

Jack couldn't tell her OMEGA worked very hard at remaining obscure. He was still absorbing the fact that Ellie had carried around a load of guilt all these years almost equal to his own.

''None of what happened was your fault,'' he countered fiercely. ''I knew the risks when I took you to bed. Given the same circumstances, I'd do it again. In a heartbeat.''

Her breath caught. She stared at him, her anger suspended, her hand fisting into a tight ball under his.

''What about—?''

She stopped. Drew her tongue along her lower lip. Forced out a ragged question.

''What about *these* circumstances?''

Jack barely swallowed his groan. He wanted her. God, he wanted her! The hunger was like a wild beast, clawing at his insides to get out.

This time there was more at stake than his career and her reputation, though. This time, her life might well depend on his ability to remain detached and alert.

''As you said, I'd best remember I'm a hired hand. I was sent here to protect you, Ellie.''

Disgust flickered in her eyes. Or was it disappointment? Before Jack could decide, she yanked her hand free of his.

"We've already had this discussion."

"Yes, we have."

"Do you have anything else to tell me about this phantom who may or may not be stalking me?"

"I wish I did."

She nodded. One quick, regal dip of her chin. "Then if you'll excuse me, I have work to do."

Jack took the hint and beat an orderly retreat. Somehow, he'd come out on the losing end of this discussion.

Ellie paced the sitting room, glaring at the computer sitting on the table, at the stacks of field notes waiting for review, at the closed connecting doors. Despite her icy request that Jack make himself scarce, work was the farthest thing from her mind at the moment.

What was the matter with her! Hadn't she learned her lesson nine years ago? Why in the world was she twisting herself into knots like this?

Over Jack Carstairs, for pity's sake! The stubborn Marine who'd considered her too young, too starry-eyed, to know her own mind. The noble idiot who'd walked away from her. The man who'd already broken her heart once.

If she let him do it again, she'd be a fool! A total, one-hundred-percent, feather-headed fool!

No way was she giving in to the heat that had flamed under her skin at his touch. *Or* following up on his startling admission that he'd take her to bed again in a heartbeat, given the same circumstances.

She had herself convinced, completely convinced, until she shoved her hands in the pockets of her skirt and felt a slip of pasteboard. Her throat tightening, she pulled out the business card the travel agent had pressed on her earlier. She stared at the embossed printing until it blurred. Crumpling the card in her fist, she whirled, crossed the room and yanked open the connecting doors.

Jack was standing at the window, hands shoved in his back pockets, staring out at the darkness. Her abrupt entrance spun him around.

"I have to know." She bit the words out. "Did you ever love me?"

"What?"

"Tell me, dammit. Did you love me?"

So bad, he'd hurt with it. In every inch of his body. Jack couldn't admit the truth then. And it was too late now. Far too late.

"What difference does it make?" he said quietly. "What's done is done."

"Bull!" She flared up, as fiery and passionate as the girl he'd once known. "It makes all the difference in the world. I want to know. I need to know."

"What you need is to go back to your room before one of us says something we might regret."

"Like what?" She advanced on him, her chin tipped to an angle he recognized all too well. "That we still want each other? That you get still hard and I still get hot every time we bump knees or hips or elbows?''

''Ellie, for Christ's sake!''

''What? Are you worried I'll bring up the fact that you wanted to kiss me down there on the river before dinner? Or admit that I *ached* for you to do it?''

She stopped in front of him. Her breasts rose and fell under the scoop-necked top. A pulse beat wildly in one side of her throat.

''I'm still aching, Jack.''

Her total honesty humbled him, just as it had nine years ago. She held nothing back. She never had. Desire jolted into him, as hot and fierce as any he'd ever felt for her. He went rigid, fighting the shock, fighting himself.

Ellie couldn't miss his reaction. Triumph leaped into her eyes. She moved closer, determined to get at the truth whether he wanted it out or not.

''I have to know.''

She raised her arms, slid them around his neck. Her breasts flattened against his chest. Her hips canted, pressing her belly into the bulge that pushed hard and hurting against his zipper.

''Did you love me?''

He couldn't lie to her. He'd never lied to her. But neither could he fully articulate the tangle of emotions she'd roused in him. He hesitated for long moments, then offered her the only answer he could.

"I would have laid down my life for you."

Her throat closed. He *had* laid down his life for her. The only real life he'd ever known. At the same time, he'd spurned her offer to do the same.

"But you wouldn't let me sacrifice my reputation or my career for you."

His jaw locked. "That was different."

She stared at him, torn between a sharp, sudden urge to whack him alongside the head and the overwhelming need to kiss the mule-headed stubbornness right off his face.

She waffled between the contradictory impulses for several moments before muttering a curse that would have shocked her students and her colleagues. Tightening her arms, she hauled herself up on her toes and fastened her mouth on his.

Jack stood stiff and unyielding under her assault, but he didn't break the contact. He didn't even *try* to break the contact. Her pulse leaping, Ellie angled her head to fit her mouth more fully against his.

Memories of other nights and other kisses exploded inside her head. Deliberately she blanked her mind and concentrated fiercely on this moment.

When she finally pulled away, Jack might have been carved from gray Texas granite. His jaw was set. The cords in his neck stood out in stark relief. His blue eyes were dark, shuttered, hiding his thoughts.

Ellie felt the first twinge of remorse, followed

swiftly by self-disgust. She'd done it again! Thrown herself at the man. Shame coursed through her, but pride kept her head high as she offered a stiff apology.

"I'm sorry, Jack. That was stupid of me. I had no business complicating an already awkward situation."

His stony silence signaled complete agreement.

Ellie forced a smile. "You'd think I'd have learned to exercise some restraint in nine years."

Actually, she had. She'd acquired a good deal of patience and restraint. She'd dated a fair number of men over the years. Had even thought she could fall in love with one or two. Yet she'd never *attacked* any of them.

Only Jack.

God, she was such a fool!

"I'm sorry," she whispered once again.

Writhing inside, she kept the smile plastered on her face and her chin high as she turned and headed for the connecting doors.

Let her walk.

The words thundered in Jack's head. He had to let her walk. If his years of experience as an undercover operative hadn't already underscored the need to maintain a clear head, Lightning had laid the issue square on the line. Jack was to keep his mind on the mission and his hands off Ellie. Period. End of discussion.

She got one step, maybe two, before he made a sound halfway between a snarl and a curse and went after her. Snagging her elbow, he yanked her around.

''We can both be sorry.''

The force of his kiss bent her backward. For a moment, Ellie thought her spine might crack. Recovering from her startled surprise, she threw her arms around his neck and fit her body to his.

Unleashed, his hunger was like a live, ravaging beast. It devoured Ellie. Consumed her. Thrilled her to her core.

This was a different Jack, she thought on a rush of wild excitement. Not the tender, passionate lover who'd teased and tormented her. Not the skilled tutor who'd schooled her in pleasures she'd never imagined. This Jack made no attempt to disguise what he wanted.

Ellie.

Naked.

Under him.

Afterward, she could never say who dragged whom down to the plush carpet. All she knew was that she was on fire by the time they hit. Every inch of her body flamed with heat. The areas Jack paid special, savage attention to blazed white-hot. Her lips. Her breasts. Her belly. The tight, aching nub between her thighs.

He stripped off her clothes first, then his own, all

the time doing things to her that had Ellie alternating between groans and breathless little pants.

She didn't lay passive. Submissiveness didn't form any part of her character. Her hands kept as busy as his. So did her mouth and tongue and teeth. Awash in a sea of sensations, she rediscovered the texture of his skin, the wiry tickle of his chest hair, the satin-smooth heat of his engorged shaft.

When he worked his hand between her thighs, she was wet and ready. So ready. Still, he primed her. The heel of his hand exerted exquisite, maddening pressure on her mound. His fingers worked a steady rhythm inside her. Ellie stood it as long as she could before lifting her body in a taut arc.

"Jack! Now!"

"No." Deliberately, he eased the tormenting pressure. "Not yet, Ellie. I've laid awake too many nights remembering how you—"

With a muttered curse, he bit off the rest of the sentence. A red flush mounted his cheeks.

Stunned, Ellie stared at the rugged planes of his face. He'd thought about her. Dreamed about her. Laid awake remembering her touch and her taste. The realization melted away the years. With them went much of the long-buried hurt and anger.

"I've laid awake, too," she whispered. "Too many nights to count."

His eyes searched hers. His jaw was clenched so tight Ellie thought it might crack. Just when she thought she'd have to take the initiative again, he groped for his jeans. For an awful moment, she thought he'd changed his mind. Frustration and chagrin welled to fill her throat with a taste like chalk.

To her infinite relief, he'd only paused to dig a condom out of his wallet. He'd protected her all those years ago, she remembered on a warm rush of emotion. He was still protecting her.

He sheathed himself with quick, jerky strokes, then rolled back to her. One hand tangled in her hair, bringing her head up for his crushing kiss. The other parted her legs and positioned his rigid member. Ellie opened for him joyously, eagerly, her heart singing a welcome even as her hips lifted to meet his initial thrust.

They made love with all the fury and twice the skill of their youth.

The first time was fast and hard. Mouths greedy, hands groping, hips grinding, they rolled over and over on the plush carpet. Ellie climaxed twice, mind-shattering orgasms that left her whimpering. Jack held back as long as he could, determined to draw out their pleasure, until Ellie took matters out of his hands. Hooking a leg, she climbed astride him, wrapped her fingers around his shaft and held him steady as she sank down, inch by satiny inch.

The second time was slower, lazier and took place

in bed, thank goodness. Ellie knew she'd sport a nice complement of carpet burns in the morning.

The third time left her completely sated and limp with exhaustion. It was well past midnight when she fell asleep, her arm flung across Jack's chest and her nose buried in his neck.

She awoke the next morning to find him sitting in the chair across the room. He was dressed all in black, unshaven, and looked more dangerous than she'd ever imagined he could.

Chapter 8

One glance at Jack's tight jaw and grim expression sent a single thought ripping through Ellie's sleep-fuzzed mind.

He was going to leave. Again.

With a flash of pure pain, she sensed that he was already regretting last night. As he'd pointed out several times, he was there to protect her. Only to protect her. Getting involved with Elena Maria Alazar—again—compromised not only his ability to do his job, it could very well cost him the career he'd carved out since leaving the Marine Corps.

Her chest squeezed so hard and tight she could barely breathe. Yanking at the tangled sheet, she bunched it over her breasts and wiggled up to rest

her bare shoulders against the wrought-iron headboard. With some effort, she managed to keep her
crushing sense of loss out of her voice.

"You're already dressed, I see. Are you going
out?"

"I've been out."

"Have you? Where?"

Her cool, almost disinterested query irritated the
hell out of Jack. He'd spent three hellacious hours,
first down at the river, searching for proof that someone had, in fact, fired at Ellie last night, then convincing the San Antonio PD detective honchoing her
case to haul his butt out of bed. Jack wanted a cast
of the fresh scar he'd found in the stone steps. Maybe
ballistics could turn up information as to the type of
bullet that had gouged it.

Finding evidence that a killer had taken aim at
Ellie was bad enough. Seeing her naked and sleepy-
eyed, sporting what looked suspiciously like a
whisker burn on the curve of her left shoulder, mag-
nified Jack's self-disgust and guilt a hundred times
over.

He'd been sent to San Antonio to keep her safe,
for God's sake! And what the hell did he do? Spent
half the night rolling around in the sack with the
woman whose life might well depend on his focus
and ability to concentrate.

If the killer had tried again...

If he'd hit when Jack was otherwise occupied...

If Ellie had been hurt…

His gut twisting, he practically snarled at her. "I told you I recognized the sound of a round fired from a silenced gun when I heard one."

She looked confused for a moment, either at his savage tone or the information he'd imparted.

"Last night," he growled, "on the Riverwalk, right when the fireworks went off. That was a shot."

The fingers gripping the bunched sheet went white at the knuckles. "Are you sure?"

"I'm sure. I found the gouge in the stone where the bullet hit."

The last of the sleepy flush left her cheeks. She stared at Jack, her eyes wide with dismay. Speculating that they might or might not have heard a gunshot was one thing, he knew. Having the brutal fact confirmed was another.

He hated the fleeting look of fear and helplessness that chased across her face. Hated even more driving home the fact that she was a target.

"From the angle of the mark," he continued tersely, "it looks like the shell ricocheted off the stone into the river. Detective Harris and an SAPD crime scene crew are down there now, trying to locate the shell and run it through ballistics."

Some of the helpless vulnerability left her face. "I can help with that! I'll lay odds my team's equipment is considerably more sophisticated than the police department's."

Dragging the sheet with her, she swung her legs over the edge of the mattress and groped for her clothes. Jack's harsh voice stopped her cold.

"Someone wants you dead, Ellie. Very dead. You're not leaving this room until I find out who."

"But…"

"The matter's not open for discussion or debate. Just so you know, I've requested backup to augment your security detail. I've also called in an expert from the company I work for to provide additional electronic surveillance and defensive countermeasures. Both team members are en route as we speak."

"Jack, be reasonable. I can't just cower here in my hotel room. Ballistics is my area of expertise. I can help. I want to help."

"I told you, the issue's not up for negotiation."

Her chin went up. "I'm not negotiating. Give me ten minutes to shower and dress."

Scooping up her clothes, she yanked the tail ends of the sheet free of the mattress and headed for the bathroom. Jack spit out a curse and followed. The shower jets were already turned to full blast when he pushed inside.

Her clothes lay in a scattered heap on the tile, along with the discarded sheet. Whirling, she snatched a towel from the nearest rack. Jack had a feeling he'd carry the image of her copper-tipped breasts, flat belly and the dark, seductive triangle be-

tween her legs around in his head for a long, long
time.

"I said ten minutes!"

"And I said you're not going anywhere."

Steam curled through the open stall door. The jets
drummed against the glass. Ellie made a heroic attempt at calm and reasonable. And failed.

"I'm not one of your troops. You don't bark orders at me and expect unquestioned obedience. I'm
an expert in my field, just as you are in yours. I'm
going to—"

"You're going to stay where I put you."

"*Put* me?"

"Don't force me take extreme measures."

Scorn flashed in her eyes. "What are you going to
do? Lock me in the bathroom?"

"I was thinking more along the lines of handcuff-
ing you to the bed."

"Oh, give me a break! I know you too well, Carstairs. You wouldn't resort to such Neanderthal tactics."

His gaze raked her near-naked form. A grim smile
settled in his eyes.

"Oh, yeah, babe. I would."

Without warning, the tension in the steam-filled
bathroom took on a whole different edge. Ellie felt
it right down to her bones. A sudden wariness that
had nothing to do with bullets or ballistics sent her
back a step. A feminine instinct older than time

screamed at her to cover herself, placate the angry male before her, defuse the situation.

Being Ellie, she did just the opposite. Another instinct, sharp and urgent, demanded she stand her ground. This was Jack, she reminded herself furiously. She'd let his hardheadedness defeat her once. She couldn't let him ride roughshod over her again. Not if she wanted him to consider her his equal. In *and* out of bed.

Spray from the open shower enveloped her in a fine mist. Steam invaded her lungs. Blinking away the drops that had collected on her lashes, Ellie looked him square in the eye.

"I wouldn't mind doing the bed-and-handcuff bit, as long as we take turns as the cuffee. But not right now, Jack. Right now I'm going to take a shower, get dressed and haul myself and my equipment down to the river. You can accept my decision and come with me, or..."

She let the sentence trail off, stalling for time while she tried to decide just what the heck *or* she could throw at him.

Jack obviously had a few ideas of his own. His eyes narrowed. The hot mist had soaked his hair and raised a sheen on the stubble darkening his cheeks. He looked wet and angry and menacing as he took a step forward.

"Or what, Ellie? You'll fire me?"

"Oh, no! I'm not letting you walk away from me again."

The retort spilled out before she could stop it. Recklessly, Ellie laid the rest of her tumultuous emotions on the line.

"We started something last night, Carstairs. Correction, we *restarted* something. I for one think we should see it thought to the finish this time."

Her heart slamming against her ribs, she waited to hear Jack's take on the matter. He declined to give one. Instead, he spun on one heel and made for the bathroom door.

Ellie's toes curled into the tiles. Fury and pain lanced into her in equal measures. "Jack! Dammit, you can't just—"

"Someone's at the door." He threw the words over his shoulder. "I'll see who it is, then we'll finish this discussion."

She hadn't heard a thing over the pelting water and the heat of her emotions. Muttering under her breath, she kicked the bathroom door shut, then stepped into the shower stall. When they finished this discussion, she wouldn't be bare-assed and still sticky with the residue of their lovemaking.

When he peered through the peephole and identified the individual on the other side of the door, Jack didn't know whether to curse or give a heartfelt grunt of relief. He settled for twisting the dead bolt and greeting OMEGA's chief of communications with a curt acknowledgment.

"You got here fast."

"Lightning put his personal jet at our disposal."

Mackenzie Blair breezed in, toting her heavy field case. She wore the uniform she favored for traveling, Jack noted: a dark blue T-shirt emblazoned with U.S. Navy in four-inch gold letters, snug jeans and serious running shoes. Few of OMEGA's special agents could keep up with the woman when she hit her stride.

She'd have a full assortment of other garments in her case, Jack knew. He and the other males at OMEGA all harbored a particular partiality for the jumpsuit she slipped into for night operations. The black nylon zipped up to her chin and covered her slender curves like a thin coat of paint.

Taking a quick glance around the suite, she cocked her head at the sound of running water in the other room. "Did I get you out of the shower?"

"No."

One brow lifted. "There must be some other reason your clothes are soaked, then."

There was, but Jack didn't offer it. His black shirt sticking to him like wet saran, he closed the door to the suite. Mackenzie dumped her case on a handy chair and turned to face him.

"Cyrene is checking in downstairs. I came right up. I've got something for you, Renegade."

Jack's pulse jumped at the intense satisfaction glimmering in her eyes.

"We IDed some interesting characters in our screen of Dr. Alazar's digital images. One in particular will catch your attention."

Punching in a code on the digital lock, she opened her field case and produced a flat silver CD. Her gaze cut to the computer sitting on the desk.

"Will Dr. Alazar mind if I use her laptop?"

Jack shook his head, although at this point he couldn't predict Ellie's reactions to anything. She'd put his back up with her stubborn resistance to his orders and thrown him for a complete loop with that business about not letting him walk away from her again.

Elena Maria obviously hadn't figured it out yet, but he had no intention of leaving her. Or letting her leave him. Not after last night. And sure as hell not with a killer stalking her.

His mouth set, he crossed the room to peer over Mackenzie's shoulder. She drummed her fingers impatiently while the laptop booted up, then sent them flying over the keys. A moment later, a scene was painted across the screen.

It was the courtyard of the Alamo. Jack recognized the low, flat building Ellie had identified as the Long Barracks in the foreground. In the background was the massive oak that gave welcome shade to the throngs of tourists wandering from exhibit to exhibit.

"There he is."

With a click of the mouse, Mackenzie placed an arrow on one particular tourist. He wore a straw Stetson and dark glasses. A camera was slung over one shoulder. He stood in the shade at the rear of the courtyard next to another man.

"It took me a while to ID him. The glasses obscure his eyes, and the hat conceals his hair color, although I doubt it's still the same color listed on the FBI most-wanted bulletin."

Well, hell! The FBI's most-wanted bulletin. That's all Jack needed to hear. The tension coiling his muscles took another tight twist.

"I finally got a hit on the scar." Clicking away, Mackenzie zoomed in on the man's profile. "See it? Just below his left ear?"

He saw it. "Unless I miss my guess, someone once took a knife to this particular tourist's throat."

"You pegged it. According to FBI reports, he got that little souvenir from a street pimp who strenuously objected to being taken out. He's a hit man, Renegade. A real professional. Suspected of killing at least ten people, both in the States and abroad."

Jack had suspected he was dealing with a pro. Knowing he was right didn't give him so much as a hint of satisfaction.

"The man's assumed dozens of different identities over the years," Mackenzie reported. "Including, we can lay odds, Mr. Harold Berger of 2224 Riverside

Drive, Austin. The FBI was *very* interested to hear he'd popped up in San Antonio. Particularly when we IDed the man standing next to him."

She zinged the pointer to a beefy, wide-shouldered man with sandy hair and a bulldog jaw.

"Meet Mr. Dan Foster. He's local, a very successful building contractor."

"What his connection to our hit man?"

"Three months ago, Foster's wife was kidnapped from their country club estate. Although there were some indications that both Fosters played around, Danny Boy appeared devastated by the kidnapping and insisted on paying the million-dollar ransom."

Eyes narrowed, Jack studied the image on the screen. Despite his size, Foster gave off a definite country club air. A designer logo decorated the pocket of his knit shirt. His khaki Dockers showed a knife crease. Gold flashed at one wrist.

"Before Foster could get the funds together," Mackenzie continued, "his wife's body turned up in a Dumpster. From the rope burns on her wrists and ankles, shredded nylons and gravel embedded in her knees, the FBI thinks she tried to escape and was shot in the process. Now, you'd expect the supposed kidnapper to bury the body or otherwise keep it hidden until after he'd collected the ransom."

"Unless he *wanted* it found," Jack said slowly.

"Right. Again, our friend Foster appeared devastated. But the Feds took note of the fact that he was sole beneficiary on his wife's two-million-dollar life insurance policy. And that he was falling behind on repayment of several major business loans he'd floated.''

The pieces fell together with startling clarity. The trashing of Ellie's hotel room, her stolen computer, the attempts on her life. None of those had anything to do with the controversy she's stirred up in town, but with the fact she caught a killer and the man who could well have hired him on camera.

''Foster must have sweated blood when he read the stories about Ellie in the papers,'' Jack guessed. ''Particularly those that went into detail about her digital scans of the Alamo and its weaponry. It wouldn't have taken more than a few calls for Foster to find out if Dr. Alazar was at the Alamo the same day he arranged to meet Scarface there.''

''What I don't understand,'' Mackenzie said, tapping a finger on the keyboard, ''is why the heck they'd risk meeting in such a public place.''

''Maybe he didn't feel safe meeting with a killer anywhere else. Maybe Scarface insisted on it, intending to blackmail Foster later by threatening to reveal his shady connections.''

''Then why would he care if Dr. Alazar caught the meeting on camera?''

''Scarface might not care, but Foster sure as hell would. My guess is he hired the guy to trash Ellie's hotel room and destroy her digital images. When word got out she'd backed them up, Foster would have no choice but to take out a contract on Ellie, too, hoping her death would scuttle her project—and the pictures she'd taken—before they ever saw light of day."

It was all speculation. Mere guesswork. But Jack knew in his gut they'd stumbled onto something.

"Did the Feds run a ballistics analysis of the bullet that killed Foster's wife?"

"I'm sure they did. I can e-mail my contact at the Bureau and find out. Why?"

"Because I'll bet you another dozen pizzas that the rifling marks on the bullet retrieved from her body will match those on the one fired at Ellie last night."

"Which makes it even more imperative we retrieve it from the river," a cool voice said behind them.

Jack grunted in disgust. Hell of a field agent he made! He hadn't heard the shower cut off. His only excuse was that Mackenzie's startling information had riveted his attention.

The new arrival seemed to rivet Mackenzie's. Her fascinated glance took in every detail of Ellie's fresh scrubbed face and damp hair before shifting to Jack's still wet shirt. OMEGA's chief of communications didn't say a word. She didn't have to. The deliberately bland expression she assumed said it all.

Unfortunately Lightning hadn't exercised the same

restraint. When Jack reported that matters between him and Ellie had taken an unexpected and very personal turn, Nick had ripped a foot-wide strip off his agent's hide.

Jack had expected nothing less. He'd also expected Lightning to yank him off the mission and was fully prepared to tell OMEGA's director to go to hell. No way Jack was leaving Ellie. He intended to stick so close to her she couldn't tell her shadow from his until he brought her stalker down.

After that…

His stomach clenched. He couldn't allow himself to think past right here, right now. Ellie's safety demanded his total focus. After would have to take care of itself. Silently, he watched her cross the room and hold out a hand to Mackenzie.

"I'm Elena Alazar. I assume you're one of Jack's colleagues."

"That's right."

Effortlessly, Mac slipped into the cover identity designed to shield her OMEGA connection. Since her extensive network of friends and acquaintances from her Navy days all knew about her background in and fascination with electronic gadgetry, she'd set up a fictitious company. Blair Consulting was listed in the Yellow Pages. It maintained a fancy home Page on the Web. Only a handful of Washington insiders knew the company's proprietor and sole employee worked exclusively for OMEGA.

"I'm Mackenzie Blair, Dr. Alazar. I own Blair Consulting. We specialize in electronic surveillance and computerized data searches. It's a pleasure to meet the woman who designed and developed the prototype for Discoverer Two."

"You know about metal detectors?"

"I'm former Navy," she answered with a grin. "We squids all harbor a secret fascination with sunken treasure. I've done my share of beachcombing."

"Then you might be interested in watching the Discoverer Two in action," Ellie said with a smile that did *not* include Jack. "I'm going to take it down to the river to help locate the shell casing you're both so interested in."

"Great!" Mackenzie enthused before Jack could counter Ellie's flat statement. "I'd love to see that sucker in operation. I understand you've loaded twenty gigabytes of metallurgical and ballistics data into its core operating system."

"Twenty-four, actually."

"Good Lord! How did you cram all that data in a portable device?"

"By compressing the reference files and—"

"Ladies," Jack interrupted. "Do you mind if we get back to the small matter of a stalker?"

Both women turned at his heavy-handed attempt to head off what had all the earmarks of an animated and lengthy discussion of bits and bytes.

"How much did you hear of what Mac had to say about the men in this image?" he asked Ellie.

Her glance flicked to the screen. It lingered on Scarface for long moments before shifting to Foster.

"Enough to make me want to hurt those bastards," she said fiercely. "Really bad. Let's get to work, shall we?"

Chapter 9

While Ellie and the young grad student on her team assembled the equipment she wanted to divert from the archeological site to the river, Jack met with the back-up agent OMEGA had sent in. Normally, Jack worked alone. The fact that he'd requested backup hadn't surprised Lightning, coming as it did on the heels of Renegade's admission that he'd crossed the line with Ellie.

After he'd finished tearing into Jack, Nick had sent one of the best. Claire Cantwell, code name Cyrene, had lost her husband to a bungled attempt to free a group of oil executives being held in Malaysia by radical separatists. Burying her grief behind a serene façade, she'd schooled herself to become one of the world's foremost experts on hostage negotiation. A noted psychologist, she was also OMEGA's most skilled agent when it came to screening crowds and identifying potential troublemakers.

Mackenzie respected and admired Renegade and Cyrene and looked forward to providing their on-scene electronics support. She'd just checked out a super-cool lie-detecting camera being developed by the Homeland Defense folks for airport use. The handy-dandy little device spotted deceivers by recording mild facial warming when under stress. She couldn't wait to have Cyrene test it out in her crowd surveillance. But when she checked into her room and made her initial on-site report, Lightning laid another task on her.

Nick Jensen's face was displayed with crystal clarity on the small screen of her communications unit. Thoughtful. A bit grim. And so damned handsome Mackenzie was tempted to drag her thumb over the trackball to blur the image a bit. She couldn't quite handle the combined impact of his navy blazer, Windsor-knotted red silk tie and deep tan this early in the morning!

"I want Foster on an electronic leash," Nick said. "He'd going to contact his hired gun sooner or later. He'll demand a progress report, or at least an explanation of why the hit's taking so long. Renegade will want to hear it when he does."

"No problem." Her mind was already sorting

through various technical options. "I'll look through my bag of tricks and see what we've got to play with."

"Good."

"Is that it?"

"For now."

"Roger."

Signing off, Mackenzie considered the best approach to Foster. Normally, field agents tagged targets. In fact, the unwritten rule of thumb was that *only* field agents made direct contact with targets. But Renegade needed Cyrene for backup on the river. There was no reason Mackenzie couldn't accomplish this little task herself.

The background dossier she'd compiled on Daniel Foster indicated he was something of a playboy who went in for the coy, kittenish type. She didn't have a kittenish bone in her body, and she wasn't sure how well she could do coy, but she'd give both her best shot.

Her first step was to trade her jeans and Nikes for strappy sandals and a sleeveless, V-neck dress with a matching short-sleeved jacket. The slinky black matte jersey defied wrinkles. It also clung to her slender curves.

After unclipping her hair, Mac dragged a brush through the shoulder-length dark mass and applied more makeup than she usually wore. A quick survey in the bathroom mirror convinced her to take a page from her mentor's book.

Maggie Sinclair, code name Chamelon, could assume a completely different personality with a few strategic accessories. At various times, Maggie had gone into the field disguised as a nun, a nuclear scientist and a high-priced call girl. On one memorable mission, she'd lifted a black lace garter belt and fishnet stockings from a shop, left a note for the owner to send the bill to the American consulate and waltzed into a smoke-filled waterfront dive that catered to gunrunners and drug lords.

What she needed, Mackenzie decided, was the equivalent of a black lace garter.

She found just what she was looking for at the department store located in the massive River Center complex adjacent to the Menger. The underwire demi-bra transformed even her modest curves into plump, seductive mounds. Additional pads pushed her breasts up so high they almost spilled out of the V-neck. More than satisfied with the result, Mackenzie charged the miracle bra to her OMEGA expense account.

She returned to the Menger and waited for the sporty little Mustang she'd arranged to have waiting at the south-side airport where Nick's private plane had landed this morning. The same valet who'd parked it in the Menger's garage less than an hour ago gawked at her dramatic cleavage when he delivered the vehicle curbside.

After she slid behind the wheel, Mackenzie placed her field case on the passenger seat and flipped down its side to access the keyboard. Dan Foster would be at work by now. According to the information she'd gleaned from her FBI contact, the two million Foster had collected from the insurance company after his wife's murder got him current on his construction company's outstanding loans but hadn't paid them off by any means. The man still had to work for a living.

She accessed the address and phone number of his office, then put in a quick call. The helpful receptionist informed her Mr. Foster was on-site at a job on San Antonio's north side. Twenty minutes later, Mackenzie pulled up at the fenced construction site.

Massive steel girders shot twenty-four stories into the cloudless blue sky. Super cranes hoisted beams to workers who appeared ant-like from the ground. Trucks raised clouds of dust as they rumbled in and out of the gate in the chain-link security fence.

Once again Mackenzie reached into her case. She peeled off the adhesive backing on a tiny, transparent disc, then stuck the disk to the back of her business card. Once attached, it became invisible. No one could tell it was there without a microscope.

She had just climbed out of the Mustang when two men exited the trailer parked beside the gate. One carried a clipboard and wore a badge identifying him as some kind of inspector.

The other was her quarry.

Her stomach did a little flip. Foster's size didn't intimidate her. Nor did his rugged good looks impress her. At all. It was just that the newspaper clippings and shots of Dan Foster the FBI had compiled did *not* do him justice.

Those grainy black-and-whites had depicted the man in a tux, his wife at his side, attending some fancy do at the country club. Or in a dark suit, his face contorted in grief as he exited a limo after her funeral.

This morning he was in boots, jeans and a hard hat. His rolled-up sleeves displayed trunklike arms that could only have been acquired by manhandling the dozers and cranes he now hired others to operate. Muscle had never particularly turned Mackenzie on, but she had to admit this guy's were impressive.

"Mr. Foster?"

He squinted through the dust. She started toward him, remembered her role and altered her stride to a hip-swinging glide.

"I'm Mackenzie Blair, president of Blair Consulting."

Foster accepted the business card she held out, but his glance made a detour to her chest and lingered for several seconds before dropping to examine the engraved lettering.

"I called your office for an appointment, but your secretary said you'd be on-site all day and suggested I catch you here."

"What can I do for you, Ms. Blair?"

"My consulting firm that specializes in electronic communications. I'm looking to expand my operations in this part of the country and would like to talk to you about the communications support you plan to put in this building."

"I've already accepted a bid from a subcontractor to wire it."

He was going with hard wire. Good. That gave her just opening she needed.

"I think you should consider fiber optics instead of wire."

"Well, I..."

"You'd be offering state-of-the-art networking capability to whoever occupies the building. And..." Her voice dropped to a throaty purr. "I guarantee I could save you a minimum of a hundred thousand dollars."

She'd pulled the figure out of a hat, a sheer guess based on the size of the project. As she'd anticipated, though, the combination of succulent Wonder curves and a possible hundred grand in savings proved irresistible.

The contractor's eyes gleamed under the rim of his hard hat. "A hundred thousand, huh?"

A teasing smile played at her lips. "I'm good at what I do, Mr. Foster."

"I'll just bet you are."

His glance dropped to her chest again before shifting to the inspector waiting patiently a few feet away.

"Look, I'm going to be tied up here for most of the day. Why don't we get together for a drink this evening and discuss all this money you're going to save me?"

Mackenzie let her smile curve into a seductive promise. "My cell phone number's on that business card. Call me."

"I will." Grinning, he tucked the card into his pocket and gave it a pat. "Talk to you tonight, Ms. Blair."

Oh, you'll be talking to me before then.

On that smug thought, she strolled to the Mustang.

A quarter mile from the site, she pulled to the side of the road and extracted a wireless earpiece. With the plastic piece tucked comfortably in her right ear, she keyed a special code into the receiver. Foster's angry voice stabbed into her head.

"...filed for those permits two months ago. I wish to hell you folks would get your act together."

Wincing, Mackenzie adjusted the volume. She'd tagged her target, temporarily at least. She'd replace the tag with a more permanent one tonight. Humming with satisfaction, she called in a quick order to

OMEGA's communications center to monitor the transmissions and drove off.

She connected with Renegade at the stairs leading to the Riverwalk. He'd planted both fists on the stone balustrade. His gaze was locked on the scene below.

The San Antonio PD had cordoned off a section of the river and commandeered one of the colorful river barges. Several uniformed and plainclothes police officers occupied the boat, which floated at the end of a long tether.

Dr. Alazar was in the barge, as well, along with her flame-haired assistant. As Mackenzie watched, Ellie slipped the heavy instrument that could only be Discoverer Two off her arm and passed it to the grad student.

"How's it going?" she asked the man beside her.

"It's not."

His face grim, Jack turned to give her a quick rundown. His startled glance zeroed in on her cleavage.

"Good Lord!"

"Hey, thanks a lot! At least Foster liked the new me."

Renegade's gaze whipped up to lock with hers. "You made contact?"

"And then some." Grinning, she tapped her ear. "He's right here, inside my head."

"Dammit, Mac, you shouldn't have tackled the

guy alone. You shouldn't have tackled him at all, for that matter. That's my job, or Cyrene's.''

"You were busy. And he was an easy mark. I'm a walking window into everything the man says or does. At the moment Danny Boy is… Hmm. It sounds like he's taking what we used to refer to in the Navy as a leak.''

"Has he talked to Scarface?''

"No. But he wants to continue *our* conversation. We're having drinks later tonight.''

"Does Lightning know about this?''

"Lightning's the one who said to tag the creep.''

She was stretching things a bit there. She knew it. Jack knew it.

"Last time I checked the field manual,'' he drawled, "tagging didn't include dinner or drinks.''

Since there was no such thing as a field manual for his line of work, Mackenzie decided to ignore the comment.

"Bring me up to speed on the salvage operation,'' she said instead, turning her attention to the barge. "What's happening?''

"Ellie laid out a search grid based on the angle of the gouge mark in the stone. They've been sweeping from left to right.'' Frustration edged his voice. "They're almost at the end of the grid.''

"They haven't found anything?''

"Are you kidding? They've found everything but the kitchen sink. That'll probably turn up, too. In the meantime, they've racked up an impressive collection of tire jacks, switchblades, car keys and coins in a dozen different currencies and denominations. But no bullets.''

"Hmm. Where's Cyrene?"

"Over there, at that restaurant. Second table to the left, by the rail.''

Mackenzie spotted the pale-haired agent at the open-air restaurant on the opposite side of the river. The elevated deck gave the agent a bird's-eye view of the barge as well as the curious crowd that had gathered to watch. With Renegade and Cyrene flying cover, Mackenzie opted for a closer view of the action.

"I'm going down to watch. I want to see Discoverer Two up close and personal.''

She had taken only a few steps before she heard a high-pitched pinging. Dr. Alazar's assistant gave an excited exclamation.

"I've got something on the screen! The digital displays indicate it's a spent forty-one caliber hollow-point casing, two hundred grain, number one hundred. Probably a Speer, although it could be a Remington.''

Brushing past Mackenzie, Jack went down the stone stairs two at a time. Part of him went tight with dread at the possibility the police might soon have evidence linking Dan Foster's murdered wife to the attempts on Ellie's life. Another part of him hoped they'd make the connection and he could convince Ellie to get the hell out of Dodge.

If he couldn't, those handcuffs were sounding better and better.

Grabbing the mooring line, Jack leaped onto the barge. It rocked under his weight and earned him a frown from the plainclothes detective and a grunt from Eric Chapman. The kid spread his legs wider to brace himself and held the detector steady over the water.

"It's showing a depth of seven and a half feet," he informed the wet-suited diver beside him.

"The water's only a little over six feet deep at this point," Ellie told Jack in an aside. "That means the bullet's burrowed into the mud."

A uniformed officer propped his elbow on the barge railing to add support for the heavy detector Eric held suspended over the river. Discoverer Two pinged noisily as the diver opened the air valve on his tanks, wrapped his lips around his mouthpiece and pulled down his face mask. Black fins waving, he went over the side with and hit with a splash. He glanced up to take a bead on the wand and dove straight down.

Shoulder-to-shoulder, Jack and Ellie peered over the railing. Mud swirled to cloud the green water. Air bubbles bobbed to the surface. The muted pops when they broke sounded so much like the silenced shot Jack had head last night that his palms got slick with sweat where they gripped the rail.

Dragging his gaze from the swirling water, he scanned the scene. He spotted Cyrene, seemingly relaxed and at ease as she sipped a frothy pink drink at a patio restaurant and let her glance drift over the gawking onlookers. Mackenzie was on the steps, dividing her attention between the voice in her head and the drama being played out before her.

Despite the added security, tension wrapped Jack in a tight coil. Scarface was out there. In one of the high-rise hotels overlooking the river. Lounging at a table in one of the restaurants. Mingling with the crowd. Watching. Waiting.

Jack could feel the killer. Smell him. He just couldn't see him. He edged closer to Ellie, angling his body to shield hers. His nerves were stretched so tight the whoosh of the diver breaking the surface damned near had him flinging her facedown in the barge.

Muddied green water streamed over the diver's mask. Spitting out his mouthpiece, he shoved his mask back on his head with one hand and held up the other.

"Is this what we're looking for?"

The expended shell gleamed in the sunlight. Unlike the artifacts Ellie and her team had recovered from the archeological site, the copper casing was clean and new and bright.

"It's a forty-one hollow point," Ellie confirmed with a single glance.

"Same caliber as the bullet that killed Joanna Foster," Detective Harris muttered.

Flashing Jack a quick glance, he dug a plastic evidence bag out of his pocket. In their first meeting, the SAPD veteran hadn't tried to disguise his cynicism about harebrained professors who stirred up more controversy than they could handle. He was coming around. Fast.

"We'll run it through ballistics ASAP," he promised Jack. "Should have a comparison between it and the bullet that killed Mrs. Foster by late this afternoon. Tomorrow at the latest."

Jack grunted, not happy with the prospect of another day's wait. Ellie didn't much like it, either. Frowning, she glanced at her watch.

"It's just a little past noon. I need to go out to the dig. I don't want to waste the rest of the day."

"Sorry. Consider it wasted."

"I'll go on out," Chapman volunteered.

After unstrapping the heavy mental detector, the young grad student swiped the sweat from his brow with a freckled forearm. The sight of the gleaming copper shell casing had sobered him…and turned him into a reluctant ally.

"Carstairs is right, Ellie. You shouldn't make yourself any more of a target than you already are."

Her mouth pursed. Jack was all set to ask Detective Harris for the loan of his handcuffs when she caved.

"All right. Tell the rest of the folks I'm sorry for leaving wrap-up operations to them. We'll convene in my room at 8:00 p.m. for a team meeting. In the meantime, I'll go through yesterday's field notes and start working on the draft report."

That was the plan, anyway. She returned to her suite, took a quick shower to wash away the sweat and stink of stirred-up river water. After a quick sandwich ordered from room service, she settled in front of her laptop and attacked the field notes, but the constant comings and goings of Jack's associates played havoc with her concentration.

With her fascination for all things electronic and near genius with computers, Mackenzie Blair was certainly an interesting study. Particularly after her sudden and rather startling transition from techno-geek to femme fatale. The calm, tranquil woman Jack referred to as Cyrene proved every bit as compelling in her quiet way.

Ellie caught only snatches of their discussion of cover points and team surveillance of Mackenzie's upcoming meeting with Dan Foster. She couldn't miss, however, Blair's rueful grin when she reported the gist of her conversation with someone named Lightning.

"You were right," she told Jack. "He had a few choice words to say about me tagging Foster."

"No kidding."

"He also reminded me I'm not—" She caught herself, threw a quick glance at Ellie and obviously modified whatever she'd intended to say. "I'm not one of you field jocks. I'm to take every possible precaution."

At that point, Ellie felt impelled to intervene. Abandoning any pretense of working on her report, she swung around in her chair.

"You don't have to do this, Mackenzie. I'm the one Foster and his hired gun may be after. You shouldn't put yourself in danger."

"Hey, don't spoil my fun. I don't get the chance to come out to play with the big guys all that often." She checked her watch. "I'd better go start getting beautiful. It could take a while."

Ellie said nothing more until Blair and the woman named Claire departed. Her eyes thoughtful, she waited for the door to click shut behind them before voicing the question hovering in her mind.

"Who are those people, Jack? For that matter, who are you?"

He took his time responding. Folding his arms, he leaned his hips against the back of the sofa. "Who do you think I am?"

"Obviously not a small-time bodyguard in need of work."

Flushing a bit at the memory of how she'd insisted

her uncle hire him, believing he might need the income, she left her chair.

"So tell me. Who are you? What do you do for a living?"

"Does it really matter, Ellie?"

The question took her back nine years. She could almost hear the echo of her fierce arguments, see Jack's stony face.

"No," she said softly. "What you do for a living *doesn't* matter. It never did."

Jack took the hit without blinking. He deserved it. More than deserved it. Considering the discussion over, she started to turn.

He caught her with a hand on her arm. Drawing her closer, he curled a knuckle under her chin.

"I'm not saying I was wrong all those years ago, you understand?"

"What are you saying?"

Bending, he brushed her lips with a kiss so gentle Ellie almost melted on the spot. When he raised his head, his expression was so serious her stomach did a little flip.

"This isn't the time or the place for promises," he said, his tone gruff. "Not with everything that's coming down on you right now. But if anyone walks away this time, Elena Maria, it'll have to be you."

Chapter 10

Ellie was still thinking about Jack's *non* promise when her team arrived from the dig. They'd shut down operations early. For good, this time.

"The deputy director of the park service called," Sam Pierce related, his craggy face both resigned and regretful. "He asked for you. I gave him your cell phone number and the number here at the hotel, but he said I could relay the message."

"Let me guess. NPS has pulled our funding."

Pierce nodded. "They left just enough in the kitty to restore the site."

She'd sensed it was coming. Given the pressure exerted by the Texas congressional delegation, the park service could hardly do anything else if they hoped to fund future projects. Still, the abrupt termination stung. Fighting a crushing sense of disappointment, Ellie listened while the others briefed her.

"We packed up all the equipment," Orin Weaver advised. "Eric loaded your van. I've got mine loaded and ready to go. I'll give you my input for the final report tonight and head home tomorrow."

The forensic anthropologist had other jobs waiting, Ellie knew. He was a frequent consultant for local, state and federal law enforcement, and his services were in demand. She couldn't ask him to stay and work gratis.

"Thanks, Orin." Forcing a smile, Ellie shook his hand. "I appreciate all you've contributed to this project."

Dr. Dawes-Hamilton wasn't quite as ready to abandon ship. "I've got some grant money back at Baylor waiting to be spent," she told Ellie. "I'll press ahead with the authentication process on the artifacts we've shipped to the university and send you a copy of my findings."

If the archeologist could use her department's grant money to authenticate the rifle and scraps of clothing found with the remains, Ellie could certainly scrape together enough funds to pay for DNA testing. Assuming, of course, the donors were still willing to provide samples.

"You'll have to decide what you want done with the bits and pieces we recovered in the past couple of days,'' Sam Pierce said. ''I imaged and catalogued them on the computer, but most of the stuff is just junk.''

The bits and pieces he referred to filled a large cardboard box. At Ellie's request, Eric lugged it in and deposited it beside her computer.

''Nothing there the park service might want to add to their collection of items found in and around Mission San Jose?'' she asked Sam.

''Nope.''

''I'll go through the box one more time. Maybe the archdiocese of San Antonio will be interested. Or the Alamo's museum director.''

''Maybe,'' Sam said doubtfully.

''If not, I'll dispose of the unwanted items when I make arrangements for the site restoration.''

Which would take her all of a day or two.

Ellie bit back a sigh. The project she'd begun with such enthusiasm and intellectual curiosity had generated nothing but controversy and was about to ignominiously fizzle out. Adding insult to injury, someone apparently wanted to fizzle *her* out with it.

Well, she hadn't completely finished with this project yet. Or with Mr. Dan Foster and his shadowy, frightening associate.

When she indicated as much to Jack and *his* team some time later, however, he flatly vetoed her suggestion that she slow roll the cleanup and shutdown operations in an attempt to draw out the killer.

"No way! You're out of here as soon as you pack up and hit the road."

"What good does it do to leave? Scarface could easily waylay me on the road or follow me home."

"You're not going home."

"Oh?"

She threw a glance at Mackenzie and the woman they called Cyrene. Both returned it with absolutely blank expressions. Obviously, this was Jack's show. They'd take their cue from him.

"All right," she said, swinging back to the man in charge. "I'll bite. Where am I going?"

"You're taking a nice long vacation at an undisclosed location."

"Don't be ridiculous. I can't just disappear indefinitely. I've got a house, a job, students who've signed up for courses that begin in less than a month."

"They can sign up for other courses. Until we bring Scarface down, I don't want you in his line of fire."

"I hesitate to point out the obvious, but I'm *already* in his line of fire. Where I'll stay until, as you say, you bring the bastard down. Seems to me you have more chance of accomplishing that right here. It's just a matter of flushing him out of hiding."

"Yeah, right. With you as bait."

Deliberately, Ellie suppressed the queasy feeling in her stomach. She was no coward, but neither was she a fool.

"Look, I'm not proposing to stroll around town with a target pinned to my back. I'm merely suggesting we turn the termination of the dig to our advantage. We can leak rumors that I'm drafting my final report. Set up a press conference. Hint that I'm going to distribute vivid images of my research and visits to the Alamo along with copies of the report. Make Foster and his hired killer sweat and, hopefully, provoke them into doing something stupid."

"It's too risky. I won't let you stake yourself out like a sacrificial goat for a cold-blooded killer. Nor do I think it's wise to reignite the anger of every hotheaded Texan who thinks you're messing with history."

Mackenzie broke her silence. "Ellie doesn't have to actually release the report to the media. All we need to do is make Foster *think* the release is imminent. I can help there."

Jack shot her an evil look, but before he could nix the plan that seemed to be forming despite his objections, Cyrene broke ranks, as well.

"When she meets with Foster tonight, Mackenzie could also let drop something about the bullet recovered from the river," Claire said in her quiet voice. "The possibility that the police might make the connection between the attacks on Ellie and his wife's murder would add significantly to Foster's stress levels.''

"The doc's right," Mackenzie argued. "I could spin all kinds of rumors. Really put Foster in a real puddle of sweat. My bet is he'll dump me like radioactive waste and head straight for the nearest phone to contact his hit man.''

"Yeah," Jack snarled. "That's my bet, too."

In the face of his fierce opposition, Mackenzie backed off. Ellie, however, held her ground.

"I guess I'm taking my cue from William Barrett Travis. I'm drawing a line in the sand. I'll take my stand here, in the shadow of the Alamo.''

"Right! And just look where that got Travis. Depending on how your final report reads, he either went down on the walls or was shot in the back of the head while trying to escape.''

Jack regretted the scathing retort the moment it left his lips. The color leached from Ellie's cheeks. Fear flickered in her brown eyes for a moment before she resolutely quashed it. Holding his gaze, she summoned a shaky smile.

"I'm not running—or walking—away."

Jack's head jerked up. Her message came through loud and clear. To him, at least.

The other two in the room sensed the sudden charge in the air. The women exchanged questioning glances, but neither said anything until Renegade conceded with a bad-tempered growl.

''All right. We'll play this out a little while longer. Mac, see what you can stir up tonight. First, though, I'd better advise Lightning on the change of plans.''

Jack had a feeling Nick Jensen wasn't going to be happy with the latest turn of events. Not only was the niece of Mexico's president offering herself up as bait for a killer, Mackenzie Blair was making an inch-by-inch transition from chief of communications to fully engaged field operative.

Jack was right.

Lightning was *not* happy.

He'd made a call to the President to bring him up to speed on the situation in San Antonio, then advised Colonel Luis Esteban, as well.

As afternoon wore into evening, Nick reminded himself that his chief of communications had gone through much of the same training as OMEGA's field agents. All headquarters personnel took marksmanship training, endured the water, jungle and desert survival courses and learned hand-to-hand combat from experts to give them an appreciation of what operatives went through in the field.

With the added benefit of her Navy background, Nick knew his comm chief could more than hold her own in just about any environment. But the gold Mont Blanc pen Maggie Sinclair had given him tapped an erratic beat as he leaned back in the leather captain's chair just past eight Washington time.

"You're not wearing a ring." Dan Foster's disembodied voice floated through the Control Center. "Does that mean you're not married?"

Nick's pen took another bounce. Foster was about as subtle as one of his eighty-ton earthmovers.

Eyes narrowed, Nick studied the scene Cyrene was beaming to the headquarters via the pen-size camera in her purse. The wall screen displayed a detailed portrait of dim lighting, gleaming wood and the couple in the booth.

The builder had hooked an arm around the back of the booth. His white shirt was unbuttoned at the top to accommodate his bull-like neck. Gold glinted on his wrist. Pure, unadulterated male lust gleamed in his eyes.

Nick could understand why. Mackenzie hadn't opted for subtle, either. If she drew in too deep a breath, she'd fall right out of that dress.

"Isn't my marital status irrelevant to this discussion?" Her husky little laugh rippled through the control center like warm velvet. "We're here to talk business."

"I make it a point to learn everything I can about the people I do business with," Foster countered with a predatory grin. "It gives me a leg up in negotiations."

"We haven't entered into negotiations."

"We might. We just might. So what's the story? Are you married, engaged or otherwise involved?"

"At the moment, none of the above. And I'd better warn you, I'm *very* ticklish in that particular spot."

Nick's pen went still.

Mackenzie waited until the builder had brought his left hand from under the table and clasped it loosely around his drink before picking up the conversational ball.

"What about you? Are you married?"

"I was. My wife died a few months ago."

"A few months ago?" With a slight turn of her head, Mackenzie let her glance drift to the arm draped around her shoulders. "I'd offer my condolences, but you seem to have recovered from your loss remarkably well."

"Joanna and I had what you might call a mutually satisfactory arrangement rather than a marriage. She didn't ask any questions. Neither did I."

"How did she die?"

"She was kidnapped and murdered."

"Good God! How awful for her. For you, too."

"Yeah, it *was* pretty awful." Making a show of pain, Foster knocked back the rest of his drink. "I still have nightmares."

Nick just bet he did. No doubt those nightmares had started about the time reports about Elena Maria Alazar's work in and around the Alamo hit the front pages.

Tucking his pen in the pocket of his camel sport coat, he leaned forward. Cyrene was providing backup for Mackenzie, leaving Renegade to guard Elena. Nick would have trusted either operative with his life. He couldn't seem to get past the fact that Mackenzie was trusting them with hers.

Grimacing, Nick remembered the strip he'd ripped off Jack for crossing the line with Ellie. Nick had better take a dose of his own medicine. Personal and professional didn't mix in this job.

"Like any big city, San Antonio seems to have a lot of murders," Mackenzie commented. "A woman staying at my hotel was shot at just yesterday. Right on the Riverwalk."

"That so?"

With apparent disinterest, Foster signaled to the waitress to bring another round of drinks. Settling against the booth, he stroked his fingers over his companion's bare shoulder.

"I heard about it from the concierge," she continued with a theatrical little shudder. "According to him, police divers recovered the spent shell casing."

Foster's hand froze.

"I have to admit, he didn't seem all that surprised that someone had taken a shot at this woman," Mackenzie confided ingenuously. "Evidently she's been stirring up all kinds of trouble. Something to do with the Alamo. Supposedly the story made all the papers. Maybe you read it?"

"No."

"Really? Well, you might see something soon.

Rumor is the woman's about to release some bomb-shell report.''

Careful, Nick thought. *Go careful here.*

''The concierge says she's reserved the hotel's ballroom for a big bash,'' Mackenzie continued air-ily. ''She's going to give some kind of multimedia presentation, complete with sound, light and digital images.''

Having neatly dropped her own bombshell, she snuggled into the crook of Foster's arm.

''Now, about the presentation *I'd* like to give you on the communications for your building. If you'll tell your secretary to provide me a set of blueprints, I can work up a detailed plan.''

''Yeah, I'll do that.'' Disengaging, Foster reached into his back pocket and dragged out his billfold. ''Listen, I'm sorry to run out on you like this, but I just remembered something I have to do.''

''Now?''

''Now.''

Tossing a bill onto the table, he started to slide out of the booth. Mackenzie halted him by the simple expedient of hooking a hand in his belt buckle.

''I want this contract.'' Her voice dropped to a seductive purr. ''I'm fully prepared to give you a special deal.''

Foster's startled glance dropped to his belt. What-ever Mackenzie's hand was doing behind the metal buckle had snagged his serious attention. Beads of sweat popped out on the man's brow. Nick felt a few pop out on his own.

"How long are you going to be in town?" the builder asked, his voice hoarse.

"That depends on you."

"I'll call you, okay?" He patted his shirt pocket. "I've still got your card. You see my secretary, tell her I said to make you a copy of the blueprints. Tomorrow, the next day, we'll, uh, get down to business."

With a smile that hovered between a pout and a promise, Mackenzie released him. Foster slid out and disappeared from the screen.

A moment later, Mackenzie winked at the camera. Her amused voice floated through the speakers.

"He might lose my business card, but until he changes belts, he'd not going to lose the bug I just stuck to his buckle. Over to you, control."

A half hour later, the team assembled in Jack's suite.

He and Ellie had listened via satellite link to the exchange between Mackenzie and Foster. Together with Mac and Cyrene, they now waited for the builder to take care of the something he'd suddenly remembered he had to do.

Foster made the call from his home just after 9:00 p.m. Shaking her head, Mackenzie adjusted the volume on the receiver.

"What a jerk!"

Amazed that the man would be so stupid as to risk calling from his home, she listened to the muted beeps of the dial tone. Although muffled, they were picked up by the bug she'd planted on Foster. The control center's computers would translate those beeps instantly into numbers.

"Yeah?"

"This is Foster. Things are happening. Things I don't like. You have to take care of that business we discussed. Like, now."

"I'm workin' it."

"Work harder!"

The phone was slammed down.

The four people in the hotel suite maintained their silence, hoping for something more. An indiscreet mutter. A short, angry tirade. Anything that might give them a better clue as to Foster's arrangements with his contract killer. All they got was the clink of glass on glass and the sudden blare of the TV.

"Well, Scarface didn't say much," Mackenzie told the others, "but we should be able to get a voice print out of it. Let's see if Control got a lock on the number Foster dialed."

Jack stood at her shoulder. His face darkened as he read aloud the message that flashed on her screen.

"The number was traced to the call notes for a cell phone registered to Harold Berger, 2224 River Drive, Austin."

Cyrene's silver blond brows lifted. "The dead man?"

Nodding, Jack cut a quick glance at Ellie before turning to Mackenzie.

"Can you work a satellite lock on the transmissions to and from that cell phone?"

"Not unless we catch a call during a broadband sweep of the entire transmission area. The chances of that range from zero to minus zero."

Jack didn't like the answer. He could see that Ellie didn't much care for it, either.

"Control will take it from here," Mackenzie advised, shutting down her unit. "If there's any further contact tonight, they'll let us know."

She rose, as did Cyrene. The psychologist cocked her head, studying Jack's grim face.

"You're tired. I'll take first watch."

"I'm okay."

"You need sleep."

"I'm okay."

"I won't let anything happen to her," Claire said gently. "I promise. And you'll be right here, a shout away."

Jack knew damned well he was operating on sheer nerves. He also knew that he wasn't about to let Ellie out of his sight tonight. Or any other night, if he had any say in the matter.

"You stand first watch here in my room," he suggested by way of compromise. "Ellie can leave the connecting door open. I'll bed down on the couch in her sitting room.''

Cyrene accepted the altered arrangements without argument. While she went to her room to collect a few things, Jack grabbed a pillow and blanket from the closet and deposited them on the rolled-arm sofa in the living room. He'd pulled out his automatic to check the magazine before he noticed the woman standing in the shadows. Hugging her arms, she stared blindly at the curtained windows.

''Ellie?''

She jumped and swung to face him. Her eyes were wide, their pupils dark pools.

''You okay?''

A shiver rippled down her spine. She didn't answer for a moment. She couldn't. The fact that she'd just heard Foster issuing her death warrant had taken some time to sink in, but sunk it had. She understood how the Alamo's defenders must have felt when Santa Anna delivered his final warning that he'd give no quarter if they continued their hopeless resistance.

Panic swept through her. She came within a breath of telling Jack that she'd changed her mind, that she wanted out of the hotel, out of the city and as far away from the Alamo as he could take her.

But she couldn't erase the mental image of that line in the sand. As much as she wanted to, she couldn't bring herself to tuck tail and run.

"I'm okay. Just a little shivery. Guess I've got the air-conditioning turned up too high."

The lie was so obvious Jack didn't bother to challenge it. Instead, he crossed the room, caught her in his arms and returned to the sofa. The cushions whooshed under his weight as he wedged his back into the corner. Settling Ellie comfortably in his lap, he gave her his warmth.

This wasn't the moment to tell her he'd also given her his heart. Not when Cyrene was moving about in the next room within easy earshot and a killer lurked somewhere in the shadows. He'd come as close to it as he dared earlier, when he told her she'd have to be the one to walk this time. She'd answered obliquely but unmistakably. That would do. For now.

Propping his chin on Ellie's head, he began to murmur the repetitive, hypnotic mantras that would ease the tension locking them both in steel cages.

For the first time in longer than he could remember, the relaxation techniques didn't work. Jack couldn't blank out the shape and scent of the woman nestled against him. Couldn't empty his mind of how near he'd come to losing her.

Again.

He didn't realize his hold had tightened around her until she squirmed and tipped her head back.

"Jack?"

Her eyes held a question, but it was her mouth he ached to answer. The tendons in his neck corded with the effort of holding back. He'd compromised her safety once by losing himself in her arms. He was damned if he'd do it again.

"Sorry," he murmured, loosening his hold. "Try to relax."

Lowering her head to his shoulder, she wiggled into a comfortable position. The movement of her bottom drove every mantra Jack had learned over the years right out of his head.

Gritting his teeth, he focused all his psychic energy on maintaining control over his body. He might not ever walk upright again after tonight, but he would keep Ellie safe at all costs.

Chapter 11

Detective Harris contacted Jack just after ten the next morning.

"We ran the bullet retrieved from the river through ballistics and sent the results to the FBI, who worked the Foster kidnapping and murder. You were right. The same gun fired both."

Jack's stomach clenched. No question now. Their conjectures had moved right out of the realm of possibility and into cold, lethal reality.

"So where does that leave us?"

"With some very excited FBI field agents who want to know just how the heck you tagged Dan Foster. They'd like to meet with both of us this afternoon. Two o'clock. Their offices are in the courthouse at 615 East Houston Street. Can you make it?"

His glance went to Ellie. She sat at the desk, a cold cup of coffee beside her. She was in jeans and a short-sleeved white shirt, its tails tucked in neatly at her trim waist. Dark circles shadowed her eyes, but her face wore a look of intense concentration.

She'd been hard at work since breakfast. Jack suspected her fierce attention to detail sprang as much from a need to keep her mind off her stalker as from a determination to tie up every loose end on her project. From the stack of field notes sitting beside the computer, he suspected she'd be at it for hours to come.

"Yes," he told Harris. "I can make it."

Cyrene would provide security for Ellie. Jack would take Mackenzie. She'd made the initial connection between Foster and Scarface and run it through her contact at the FBI. She'd also had two face-to-face sessions with Foster. The FBI guys were going to want to hear about those. And about the tag she'd put on the builder.

Mackenzie would know how to finesse that bit of electronic eavesdropping. OMEGA took its direction directly from the President and wasn't bound by the same rules and restrictions when it came to field operations as other government agencies, but it didn't hurt to head off jurisdictional disputes at the pass.

Cyrene was one of OMEGA's best. Jack could trust her to keep Ellie safe. Still, he had to force himself to the door after lunch.

With Jack gone, the suite seemed emptier, the afternoon endless.

Cyrene curled up on the sofa with a spy novel. Ellie made calls to several companies for estimates to fill in the excavation site. She also called each of the volunteers, thanking them for their assistance at the dig before putting the final touches on her report.

As she scrolled through the pages, she fought another sharp stab of disappointment. She and her team had come so close to fitting the pieces of the puzzle together. She hated to end the project by offering supposition and conjecture instead of fact.

Setting aside her personal feelings, she forced herself to take a critical eye to the report. She'd fine-tuned the sections detailing the discovery of the remains, the assembly of the team, the recovery of artifacts and the on-site authentication processes the team had employed. She'd add Dr. Dawes-Hamilton's laboratory results later.

The section dealing with the remains was the hardest to work on. She'd already incorporated Dr. Weaver's anthromorphical analysis, which included the basic physical features as extrapolated from the skeletal characteristics.

Male. Caucasian. Average height for his time. Age thirty to thirty-five. Indications of incipient arthritis, with some degree of bone degeneration in joints.

Propping her chin on her hands, Ellie stared at the terse summary. The shadowy figure of a Tejano formed in her mind. He didn't wear buckskins and rough frontier garb as depicted by Hollywood in its movies about the Alamo, but a broadcloth suit such as a doctor or lawyer might have donned. His face was shaded by a wide brimmed-hat to protect it from the fierce Texas sun. He grasped a double-barrel shotgun in one hand.

Who are you? she wondered for the hundredth time. *Did you escape the Alamo? If so, when? Before the final assault or after?*

Blowing out a long breath, she hit the laptop's keys.

By three o'clock the walls were starting to close in on her. Abandoning the computer, she decided to attack the cardboard box Sam Pierce had deposited on the floor. It took all her concentration to remain focused on the objects she pulled out to examine and verify against the inventory.

None of them appeared to hold any real historical significance. A broken snaffle bit. Several coins. A rusted tin plate. What looked like a piece of a plow-share.

At the bottom of the box, she found the dented silver disc Jack had turned up during his stint with Discoverer Two. Evidently the National Park Service hadn't considered the item worth salvaging. It was tarnished almost black, pitted all the way through and not anywhere near as valuable as the solid silver bracelet circling Ellie's wrist.

She'd never given Jack anything in return, she realized. She'd never had the opportunity. She'd only seen him once after he slipped the two-inch band on her wrist, and that was when she'd stormed into to the U.S. Embassy compound to engage in a furious, one-sided argument with a certain hardheaded Marine.

The small, dented concho wasn't in the same class as the expensive bracelet, but polished, it might make a keepsake for Jack. Something to remind him of these days in San Antonio—as if either one of them would need reminding!

Fingering the disk, she dialed housekeeping. "This is Dr. Alazar in Room two ten. Would you please send up a small jar of silver polish and a soft cloth? Yes, silver polish. Thanks."

Claire looked up from her book, her glance curious.

"Jack found this out at the site," Ellie explained, displaying the bit of silver. "I'm going to clean it up for him as a souvenir."

A maid delivered the requested items. No doubt the Menger's management was wondering just what Dr. Alazar was up to now. After passing the woman a generous tip, Ellie went to work on the concho.

Gradually, the tarnish disappeared to display an intricate pattern stamped into the silver. The design was extraordinarily artistic, with scrolls and swirls and a tiny oak leaf cut in the center. The oak leaf wasn't a traditional Mexican symbol. It struck her as more like a design a silversmith would do for one of the Tejanos.

A vague memory stirred in the back of her mind. She'd seen a design like this before. She was sure of it. But where?

Puzzled, she took it to the desk. A search of her database turned up no images that matched it. Only after a second lengthy search did she remember the design stamped into the silver work on the shotgun she'd photographed at the Alamo.

A touch of the old excitement fluttered in her veins. Pulling up the image of the double-barreled shotgun, she examined the elaborate scrollwork on the sidings and butt plate.

Yes! There it was! A small oak leaf in the center of the scrollwork.

Her excitement taking wing, she pulled up images of the gun they'd found some yards away from the skeletal remains. The silver was still tarnished, the design difficult to decipher, but Ellie could swear it was the same.

Okay. All right. What did she have here? Not a whole lot, except the possibility that the smith who worked the silver facings on both guns might very well have crafted the concho Jack had found.

Once more she attacked the computerized files.

The minutes ticked by. Undaunted, Ellie conducted search after search before she found a reference to Josiah Kennett, one of the Alamo's more obscure defenders. Or more specifically, to the silver conchos on Josiah's Kennett's hat.

Suddenly, Ellie remembered the miniature portrait of an unsmiling young man, his collar tight around his neck and his face shadowed by the wide-brimmed hat favored by Mexicans and Tejanos alike. She'd seen his miniature in the Alamo, right next to the man's tattered Bible.

The thrill she always felt when the pieces of a historical puzzle began to fall together gripped her. Closing her fingers over the silver disk, she swung around in her chair.

"When's Jack going to be back?" she asked Claire.

"I don't know. Soon, I would think. Why?"

"I need to make a quick visit to the Alamo. I think I may have a clue to the identity of the remains that my team and I recovered. I won't know until I get a shot of a portrait in the museum and enlarge it."

"It's not a good idea for you to leave the hotel," Claire countered gently. "Not until Jack gets back, anyway."

Ellie had no intention of taking a step outside the Menger without Jack. "Can you contact him? Find out where he is?"

"Of course."

Slipping a small cell phone out of her pocket, she pressed a single button.

"This is a secure instrument," she said with a smile as she put the instrument to her ear. "Mackenzie would take it as a personal insult if anyone ever eavesdropped on one of us."

Like Mackenzie herself was doing to Dan Foster. Recalling the builder's terse call last night, Ellie almost changed her mind about leaving the confines of her hotel room. A cowardly little voice inside her head whispered at her to hunker down behind strong barricades and stay there until it was safe to come out.

She couldn't cower behind drawn shades and closed doors forever, though. And a determined foe could breech even the strongest walls...as the defenders of the Alamo had learned all too well.

Shoving her hands in her pocket, she listened to Claire's side of the conversation with Jack. Evidently, she'd caught him and Mackenzie on their way back to the hotel. His first instinct was to flatly veto Ellie's request for a quick trip next door. His second, to acknowledge the bitter truth. If two OMEGA agents backed-up by their chief of communications couldn't keep her safe, no one could. Period. End of story.

"He'll meet us in the lobby in fifteen minutes," Claire advised. "Hang loose while I run a check of the halls and the elevators."

Her movements graceful and unhurried, she hooked her purse over her shoulder and exited the suite. In her gray pleated linen slacks, narrow belt and sliky green blouse, she could easily pass for one of the hotel's well-heeled guests instead of a highly specialized protective agent.

At least that's what Ellie assumed she was. One of these days, she vowed, she'd have to pin these people down on exactly who they worked for. Pacing the room, she rubbed her thumb over the silver disk and waited in mounting impatience for Claire's return.

"All clear," she advised after a short absence.

Snatching up her camera and a curled-brim crushable straw hat, Ellie hurried out the door.

Jack and Mackenzie met them as they stepped out of the elevator. He didn't have much to say about his visit to the FBI and Ellie knew better than to probe for details in such a public place. He did, however, want to know what the hell was behind the urgent visit to the Alamo.

"This."

Pulling her hand out of her pocket, Ellie uncurled her fingers. "It's the concho you found at the excavation site. Look at the design. I've seen it before, Jack. I'm sure I have. I just need to verify where."

He shook his head but could tell from the suppressed excitement in her voice that she thought she was on to something.

"Okay. Just stay with me, and do exactly what I say the instant I say it. Cyrene, you take point. Mac, you've got rearguard."

With Claire strolling ahead and Mackenzie trailing behind, they walked outside. After the controlled chill of the hotel's air-conditioning, the muggy Texas summer hit them like a baseball bat. Hastily, Ellie slipped on sunglasses and tugged her hat lower on her brow to shield her face. Her skin began to dew before they covered half the distance to the monument next door.

The usual crowd milled around Alamo Plaza, snapping photos in from of the mission and slurping up ice-cream cones purchased from near-by vendors. The hair on the back of Ellie's neck prickled as her glance roamed over the tourists. Was Scarface lurking among these camera-laden sightseers?

Her pulse skittered when she caught a glimpse of a straw Stetson similar the one the killer had been wearing when she'd unintentionally photographed him with Dan Foster, but the face beneath the brim belonged to a short, stocky man of Hispanic descent. He carried a baby in one arm and had looped the other around his young son's shoulders.

Blowing out a sigh of relief, Ellie pushed through the door set in the massive walls. Once inside, a welcome wash of cool air surrounded them.

"Oh-oh!"

Elle's murmured exclamation put Jack on instant

alert. Claire's head whipped around. Her hand disappeared inside her purse. Mackenzie hurried up to add to the living shield around Ellie.

"Do we have a problem?" Jack asked softly.

"Yes," Ellie whispered, "but not the one you're worried about. See that docent?"

All three agents eyed the gray-haired volunteer cheerfully passing out brochures.

"If she recognizes me," Ellie whispered, sliding her sunglasses back up the bridge of her nose, "she'll call out the palace guard. Would one of you distract her long enough for me to slip by?"

Claire had no difficulty claiming the docent's attention. A simple question about the age of the wood beams overhead had the volunteer craning her neck to point out original iron nails and peg-joints. Ellie kept her face averted and whisked right past.

Once inside the courtyard, the ripple of excitement she'd felt earlier in her hotel room returned. History was both her profession and her passion. Solving the mystery of the remains found in a creek bed five miles south of the Alamo might not rank up there with discovering the Dead Sea scrolls or deciphering the Rosetta Stone, but putting a name to the man who died alone and unmourned would afford her immense personal satisfaction. Consequently, she paced in a fever of impatience until Claire re-joined them.

"The exhibit I want to see is in that long, low building."

Cyrene, you stay outside and surveil the crowd,'' Jack instructed, slipping a hand under Ellie's elbow. ''Mac, I want you at the entrance.''

Nodding, both women took up their posts.

As she and Jack entered the Long Barracks, Ellie kept a wary eye out for Dr. Smith. The museum director had insisted she submit written requests for further access to the private collections. He hadn't said anything about the public exhibits, but she wasn't taking any chances.

The display case containing Josiah Kennett's tattered Bible and miniature was in a small room filled with artifacts belonging to the Alamo's lesser-known defenders. Ellie's gaze shot straight to the hat shading Kennett's young, unsmiling face.

A narrow leather strap banded the crown. Ellie's breath caught as she noted the silver conchos ornamenting the band. Given the small size of the portrait, she couldn't tell whether or not the design included a small oak leaf.

A quick glance around the room showed she and Jack were alone. A clutch of tourists peered at exhibits in the room across the hall, but for the moment at least, Ellie had Josiah Kennett all to herself.

''I just need a few pictures,'' she said, excitement simmering in her veins.

She was reaching her digital camera when Jack's cell phone gave a discreet ping. Sliding it out of her pocket, he glanced at the digital display.

"It's Mac."

Flipping open the phone, he tried to acknowledge the call. A frown creased his forehead. The static coming through the line was so loud even Ellie could hear it.

"Something's breaking up my transmission," Jack muttered. His gaze snagged on the intrusion detection device mounted above the exhibit cases. "Probably the infrared beams from those security alarms."

"Probably," Ellie agreed, absorbed by the contents of the exhibit case. "The Alamo is more wired than Fort Knox."

Jack glanced down the way they'd come. The halls were clear. The rest of the tourists had moved onto another section of the museum. Mac was right outside, ten steps away. Jack could keep Ellie in sight while he checked with Comm on the transmission problems.

"Do not leave this room," he ordered tersely. "I'll be right back."

He took two steps down the hall. Caught a faint whisper of sound. Sheer instinct spun him down and around.

There was a soft pop. A fiery explosion of pain. With a small grunt, Jack took the bullet.

Unaware of the lethal drama taking place just paces away, Ellie fiddled with the settings for her camera and snapped away. She'd have to do more research on Kennett. Verify where he came from.

How he ended up at the Alamo. If possible, determine what weapons he was carrying when he joined the ranks of defenders.

Humming, she zoomed in on the miniature. Only then did the significance of the small leather pouch slung over Kennett's left shoulder sink in. On closer examination, she decided it could well be a courier's pouch, like those carried by army scouts. Identical, in fact, to one she'd seen in a portrait of James Allen, the sixteen-year-old courier who carried Travis's last, desperate appeal for reinforcements out of the Alamo on March 5th, the day before Santa Anna attacked in full force.

She knew from historical documents that Travis had sent out a number of couriers, some identified by name, some not. James Butler Bonham, a lawyer and fellow South Carolinian from Travis' home county, had tracked down Colonel James Fannin at Goliad. Captain Juan Seguin carried an appeal directly to Sam Houston. Young James Allen made that last, hopeless ride.

As she tried to recall references to the other, unnamed couriers, the possibilities burst like fireworks in Ellie's mind. Maybe Travis had gleaned intelligence warning of the imminent attack. Maybe he'd worried one courier might not get through enemy lines. Maybe he'd sent two, sacrificing badly needed firepower in the hope that one of them would make it. Maybe young Kennett wasn't fleeing the massacre on March 6th, but trying urgently to prevent it.

She'd have to go back through the inventory of artifacts recovered at the dig. Check to see if there was any bit of metal or scrap of rotted rawhide that might have come from a pouch. Snapping away, she recorded several more digital images. The creak of a floorboard behind her had her whirling to share the exciting possibilities with Claire and Jack.

It wasn't Jack who stood in the doorway, however. Or Claire. It was a tourist in mirrored sunglasses and a black ball cap emblazoned with NYPD in gold letters. Ellie took in the reassuring lettering and started to smile a welcome. Her smile turned into a sick gulp when she noticed the white scar tracing a path in the tanned folds of the man's neck.

"Hello, Dr. Alazar."

She didn't need the faint mockery in his greeting—or the long, lethal silencer screwed to the muzzle of the pistol in his hand—to know she'd come face-to-face with her stalker.

"Jack!"

Her frantic scream bounced off the thick walls.

"Your friend can't hear you," Scarface said with a grim smile. "He can't hear anything."

Despair knifed into Ellie, so sharp and lancing she almost doubled over.

"No!" she moaned. "Dear God, no!"

"Yes," the thug taunted. "And now…"

"You bastard!"

Acting from sheer animal instinct, Ellie reached behind her and smashed her digital camera into the glass exhibit case. Before the first, shrieking alarm had filled the air, she brought her arm forward and flung her camera at Scarface.

What was left of the glass exhibit case behind her shattered. Ellie didn't hear the gunshot over the screaming alarm, didn't even care that his first shot had missed. Fingers curled into claws, she launched herself at the man.

She had to get past him, had to get to Jack....

Before she reached him, there was a bright flash. An unseen force propelled her attacker into the room. He collided with Ellie, took her down. Frantic, she tried to scramble out from under his dead weight.

"Ellie!"

The hoarse croak came from above her. A fist reached down, yanked at the weight crushing her into the floor. The instant she could wiggle free, she rolled onto all fours. Broken glass cut into her hands and knees. The alarm shrieked like the hounds of hell, but Ellie felt nothing, heard nothing but a roaring rush of joy.

Jack! It was Jack! Blood flowered like a bright, obscene hibiscus on his shirt. His face was dead white. But his eyes were feral as he went down on one knee beside her, keeping his weapon trained on the man sprawled in a growing puddle of blood the whole time.

"Were you hit?"

She saw his mouth move. Saw, too, the near panic in his eyes as they raked her from head to foot.

"What?"

Mackenzie raced into the room at that moment, followed a second later by Claire. Ellie saw the weapon in their hands, saw their lips moving, but couldn't hear anything over the deafening clang.

Jack motioned to Claire to keep Scarface covered and whirled back to Ellie. "Where were you hit?"

She shook her head, unable to hear but grasping the reason for his fear. Blood splattered her white blouse and drenched her jeans from the knees down.

"I'm okay!" she yelled. "But you..." Frantic, she fluttered her sliced palms at blood-drenched shirt. "You've been shot!"

The alarm cut off abruptly. Her ears ringing, Ellie tried to understand what Jack was saying as he gently grasped her wrists.

"It looks worse than it is. Damned bullet ricocheted off the bone and took me down for a few moments, but it went clear through."

Mackenzie's sneakers crunched on the glass as she crouched down beside them. "Just hold still," she instructed, "we'll get you patched up and..."

The sound of running footsteps cut her off. Jack chopped a hand in the air, motioning her to one side, and shoved Ellie behind him. Claire slammed her shoulder blades against the wall, where she could keep both Scarface and the door covered. Ellie tensed for another attack.

Dr. Smith burst in. His jaw dropping, the pudgy museum curator gaped in disbelief at the carnage. His wild gaze flew from the unconscious figure on the floor to Claire, to Jack. Finally, to Ellie.

Red suffused his cheeks. His eyes bugged behind his glasses. He sputtered, choked, spit out Ellie's name like a curse.

"Dr. Alazar! I should have known! What in God's name are you doing?"

The combination of stark terror and relief so deep and sharp it ate like acid into her bones had her snapping right back.

"What does it look like we're doing, you twit? We're fighting the second battle of the Alamo."

Chapter 12

Keeping a tight lid on the shoot-out at the Alamo required the combination of Renegade's forceful personality and Lightning's political influence. There was no way they wanted Foster to know his hit man had gone down. Not yet anyway.

Dr. Smith went tight-lipped with indignation and disapproval when informed that the President's special envoy had placed a call to the head of the Daughters of the Texas Revolution. She had agreed that this unfortunate attack on the niece of the President of Mexico was a matter for the police, not the press.

The various law enforcement agencies involved

concurred. Wheeling Scarface out of the Alamo on a gurney, they informed the gawking tourists that there had been an accident. He died in the ambulance on the way to the hospital without recovering consciousness. His demise left a frustrated Detective Harris and two very disgruntled FBI agents with no clue to the hit man's real identity. Or with anything linking him to Daniel Foster except Ellie's photograph.

"Which," Claire said later that evening in Ellie's hotel suite, "Foster's lawyers will argue is merely a chance juxtaposition of two visitors to a popular historic landmark."

"Yeah, right," Mackenzie groused. "Some visitors."

She took a turn around the sitting room, hands shoved into the front pockets of her jeans. Her Nikes left tracked imprints on the plush carpet. The sex kitten who'd nestled up to Foster at the bar last night was gone. In her place was a woman imbued with a sense of purpose.

"We all know Foster hired that bastard to off his wife. We just can't prove it. There's no record of money transfers from his bank to suspicious accounts. No traceable phones calls besides the one we intercepted, and that was made to a cell phone we *think* belonged to Scarface but can't locate, as he didn't have it on him when he died."

Ellie sat quietly in an armchair, her bandaged hands tucked loosely around her waist. More bandages showed beneath the hem of her shorts, padding her knees. She couldn't get quite as worked up as Mackenzie over Daniel Foster's probable guilt. Not just yet. She was still recovering from the trauma of dodging the assassin's bullet.

Jack had remained quiet since they'd returned from the emergency room, too. As he assured her, the bullet had merely glanced off his clavicle. Luckily, the bone hadn't shattered. The entrance and exit wound were clear. He'd refused pain pills and now listened to the others with every evidence of attention, but his glance shifted to Ellie at frequent intervals, as if to make sure she wasn't about to keel over from blood loss or delayed shock.

"Foster's got to be a mass of raw nerves right now," Mackenzie continued. "He'll be expecting a call from Scarface with confirmation he's done the deed. Every hour that goes by without word is going to torque up the pressure on Danny Boy. Sooner or later, he's going to do something stupid. I say we make it sooner."

"I say we let him sweat," Jack countered. "For tonight, anyway."

"Yes, but—"

"I agree with Renegade," Claire said, rising from her chair with fluid grace. "As long as the incident at the Alamo doesn't leak to the press, Foster will think Scarface is still on the hunt. That puts the advantage squarely in our court. Let's use the time to think through our next moves."

Hooking an arm through Mackenzie's, Cyrene gently but firmly steered the younger woman out. Jack followed them to the door, shot the dead bolt and armed the intrusion detection alarm he'd rigged when he'd arrived. The immediate threat to Ellie had been eliminated, but he couldn't shake an edgy sense of incompleteness. She still had to wrap up the last details of her project. He still had to decide whether to go after Foster or leave him to the locals.

Then there was the small matter of where he and Ellie went from here.

Tonight wasn't the time to talk about it, though. His wound hurt like hell and Ellie looked ready to drop. Her shoulders drooped. Fatigue left shadows like bruises under her eyes. If that weren't enough to rouse Jack's fiercely protective instincts, the bandages on her hands and knees would have done the trick.

"You should get some sleep," he said, his voice gruff with concern. "You've had a hell of a day."

"It was rather eventful." A faint smile feathered her lips. "Do you think Dr. Smith will ever let me set foot inside the Alamo again?"

"I'd say you'll have to do some real sweet talking first."

"Maybe he'll relent when he hears my theory about young Josiah Kennett."

"Maybe. In the meantime, I suggest you forget Smith, forget Kennett, forget the second battle of the Alamo and crawl into bed."

"I might, if you crawl in with me."

Her smile deepened, starting an ache almost as fierce as the one in Jack' shoulder.

The docs said you should rest," she reminded him, using her bandaged hands to lever herself awkwardly out of her chair. "Let's go to bed."

Yeah, right. As if he'd get any rest lying next to Ellie. Particularly when she stopped beside the bed and lifted her hands helplessly.

"You'll have to undress me. I can't work my shirt buttons with these bandages."

Jack's throat went dry. "I think I can manage that."

"I think you can, too."

His blood was pounding, but he kept his touch gentle as he unbuttoned the linen camp shirt Claire had helped her into after returning from the E.R.

The docs had assured Jack they'd extracted all the glass shards from Ellie's palms and knees, and that the cuts weren't deep enough to require stitches. Yet the gauzy bandages were a grim reminder as he eased the shirt down past her elbows.

If he hadn't caught that faint whisper of sound and dodged the assassin's bullet, if Ellie hadn't won a few precious seconds by flinging her camera at the killer, she might have been the one wheeled out of the Alamo on a gurney. The thought made his chest squeeze so tight he couldn't breathe.

She didn't seem to notice the sudden constriction in his breathing. Heeling off her shoes, she kicked them aside and waited patiently for Jack to start on her shorts.

By the time he'd stripped her down to her bra and bikini briefs, more than just his chest was tight. Hard and aching, he skimmed a knuckle down the hollow of her belly.

"You sure you don't want another of the pain pills the docs prescribed?"

"I'm not feeling any pain at the moment. My sleep shirt is over there, on the chair."

Jack retrieved the scrap of cotton. The damned thing had put in him a sweat the first time he'd seen her in it. He was feeling pretty much the same effect now. Ignoring the painful pull in his shoulder, he eased it over her head.

"Now you," she murmured.

Ellie's throat closed as he eased off his shirt. The neat bandage wrapped around his shoulder brought the afternoon's horror rushing back. Inching sideways on the bed, she made room for him.

"Fine pair we are," he said with a wry grin. "Come here."

Slipping his uninjured arm under her, he brought her closer. Ellie cradled her head in his good shoulder. Her palm rested on his chest. Beneath her fingers was the strong, sure beat of his heart.

"This afternoon," she whispered, "when Scarface said you couldn't hear my scream. I thought...I thought I'd lost you."

"I thought the same thing when I barreled through the door and saw you go down."

Curling a knuckle under her chin, he tipped her head up. His eyes held hers.

"A few nights ago, you asked if I'd ever loved you. I've never stopped, Ellie."

"Oh, Jack!" She wanted to weep with the joy and the sharp, stinging regret. "We wasted so many years. So many days and nights we could have shared."

"I know." His thumb brushed her cheek. "I don't plan to waste any more."

She hooked a brow. His teeth flashed in a rueful grin.

"After tonight," he amended. "Go to sleep, sweetheart."

The bright bubble of joy was still with Ellie the

next morning, when she bundled into one of the hotel's plush terry-cloth robes, made a futile attempt at
wielding a hairbrush, and ambled into the sitting
room in search of Jack and coffee.

She found both, as well as two other men. One
was a stranger. The other Ellie recognized immediately.

"Colonel Esteban!"

"Elena. It is good to see you again."

Moving with the grace of a jungle panther, he
came forward and bowed over her hand. Ellie had
met him on several occasions during her visits to her
aunt and uncle, yet even her awareness of the shadowy world the colonel worked in couldn't blunt the
impact of his dark eyes, luxuriant mustache and Cae-
sar Romero smile. Ellie might have fallen in love
with Jack Carstairs all over again, but she wasn't
blind. Nor was she oblivious to the tension in the air.

Frowning, she threw a quick, questioning look at
Jack. He had obviously rolled out of bed well before
she did. Showered and shaved, he filled a cup with
black coffee and carefully passed it into her bandaged hands.

"How's your shoulder?" she asked.

"Hurting but healing. How are your hands?"

"The same."

Downing a grateful sip, Ellie returned her attention

to the colonel. "It's good to see you, too. What are you doing in San Antonio?"

"Your uncle sent me. He was informed of the unfortunate incident at the Alamo and wishes to be assured you took no serious hurt."

"I'm fine."

The colonel's glance drifted to the white gauze.

"I just took a few cuts and bruises," Ellie said. "Really. You can tell Uncle Eduardo I'm up and walking and ready to get back to work."

"Perhaps you should tell him yourself. He would like you to come stay in Mexico until the U.S. authorities take care of this bastard who wants you dead."

"We were discussing that last night. Getting hard evidence against Daniel Foster could take months, even years. I can't—correction, I *won't*—run away and hide that long."

The stranger had said nothing, but her protest brought him forward. He was a tall man, dressed with casual elegance in knife-pleated gray slacks and an Italian knit sport shirt.

"We don't believe it will take as long as that, Dr. Alazar."

"And 'we' are?"

"Sorry. I should have introduced myself sooner. I'm Nick Jensen, special envoy to the President of the United States."

Ellie had spent enough summers with her uncle to have a good grasp of the various levels of bureaucracy inherent in any government. Despite that background, she didn't have a clue what a special envoy did.

Jensen didn't enlighten her. "Like your uncle, the President is concerned for your safety. That's one of the reasons we sent Renegade—Jack—to protect you."

"You sent him? But I thought—that is…"

"That your uncle hired him? Let's just say it was arranged through my office."

Well, she'd already figured out Jack Carstairs wasn't the down-at-heels gumshoe she'd first thought him, but the fact that he worked for the special envoy to the President of the United States took some getting used to. Struggling with the mental readjustment, she picked up on Jensen's comment.

"You said concern for my safety was one of the reasons you sent Jack to San Antonio. What were the others?"

"Quite frankly, the President also worried that the ill will displayed toward you could erupt into ugly anti-Mexico sentiments, possibly derail the North American Free Trade Association Treaty. Neither Mexico nor the United States wanted to see that happen."

A sick feeling curled in Ellie's stomach. She didn't look at Jack. She couldn't.

"Let me get this straight," she said slowly, the coffee cup cradled in both hands. "You—all of you—got involved in this mess because political issues were at play?"

"Political issues are always at play," Jensen said, "but your safety was the overriding concern, of course."

His rueful smile might have charmed Ellie under any other circumstances. At the moment, she was too numbed by the thought that she'd been a political pawn in a game she'd known nothing about.

"Of course," she echoed dully.

"It's still the overriding concern," Jensen continued smoothly. "Foster has already demonstrated the lengths he'll go to. He hired one killer. There's nothing to say he wouldn't hire another. The President thinks you should consider your uncle's offer. Or at least let us take you to a safe house until Jack and the others put Foster on ice."

"I see."

Carefully, she placed the cup on the sofa table. She felt frowsy and frumpy and at a distinct disadvantage facing Esteban and Jensen in her bare feet and bathrobe. But those feelings paled beside the ache that formed around her heart when she turned and saw Jack's face. There was no sign of the tender lover in his stony expression. No spark of warmth in his cool blue eyes.

"What do you think? Should I leave San Antonio?"

"Yes."

She waited for some softening of the hardness in his face, some indication another separation would rip him apart as much as it would her. When he didn't so much as blink, Ellie's hurt took a sharp right turn into anger.

No! Not again! Jack Carstairs had gone all stubborn and tight-jawed and noble about what was best for her nine years ago. No way in *hell* she was going to let him do it again!

Her spine snapped straight. Matching him stare for stony stare, she made her position ice clear. "You said I'd have to be the one to walk away this time. I told you then and I'm telling you again, I'm not walking. So you can just deal with it. All three of you!"

On that note, she exited the scene. Slamming the bedroom door behind her was childish and unnecessary, but it gave Ellie intense satisfaction.

The thud reverberated through the sitting room. Esteban and Jensen stared at the closed door for some moments before turning to Jack.

"You were right," Nick conceded with a grin.

"She didn't take kindly to the idea of being hustled out of town. We'll have to fall back and regroup."

Luis Esteban wasn't quite as ready to admit defeat. Smoothing a palm over his lustrous black hair, he gave the closed door a disgruntled glance. "You must speak with her, Carstairs. Convince her to leave. You and I, together we will handle this Foster."

"You and I?"

"President Alazar has suggested I remain in San Antonio to, ah, provide whatever assistance you might require."

Hell! That's all Jack needed! A watchdog hired by Ellie's uncle looking over his shoulder, second-guessing his every move. The urge to tell the colonel just what he and Eduardo Alazar could do with their so-called assistance rose hot and swift in Jack's throat.

He swallowed the words, right along with his pride. With Ellie still at risk, he wasn't about to turn away any help. Lightning made the bitter pill easier to take when Jack had assembled Comm and Cyrene in his suite some fifteen minutes later.

"Luis Esteban worked a hairy mission with Maggie Sinclair some years ago," he said by way of introduction. "She and Thunder both came to my office to meet with him a few weeks ago. The colonel's gone into the private sector now, but he's still one of us.''

That was all the endorsement Mackenzie required. ''Anyone Chameleon considers a good guy *is* a good guy in my book.''

Her unconditional acceptance won her a quick, slashing grin from Esteban. Those gleaming white teeth and glinting black eyes sent the gulp of coffee she'd just taken down the wrong pipe. Choking, Mackenzie rattled the cup onto the table, splashing lukewarm liquid on the polished surface.

Claire was more reserved in her reaction to the newcomer. Reaching across to pound her sputtering colleague on the back, she gave the colonel a cool, assessing look.

Esteban's gaze was considerably warmer. Where in God's name did OMEGA recruit these women? Maggie Sinclair was in a class by herself. The one called Mackenzie possessed a lively animation and a quick wit. But this one, this mature, composed beauty, stirred his blood in a way no woman had since... Well, since Maggie Sinclair.

He'd have to find out more about her. His resources might not reach as deep or as far as OMEGA's, but he could still access information when he wanted it.

''So why are you and the colonel here?'' the dark-haired Mackenzie asked Lightning when her fit of coughing subsided. "What's the plan?"

"The plan is, ah, under review at the moment. As to what Colonel Esteban and I are doing here... We flew down to convince Dr. Alazar she shouldn't take any more risks."

"Well, darn!" A look of acute disappointment crossed Mackenzie's expressive face. "I wish I'd been here to hear Ellie's response to that."

Even Cyrene was amused. "Renegade made the same argument. Apparently you two didn't have any more success than he did."

"We'll try again," the colonel assured her. "She must realize we have only her best interests at heart."

Her best interests.

The words clanged like a klaxon in Jack's head. He'd uttered them himself. More than once. For the first time, he recognized how pompous and patronizing they must sound to Ellie. As if she weren't intelligent or rational or mature enough to recognize her needs.

He still wanted her out of San Antonio. His overriding instinct was to shield her, to safeguard her from all harm. If anything, the shoot-out at the Alamo yesterday had reinforced the edgy feeling that she wouldn't be out of danger until they nailed Foster.

Jack had finally learned his lesson, though. He couldn't make her decisions for her. Nor could anyone else. It was time he acknowledged that fact. Past time.

"Why don't we get Ellie's input into the revised plan?"

The suggestion earned him a frown from Esteban, a curious glance from Lightning and an emphatic second from Mackenzie. Claire sent her approval in the form of a small nod.

Crossing the room, Jack rapped on the bedroom door. "Ellie? We want to talk to you."

The door swung open. She emerged from the bedroom wearing crisp linen slacks, a sleeveless turquoise top and a decided air of authority.

"I have a few things to say to you, too." She made a quick sweep of the room, nodding at Claire and Mackenzie. "Good, you're here. I won't have to repeat myself."

Moving to the center of the sitting room, she tucked her injured hands under her crossed arms.

"All right, listen up. Here's what we're going to do. I'm going to finish my research into Josiah Kennett and coordinate the final report with my team. That should take twenty-four hours, less if I get right to it. Then I'll release the team's findings. Right here, in San Antonio. We'll gather the public forum Mackenzie hinted to Foster about and blow it up big.

Invite the media. The mayor. The city council. Influential members of the business community and country club set. Including," she announced grimly, "one Dan Foster."

"Oh, this is good," Mackenzie breathed. "Really good! Danny Boy will go ballistic when he gets the invite."

"We'll hold the reception here at the hotel," Ellie continued, directing her comments to the three men, daring them to object. "It's short notice, but we have to hope they can accommodate us. I'll work the crowd at the reception. I'll also contrive to get Foster alone at some point. You," she said, pinning Jack with a look that could have cut glass, "will come up with some scheme to get him to incriminate himself."

"I think I can manage that," he drawled.

"Good!" With the air of one who's firmly in charge, she surveyed the group. "Does anyone have any questions or comments?"

"Just one," Nick said in the short silence that followed.

Ellie braced herself for an argument. To her surprise, Jack stepped between her and the President's special envoy.

"We're doing this her way, Nick."

His firm, no-arguments tone had Ellie blinking. A few moments ago, he'd stated flatly that he wanted her out of San Antonio. She still hadn't quite recovered from the hurt of knowing he'd been following a political as well as a personal agenda all this time.

Now he was not only acknowledging her right to make her own decisions, it sounded as though he was fully prepared to sacrifice a second career for her. Thoroughly confused, she couldn't decide whether to whoop in delight or warn him to back off, fast.

Not that he would have listened. From the set to his jaw, it was obvious Jack had no intention of backing down.

"Ellie's had her baptism under fire," he told Jensen. "She's earned her spurs. We're doing this her way or not at all."

Once again, she was surprised. Instead of taking offense, Jensen merely nodded.

"You're in charge on this mission, Renegade. You call the shots. I was simply going to offer my restaurant as an alternative site for the big announcement. It will hold as many or more than the hotel's ballroom and give us better control over security."

Ellie blinked. "You own a restaurant?"

"Actually, I own several."

"Try several dozen," Mackenzie muttered. "Ever hear of Nick's?"

"Good heavens, yes! There's one in Mexico City. In Acapulco, too, I think."

Mackenzie held up a hand and ticked off a few

others. "And Paris and Rome and Hong Kong, New York, Vegas, Palm Springs. You'll find a Nick's about everywhere the rich and famous gather."

"And none of them," he commented with a glinting look in her direction, "serve sausage, double pepperoni and jalapeño pizza."

"Too bad." She tossed the words back. "You won't get my business unless you diversify your menu."

"We'll have to talk about that. Along with the expanded operation role you've assumed on this mission."

"Uh-oh." Mackenzie's brows waggled. "This doesn't sound good."

"Let's go to my room, shall we? I had Mrs. Wells book one just in case I decided to stay." He gave the others a polite nod. "If you'll excuse us."

With the exaggerated air of a martyr about to meet her fate, Mackenzie preceded him to the door.

Chapter 13

Mrs. Wells hadn't just booked Lightning a room. She'd reserved the presidential suite.

Of course.

The palatial five-room suite took up most of the top floor and gave stunning views of the Alamo. Ornate furnishings from a bygone era made Mackenzie feel as though she'd stepped into the bustling days of Texas before the turn of the century, when cattle was king and Judge Roy Bean's Lillie Langtry thrilled audiences from coast to coast. The massive antique sideboard that housed a bar and entertainment center had been carved from some dark, brooding wood. So had the canopied four-poster she glimpsed in the bedroom. The thing looked like it could comfortably sleep six!

"Forget the ballroom and your restaurant," Mackenzie commented. "You could fit the mayor, the city council, the entire country club set and every news crew in Texas in this suite."

"Let's talk about a certain member of that country club set." Tossing his room key onto the sideboard, Nick leaned his hips against it and slid his hands in the pockets of his gray slacks. "You got pretty chummy with Foster at the bar the other night."

Airily she waved a hand. "All part of the job, chief."

"But not part of your job. When I instructed you to put a tag on the man, I didn't say to do it yourself."

"You didn't say not to, either."

"Don't play games with me, Comm."

The whip in his voice brought her snapping to attention. "No, *sir!* I would never do that, *sir!*"

Nick eyed her for long moments. The coins in his pocket clinked as he jiggled them in one hand.

"Did any of your Navy commanders ever consider a court-martial?"

"One or two." Grinning, she abandoned her exaggerated pose. "I was usually shipped out before matters reached that point."

"I may just ship you out this time, too."

"That's your option," she agreed breezily, refusing to admit this annoyed, unsmiling Nick was just a little bit intimidating. "But I was thinking our friend Foster might want a date for the big do. Someone who can give him an alibi when his hired gun shows up at the party.''

''Why would he think Scarface will show?''

''Well, I sorta figured I'd tell him.''

Lightning's eyes narrowed. The coins clinked again. Mackenzie held her breath until he broke the small silence.

''How?''

She was on her turf now. Confident, eager, she sketched her idea.

''We got a voiceprint on Scarface when Foster called him. It's not much. Only a few words. But we can digitize the sounds and run them through a phonetics databank, then use a synthesizer to imitate his exact intonation. Tweety Bird could chirp into the phone, and Foster would think it was his hired killer.''

He didn't argue her skills. No one could. When it came to electronics, she was the best.

''Think about it, chief. Foster will want to attend the function to make sure the hit goes down *before* Ellie makes her announcement and releases her report to the media. But he'll need an alibi, someone who can swear he was otherwise engaged when it happens. I'll be that alibi. I'll also make sure we get our boy on tape when Renegade figures out how to get him to incriminate himself.''

Lightning wasn't convinced. ''There's a good

chance Foster already paid for one death and is working on a second. I don't like the idea of my chief of communications turning up number three on his list.''

''Aww. Are you worried about me, boss?''

''Worrying about OMEGA's operatives comes with the title of director, Blair, but you're adding a new dimension to the mix.''

Mackenzie would have had all four incisors yanked without the benefit of anesthetic before she admitted to the thrill his sardonic reply gave her. Still, she couldn't hold back a smug little smile as she sashayed to the door.

''I'll get my folks at headquarters to work running the voiceprint through the phonetics database.''

While Jack accompanied Nick to his San Antonio bistro to perform an initial security assessment, Ellie got to work. Her bandaged hands made things awkward, but she spent several hours engaged in a flurry of phone calls and e-mail exchanges with universities, libraries and genealogists. Finally, she tracked down the clerk of Kearnes County, Texas, where Josiah Kennett's family had reportedly homesteaded. After a hand search of county records, the clerk located an eighty-seven-year-old great-great granddaughter of Kennett's only sister.

Ellie got Dorinda Johnson's number from information. To her delight, the woman who identified herself as Dorrie answered the phone. She sounded frail but had no difficulty grasping Ellie's background and interest in the tumultuous events of 1836.

"I remember my great-granddad telling us about the Runaway Scrape," she said in a wavery, paper-thin voice. "That Generalissimo Santa Anna you mentioned came up with a plan to move foreign settlers to the interior, replace them with Mexicans and cut off all immigration. Said he was going to execute every foreigner who resisted. After the Alamo and the massacre at Goliad, I guess the American settlers round these parts figured he meant business. Every one of 'em, including my great-great-granddaddy, abandoned their land and skeedaddled over the border to Louisiana."

If Ellie remembered correctly, the frantic scramble labeled the Runaway Scrape took place in early April, a month after the Alamo fell and just weeks after Colonel James Fannin and his force of four hundred Texians surrendered to Santa Anna. Under the mistaken impression they would simply be expelled from Mexico, the Tejanos were marched back to Goliad, where Santa Anna had them summarily shot.

Word of the massacre spread across Texas like prairie fire. Frightened settlers loaded everything they could into wagons and rushed helter-skelter for the U.S. border. Soldiers in Sam Houston's ragtag army abandoned ranks in droves to assist their fleeing families. Houston was left with only a little over nine hundred volunteers to face Santa Anna's well trained, well equipped and—until then—victorious army.

"Great-granddaddy said his grandpa's cabin was burned to the ground," Dorrie related, "but he came back and rebuilt after Houston beat the pants off Santa Anna at San Jacinto."

"Did your great-grandfather ever mention a great-uncle named Josiah Kennett?"

"Seems like he did, but I don't recall much about him, 'cept he died at the Alamo."

"Are you sure?"

"Well, that's what we were always told. I've got some old family pictures and letters stashed in a trunk up in the attic. I think there's one in there that talks about Josiah. Might take me a while to get to it, though. Doc says this new hip of mine isn't ready for stairs yet."

"That's all right!" Ellie said hastily. "Please don't go up to the attic."

She did some quick thinking. Kearnes County was less than an hour's drive from San Antonio. She could get out there and back by late afternoon.

"Would you mind if I drove out to your place and took a look through that trunk?"

"You come right ahead, missy. I'd enjoy the company."

Snatching up a pen, Ellie jotted down directions to her place. "Thanks. I'll be there by two-thirty or so."

Trying to contain her excitement, she filled the time until Jack's return by negotiating a contract for the site restoration and drawing up a list of invitees for the reception.

Mackenzie pounded on her door just before noon, every bit as excited and even more impatient for Jack and Nick's return. They arrived at the Menger a while later. Ellie wasn't quite sure how the colonel had managed to become a permanent member of their little group, but the others seemed to have accepted his presence.

Plugging a microphone into a small gray box, Mackenzie claimed their immediate attention.

"Wait till you hear this."

Her eyes gleaming, she spoke a few phrases into the microphone. The synthesizer translated the words into a deep rasp. The result sounded so much like the man who'd attacked Ellie in the exhibit room that goose bumps raised on her arms.

When the raspy echo faded, Mackenzie looked across the mike at Ellie. "You're the only one of us who heard him live. What do you think?"

"I think it's amazing. And just a bit scary."

"Good!" Her glance went to Jack. "Want to make the call to Foster?"

"Let's work out the wording, then you can go for it."

A few minutes later, Mackenzie dialed Foster's

private number. When an answering machine clicked on, she rasped out a brief message.

"Word on the street is our friend plans to release her report tomorrow night. I'll be there to make sure it doesn't happen."

Ellie knew it was a ploy. She was standing right there, had watched Mackenzie mouth the words. Yet the threat sounded so ominous that she had to work to match Mackenzie's smug grin when she cut the connection.

"There! That'll up Foster's pucker factor. I'll wait till he gets his invitation to the soiree to make the next call."

Recalled to her part in the drama, Ellie produced the list she'd worked on earlier. "Believe it or not, I convinced Dr. Smith to help me pull it together. The man's so eager to see me leave town—and so relieved that it looks like I'm not going to rewrite the history of his Alamo—that he actually volunteered the names of the high rollers who've contributed to the Alamo Restoration and Maintenance Fund."

She met Jack's glance.

"Foster's wife was one of the contributors."

A savage satisfaction glittered in his eyes. "That gives us the perfect rationale for including the bastard among the invitees. Think you can notify everyone on the list today?" he asked Mackenzie.

"Consider it done. I'll zap the list to my people

at headquarters. Given the short notice, they'll have to fax the invites. We'll make sure it looks as though they came from Dr. Alazar. As soon as they're out, I'll put in another call to Foster and offer myself as his date. Then,'' she announced, ''I'm going shopping.''

Jack hooked a brow. ''Again?''

''Again. The results of my last expedition seemed to impress Danny Boy. This time, I'll pull out all the stops and knock him off his feet. Literally.''

''No, you won't.''

Jack's reply came hard and fast, preempting Nick's.

''Foster's mine. All mine. No one knocks him off his feet but me.''

Faced with his vocal opposition and Nick's tight frown, Mackenzie backpedaled. ''Okay, okay. He's all yours. But I still need to go shopping. I didn't bring anything suitable for a black-tie affair. How about you, Claire? Ellie?''

The psychologist's gaze drifted around the small group. It didn't linger on Luis Esteban for more than an instant, but whatever she saw in his face caused her to incline her head in a graceful nod.

''I'll join you.''

''Ellie?''

''I can't make it this afternoon. I want to drive down to visit a fourth-generation relative of one of the Alamo defenders.''

The excitement she'd felt at the start of her project seeped into her veins. Her face eager, she turned to Jack.

"She lives in Kearnes County, less than an hour from San Antonio. She thinks she has some letters in her attic that contain information about Kennett. I'm also hoping I can talk her into providing a DNA sample. Will you go with me?"

The first real smile she'd seen in days crept into his eyes. "Try going anywhere without me."

The trip through the South Texas countryside was just what Ellie needed. After the stress of the past weeks and the sheer terror of the attack in the Alamo, the wide-open plains rolled by with soothing monotony.

Jack was at the wheel of the rented Cherokee. His eyes shielded behind mirrored sunglasses, he kept a close watch on the rearview mirror. They weren't followed this time. Nor did they engage in any high-speed chases. Gradually, even Jack relaxed.

They drove south on 181 for some forty miles, roughly paralleling the course of the San Antonio River as it meandered to the Gulf. Just past Hobson, they turned onto a two-lane county road that ran straight as an arrow between fields fenced by barbed wire. Ellie consulted the directions she'd scribbled down earlier.

''Dorrie said her place was three point four miles down this road.''

Nodding, Jack took a fix on the odometer. Three point four miles later, a dented mailbox atop a weathered post proclaimed the Johnson place.

A dirt track led to the house, perched on a slight rise a quarter mile from the road. The Cherokee jounced over deep ruts. Dust swirled in a long plume behind, announcing their arrival long before they drove over a cattle guard and pulled into the yard.

The original structure must have been constructed in the early Texas dogtrot style, with separate sleeping, cooking and eating quarters on either side of a walk-through breezeway. Native stone walls enclosed the original sections, but succeeding generations had tacked on clapboard additions and enclosed the breezeway.

Leaning heavily on a walker, Dorrie Johnson hobbled out to greet them. Shaded by the tin roof that extended over the front porch, she was a tiny figure in a bright yellow blouse, denim jumper and sturdy sneakers. To Ellie's consternation, she'd prepared a small feast for her visitors.

''My molasses cookies won first prize at the county fair for near onto three decades,'' she announced smugly. Her walker thumping, she led Jack and Ellie into the front parlor and waved at them to have a seat. ''The pecan crop wasn't all that good last year, though, so I baked up a sweet potato pie, too."

Jack didn't appear to find any fault with the pecans. He consumed a plateful of cookies, washing them down with sweetened iced tea, before tackling a hearty sampling of pie. Ellie was too enthralled by the memories Dorrie shared of her family to do more than nibble at the rich sweets.

"Salathiel Charles Kennett and his bride homesteaded this place in twenty-eight. Hauled everything they owned west in a covered wagon. Like I told you, they left in a hurry in thirty-six."

At Jack's questioning look, Ellie explained the Runaway Scrape.

"They came back, though," Dorrie continued complacently. "One of their offspring or another's been squatting on this patch of dirt ever since."

"Do you know where Salathiel hailed from?"

"He was from Alabama. Barbour County, best I recall. His wife was from Sparta, South Carolina. Dorinda. Dorinda McLaren. Want to guess who I was named for?"

Ellie jerked upright in her seat. Ignoring the playful question she fired one of her own.

"Your kin came from Sparta?"

Dorrie's eyes twinkled. "Didn't I just say so, missy? I'll admit I'm getting a mite forgetful these days, but I can pretty well remember the words that just popped out of my mouth."

"Yes, of course. I'm sorry. It's just that... Well, William Barrett Travis, the commander of the troops at the Alamo, moved to Texas from Sparta, South Carolina, too."

"You don't say!"

Carefully placing her iced tea on a coaster, Ellie scooted to the edge of her seat.

"Historical documents indicate Travis arrived at the Alamo armed with a double-barreled shotgun, among other weapons. There's one on display up there in San Antonio bearing a mark that traces to a gunsmith in Sparta. I found another buried in a creek bed some miles south of the city with the same mark. We're trying to determine who that gun belonged to."

"Don't know that I can help you there, missy. Seems I remember great-granddaddy talkin' about a shotgun *his* daddy carried west with him. Could have been made by that gunsmith you're talking about, but I don't know what happened to it."

"Could he have given it to his brother, Josiah, to take with him when he joined the Texas Army?"

"I 'spose so."

"Maybe there's something in those letters you told me about that will give us more information," Ellie hinted.

"Maybe," Dorrie said doubtfully. "You're welcome to crawl up to the attic and take a look."

The tin roof trapped the heat and held it under the eaves. Dust motes danced and swirled in the hazy light cast by the bulb dangling at the end of a long cord.

Switching on the flashlight Dorrie had provided for extra illumination, Ellie stepped over bundles of old *National Geographic*s and stacks of yellowed sheet music. A zigzagging course through the treasured junk of several generations took her to the steamer trunk pushed under the eaves. Leather peeled in strips from its sides and humped top. The rusted hasps were sprung and hung uselessly on their hinges. Grunting, Jack used his good arm and worked it out far enough for Ellie to raise the lid.

She gasped in delight. He swiped at a trickle of sweat and groaned.

"It's going to take hours to go through all this stuff."

"It might take you hours," she retorted, the historian in her affronted by his lack of faith in her abilities. "I know what I'm looking for. Just pull up that crate, get comfortable and hold the flashlight steady."

Jack did as ordered. Hunkering on the sturdy crate, he planted his elbows on his knees and aimed the beam of light at the yellowed letters, old newspaper clippings and faded family photos.

Her still tender knees made kneeling impossible, so Ellie sat cross-legged beside the trunk. Despite the bulky bandages on her hands, or maybe because of them, she handled the clippings and documents with extreme care. She skimmed each with a keen eye before setting it aside. Inch by inch, the stack beside her grew.

Jack found the woman digging through the trunk far more intriguing than its contents. She probably didn't have any idea how beautiful she looked to him at this moment. Dust swirled around her. Sweat glistened on her forehead and upper lip. White streaked her hair where she'd caught a cobweb. She was totally absorbed by those yellowed scraps of paper, as thrilled by the past as Jack was nervous about the future.

He'd dropped enough hints. Hell, he'd come right out and admitted that he'd never been able to get her out of his head or his heart. He'd had to work to say the words. He'd never told any woman he loved her, Ellie included.

He was pretty sure she loved him, too. She'd told him flat out she wasn't wasn't walking away from him. And she certainly held nothing back the night she'd flamed in his arms. Yet Jack wanted to hear the words. Needed to hear the words.

''Ellie.''

''Hmm?''

''Last night…''

She glanced up then, curiosity warring with impatience to get back to the letter in her hand.

"What about last night?"

"I meant what I said. I've never stopped loving you."

The words hung on the suffocating air. Chewing on her lower lip, Ellie considered his quiet declaration.

"Last night," she said after a long moment, "I believed you. For a moment this morning, I had my doubts."

"I know. I saw the hurt in your eyes when Lightning brought up that business about the treaty. You have to know politics have nothing to do with what's between us."

"To quote your friend Lightning, political issues are always in play. They certainly were nine years ago."

"But not this time. Marry me, Ellie."

"What?"

"You said it yourself. We've wasted too many days and nights already. Marry me. Here in Texas, or in New Mexico or wherever we can get a license with the least hassle and delay."

Helplessly, Ellie gaped at him. Sweat trickled down his temples. With the flashlight's beam backlighting his face, he looked like a character from a B-grade horror flick. She couldn't believe the man had chosen this hot, musty attic to ask for the commitment she'd ached to give him nine years ago, but she wasn't going to argue the time or the place. As she'd told Jack, she knew her mind then and she knew it now.

"Yes," she said simply. "I'll marry you. Whenever and wherever you want."

With a small, inarticulate sound, he bent to seal the agreement. The kiss left them both breathless and several degrees hotter than before.

"Better finish with that trunk," he warned with a crooked grin, "or Miss Dorinda might hear some strange thumps coming from her attic."

Chapter 14

Ellie found the prize she'd been searching for near the bottom of the trunk, tucked inside an old Bible. The yellowed, folded sheet had torn at the creases and almost came apart in her hands. Carefully lifting the bottom edge, she took one look at the signature and gulped.

"Here." Her hands clumsy and trembling in their gauze wrappings, she passed the letter to Jack. "I don't want to take a chance on tearing this further. Unfold it, will you, and hold it so I can read it."

Trading the letter for the flashlight, he lifted the folds and tilted the letter toward the beam. Ellie came up on her knees without so much as a blink at the pain and leaned on Jack's thigh. Her heart thumping, she peered at the spidery script.

March 5th
1836
Elijah—

I don't have time for more than a few lines. The colonel's sending me & another out shortly. God willing, one of us will make it through & bring back reinforcements. If there are none to be had, I'll rejoin my company here at the Alamo.

Ammunition's running low, but I still have enough for pa's short-barrel to give a good accounting. She fires as true as the colonel's. Guess she should, seeing as the same smith cast both.

They're calling for me now. I'll leave this letter with the captain's wife, as many of the company are doing. She's promised to see them delivered if she survives the attack we all know is coming.

Yr brother,
Josiah Kennett
Private
Texas Volunteers

Ellie's throat ached at the letter's simple poignancy. The satisfaction of knowing she'd found the last vital piece of the puzzle didn't begin to compare with the admiration she felt for Kennett's courage and sense of duty.

"James Allen made it to Goliad," she murmured, leaning against Jack's knee, "but Fannin delayed sending troops until it was too late. I wonder where Josiah was headed."

"Guess we'll never know." Carefully, he folded the letter. "Do you think Dorrie will agree to contribute this to the collection at the Alamo?"

"I hope so!"

Dorrie not only agreed to let Ellie take the letter, she also cheerfully provided a DNA sample. After rolling a cotton swab around in her mouth, she stared at the tip for a moment before dropping it into a plastic baggie.

"You sure that's all you need?"

"If that doesn't do it, we know where to find you."

Ignoring Ellie's protests, Dorrie thumped out to the porch to see them off. "Y'all come back any time."

"You promise to bake more of these and we will," Jack said, carrying the bag of molasses cookies the older woman had pressed on him with the same care Ellie carried her bagged letter and DNA sample.

Ellie occupied the hour's drive to San Antonio plotting how best to rush through a DNA test. Jack expressed far more interest in obtaining the blood test required for a marriage license.

He solved the first problem by swinging by the

federal courthouse. Tracking down the two FBI agents he and Mackenzie had met with the previous day, he traded an update on the Foster situation for a promise to strong-arm their lab into an overnight DNA analysis.

He took care of second problem with a stop at the emergency room where Ellie's cuts had been treated two days ago. Her eyes widened when he pulled into the lot.

"Jack! You were serious? You really want to get married right away?"

"This afternoon, if we can talk the doc into doing the blood work and track down a judge to waive the three day waiting requirement. Why? Are you having second thoughts?"

"No! But my mother, my aunt and uncle... They'll be crushed if we don't invite them."

Jack gave her a wry look. "Your uncle Eduardo, huh?"

"Uncle Eduardo," Ellie said firmly. "He might not be able to rearrange his schedule and fly up here on short notice, but for all his overbearing ways, he's been as much a father to me as an uncle. I have to invite him. And, well..."

She fiddled with the plastic bag holding Josiah Kennett's precious letter. The mere thought of joining her life with Jack's sent excited anticipation racing through her veins. After so many years, so many hurts, the future held all the promise their past had cut short.

Ellie didn't want anything to spoil their day. Anything.

"Let's think about this waiting period. If we work things right in the next twenty-four to thirty-six hours, we can go off on a nice, long honeymoon with no loose ends left dangling."

"Like Josiah Kennett," he said with a smile.

"And Daniel Foster."

Jack kept the smile on his face, but it took some doing. At this point he couldn't say how much, if any, of his urgent need to make Ellie his stemmed from an instinctive, gut-deep desire to give her every protection a man can give his woman. All he knew was that he didn't like the idea of Ellie going head-to-head with Foster. At all!

From all indications, the bastard had arranged the murder of one woman. If pushed to the wall, he might take matters into his own hands. The man was big enough, ruthless enough, desperate enough to pull the trigger if he thought he could get away with it.

Jack would just have to make sure Foster knew he couldn't get away with it.

"All right," he conceded. "We take care of the loose ends, then we get married."

After that, it seemed to Ellie as though events moved with the speed of light.

Anticipating a wedding, preparing a public announcement of a major historical find and rehearsing responses to several different scenarios involving Dan Foster took up the rest of that evening and most of the next day.

RSVPs came pouring in. All the local TV and radio stations were sending crews. The mayor and most of the city council intended to make an appearance. Almost every local member of the Alamo Restoration and Preservation Foundation accepted—including Daniel Foster.

As it turned out, Mackenzie didn't have to place a second call to Foster and inveigle an invitation to be his date. He called her. Listening to the tape of their brief conversation gave Ellie a distinctly queasy sensation. If the man was driven by anything more than a desire to show up with a gorgeous female draped over his arm, he hid it well.

Gorgeous, he'd certainly get. Mackenzie had made good on her promise to do some serious shopping. The midnight blue sheath she displayed to Ellie dipped dangerously low in the front, even lower in back.

Claire, too, had found the perfect gown to complement her silvery blond beauty. The shimmering turquoise silk was strapless, banded with silver sequins at the bodice and split up one side. Ellie had no idea how the woman would hide anything, much less her neat little revolver, under that whisper of silk. Smiling, Claire admitted that a holster strapped to the inside of her thigh made gliding across a room an exercise in extreme care.

Forcefully reminded of her woefully inadequate wardrobe, Ellie coerced the two women into a return trip to the elegant little boutique they'd discovered in River Center mall. Those sixty minutes turned out to be among the most expensive of Ellie's life. She ended up purchasing not only a gown for the reception that night, but a cream-colored silk suit perfect for a wedding, a flame-colored chiffon nightdress that clung to her every curve and lacy underwear designed more for seduction than for comfort.

Mackenzie took one look at the scraps of lace and promptly bought two pair for herself. Even Claire was convinced to splurge on the outrageously extravagant panties.

"Now I really won't be able to walk straight," she said with a rueful smile.

"Maybe not," Mackenzie returned with a grin, "but you'll sure have the colonel wondering why. You notice he hasn't taken his eyes off you since he arrived?"

"As a matter of fact," the psychologist replied serenely, "I have."

The happy saleswoman was ringing up their purchases when a cell phone rang. All four women checked their phones. Ellie flipped hers open.

"Dr. Alazar. Yes, I can hold."

Gnawing on her lower lip, she waited for Janet Dawes-Hamilton to come on the line.

"Ellie?"

"Yes."

"As you requested, the FBI sent me the results of the DNA profile their lab worked up for you. I just ran it against the samples we took from the skeletal remains."

"And?"

"We have a match, girl!"

Whooping, Ellie danced around her startled companions.

The shopping expedition and thrilling report from her colleague succeeded in holding Ellie's nervousness at bay for an all-too-brief hour. It came rushing back when the three women returned to the hotel and got caught up in the flurry of last-minute preparations for the function that night.

Jack insisted Ellie rehearse a variety of different responses for if and when she confronted Foster. The responses ranged from merely smiling and letting Foster do all the talking to dropping facedown on the floor if his hand moved so much as an inch toward his tux or pants pocket. After the third or fourth drop, she was a bundle of raw nerves. Pleading the need to review her speech a final time before dressing, she escaped to her bedroom.

Jack knocked on the connecting door at the time

they'd set as the time to leave the hotel. Ellie had just finished putting the final touches to her makeup. Thankfully, the cuts on her palms had healed enough for her to leave off the bandages. A light application of pancake makeup muted most of the scabs. Fighting a panicky flutter of nerves, she tucked a stray curl into the feathery cluster on top of her head and opened the door.

"Oh, my!"

Nine years ago, she'd taken one look at a tall, broad-shouldered Marine in his dress blues and immediately decided to wrangle an introduction and a dance. When Jack had arrived at the Menger, his rugged informality had at first surprised her, then stirred her senses.

This Jack rocked her on her heels.

His tux might have been cut by the hand of a master. The black broadcloth showcased his broad shoulders. Silver studs winked at the front of his snowy white shirt. A satin cummerbund nipped in his trim waist, and a matching satin stripe ran down the outside of his pants legs. What struck Ellie even more than the elegance of the formal attire was the casual ease with which he wore it.

"Where did you get a tux to fit you on such short notice?" she asked when she recovered her breath.

"Nick had it delivered. Compliments of the same tailor who rigs out his waiters."

If Nick Jensen's employees waited tables in hand-tailored tuxes like this one, it was no wonder dinner at one of his glitzy watering holes reputedly cost more than the down payment on a four-bedroom house.

"You look incredible," Ellie murmured.

"*I* look incredible?"

Jack's glance made a slow journey down her length. Just as slowly, he brought his glinting gaze to hers.

"You're going to have every man in the room tonight wishing they could go back to school and take more history courses."

Ellie had to admit the slinky silver lamé gown was about as far from academia as anything could get. The plunging halter top left her shoulders and back bare, while the pencil-slim skirt clung to her hips and glittered with every step. Paired with the silver bracelet Jack had given her nine years ago and dangly silver earrings, the effect was pure Hollywood.

If she'd had more time to deliberate and less on her mind, she might have chosen something more restrained, more dignified. The gleam in Jack's eyes made her glad she hadn't.

"I have something I want you to wear tonight," Jack said. Sliding his hand into his pocket, he produced what looked like a thin transparent patch.

"What is it?"

"A wireless transmitter, compliments of Mackenzie."

His knuckles warm on the slope of her breast, he stuck the tiny device to the inside folds of the halter top.

"Don't take this off tonight. For any reason."

"I won't."

He hesitated a moment, his fingers lingering on her warm skin before reaching into his pocket once more. This time he produced a little box bearing the logo of the jewelry shop just off the Menger's lobby.

"I was going to wait and let you pick out the ring you wanted, but I saw this downstairs and thought it would match your bracelet."

"Oh, Jack! It's beautiful!"

The diamonds were channel cut and set flush in a narrow platinum engagement ring. A wider wedding ring of beaten platinum nestled in the black velvet below the diamonds. Leaving the wider band in place, he popped the box shut and slipped the diamonds on her finger.

Ellie waggled her fingers, marveling at the fiery sparkle. She couldn't quite believe so much was happening so fast!

"I've got a gift for you, too," she told him. "Nothing near as beautiful as this ring *or* my bracelet, but... Well... Wait here a minute."

Hurrying into the sitting room, she retrieved the silver concho.

"I thought you might like this as a souvenir. It's the concho you found at Mission San Jose."

Pleasure softened his features as he worked his thumb over the intricate design. "Don't you need it to substantiate your findings?"

"Not with Josiah's letter and Dorrie's DNA sampling."

"Then I'll keep it."

Sliding the concho into his breast pocket, he drew her forward. His kiss was long and hard and went a long way to calming Ellie's jittery nerves. The reassuring smile he gave her helped, too.

"Time to go. Are you ready?"

She drew in a shaky breath. "As ready as I'll ever be."

Nick's more than lived up to its reputation.

The restaurant occupied the entire top floor of one of San Antonio's tallest buildings. An outside glass elevator whisked patrons upward while providing stunning views of the Riverwalk and the floodlit Alamo. Guests stepped out of the elevator into an eagle's aerie with a spectacular three-hundred-sixty-degree view of the city. Floor-to-ceiling glass panels stood open to the night to allow easy circulation between the dining area and the mist-cooled balcony.

Ellie had never been to a Nick's, but understood they were famous for incorporating local culture and cuisine. This particular establishment offered the best of Texas with a distinctly Hispanic flavor. Discreetly lighted niches displayed museum-quality pieces of

sculpture and art depicting the rich heritage of the
area. The wine cellar, she'd been told, stocked some
fifteen hundred labels, including a number of rich,
hearty Texas reds bottled in Hill County vineyards.

For tonight's bash, the lush greenery that provided
diners an illusion of privacy without impeding their
view had been removed, as had most of the tables.
This was a stand-up reception with an open bar and
a lavish spread of hot and cold delicacies, subsidized
by the restaurant's owner. Good thing, as Ellie knew
the pitiful bit of funding that remained in the project
kitty wouldn't have covered the drinks, let alone succulent Gulf shrimp sautéed in a white wine sauce,
bourbon seared beef tenderloins, and a *carne asada*
with the most delicate, delicious aroma she'd ever
sniffed.

A good number of guests in black tie and glittering
cocktail dresses and gowns had already assembled.
Conversation hummed. Ice clinked in glasses. Tux-
clad waiters floated between groups refilling glasses
and plates. Her palm clammy where it rested in the
crook of Jack's arm, Ellie skimmed a quick glance
over the assembled guests in search of Mackenzie
and her escort.

Foster had picked Mac up at the hotel twenty
minutes ago. Ellie had been kept out of sight, but
Nick, Jack, Claire and Colonel Esteban had observed
the pickup from different vantage points. Claire and

Luis had trailed the couple in Luis's rented Lincoln. Both couples should have arrived by now.

A fact that obviously played on Nick's mind when he greeted Ellie and Jack.

"Comm's playing her part to the hilt," he informed them. "She managed to talk Foster into a detour on the way here, ostensibly to show her another building he constructed."

Annoyance darkening his blue eyes, Lightning flicked the cuffs of his dress shirt. If the stark black and white of formal dress tamed Jack's rugged good looks, Nick Jensen wore his like he'd been born to them.

"From the tenor of the transmissions we're receiving," he said with something less than his usual urbane charm, "she's succeeded in upping the man's pucker factor by several degrees."

She was certainly upping Ellie's. The delay set her nerves snapping and sparking like downed electrical lines. She longed to snatch one of the crystal champagne flutes from the tray a smiling waiter presented, but she knew she had to keep a clear head.

Instead, she sipped at the glass of Perrier Nick procured for her with a single word to the waiter. The overhead lights shot brilliant sparks off the diamonds on her hand as she lifted the heavy crystal goblet. Nick's glance went to the ring, then to Jack. A smile played at his eyes, but he said nothing.

"There's the mayor," he commented. "As host for tonight's event, I'd better greet him."

"And I should look over the layout for the presentation," Ellie said to Jack.

Nodding, he led her to an area cordoned off by black velvet ropes. Rows of straight-backed chairs emblazoned with a gold N faced a raised platform. A wall-size screen would be lowered from the ceiling behind the podium on the platform.

Gulping, Ellie clutched her little silver lamé evening bag. Inside were a lipstick, a compact and a CD in a thin plastic case. She'd boiled down all her weeks of work, all the hours at the dig and at the Alamo, all her team's collective research into a dramatic slide presentation. It was astounding how much history could be crammed onto a single CD.

Her fingers tightened on Jack's arm. "Do you think I'll actually get to present the findings tonight?"

"Yes. Just play this out the way we rehearsed. Exactly the way we rehearsed."

She felt like a Ping-Pong ball bouncing between the public drama of her presentation and the very private, very tense drama with Foster.

"I just hope the rest of the team arrives in time," she said nervously.

Orin Weaver had made arrangements to fly to San Antonio. Janet Dawes-Hamilton was driving down from Waco. Sam Pierce had indicated he'd show, too, and had coerced the National Park Service regional director into coming with him. Ellie had made sure invitations went to each of the volunteers, as well. The only member of the team she hadn't been able contact was Eric Chapman. The grad student was on the road somewhere between San Antonio and Albuquerque and not answering his cell phone.

If her team was still arriving, most of Jack's was already in place. Nick circulated among the crowd, greeting the mayor and other dignitaries with an ease that astounded Ellie considering the fact that he was also receiving a steady stream of transmissions from his headquarters. She couldn't begin to imagine how he separated the mayor's polite patter from the voices feeding into his right ear.

She spotted Detective Harris on the far side of the room, tugging a finger at the tight black bow tie encircling his neck. Jack had indicated upward of a half dozen more of SAPD's finest would be in attendance tonight. Ellie thought she recognized one of the FBI agents she'd met yesterday. The other was here, as well, but she couldn't see him in the growing crowd.

The media had turned out en masse. Banks of TV cameras stood ready opposite the podium. Reporters with mikes and Minicams vied for space and the best backdrops in the roped-off area reserved for interviews. They understood Ellie and her team wouldn't be available until after the presentation but were managing to capture other VIPs on tape.

"Guess we'd better circulate," she murmured, dragging in a shaky breath. "At least until Mackenzie and her date make an appearance."

They arrived less than ten minutes later. Claire and Luis Esteban drifted in almost on their heels.

Ellie sensed rather than saw their entrance. Jack's arm went taut under hers. The skin pulled tight across his cheeks. Gulping, she saw his eyes narrow as he tracked his prey.

She turned slowly, searched the crowd milling at the entrance for a glimpse of a midnight blue gown. Mackenzie floated into view a second later, clinging like a burr to Dan Foster.

The builder's face was ruddy above his black tie. Even from this distance, Ellie could see the sheen of sweat at his temples. His eyes darting around the restaurant, he dragged a folded handkerchief from his pocket and dabbed his forehead.

Across the room, his gaze locked with Ellie's. His hand froze in mid dab for a second, maybe two. Abruptly, he stuffed the handkerchief in his pocket and turned away.

After so many hours of clawing tension and dread, trapping Daniel Foster in the net he had woven proved embarrassingly easy. Almost anticlimactic.

Mackenzie played her role to perfection. While the entire team watched from various vantage points, she snuggled up to Foster, whispered coyly and did everything but stick her tongue in his ear to add to his obvious edginess.

Nick Jensen, Ellie saw in a quick glance, didn't appear to fully appreciate her performance. Like Jack, he tracked the builder's progress around the room with narrowed eyes.

Foster was obviously searching the crowd, looking for one face in particular, growing more tight-jawed by the moment when he didn't spot it. Since a good number of guests had drifted onto the balcony to enjoy the view, it didn't take much work on Mackenzie's part to steer her escort there, as well. With seemingly effortless ease, she maneuvered him to the corner Jack had chosen earlier. A bend in the building left that particular niche shielded from view of most of those inside. The wrought-iron lampposts scattered around the balcony cast only a dim spear of light in that direction.

It was barely enough to illuminate Mackenzie as she withdrew her arm from Foster's and pantomimed powering her nose. Distracted, he gave a terse nod. A moment later, a stunning figure in midnight blue floated past Ellie and Jack on her way to the ladies' room.

"All right, you two. He's all yours."

Swallowing, Ellie swiped her hand down the sides of her dress. Her damp palms slid over the glittering metallic material. Too late, she realized that she'd left smears of the makeup she'd used to cover the ugly scabs on her hands.

Wondering how in the world she could even *think* about such trivia at a time like this, she started forward.

Jack held her back. "Remember how we rehearsed it. If he lifts so much as a finger, you hit the deck."

"Don't worry! I'll go down like the *Titanic*. Now let's get this over with."

The scene that followed might have been scripted. When Ellie moved into the circle of dim light cast by the wrought-iron lamppost behind Foster, the builder reacted just as Claire had predicted he would.

His eyes turned wary. His shoulders went taut under his tux. But no one watching from more than a few feet away would see anything but affability in his smile.

"Mr. Foster?"

"Yes."

"I'm Elena Alazar. I understand your wife was one of the leading contributors to the Alamo Restoration and Preservation Foundation. I just wanted to say how very sorry I was to hear about her tragic death."

"Thank you."

"I know there's been some concern on the part of other foundation members about my team's findings. I just wanted to assure you that…"

With a show of concern, Ellie took another step

forward. That was as close as she dared get to the man whose knuckles had gone white where his hand gripped the balcony rail.

"Mr. Foster? Are you all right?"

His glance was riveted on something just beyond her. She didn't have to look around to know it was the gleam of a long, lethal silencer.

"Are you crazy!" Foster whispered, frantically searching the shadows behind the gun. "Not here! Not with me standing two feet away from her!"

"Mr. Foster, what in the world? Oh!"

Ellie froze as something hard jabbed into the small of her back.

"Don't make a sound," a deep voice rasped from behind her. "Or a move. One twitch and you're dead."

She didn't have to fake the ice that crystallized in her veins. The press of that gun barrel against her bare skin was all too real. The voice so eerily like the one at the Alamo that Ellie couldn't breathe, much less twitch.

Foster fed on her fear like a jackal feasted on carrion. With a snarl, he pushed away from the railing.

"For Christ's sake, keep her here in the shadows until I get across the room. Then do it right this time and blow the bitch away."

"If I blow anyone away," Jack answered in his own voice, "it'll be you."

His jaw dropping, the builder whirled back. "What the hell...?"

"Take one step." With a savage smile, Jack stepped out of the shadows. "Just one."

The beefy contractor was no fool. He froze right where he was. With a grunt of acute disappointment, Jack raised his voice.

"Did you get that, Comm?"

Mackenzie sailed through the glass door. Nick, Claire, Esteban, Detective Harris and the FBI man crowed right on her heels. Behind them, TV crews scrambled frantically to aim their cameras and lights.

"We all got it," she announced, shooting Foster a look of utter scorn. "I broadcast the murdering bastard live."

Epilogue

Washington, D.C.,'s muggy July had given way to a surprisingly pleasant August when Renegade ushered his new bride up the steps of an elegant town house set halfway down a shady street just off Massachusetts Avenue.

Ellie had already met a good number of Jack's friends and colleagues. Men and women with curious code names like Jaguar, Cowboy, Artemis, Chameleon and Thunder had converged on San Antonio, families in tow, for the wedding that had taken place at Mission San Jose the day after Ellie gave a name and a history to the solitary solider who'd died so many years ago on mission grounds. In addition to that lively group, a whole contingent of Marines showed up unexpectedly. Square-shouldered and spit-shined, they stated emphatically that they had to see their old Gunny take the plunge with their own eyes.

Jack's friends weren't the only ones who crowded into the beautiful old church. Ellie's team had showed up *en masse*. A tall, handsome Marine escorted a beaming Dorrie Johnson to her pew. The First Lady of Mexico and her sister-in-law occupied the front pew on the bride's side.

The media had turned out, too. Dr. Alazar, one was heard to proclaim, sure provided *great* copy. TV Minicams whirred and cameras flashed as the President of Mexico escorted his niece down the aisle.

The wedding supper that evening was held on a string of colorful barges floating along the San Antonio River. Candles winked in crystal chimneys. A mariachi band serenaded the guests. Nick's catered the food and wine. It was, Ellie had decided, the perfect ending to her visit to San Antonio and her quest to discover the identity of a fallen Texas hero.

It was also, she thought on a flutter of pure happiness, the perfect beginning for her new life with her own particular hero. A beginning that included a honeymoon in the Pyrenees, where she intended to entice Jack into exploring the mysteries of some recently discovered ice-age cave paintings.

First, though, he'd insisted on a stopover in Washington. It was time, he'd stated, she understood exactly what he did for a living.

The tour a smiling Nick Jensen gave Ellie of the offices of the special envoy didn't shed any particular light on the subject. Not until he ushered her and Jack into an elevator hidden behind a walnut panel fitted with a titanium insert and whisked her up to Mackenzie Blair's domain did she grasp the significance of that bulletproof shield. The door slid open to reveal a state-of-the-art war room.

"Good grief!" Stunned, Ellie took in digital displays that took up three of the four walls. "What is this? An alternate command center for the Joint Chiefs of Staff?"

"They wish!" Her eyes sparkling, Mackenzie waved a proprietary hand. "Nope, this is all mine."

She caught Nick's hooked eyebrow and made a slight correction.

"*Mostly* mine. Come on, I'll show you around."

Dazed, Ellie was treated to a detailed description of the control center's futuristic array of electronics, a visit to the field dress unit, a view of weaponry at the firing range that would have challenged even the data stored in Discoverer Two, and finally a highly sanitized briefing of OMEGA's charter.

Enough of its mission came through, though, to make her frown and swing around in her chair.

"This is what you do, Jack?"

"It's what I did," he answered quietly. "What I do from here on out depends on you."

Startled, Mackenzie and the other agents present at the briefing flashed a quick look at Lightning. He shook his head, signaling that this was news to him, too.

"I don't want you worrying every time I walk out the door, Ellie, or wondering if I'll come back. I came here today to terminate my membership in this elite club."

Relief washed through her, followed immediately by the sharp sting of regret. She'd cost Jack one career. Now he was giving up another for her. Her smile wobbly, she opted to continue this discussion without an interested audience.

"We'll have two weeks in the Pyrenees. Why don't we talk about it there?"

The wolfish grin that slashed across Jack's face said more clearly than words that his plans for those two weeks didn't include a whole lot of talking. Nodding to the others, he escorted Ellie out of the control center.

Mackenzie folded her arms. Toe tapping, she stood beside Lightning and watched the two leave. She liked Ellie. Liked *and* respected her. But she wasn't happy with the idea Renegade might not rejoin the ranks of active operatives. Mac considered each and every one of them her personal responsibility.

"Do you think he'll really give up OMEGA for her?"

Nick slanted her an enigmatic look. "Wouldn't you, for the right man?"

The glint in his blue eyes closed Mackenzie's throat. She had to take in a quick gulp of air before she could inject the right note of nonchalance into her reply.

"Maybe. Maybe not. Guess I'll just have to wait for the right man to make his move and see what happens."

Nick's amused glance followed her across the control center. "I guess you will," he murmured.

*   *   *   *   *

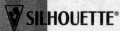

Romantic reads to

Need, Want

International affairs, seduction and passion guaranteed
8 brand-new books every month

Pure romance, pure emotion...
4 brand-new books every month

**Pulse-raising romance,
– heart-racing medical drama**
6 brand-new books every month

**From Regency England to
Ancient Rome, rich, vivid and
passionate romance...**
3 brand-new books every month

Scorching hot sexy reads
4 brand-new books every month

*Mills & Boon® books are available on the **first Friday of every month** from WHSmith, ASDA, Tesco and all good bookshops.*

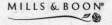

MILLS & BOON®

M&B/SIL/GENERIC a

satisfy your every
and Desire...

Two passionate, dramatic love stories in every book
3 brand-new books every month

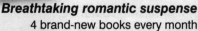

Life, love and family
6 brand-new books every month

Breathtaking romantic suspense
4 brand-new books every month

Passionate and thrilling romantic adventures
6 brand-new books every month

Enjoy the drama, explore the emotions, experience the relationship
4 brand-new books every month

*Silhouette® books are available on the **third Friday of every month** from WHSmith, ASDA, Tesco and all good bookshops.*

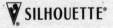 **SILHOUETTE®**

M&B/SIL/GENERIC b

SILHOUETTE®
Desire™ 2 in 1

ENGAGEMENT BETWEEN ENEMIES
by Kathie DeNosky
(The Illegitimate Heirs)

After a scandalous rumour erupted, honourable tycoon Caleb Walker made employee Alyssa Merrick an offer she couldn't refuse...

TYCOON TAKES REVENGE by Anna DePalo

Infamous playboy Noah Whittaker gives gossip columnist Kayla Jones a taste of her own medicine, but finds that love is far sweeter than revenge.

※

THE MAN MEANS BUSINESS by Annette Broadrick

Business was millionaire Dean Logan's only thought until his loyal assistant, Jodie Cameron, accompanied him on a passionate Hawaiian vacation and put marriage on the agenda!

DEVLIN AND THE DEEP BLUE SEA
by Merline Lovelace
(Code Name: Danger)

Helicopter pilot Elizabeth Moore thought sexy stranger Joe Devlin was a mystery to solve—and if she hadn't just been jilted, she might have made an effort to uncover *all* his secrets!

※

BABY, I'M YOURS by Catherine Mann

Three months after their whirlwind affair, Claire McDermott discovered she was carrying Vic Jansen's child and that she wanted more than just an honourable offer of marriage...

HER HIGH-STAKES AFFAIR by Katherine Garbera

An affair between them was strictly forbidden, but when passion struck Raine Montgomery and rich, sexy Scott Rivers under the bright lights of Las Vegas, it was on the cards!

On sale from 19th January 2007

Visit our website at www.silhouette.co.uk

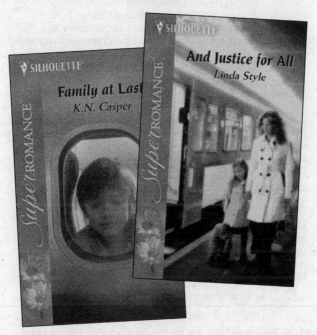

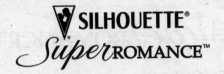

SILHOUETTE®
*Super*ROMANCE™

A HEART AS BIG AS TEXAS by KN Casper
Home to Stay

Kayla is thrilled to be part of Homestead's Home Free programme—and establish a vineyard and in turn help revitalise a dying town. But hard work isn't enough to make her venture a success, and she must find out who wants her gone and why they are desperate enough to resort to sabotage.

EXPECTANT FATHER by Melinda Curtis
9 Months Later

Becca Thomas is thrilled to discover she's pregnant—even though it means bringing up her baby alone. She doesn't expect to run into the father again—and she certainly doesn't expect a carefree younger man like Aiden Rodas to *want* to be a father. Little does she know…

NOT WITHOUT CAUSE by Kay David
The Operatives

Meredith Santera is the leader of the Operatives, putting the needs of others in front of her own. Which means that she chose the job over a relationship with Jack Haden. Now her job is putting her in contact with Jack once again. But this time they are on opposite sides.

A SECOND CHANCE AT LOVE
by Brenda Novak

After finding out that her husband had another woman in his life, Elizabeth O'Connor opens a chocolate shop in a new town with her two children. Carter Hudson isn't part of her plan. But gradually, Liz realises she likes having Carter in her life. However, Carter seems to have secrets in his past, secrets that apparently involve a woman…

On sale from 19th January 2007

Available at WHSmith, Tesco, ASDA,
and all good bookshops

www.silhouette.co.uk

❦ SILHOUETTE®

SPECIAL EDITION™

A MONTANA HOMECOMING
by Allison Leigh

When Laurel Runyan came home, finding her first love, Sheriff Shane Golightly, as a neighbour was a surprise. Was Laurel ready to give her home town—and Shane—a second chance?

THE BABY DEAL
by Victoria Pade
Family Business

For Delia McRay, hooking up with Chicago playboy Andrew Hanson on a Tahitian beach was a fantasy come true. But when Hanson Media met with Delia's company months later to land her account, there was a pregnant pause…

LUKE'S PROPOSAL
by Lois Faye Dyer
The McClouds

When Rachel Kerrigan sought Lucas McCloud's help to save her family's ranch, he thought of their fleeting youthful kiss and agreed. It was strictly business and the old family feud wouldn't matter…

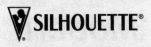

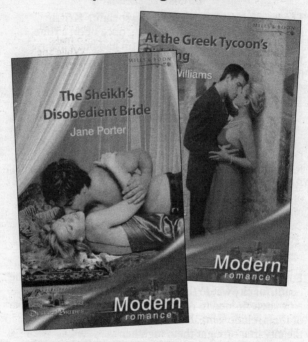

0107/01b

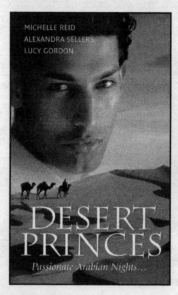

NEW from M&B™ by *New York Times* bestselling author DIANA PALMER

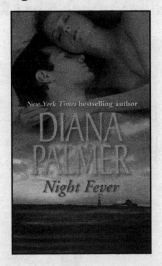

A dazzling novel that will leave you breathless…

At the tender age of twenty-four, Rebecca Cullen already has her hands full with a full-time job, raising two teenage brothers, supporting her elderly grandfather and tending to the family farm. When her troubled brother Clay is arrested, Rebecca's complicated world falls apart and the last thing she needs is arrogant, but devastatingly attractive, lawyer Rourke Kilpatrick prosecuting her brother…

On sale 5th January 2007

Available at WHSmith, Tesco, ASDA, Borders, Eason, Sainsbury's and all good paperback bookshops

www.millsandboon.co.uk

M&B™

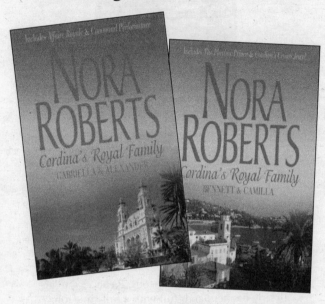

Flowers make great gifts...until they wilt.
Chocolates are always popular...calories are not.
Baby daughters are just adorable...but they grow up!

SUSAN MALLERY &
JENNIFER ARCHER

A Mother's Day

Carly and Cici have both tried Plan A – being
perfect wives and mothers. Now they're about to
start over...with their darling daughters.

**This collection of brand-new stories is the
perfect gift for Mum – or yourself!**

Available 2nd February 2007

*Available at WHSmith, Tesco, ASDA,
and all good bookshops*

www.millsandboon.co.uk